BLACK DAWN

Davenport Series

BRETT DIFFLEY

PROMINENT
BOOKS
EDGE

5830 E 2nd St, Ste 7000 #9983
Casper, WY 82609
USA

Words from the author

THERE'S A DIFFERENCE BETWEEN READING a good action-adventure, and feeling it. If you feel it, you get totally immersed in the story and its characters—feeling the joy and sorrow. As a writer, this is important not only for the entertainment value, but also in the challenge itself. Can I take the reader away? Make them part of the story? Can I hold their hand and take them on an emotional journey? This is the goal of most books, to varying degrees. Simply put, a good storyline, and its characters are like the layers of an onion, peeling back with each turn of the page. If the book is good, it will lure the reader into wanting more, and therefor continually draw them towards the proverbial center of the onion. This is the definition of a good thriller—and the making of a good rollercoaster ride.

If you are a first time reader to the Davenport Series, I'm envious of you. It's an action adventure series like no other, leaving you thrilled and entertained with each turn of the page. However, I encourage you to start with book one—**Perfect Plan**—to understand the dynamics of the evolving storyline, the multiple plotlines, and more importantly the characters, who you will both love and hate. With that being said, each character's backstory, detailed and descriptive in book one, will be greatly reduced by book seven— **Treacherous Paths**.

I think a writer needs to evolve with the reader. Plots are rarely one dimensional in real life, so in keeping up and challenging the reader, my stories are generally multifaceted. Now my question to you…Do you stop after peeling that first layer? If not…enjoy the ride!

About the Author

Author- Brett Diffley

Born in Anchorage, Alaska.

Raised in Tri-Cities, Washington.

Graduated from Finley High School

Living in Big Timber, Montana

ADVENTURE LURKS IN THE SOUL of each of us to varying degrees, and there are some of us that seek it out, making us better for it. It's these experiences that give him incites as a writer, and it's his overwhelming creativity that makes him a great story teller. In addition to writing, Brett is also a fixed-wing pilot, helicopter flight instructor, commercial diver, professional dog trainer, self-employed entrepreneur (patented a line of water toys, and wake training-board), commercial crab fisherman in Alaska, and commercial fisherman in several areas. Most recently, he is the author of the Pinnacle Award winning Davenport Series.

Please visit Brettdiffley.com for updates

Perfect Plan
Perfect Plan II
Black Tide
Black Dawn
Safe Passage
Storm Warning
Treacherous Paths (2025)
Chance (2025)
Terror Effect (2025)

Dedication

"When a father gives to his son, both laugh; when a son
gives to his father, both cry"—William Shakespeare

"It is easier for a father to have children than for
children to have a real father"—Pope John XXIII

"I'm a father; that's what matters most. Nothing
matters more"—Gordon Brown

*****

RAISING A CHILD CAN BE a scary proposition, and I think Luther Vandross's song *Dance with My Father* couldn't have been more eloquently stated when seen through the eyes of a child. So what defines a good father? What makes him a good parent where so many fail? How can one man be so dedicated, inspirational, and compassionate, and others not? Doesn't a child deserve a decent father? Imagine…if you will…the possibilities if we lived in a world where every child had the guidance of a good father. This leads to my dedication, and of course this relates to the animal kingdom as well.

There are many species of animals known for their unwavering parenting skills, but I've chosen the Adelie penguin. Living in the sub-zero Antarctic conditions, these fathers are unquestionably dedicated animals. Their first task is traveling over three thousand miles to the nesting site where they have nested year-after-year. Then they prepare the nest to keep the eggs off the ground. After the female lays the eggs, she rarely leaves the nest due to the extreme temperatures. That leaves hunting for fish and krill, and the perils of defending the nest the male's sole responsibility. This he will do to the death, and often does, especially against leopard seals—a cunningly voracious predator in the Antarctic, and known to shake young penguins from icebergs. And this says nothing of killer whales, where male Adelie penguins have been known to enter the water to draw the huge carnivores from the nests. Most don't return—an example of fatherly instincts at its best, and a commitment like none other. Unselfish and devoted, these fathers' unsaid mantra could easily be *family first* or even *purposeful sacrifice*.

So is it instinctual or just genetics?

More recently, I read a true story about a young father who lived in Kenya. Shortly after his daughter was born, his wife fell ill, and he became the sole parent. Touchingly sad, it might very well be the definition of fatherhood. It's a story, much like the penguins in regards to *sacrifice and purpose* because it happened in a world where famine was rampant, and where a man seen carrying a baby was taboo; a place where most fathers abandoned the child. So again, how can one man be so dedicated and inspirational to his children, and others not?

To further the story, he never had enough to eat much less enough food for his infant daughter. This forced him to beg on the streets so his precious daughter could not only eat…but eat first…and usually alone. And to prove how little food there was, he wasted away, hardly taking anything for himself because whenever he found food, his daughter came first. As a result, he grew sickly and malnourished, but he didn't care, as long as his baby survived. This was a father who was willing to pay the ultimate sacrifice for his daughter. And he did. But his child survived. To me, it's a story that embodies the true meaning of 'fatherly love and dedication'. There are others too: a father who threw his child out of the way of a speeding vehicle, another jumped into a full septic tank to save his young son by standing on the bottom and holding him high enough to breathe even though he himself would never inhale again, or the trapped father who pushed his young son out the window of their upturned car as it filled with water.

Too often these stories go unnoticed, but make no mistake they're never forgotten in the eyes of that child left behind. Much like the Adelie penguins, these are all examples of *sacrifice and purpose*, and gives a whole new meaning to Father's Day.

Black Dawn is dedicated to these great fathers of this world, be them small or tall, large or thin, two legged or four. It's dedicated to those that have sacrificed, or willing to sacrifice all, in an obligation to their children and their children's children. Not dependent on the color of their skin, feathers, or even fur, these fathers are the ultimate inspiration and should be commended. Unselfish and without regard, their commitment and strength of character is unwavering, and for this, the world is a much…much…better place.

*****

"No child should be beyond a fathers gaze"—Brett Diffley

*****

Hope you enjoy *Black Dawn*!

Prologue

T HE MID-DAY SIDEWALK TRAFFIC BUSTLED at the intersection of New York's Broadway and Liberty streets. Shoppers came and went from numerous store fronts and offices located in the surrounding downtown skyscrapers. A man watched them, along with the flow of bumper to bumper traffic. He was heavily bearded, in a rumpled torn trench coat, and high necked cotton sweater. His name was Tom Spears. A gentle looking man, he sat at the base of the twenty-four-story Westinghouse Building between the entryway and Bank of America. Dressed to blend into the ubiquitous city street-life, he wore a dirty grey-knit beanie on his head and a pair of military-green surplus pants.

Without lifting his gaze, Tom thanked a passerby for dropping a quarter into an open violin case between his knees. For most he was nondescript, seen yet unseen, as they stepped around his outstretched legs or tripped over his duct-taped shoes. But his shoddy, unsavory, appearance was only an illusion. With his head tilted forward, his long disheveled hair masking his keen eyes, he was alert and aware, and continually scrutinizing his surroundings.

A horn honked as a yellow cab stopped in front of the building. The back door flew open, and a leggy blond in heels and a short tan skirt exited. She bent over and handed the driver some money through the passenger window. As the taxi merged back into traffic, she straightened, smoothed her skirt, and approached the doorman. "Hi, Henry."

"Hi, Mrs. Averton," he replied with a smile and opened the door.

"Has Frank been in yet?" she asked. "The once-a-month meeting is today and I wanted to get in early."

"No, ma'am," he replied holding the big glass door open, and letting her pass by. "You're the first."

Tom listened closely. In a few short hours as a vagrant, he already knew a great deal about the comings and goings of the building. For instance, Henry the doorman was approaching his sixtieth birthday, a widower, and single. He was also lactose intolerant, a recovering alcoholic, and had a dog name Beau. As for Michelle Averton, she was a single, thirty-six-year-old attorney with an office on the uppermost floor, and not by coincidence, on the same floor as Frank Manatone, the crime boss for all of New York.

Tom knew the floor and the building well. After all, years ago he had been employed by the Manatone family himself, and at one time had even been part of the protection detail for Frank Manatone. The other two men at the time were Mike Rauls and Micky Trevor. Tom sighed heavily with thoughts of his dead friends. The two had disappeared over a month ago—two weeks before his wife Tanya had been taken.

The pain from the loss of his wife came back in a wave of agonizing anguish. Like a wrecking ball in his brain, he took a shuddering breath.

She was gone forever, it wasn't a dream.

But it was a dream, a nightmare of the worst kind. The questions soon followed, repetitive and merciless, without reprieve. *Could he have done anything different? Could he have saved her? Would things have turned out differently had he taken her out of that room right away...*

For six days Tom had tracked her through a GPS chip hidden in the locket she wore around her neck. Made of solid gold, he had given her the special gift shortly after they were married. Hand crafted and uniquely designed, it had cost him a small fortune. But the price meant nothing to him. The value was not only in his complete and undying love for her, but also for her peace of mind. Having been abducted as a child, used in sex bondage, and forced to live for more than ten years as a human slave, it would help ease any remaining fears for her. But that was only part of it. The pragmatist in him was the other. As a liaison for Crude Technologies, and dealing primarily with foreign diplomats in various countries, she was exposed and vulnerable. Probably more for him, the gift was a comforting gesture, and his lone requirement at the time was that she never take it off. It was the only time in their entire relationship he had asked her for anything. And when he'd explained why, she never did.

Unknown by her captors at the time, this had allowed him to close on her position as they headed east from Washington State, zigzagging across the United States. It was a good thing too, because at that point he still had no idea who had taken her or why. All he had to go on was a glowing dot on a laptop map. Then on the evening of the sixth day, the blipping signal had finally stopped just outside of New York City, and when it did, he not only found those answers…but his wife.

Like a dagger twisted into his heart, guilt struck him again and if he could go back to that moment two weeks ago, he would never…ever… have left her side…

Chapter 1
Darkness

TANYA DEMITRY-SPEARS STOOD IN THE middle of the dimly lit room. Small and cool, it had the hint of dampness, and there wasn't any heat. But at least she wasn't tied up anymore. She rubbed her wrists where the strap had reddened the skin. She was still in her two piece grey suit she'd been forced to put on; the fabric soiled at the arms and knees from being in the cargo van.

How many hours had it been since she arrived? She massaged her tired grey eyes with dirty fingers. She couldn't even be sure how many days it had been since she was taken. Only now, the blurriness of the trip was beginning to fade. After being taken from her home in the dead of night, she had been put in the windowless van, drugged, and thrown onto a slim foam mat on the floor. Most of the way she had slept. The only time they had stopped was to go to the bathroom, and that was usually only for a minute, relieving themselves beside the idling rig.

She remembered thinking how organized her abductor was too. His every action, his every move, from abduction to getting here, had been careful, methodical, and planned out. Nothing had been left to chance, including stopping at any public areas. Food and water had been in a large ice-filled cooler, and there was enough for a week or more. Even getting gas had been all but eliminated. Except for the last day, he had used the twenty fuel-filled gas cans that had been loaded into the back of the van beforehand. But while sharing the van's confined space for those days, she did manage to get some occasional information along the way…albeit very little.

On two separate occasions during the long journey, she had woken to hear her abductor talking on a cellphone—a disposable, with the freshly opened packaging thrown on the floor by his seat. At the time, it had been difficult for her to stay focused and eavesdrop on the conversation—to fight the need to go back to sleep. Both times, she had only managed to stay awake for fleeting seconds, but she did learn he was returning to New York. She couldn't know whether that was the state or the city, but apparently…in either case…New York had something to do with where they were going.

Then late last night they had finally arrived, and after putting a white canvas bag over her head, he had calmly guided her through several doors, down the stairs, and put her into this room. Before leaving, he had removed the bag, freed her hands, and given her a blanket. It was also the only time he had spoken after being taken—two words to be exact; "get comfortable."

The tone had been soft spoken and without malice, but Tanya still had the right to know what was going on. A few hours later he had returned, bringing her a plate of food, and telling her of the security measures in place. These included cameras throughout the complex, and glass-break sensors, which he told her about after breaking numerous lightbulbs in the hall outside her locked door. More telling, and even chilling, was the food he'd brought. "Her favorite," he had said. "Your eggs are over easy the way you like them. I also know you prefer sausage over bacon, and milk over juice." That's when she learned the abduction hadn't been random, and true fear had struck her. In fact, the man had been studying her, and if she hadn't already been sitting, her knees would have buckled right then and there. This meant, at the very least, he had been following her—them; her and Tom. He also told her that he meant her no harm, and that her abduction had been planned for more than six months with no detail being overlooked. But she still didn't know why, and when he left, he had taken her shoes, saying he would answer her questions when he returned. That had been several hours ago. She held her breath to calm herself, wrapping her arms tightly across her chest. She felt so alone, and the air, stagnant and suffocating, wasn't helping.

She glanced around the small cement room that had become her cell.

There were no windows, and the only light, ebbing and flickering inconsistently like powered by a generator, came from a single glowing bulb on the ceiling. In the corner was a small steel framed bed, without bedding, the mattress grey and stained. Next to it, on the floor, was a five gallon bucket with a lid, and a roll of toilet paper. On the bed was the old wool blanket that he had supplied. She picked it up, snap-shook-it once and wrapped it tight around her shoulders. Even though it smelled of storage, and the red-woolen fabric felt rough on her skin, the warmth was instantly comforting. But it did little to dispel her heightened emotions.

Like the suffocating effects of an avalanche, her chest welled and then constricted, leaving her with the urge to cry. It came from the loneliness that settled on her like a recurring weight on her soul.

Don't cry. It'll be okay, she thought, trying to convince herself. *It's not the same. It's not!*

But the distant memories of being taken from her Odessa home in the Ukraine, abruptly struck her in an explosion of emotions like a giant wave into a cliff face.

She sat on the bed, slid back against the wall, and wrapped her arms tightly around her knees.

The abduction had been long ago but the clarity remained. Taken at the tender age of seven, she had been quickly smuggled out of the country, and months later forced to become a sex slave for the Akmalit brothers in rooms much like this one. For years she lived like this, at the mercy of her capturers, repeatedly raped, beaten, and starved; rarely being allowed to see the light of day, much less leave the cell she was in at the time.

She wiped away the single tear that rolled down her cheek. Such was her life back then.

The company was Corporate Affairs—a worldwide conglomerate that made millions legally, and billions illegally in the slave market. The owners were the Akmalit brothers, and between the two of them, they turned their slave marketing trade into a prolific global network; unknown legally, but renowned illegally. It was Kalam Akmalit's sharp mind that drove Corporate Affairs forward both financially, and in flexibility. Every move he made was careful and measured. On paper it was a legitimate company with several hubs around the world, making its money by showing other corporations how to hide theirs. Not by coincidence, their global reach also gave them unlimited access to what motivated the company most; children, to be bought, used and sold at their discretion.

Secrecy was the key to this success, and it was Kalam's brother, Kalib, who continually added abductees to the corporation's commodities. Like his brother, this was *his* forte. From the processing teams that found the targets, to design and implementation, he took every aspect into account down to the smallest details, such as looks, background, and even the family's resources if their child disappeared.

It all mattered.

Once a plan was instigated, another team took care of the abductions and subsequent accidents. Some abductions were as simple as a van grab, but others were so cleverly thought out it took weeks to coordinate. And because the ruse was orchestrated to point towards accidents or runaways, the disappearances never came back to them; no trace of foul play, and no evidence for police to follow. The rest was semantics and big money, putting them into the system and becoming a commodity people paid for. It had been the only life Tanya had ever known.

But the bondage didn't stop there. In fact, it was only the first phase in a Corporate Affairs' system that had been—if nothing else— the quintessence of efficiency; the system coordinated and continually adapting as children grew into adults. The next phase was processing the young adults into the labor force as working slaves. From servants to physical labor, this was their destiny. Even planned pregnancies were thought out, where babies were sold at a very high price to adoption companies. Then the mothers became members for life because of threats to them or to their child. It kept most in line, and the money rolling in for the company.

So at age twenty-two she had outlived her usefulness as a sex slave, and was sent to a breeding farm, where ten months later she gave birth to a baby girl—a healthy child who was taken shortly after birth. Then the threats to her newborn began and she was sent into forced labor, working at Savory's Spa as a masseuse for the next seven years of her life. But the "accidental" death of a man named Frank Teeds at the spa wasn't to be overlooked. It had happened while she was on duty and she became expendable. So she was sent to Texas and chained in a basement for her final days on earth. But her circumstances soon changed, thanks to two strangers: Reed Davenport, and her future husband, Tom Spears. The two had been at the center of her rescue, and also the destruction of Corporate Affairs.

Most damaging of all during that time was the potential loss of her daughter. She had no idea where to even begin looking for her. It was the final piece of a never ending nightmare from her past. A convulsive sob shook her, threatening her resolve.

Her child, her beautiful child, taken away. But even this wasn't to be the true pinnacle of her loss. That came later with the dashed dream of the two of them being reunited again.

To that point of her life, she had held out hope, living each day with only one goal and one reason to live; to be reunited her daughter again. But like a fading mirage over the desert, this turned out to be only an illusion…wishful thinking…a dream.

Tom had been the one to deliver the unimaginable news. After being rescued from the basement of horrors, and lying in a hospital bed, he had come to Tanya to tell her of her daughter's unimaginable fate.

It came at a time while he was searching for another abducted girl aboard the container ship *San Paulo*. And it was there—a chance encounter—that Tom had briefly met her brown eyed little girl. She was locked in a container with other children that were being secretly shipped to New York. Tom had tried to intervene but it wasn't to be because of a hurricane that was ravaging the decks—a storm that ultimately sent the ship to the bottom.

She thought about her husband.

Long before they were even a couple, and shortly after their escape from the basement, he had told her of her daughter's unimaginable fate. They were in the hospital recovering from various injuries when he had approached her, and summoned the courage to tell her what he believed to be true: that he'd seen Tanya's cloned image in the form of a little girl imprisoned in a container, which ultimately went over the side during a hurricane. Tanya still remembered the plagued, distraught look on Tom's face and also his conviction when he told her the truth about her daughter. The devastation in his eyes could only be matched by his tormented heart. She would never forget that torn man, a stranger weeping in front of her, tortured by a portion of the past that wasn't even his to bear. To this very day, it was a suffocating pain that cleaved his soul. He did his best to keep it hidden, but it left him drenched at night in nightmarish sweats knowing he hadn't saved her—the daughter that neither of them had had the opportunity to know.

She had often thought about his words, the story of her daughter's final days; *the truth,* he called it. For better or worse, it was the only image that remained for Tanya: "The container was pitch black," he had begun, "except for the flashes of lightening as the hurricane lashed out. It was only after I turned on my flashlight that a small face appeared in its beam—a child no more than seven with big brown uncertain eyes and thick brown hair…" He'd stopped then to look at her. "Your hair…and your eyes…" he had clarified, his voice shaky but confirming.

"She was something though," he had continued. "Even with the tear troughs that ran down her dirty cheeks, she was a vision of loveliness—of strength in a world full of chaos. She was squatting next to me; not smiling, but she wasn't afraid either." His lip had quivered, but he had forced a smile. "At seven, she was probably the person in charge, and reassuring the others…"

There was much more to his story, but this was all her motherly instincts could take. So instead, she focused on the words she held most dear. *Her child wasn't afraid.*

With that, she stood abruptly, wiping her sorrow on her sleeve, and spoke out loud. "Now it's my turn—my little angel—to be brave."

"Be brave," she repeated again.

Optimism touched her. Unlike the Akmalits basement, where she had waited to be tortured and killed, her husband would come for her, and that certainty fed her resolve. He had always been the source of her strength, the stout ship in any stormy sea.

He would be again too!

She closed her eyes and reverently touched the small gold locket around her neck. It was a gift presented by Tom after their wedding. Made from pure gold, the polished surface was curved, embedded with two hearts intersecting, and inside each were their initials—the first a D for her maiden name of Demitry, and the second an S for Spears. And inside the small compartment was a flat polished plate with the inscription; *Forever.*

His lone requirement at the time of the gift, was that she never take it off. It was the only time in their entire relationship he had asked her for anything. And when he'd explained why, she never did. She now gripped it like her life depended on it.

She heard a distant sound and her eyes flared open. It was the hollow drum of footfalls coming down the steel steps, the opening and closing of a door, and finally the crunching of glass as he walked down the hall to her door. Remaining on the bed, she cringed at the abrupt sound of a key being placed in the lock, and watched the doorknob being turned. Then the big steel door slowly swung open, squeaking on seldom used hinges, and there before her once again was her abductor.

He wore jeans and a brown windbreaker over a white button-down cotton shirt. In one hand, he held a tray of food, and in the other a folding chair.

She studied him for a moment. He was middle aged, hair close cropped and grey, his eyes the darkest blue. His physique was toned, muscular, and he walked with purpose. A handsome man even now, with high cheekbones and a square jawline.

"Once again, I apologize for the crude treatment." His words were confident without rancor. "It's unfortunate, but I hope some hot food will appease a little of that discomfort." As he stepped inside, the smell of cigarettes filled the room. It was a reeking smell, and she vaguely recalled the wafting smoke that continuously floated around the interior of the van.

Her gaze shifted to the doorway, her only escape route. Beyond it, the darkened corridor disappeared left and right, the walls cement just like her cell. Again she wondered where she was being held.

After flipping open the chair and positioning it in near the bed, he put the tray of food in front of her and removed the old one, setting it on the floor.

Half starved, the aroma of the food made her stomach growl and she glanced at the tray. On it was a burger and fries; the hamburger, no doubt, minus pickles and onions the way she liked it.

"Thank you for eating something," he began, looking at what remained of the eggs and hash browns on the tray on the floor. "You'll need your strength in the coming days." His face relaxed into a smile, and he pointed at the chair. "May I sit?"

He was asking her permission? She nodded warily, and brushed back a strand of hair from the disheveled bun on her head.

He sat facing her. "Please excuse my indulgences, I've been looking forward to meeting you…talking to you. This situation is very unique, and I find myself captivated by both you and your husband."

Being in close proximity, and above the pungent odor of cigarettes on his clothing, she could smell the faint odor of coffee on his breath. "Who are you, and why am I here?" she asked firmly. "There must be some mistake."

"Of course," he replied, nodding. "But there is no mistake. Your husband and his past is why you're here. So I'll enlighten you on your situation."

His non-confrontational tone caught her by surprise. She nodded toward the tray, masking her uncertainty in a favorable tone. "Thank you for your kindness…"

He held up a hand to stop her. "My name is Bishop Styles, and I'm many things, but not an animal…and your thanks is meaningless to me," he said calmly, but with fervor. "I study, gather, and absorb. This is what I do. Each time I'm here, I learn even more about you. It's in my nature, not to mention, my line of work to constantly evaluate and store useful information." His brow furrowed slightly, but his tone remained nonchalant. "So let's be clear, don't let my appearance, or perceived *kindness* fool you. I'm a very bad man Mrs. Spears, and I've done more evil in my short existence than a lifetime of twenty." His words were revealing, more than cavalier. Not brazen but confident. "From the assassination of one, to the killing of many, I strive for perfection— the challenge, the elevating of talent. Like a math professor dissects an equation, I learn a person's strengths and weaknesses, equating the probability of success and then instigating a plan. Sometimes this requires brute force, with little time needed to prepare. Other times a softer, more subtle approach is needed, but I can tell you, the volumes of preparation remain the same." He leaned forward on his elbows, his eyes focused.

She felt even more uneasy. His penetrating stare was almost like he could see right through her, so to gain separation, she moved to the furthest corner of the bed with the blanket still held tightly around her.

"Before enlightening you on why you're here, let me educate you further about me and my world. It will help you broaden your scope of who you're dealing with, eliminating any further misleading illusions you might have. To be blunt," he said, getting right to it, "I'm a professional killer. My world begins with a contract, and ends with the fulfillment of that contract. These vary in many ways from the amount of upfront money, to the method; from small to the more elaborate that require certain stipulations. A perfect example of *elaborate* happened last year, in which I was hired to kill one man. Unfortunately, due to stipulations, many more people had to die to accomplish this." He lapsed into silence, before continuing, "Do you remember Malaysian flight 340?"

She nodded without speaking. Of course she remembered the tragic accident. It was all over the news for months with various speculative reports from terrorism to an in-air catastrophe—even a hijacking by the crew was mentioned. But nothing was ever substantiated because the plane was never found.

"The plan went flawlessly," he continued. "At 30,000 feet the pilot, distraught from his failed marriage, began a chain of events that would eventually lead to its disappearance." He nodded, his face impassive. "This is my world, Mrs. Spears, much like yours is mine now."

I'm his world? Is that what he just said? She tried to blink away her concern. *And what did any of this have to do with Tom?* Riveted to his words, she was still trying to understand why she was here—in the same room—with a professional killer.

"This is just one example to let you know that I won't hesitate to kill you." His face softened. "You should also know that you're not my intended victim, but much like the rest of the people on the plane, you could become expendable."

Tom was the target!

The understanding struck her like a thundering punch to the midsection and suddenly she couldn't breathe. She wanted to scream… *Why? Why was this happening?* She held her composure in check, and fought the dreadful thoughts now going through her brain as he continued speaking—speaking like he wanted to explain his reasoning's.

"In regards to the plane, the family that hired me made it quite clear. It was to look like an accident, his body unrecoverable, with no connection back to the family." He shook his head slowly. "You could never guess, or appreciate the enormity of accomplishing just one of these conditions, much less three." His voice faded, his look becoming distant.

Tanya noticed his pause and the subtle flicker…of something…in his blue eyes. For an instant he wasn't as calculating—like something much less threatening was trying to emerge.

"The information gathered," he continued, "requires tireless research, much like what I've learned about you and your life, because knowing the person is half the battle. This particular contract was for a man named Jimmy Tsang—a Chinese immigrant and a land developer with ties to both the Chinese mob, and an unscrupulous government. But in the end, neither had anything to do with his death. That came solely from his own family. Their reason? A last will and testament was being drawn up, and upon his death, his considerable wealth was going to be dispersed well beyond the immediate family. They couldn't have that. So they examined the verbiage in the new documents for weakness, and found what they were looking for in a clause under Abduction for Ransom. As fate would have it, this stipulation was added by Jimmy Tsang himself to keep the new parties beyond the family from being overeager; to keep them honest. But he should've looked much closer to home. Simply stated, if Mr. Tsang were to disappear for any reason, and the body unrecoverable, the final declaration would become null and void. Should this happen, and by Chinese law, the entire wealth would revert back to the immediate family.

"So after months of research, while monitoring Mr. Tsang, his lifestyle and his continuous overseas trips, I made my first move towards an airline accident, surveying carriers to find the perfect crew—the breakdown meticulous.

"Months later it was finally time to approach the captain I liked for the job, and when I did, I also knew everything about his life as well, his family, and even the name of his dog. I found his weakness *in that knowledge*. In this case, it was his wife's infidelities; something he had no knowledge of at the time. So I supplied him with photos—graphic photos—that left little to the imagination." His face remained neutral, his words matter-of-fact, monotone, showing neither pity nor bravado.

"For the next three weeks I waited for the right moment, letting his shock ferment into anger. Then we struck a deal; although not the one I had foreseen. When I offered a trade to kill his wife, in exchange for the enlistment of his services, he spurned me. He said something about his Chinese heritage, and that her dishonor was his alone to carry— his burden, not hers." He cocked his head curiously. "Although, even now, *that honor* seemed a bit askew to me because of his willingness to kill several hundred men, women, and children, instead of just his wife. But be that as it may, the outcome would have still been the same, and we came to an agreement involving an off-shore account set up for his children. Dispersed in small increments after a two year period, this would thereby negate any provable fault or liability towards the captain, leaving only endless speculation surrounding a terrible tragedy.

"So on March 9, 2014 the Malaysian flight took off, and somewhere over the China Sea, the captain made a two-minute call to his wife—a final requirement of his, which I arranged through an untraceable phone. Records would later show he made the call to someone, but nothing to substantiate or indicate a suicide was in the making.

"As to what was said in the conversation, I have no idea. But shortly afterwards he turned off the transponder, pulled the fuse for the oxygen masks, and killed the other two crewmen in rapid succession with a four round derringer I supplied—a weapon the captain simply walked through security. Then he cracked the cockpit door and put a bullet through the front glass, instantly depressurizing the aircraft." Bishop shrugged. "Whether he had time in the ongoing rush of air to use the last bullet on himself, I can't be sure, but it was obviously immaterial. With the rapid decompression, and with no oxygen masks deployed for either the passengers or crew, unconsciousness happened in less than thirty seconds—death in under two minutes. But what I couldn't have foreseen, and learned afterwards, is the Boeing 777 relies heavily on autopilot because it's so difficult to fly. So when the decompression occurred, the rest of the emergency equipment went online, dropping the jet in a rapid descent that would've been reminiscent of coming down the world largest rollercoaster at three hundred miles an hour.

"Three minutes later the auto pilot leveled out at two thousand feet, but by then it was too late. With no one left to make a course change, the autopilot resumed a preset track, sending the jet over the Indian Ocean, and four hours later it ran out of fuel and crashed—never to be seen or heard from again." He shrugged. "Contract fulfilled; two hundred and thirty nine people—men, women, and children—killed for the sake of stipulations made for one man." He sighed somberly. "It wasn't something I wanted to do, but it changes little. I'm a killer, just like your husband once was…"

Their eyes met, and she saw the change in him occurring again, indistinct, rising from the depths of his dark eyes like a shadowy image from the bottom of a darkened pool. Was it regret…empathy…or a simple understanding of the evil he had done?

"In many ways I'm envious of your husband. He found a way out of this violent life, and more importantly kept what was left of his compassion. It's important. This is a life that continuously erodes at that fabric. With me, it's an intoxicating rush to dissect the problem and come up with the perfect plan in any scenario. But much like the day after a hard night of drinking, it comes with the consequential hangover. This is where that erosion starts; small at first but growing with age. Early on, I believed I could block it out. But you can't, the death consumes you a piece at a time—a death at a time. Your husband knew it, and walked away. And in doing this, regained some of the person that was lost after the death of his family."

She did little to hide the disparaging information he had of their lives that now obviously included Tom's previous family. It wasn't surprising considering everything she had learned about flight 370. *That was the point, wasn't it? To show her that he was prepared and organized, even down to the intimate details of Tom's past?*

But as a devoted wife, in a loving relationship, she had her own grasp of Tom's past. In fact, he was very forthcoming, wanting no surprises between them. If she asked, he told her—good or bad— even the ugly secrets from his dark background. This also included a conversation they had about another chance meeting with her. One that had two strangers—she and Tom—passing in a hallway at Savory Spa shortly before Frank Teeds died. Unaware at the time, she only vaguely recalled passing a large man dressed in a maintenance uniform, but Tom had revealed it to her, letting her decide who he really was. Her decision had taken less than a heartbeat…the blink of an eye…and decisively faster than a flash of an energized lightning bolt. She remembered it fondly because that malevolent past wasn't the man she knew and loved with all her heart. He wasn't a killer *by this man's* standards, and unlike him, wouldn't have intentionally killed hundreds of people. It wasn't in him, and that was displayed and replayed over and over, night after night, in his inability to save the children inside the container. No, the past was the past, and much like hers, it was better left alone.

A defusing smile crossed his lips when he noticed her defiant stare. "Yes, I even know all about that fateful night that forever changed his life. It was a sad situation, his life set on a new path when his wife and precious child were killed by the hand of a drunk driver."

She watched him as he spoke; puzzled. *It was a sad situation?* He was a contradiction of emotions, showing brief flashes of empathy in-between long bouts of controlled, and unemotional dialogue. Case in point. She watched him revert back again; measured…detached…but respectful.

"Several months later, he took that new path. After killing those responsible, he started a new job and life in New York; the same people who coincidentally have me hunting him now. But instead of finding pity in a bottle, or some other addiction to help cloud the past, he found a different conduit in shutting down the painful memory. Killing became his life, and soon his deadly reputation grew. Seldom seen, and never caught, Tom Spears became an enigma, and the Shadow—the killer of men—was born."

A charismatic glint appeared in his blue eyes and he sat back, slapping his knees in a lighthearted demeanor, his tone upbeat. "I met him once you know—your husband. It was long ago in New York, when his reputation as *an elite* was at its peak." His words were complimentary, and he smiled. "He was eating breakfast at some no-name restaurant when I walked up, introduced myself, and asked if I could join him." He grinned. "You should have seen the look of surprise…caution…and even curiosity on his face. It was a moment I'll never forget. In the end though, caution won out, and Tom gripped the small pistol between his legs that much tighter." Bishop shook his head, his eyes bright and glowing with the memory. "It was a natural reaction of course, and I understood completely." His face flushed in amusement. "He actually kept me standing in the aisle until I explained the visit was only a courtesy; to let him know I was going to be doing some work in his back yard so-to-speak. Then after an awkward moment of silence, he *begrudgingly* allowed me to join him. We only chatted for a few minutes, but I found him to be intelligent, articulate, and with good instincts. Of course, all this was a given, considering his proven success. Even if it was unconventional."

He nodded, still smiling. "Did he ever tell you about his contracts? Or the stipulations he, himself attached?" He laughed out loud, a sound rich and full of life like two close friends sharing a touching moment.

But this wasn't with friends and the lighthearted—suddenly friendly—demeanor seemed out of character to Tanya. *Or did it?* she wondered. *Was this the person he once was…the consequences of erosion he talked about?* She believed it was, and the coping mechanism he had spoken of wasn't booze for him either, his addiction was the cigarettes. That was now obvious. Adding to this knowledge, she realized he was inspired by Tom, and now gripped with indecision, trying not to care… to remain detached…but losing emotional ground. *Is this why he wanted to talk…possibly to make amends. But for what?*

To keep from being drawn in, Tanya forced herself to look away from his friendly eyes. She needed no reminder that he was a killer and that she remained a prisoner. But even this had caught her off guard.

He seemed not to notice her unease and continued talking, his words becoming charismatic like his alter ego had been found. "*His stipulations* were to limit any killing to what he perceived as pure-evil. That meant no unfaithful husbands or wives, or even the junior executive wanting to become a *senior executive* by dispatching a workmate." His warm smile lingered like swirling bubbles in a comforting bath. "I mean, hells bells, those two alone would cut my *lucrative* business in half."

It became clear to her that he related to her husband—admired him. Relief touched her, now thinking Tom wasn't the target...*Was he? Or was it just hope?* She wanted to ask, but she was fearful of his answer.

He became quiet for a moment before speaking again. "Honestly, the more I studied your husband the more I liked him." His eyes showed sincerity, and he spoke with candor. "I find he's a rarity in so many ways—a killer, but also a difference maker; deadly, but also compassionate. I also think his past wasn't a liability. In retrospect, I believe it was an attribute, because it was always about the two drunks that had killed his family. Those two men—a father and son—had made a mockery of the flawed court system and his past life. So in his own way, he was cleansing his soul, while giving purpose to his life.

"Then another course changing event occurred when a man name John Wilks hired him to find his daughter, which he did, and that led to you." He paused, his manner engaging, but his eyes becoming clouded.

She saw it again, even before he spoke. The change back to the cold, calculating, and culpable personality, was as vivid as flipping a light switch.

"So to answer the question as to why you are here. It happened years before, when that same John Wilks had hired your husband to kill a lowlife by the name of Frank Teeds—a loan shark who was squeezing John for a debt incurred by his gambling brother. Unfortunately, Frank Teeds was the cousin of Frank Manatone, crime boss for the Manatone family in New York, and also my present employer. Making the situation even worse, it appears Tom did the killing while being employed by that same syndicate. Now I've been paid to right that wrong." He gave her a lingering look like he was pondering his next words. "Remember the stipulations I told you about?" He didn't wait for a response and continued. "Like the Malaysian flight, one variable can change everything. This is the case now. In regards to you, a stipulation was made that before killing him, you are to die in front of your husband—a tradeoff; a family member for a family member."

She couldn't breathe, her hands became rigid, bunching the blanket over her chin.

He stood, folding the chair. "But like I said, the two of you captivate me because your lives are relative to my own. So this has changed," he reassured her. "I will deal with the ramifications of not hurting you later, but your husband is a different story. As you've figured out, I know everything there is to know about him; his strengths and weaknesses. In short, you're here because that's you. Both in strength and weakness, you're his undying love, his eternal flame, the woman that took him from his violent world, and healed the wounds that came from the death of his previous family. So he'll come, and if there's one thing I've learned about him, no apocalyptic event—seismic or climactic—is going to change this." He shrugged. "And there lies his weakness." He spoke with confidence, his words becoming direct. "When he does, I'm going to put a bullet between his eyes." He turned before closing the door. "But for what it's worth, I can honestly tell you, I'll take no joy, or satisfaction in killing Tom Spears."

One last flash.

Chapter 2
Kingpin

"WE HAD AN AGREEMENT, A deadline, you're out of time," Frank Manatone said into the phone, his harsh words critical of past performance. "I made it quite clear—as you made it clear when I paid for your services in advance." Agitated, he stood, and looked out the large office window that overlooked the New York City skyline. From the 24th floor of the Westinghouse Building, he had a sweeping view from Battery Park and the World Trade Center Memorial Foundation in the south, to the Children's Museum north, and beyond them to the shimmering waters of the Hudson River. "You have twenty-four hours to bring Tom Spears to me. No more excuses!" He hung up, and pushed the intercom button for his secretary. "Get me my son. Now!" He took off his spectacles, tossing them on the desk and went back to the window. The sun was breaking through a grey overcast sky, and glinting off the distant World Trade Center's windows.

He ran a hand over his short cropped grey beard. Then he caught his reflection on the window. He looked bone weary. His eyes were hollowed and dark rimmed, his wrinkled skin pale and almost translucent. For the last year he had been telling himself it was time to retire, and now he was ready but for one thing…one person: Tom Spears.

At one time, the man had been part of his exclusive family, part of his life, and part of his inner circle. That's what agitated him most. Tom was like blood, and making the betrayal worse, he had genuinely liked the man. Not only had he been trusted as a bodyguard, but also as a personal friend.

He shook his head.

The killing of Frank Teeds, his late brother's only child, was one thing, but not near as galling in his mind as having it perpetrated behind his back. It showed no respect. Why hadn't Tom come to him? Hell, he might have taken care of it himself had the reason been just. After all, Frank Teeds wasn't without faults. He liked to do as he pleased, even taking his mother's last name for no other reason than to rile his father. In fact, he didn't have a decent bone in his entire body. To further that, the real surprise to all who knew him, wasn't that he died before his fortieth birthday, but that he died of natural causes. At least that's what Frank himself had thought for more than ten years; the death being from a heart attack at Savory Spa. Now he knew the truth, and this was about being disrespected—a matter that couldn't be tolerated in this business. Otherwise it opened the door to further discord and chaos. "He could've come to me," he mumbled with fervor. "But no. He chose to be deceitful…right under my nose…while collecting a paycheck and drinking my booze."

No! Tom Spears was going to pay…and pay dearly!

With the disloyalty, Tom's character and past deeds also came into doubt. How many more lies were there? How many more transgressions? He found it hard to believe this was only a onetime affair. His thoughts went back to the bust off the Florida coast. Could Tom have been involved? Even now, the confiscation of millions of dollars in drugs and property was hard to forget. On that day, the Fed's had swarmed into town, along with the DEA, when one of the Family's shipments had run into trouble; a three-hundred-thousand-dollar Top Gun cigar boat—fully loaded with both cocaine and bails of marijuana—had collided with a submerged log while skimming across the surface at more than 140 mph. The log had done little to the Kevlar hull, but the collision had launched the thirty-eight foot vessel into the air where it flipped several times before coming to rest upside down. The first vessel that happened on the scene was a Crude Technologies tug, and a short time later so was the DEA, who confiscated the drugs, and arrested the men in the water. More arrests soon followed. From Florida to New York, more than thirty people had been charged by the time the investigation finally closed, including several of his own lieutenants here. Did this have anything to do with Tom, or was it just paranoia? He couldn't be sure. It had been several years ago, and long before Tom had started working for Crude Technologies. But the fact still remained, it was the same Crude Technologies that was involved. Coincidence? *Not hardly*, he thought. And if nothing else, Tom Spears would become the scapegoat.

The intercom buzzed, followed by his secretary's voice, "Your son is on line one, sir."

He lifted the receiver and pushed the flashing button. "Tony. Where are you?"

There was a moment's pause, then stuttering, "I'm in Queens…"

"I thought you had control of this Spears fiasco," he interrupted. "I just got off the phone with the…" he paused, catching himself, "the Baker…" using a synonym in case his phone was tapped again by the FBI, "and I want to know why my order hasn't been delivered?" He could barely contain his anger and continued, "It's been weeks. There was a time when deliveries were made on a daily basis, and those weren't paid in advance!"

"It's under control," Tony replied, sounding intimidated, "just a little more time."

"More time? You…" he began, then stopped himself before calling his son a flaming queer, which he was. "You are out of time. I want this done. That means I want the people involved dead, their children dead, their children's children dead, and I want their fucking dog's head on a pike! Are we clear?" He slammed the phone down once more, hoping to hell that the phone line wasn't actually tapped. But his son brought out the worst in him. Dealing with mob related issues was hard enough, but to know your son was a flower toting, pink leotard, instead of the heir-apparent to one of the biggest crime families in the United States, if not the world, was almost too much to bare. "Flaming queer," he said with disgust, "seems fitting he's in *Queens*."

Even his son's soft voice annoyed him. "What the hell is up with that anyway?" he growled out loud. "You take it in the ass and it affects your vocal chords?"

His hands were visually shaking as he leaned heavily on the desk. Of course he had seen the signs at an early age. Before Tony's eighth birthday, he had caught him in the closet looking at nudie pictures of men in a magazine, and then of course, there was the limousine fiasco as a teenager. That's when the dreaded family secret had come out. It happened after Tony had eaten dinner with another boy from school. Upon returning to the limo, Tony had conveniently given his security detail time to go eat themselves. An hour later, intermittent squeals of pain had been heard coming from the back. So his team had investigated, and not long after that, the nickname 'Little Mouse' was coined. It didn't get any better as he grew older either. As it turns out, killing young female prostitutes, and even classmates, seemed to give him great pleasure, too. But considering the family business, Frank had been willing to live with those. Hell, killing was an attribute.

Being gay however, was another matter altogether. *One of the biggest crime families in the world,* he thought, *left in the hands of a man known as Little Mouse, and worse yet, the killer of women.* It was as embarrassing as it was maddening. But what choice did he have? Tony was his only heir. His only child. Good thing for Tony, too. If there had been a sibling, Tony wouldn't have lived past limo-night.

He took a deep calming breath, stood, and grabbed his overcoat off the coatrack. It was time to get some air and maybe a late lunch. Leaving his office, he passed his receptionist, who was hard at work sitting behind a metal grey desk. At age fifty-six, she was a coarse looking woman with short red hair and a long nose. "I'll be back in an hour," he said curtly, and went out the door.

To each side of the elevator, and sitting in chairs, were his two bodyguards. Both men were in suit and ties, broad shouldered, and grim faced. They stood in unison. "Where to, boss?" the bald man on the left asked with a heavy Jamaican accent. His name was Charley Mack. A huge black man pushing the scales at more than 390 plus pounds, he was smiling, his gold tooth glinting in the overhead lighting.

"I need some air, Charley," Frank answered. As he approached the elevator, the doors opened and Michelle Averton stepped out. Thanks to Frank, she was the only other tenant on the entire 24th floor.

Frank gazed at her approvingly.

She was dressed in a short sleeved white button-down blouse, and a tight fitting skirt that showed off her shapely ass and slender legs. Her blond hair was pulled back into a pony tail, and she smiled. "Hi, Frank," she said stepping up and kissing him on the cheek. "You going to get something to eat?" she asked, lingering in front of him as Charley kept the door opened with his big hands and sausage-like fingers.

His recent appetite for food and fresh air, wavered upon seeing her. Michelle Averton was as sexy as she was smart. She was also ambitious… very ambitious. This, Frank had taken full advantage of shortly after she had represented him in a drug smuggling conspiracy charge four years earlier. In winning the case, Frank had shown his appreciation by setting her up with her own firm here on the same floor as him. But the gesture wasn't about adding an exclusive lawyer for his less than law-abiding businesses. On the contrary, he had much more in mind than professionalism. So with promises of continual work and big money, he had cornered her in the elevator that same day, and had her perform oral sex on him right then and there. The funny thing was he had been more than willing at the time to force himself on her, but that hadn't been necessary. As it turned out, she had been more than a willing participant. That had set the tone for her current and future obligations toward him. Now when he felt the urge, he did as he pleased, whenever he pleased. She was his to control. Of course it didn't hurt that she lustfully craved Frank's dangerous persona both energetically and enthusiastically. It was a thrill to her; the perfect relationship.

Relationship? The thought almost made him chuckle. She was no more than a toy to him—a convenience—and his to throw away. But as far as she or anyone else was concerned, she was exclusively his mistress. He sensed she liked that too, knowing he wouldn't be tolerant of another man in her life; a deadly mistake to be sure.

He brushed her cheek with his palm. Feeling her soft heated skin, he was tempted to drag her into the elevator right then, and lift that tight skirt. It would do wonders for his present state of mind.

He leaned in close to her neck. "Just going out to get some air," he said, filling his lungs with the subtle, yet intoxicating, scent of her lavender perfume, "but I'll need you a little later." It wasn't a question, and she understood, nodding and obediently tilting her head to the side so he could kiss her exposed neck.

He stepped onto the elevator.

When he entered the lobby, his two bodyguards were off each shoulder. "Let's go for a walk," he said over his shoulder to Charley. "Maybe we can stop by Mashones on the way back." The black man grinned. Mashones made some of the best deep-dish pizza in town.

*****

Tony Manatone gripped the phone with a shaky hand long after Frank hung up. He had been treated like this his entire life, and he was tired of it. "Soon old man, I'm going to make you eat those words!"

"Now is that anyway to talk?" a man's voice asked from behind. "Seems to me your money would be better spent with less time on the phone." Tony was naked, and the man ran his hands across his narrow shoulders before teasingly moving to his pierced nipples.

With a show of defiance, Tony stopped him half-heartedly as the muscular stranger pulled on the small golden rings. "Stop. I need to go," he said squirming. "There is…something I need to have taken care of."

"No!" the man snapped harshly into his ear. "I know what you like, and the only thing you'll be taking care of at the moment is me." He grabbed him by the hair and threw him forward onto the bed.

Anger coursed through Tony, but it had little to do with what the man was about to do to him. On the contrary, he waited on all fours, while thinking of his own fantasy; the killing of Frank Manatone. His father would never see it coming, and the thought of killing him was almost orgasmic. Feeling the shifting weight on the bed behind him, he dropped acceptingly to his elbows but continued to think of the many ways to kill his father and the plan already in motion.

Chapter 3
The Hunt

TOM LOOKED AT HIS WATCH. It was shortly after eleven PM. Having finally caught up to his wife's abductors, he was in Brooklyn, NY, and staring at the Red Hook Grain Terminal. Long since abandoned, it was located in a rundown warehousing district along the back of the Henry Street Basin—a manmade waterway near the mouth of the Hudson River that connected to the Gowanus Canal. This was disconcerting, not in the location, but due to its close ties to the mob, and more specifically the Manatone syndicate. It was also a building Tom knew well.

During his ten year tenure with the notorious mob organization, he had been there on at least a dozen occasions, and usually for nefarious purposes. Its secluded location garnered the utmost privacy, and thus the main reason the property was kept on the books and never sold. Which now begged the question, why was Tanya brought here? At first he was alarmed, knowing the buildings' true hidden purpose. But he dismissed the thought. There was no reason to believe the abductor would have driven all the way across the United States just to kill her here. No, there was much more to this than met the eye.

His thoughts went back to the Rickter's. This was the family Reed Davenport and Crude Technologies believed responsible for taking the mysterious black torpedo back in Washington State. They were fanatics, but he had never been sold on the idea that they were involved with the kidnapping of his wife. To abduct her was personal and Tom had no ties to the Rickters at all. However, the biggest crime family in New York, and the world, was another matter entirely. So in retrospect this new information was indeed a surprise.

But how did this help him?

With thoughts now of deceit, he closed his eyes for a moment. So if the Manatone's were now the culpable party, what did this have to do with him or Tanya? Did this give him any more answers? He couldn't be sure. He knew they owned the building, but were they guilty? What would they gain? There had to be something. His thoughts drifted to the intrusive cigarette smell left in his house after Tanya had been taken. The brand had been familiar to him, putting him on high alert. He knew of only one man who smoked them. His name was Bishop Styles—a deadly assassin that went by the name of The Duke. They had met only once, years ago, and the unforeseen encounter was hard to forget. While eating breakfast at a small café in New York, Bishop had strode up to his table and asked to sit down. Reluctantly, and warily, Tom had accepted. Turns out, Bishop had only wanted to let Tom know he was in town to fulfill a contract, and the visit, merely a professional courtesy. And it was in that five minute conversation, Tom reflected now…more so on the fact that the man was a chain smoker. Not hard to deduce at the time, the assassin reeked of cigarette smoke. But not just any brand. These were more expensive. His preferred variety was Visol Morris. Bridging the gap between cigars and cigarettes, it was longer, wrapped in brown paper, and had a distinctive sweet smell. It was that distinctive odor Tom had smelled in his home.

If the assassin known as The Duke was involved, was he working alone, and just using this known site for his own personal use?

No, Tom thought, *with or without Bishop, the Manatone's had to be involved.*

It was the only scenario where the parts of this puzzle came together. After all, he was in the crime family's home state, sitting next to one of their buildings, and Bishop Styles had been previously hired by the Manatone's on more than one occasion. *But again*, he thought skeptically, *what would the crime syndicate—much less an assassin known as The Duke—want with him or his wife?* It didn't make sense, other than it was beginning to look like it had something to do with his distant past.

He rubbed his burning eyes, finding it hard to concentrate. The lack of sleep was catching up to him and he blinked several times to clear his blurry vision. After starting out in Washington State, it had been a long zigzagging trip across the United States due to the captors sticking to lesser-used routes to avoid any police presence or alerts. At least that's what Tom had assumed.

How many days had it been? Five or six?

Several times he had closed the gap, but they never stopped long enough for him to catch up. It had been frustrating. However, he did manage to close to within three hours one time, but unfortunately that number then swelled to more than twelve when, after driving two days straight, he was finally forced to sleep alongside the highway. Then he had closed the gap again when they themselves had to stop for a couple hours to sleep. This leapfrogging back and forth was telling to Tom, and confirmed it was only one man. Otherwise they would've rotated the driving duties, and never stopped for anything longer than a few minutes. It was at one of those moments when he had been tempted to call the police, to get them to intercept the vehicle when it was stopped. But he had dismissed the idea immediately. Aside from relying on the police for Tanya's safety, he would've given away his only advantage, which was the ability to track her.

He ran a hand over his unshaven face. According to 'the last reported position' on his laptop, his wife was no more than six hundred feet away. But without anything current, he knew it was misleading. After all, the GPS chip only generated the signal. It didn't broadcast it. To accomplish this, it piggybacked off the cellphone network. This allowed for broader range, but it also had its faults, such as 'reliable wireless coverage', and/ or no cellphones in the immediate area. Both created lapses in coverage, and that was no more apparent than when he passed through the broad state of Texas on Highway 10. There, with only uninhabited, sagebrush-covered plains for miles and miles, the signal had been sporadic at best, and sometimes nonexistent. Making that situation even worse, it had also been at night with fewer cars and therefore phones.

He looked at the map on the laptop again. According to the time stamp of her last reported position, it had been ten hours ago. That meant—if she was still indeed wearing the locket—she had been taken into a 'no-service dead-zone'; probably the basement.

Parked on the shoulder of Columbus Street—a seldom used port road along the granary's western perimeter—he studied the building further. Even in the dark and a quarter mile away, the uninhabited building was massive. At more than four hundred feet long and two hundred wide, it was twelve stories tall, and that didn't include the apexes on both ends of the building that went up an additional six floors.

Inside the tall complex he couldn't see any lights much less any signs of life. The same held true with the exterior where the only illumination came from two light poles at the northern end of the building over the old parking area. In the faint glow, Tom could see several forty-foot-trailers still haphazardly parked on the broken a dilapidated blacktop. Left long ago, most were derelicts, and either leaning from broken landing gear, or flat tires. The only other lighting came from the floodlights of the nearby gravel pit. It was another syndicate-owned operation. Between the two, Tom could only venture a guess as to how many bodies had been either buried or sent to a water grave here. But he knew the number was high. In fact, it had become known in the underworld as the perfect dumping ground.

His eyes flicked to the well-lit gravel pit. The main gate, and the only road in and out of the Red Hook Grain Terminal, was there. So his options were limited. To remain unseen, his obvious choice—if he had more time—would've been to approach via the waterway on the far side of the building. But with circumstances as they were, he couldn't waste the time acquiring a boat. So his only option was to continue on foot.

He got out, and opened the back door of his Subaru outback. From his suitcase he removed a dark windbreaker and black stocking cap. After putting them on, he closed the door and stepped to the back of his car. He opened the hatchback. Under a blanket, was a duffle bag, and from it he grabbed four extra magazines for his Glock. He put them into the back pockets of his jeans, and also grabbed a flashlight, stuffing it into his waistband.

Pausing a moment, his gaze drifted over his intended route. A huge community park bordered the property, and in front of him were two grass-covered soccer fields. Set end to end, they were unlit, and if he skirted them, the darkened tree line would conceal his approach. Then at the end of the park he would have to climb a ten foot chain-link fence to access the grain terminal. Even with the razor wire at the top, it seemed simple enough. He already knew it was the only security measure for the entire complex; a deterrent mainly to keep kids and vagrants out. So to contend with the razor wire, he opened the passenger door behind the front seat, and threw one of the rear floor mats over a shoulder

Now ready, he closed and locked all the doors, zipped up his windbreaker, and headed out.

Thinking optimistically, his heart warmed with thoughts of his wife. His first priority would be to find her and to get her safely away. Then later, he would deal with the people responsible. On that, there was no question.

Chapter 4
Athletic Club

AFTER HEADING NORTH ON INTERSTATE 678 towards Queens, Bishop Styles took the next off-ramp, which arced him west onto Highway 495 towards New York City. At the Long Island City exit, he left the highway and dropped down to the surface roads in a depressed area of Queens. It was the old warehousing district, and the traffic became nonexistent. A few minutes later he was driving along Vernon Street, with the East River on his left. He passed several dilapidated warehouses, before slowing in front of a building with Queens Athletic Club painted on the wall; the black paint weathered, chipped and bubbling.

It had been several weeks since he was last here. On that day he had come to the Club to accumulate more information on Tom Spears. Of course that was at the expense of Tom's longtime friends Micky Trevor and Mike Rauls, who had also been previously employed by the Manatone's, and then killed by Tony Manatone himself.

As Bishop listened to the soothing sounds of Mozart playing in surround sound, he thought about their deaths. Not that it made much difference to him in the broad scope of things, but had their deaths been that valuable? Had he learned anything more than he'd already known at the time?

No, he thought, without emotion. But that's not to say he didn't find a sliver of weakness to use against Spears. In fact, their complete loyalty had said plenty about the relationship between the once vaunted assassin and them. Getting allegiance from people demands trust, and the two were willing to give up their lives for their friend…and they had. It was a quality Bishop had never experienced himself. Not once, aside from his dead mother, of course.

With thoughts of his mom, the craving struck him again, and he picked up the pack of cigarettes from the passenger seat. The lifelong addiction—started the day his mother had passed away—gave him peace without dulling his senses. But it came at a cost, both emotionally and physically; his mother a testament to that knowledge. He remembered that traumatizing day vividly, and thought about it often—the cigarettes and her life entwined in one memory.

He had been only eight years old at the time, sitting in the waiting room at the Saint Mary's Hospital in Manchester, England. His mother's sister was there, outside the cancer ward, and the prognosis wasn't good. Burned into his memory was the smell of medicine that hung in the air, the white washed walls, and the doctor in a green smock talking to her. Words like aggressive, lung cancer, and terminally ill were mentioned. But he had already known this. After being diagnosed two months prior, he'd assumed the doctors would fix her…could fix her. Why wouldn't he? He was eight, an only child who still believed in the miracle of Christmas. So the shock of her passing later that same evening hurt like nothing he had ever felt before. It left him confused, with more questions than answers. After all, where would he go? They didn't have money, and for that matter, his mom struggled daily just to get food on the table. Even worse was her sister's situation, raising three kids of her own, and a non-working drunk for a husband. So who would take care of him? All he'd ever had was his mother. In panic, he had even thought about his father, but he was nothing more than a name from her past, seldom spoken, and a person he had never met. Truth be told, there was no one he could count on beyond his mother. She was his family; his only family.

Then just like that, she was gone, leaving him alone, and angry. With no one to blame, he focused his young imaginative mind on the cigarettes, relating to them like a living entity—a bully on the playground, a dragon; a beast that had killed his mom. This gave him the strength to confront a faceless foe, and like a child avenging his mother, he took her opened pack to the parking garage to confront the demon that had put such emotional pain in his heart. Without looking beyond the ending day, or even knowing what to expect, he would fight it on its own terms. To his naive mind, it wasn't a long term habit that caused her death, or a malignant growth that had started decades prior. No, to him, she had been taken in a short span, and he needed to know why. So he went to the second floor, and stood against a cement piling between two cars. In the distance he could see Whitworth Park, hazy in the receding light. His heart welled further. The two of them had been there several times, even playing Frisbee in the rain one day.

He took one more look around for any adults that might stop him, but the floor was deserted, even tranquil, except for the cars passing by outside. With his head down, and tears streaming down his cheeks, he took one out with shaky hands and attempted to light it. But he was unfamiliar with the process, and it went out on the first try. The second time wasn't much better, but he blew on the smoldering end until it grew hot and glowed red.

When he was ready, he drew a sleeve across his eyes to clear away the tears, and put it to his lips. Then he paused for a moment as fear touched him. What if the demon took him too, right now? What if he just fell over dead? He fought back the rising panic, his heart racing even faster when his tongue touched the filter. It had a papery taste, along with a cool mint flavor that seemed to coat the inside of his mouth. He blinked hard several times, fighting the urge to just throw it on the ground and crush it under a heel. But then the anger flared again, and he swallowed his fear.

The first puff had seared the inside of his lungs, forcing him to double over and cough repeatedly. The same held true for the second and the third, but he fought through the pain, allowing it to replace his emotional anguish.

That's where it had begun.

Two days later was the funeral, and by then, he had managed to finish the pack of twelve—a victory in his young confused mind. But those victories became smaller as days turned to months, months to years, and a cigarette a day becoming two packs a week; transitioning from an angry youth with good intentions, to an adult with an addiction caused by trauma.

As he eagerly looked at the pack now, he could smell the subtle, yet alluring, aroma of tobacco nourished by the warmth of the fading sun; its scent, fresh and enticing, making his mouth water with pangs of desire for the mentholiptic-nicotine taste. He shook his head at the weakness. There was nothing desirable about the habit. It made his clothes and everything around him, smell like smoke; not to mention what it was doing to his insides—a disparaging thought he didn't want to think about. So he used the confliction to force the temptation from his mind, and placed the pack back on the seat.

He turned onto a side street and then the alleyway in the back. Always on alert, his eyes were constantly scanning for possible threats. In this case it was the windows above, and any darkened hiding places along both sides of the narrow one-way alleyway. He stopped next to a steel door that read "Employees Only".

His thoughts went back to loyalty again, and how it related to Tom's wife, Tanya. It was the same with her. She would die for him, of that he was sure. Not that he wanted to, but would she give up answers under physical duress?

Oh yes, that was also unquestionable. But fortunately for her, there were no answers she could supply that he didn't already know.

"Loyalty," he mumbled, "breeds loyalty." That meant Tom Spears would be coming soon. He grinned slyly, his fingers strumming the steering wheel. *What was her husband doing now?* he wondered. *And where was he looking?* Not that it mattered. After all, Tom would have nothing to go on, and up to now, no trail to follow. His first instinct would be to think the Rickter's were involved. After all, Tom Spears worked for Crude Technologies; the oil-cleanup company responsible for uncovering the Rickter global-plot behind the mysterious black torpedo.

But things weren't as they appeared.

Suffice it to say this would have Tom Spears and the police, going around in circles like dogs chasing their tails. That's why Bishop had made no effort to contact him yet. In letting him stew aimlessly without direction, Tom would become all-consumed and eager for word…any word…of his wife. At least this is what Bishop was counting on because with eagerness came inevitable mistakes.

After turning the engine off, he stepped out of his 2016 Cadillac CTS, closed the door, and paused a moment to take one last look around. Satisfied, he wrapped his knuckles twice against the locked steel door. While he waited, he unclipped the shoulder holster under his windbreaker. In it was a 9mm Beretta. He also rested his hand comfortably on the handle of a snub-nosed .38 revolver at the back of his waistband.

He heard shuffling feet on the inside floor, and the door being unlocked. It opened a crack, paused a moment, then opened all the way. Just inside the doorway were two grim faced men. Bishop recognized them. Both had assisted in the apprehension, interrogation, and subsequent torture of Mike and Micky.

"He's in the back, Mr. Styles," said the man Bishop knew as Jimmy. He was dark haired, muscular, with a wicked four-inch scar that started at the top of his forehead and moved up into the hairline. Adding to his menacing appearance, he had a recently broken nose that remained swollen and hooked to one side. His eyes were still slightly blackened as well—all thanks to Micky Trevor's big right hand when he and Mike Rauls were accosted from this very alleyway.

The blond haired man next to him nodded. His name was Tim. He was narrow shouldered, wore an old Yankees baseball cap, and like Jimmy, was in his mid-to-late twenties. "You'll find him in the locker room." He held a menacing looking bat and pointed it down the hall; his movements tentative and stiff. It was another injury sustained in the confrontation with Mike and Micky—a blow delivered by Mike with a three foot piece of two-by-four, cracking the man's ribs.

They stepped aside, and waved him in. However, in this situation, Bishop didn't like anybody walking behind him. So instead, the assassin waved them ahead of him. They obliged, and Bishop—always overcautious—followed, with his hand remaining around the pistols grip at the small of his back.

They followed a short hallway that opened into a large chamber. This is where the workout equipment used to be, but all that remained now was a rubbish pile at the center of the room from the stripped interior walls. Passing what was left of the crumbling front desk, they made their way toward the locker rooms. Here, the pungent odor of broken plumbing filled the short hallway. But that wasn't all. Also carried in the stagnant air was the smell of decomposition—an odor Bishop Styles was all too familiar with given his line of work.

A short man in a grey Armani suit was waiting for them outside the men's locker room. He had slick black hair combed back behind the ears, and a long birdlike neck. His name was Tony Manatone, and his fine-boned face and soft features looked almost feminine as he smiled. "Mr. Bishop, glad you could make it." He held out his hand, but Bishop didn't return the gesture. It was yet another habit born of self-preservation to keep both hands free. Besides, he preferred holding the pistol, and he didn't like the man anyway.

Tony's hand tentatively dropped back to his side.

"You needed to talk to me," Bishop snapped with a glare. "What is so important that this couldn't be done through normal channels?" In most cases, the standard way of communicating with Bishop had been through a pre-agreed series of numbers sent as text to a burner phone. Then Bishop would respond at his discretion. So this was not only out of line, but the second of two direct calls in one day, with the first being the angry call from Frank Manatone himself. One call was bad enough…but two on the same day?

Bishop took a deep calming breath, his tolerance coming to an end. *This was the problem with people in a position of perceived power,* he thought with distain. *They were impatient, and borderline disrespectful—a word they only used when it suited them. And hunting Tom Spears, by coincidence, was the perfect example of this hypocrisy.*

Tony Manatone remained tentative but cordial. "My father…and his plan…is what I wanted to talk to you about."

Bishop's face turned cherry red. He assumed this had to do with Frank Manatone's harsh words, and if that wasn't bad enough, he didn't like to be second guessed. "As I told your father, the table is set and the plan is in motion." Anger flaring, his hand tightened on the hidden pistol. "You paid for a job and it's getting done." He leaned in, eyes narrowing. "There's a fine line between 'customer' and 'liability', and you are crossing that threshold. Any more contact outside of regular channels and I won't hesitate…"

Tony eyes flared and he held up both hands. "No…no…you misunderstand." He stepped back with genuine fear. "I came here to offer you another contract above and beyond your current obligation." He swallowed hard, and after a moment's pause continued. "I'd even pay you double…that is…on top of what you've already been paid."

Bishop had only worked with Tony Manatone once, and that was during the interrogation of Mike Rauls and Micky Trevor. He found him to be reckless, even careless, and more than anything else, the man couldn't be trusted. With that in mind, he knew who the young Manatone wanted dead. Without question, it was Mr. Manatone himself. It explained, even justified, the reason for this unsolicited secret meeting. Any hint of what Tony was up to, and the young heir would be dead within the hour. His eyes narrowed as he became more controlled. "I have a hunch who this one person might be. Are you sure this is a road you want to travel? Once word gets out…"

Tony held up a hand and smirked. "That's the beauty of what I have in mind. It won't."

Bishop cocked his head. "I'm listening."

Tony nodded to Jimmy and Tim, who were leaning against the nearby wall. "You two go back and guard the front door." After they complied, Tony gestured for Bishop to follow him into the men's locker room.

As they entered, the crunching sound of broken glass under their feet echoed off the cement walls. To their right was the bathroom area, and the source of the glass covered floor. Where once the mirrors hung, now only shadowed rectangular stains remained on the faded wall, and below them, even the row of sinks had been shattered. The toilets were in similar shape, and somewhat to blame for the putrid smell. But only partially. He looked over at the claw foot tub beyond the graffiti covered lockers. It was at the center of the room and placed over a drain on the iron-grey cement floor. In it, and sitting in a yellow-tinted soupy-fluid, were the remains of Mike Rauls and Micky Trevor. After three weeks, their decomposing bodies—sitting upright on each end—were blackened like charred marshmallows, and deflated; their melting organs and fluids augmenting the thickening contents of the tub. Adding to the nightmarish scene was their decaying flesh, which not only sagged like melting wax, but left them with open jaws and eerily haunting grins.

Bishop didn't much care one way or another what they did or didn't do with the bodies, but it did confirm another truth about the young Manatone. In his growing list of undesirable traits, he was…in all probability…completely mad, and the stench only added to Bishops irritability. After surveying the room once more, he relaxed, and brought his gun-hand back to his side. "Speak. You have one minute."

Tony nodded, and spoke with a nervous tremor. "I'd like the killing of Spears to proceed, but only after you've killed my father." He swallowed hard again, his Adams apple bouncing like a yoyo in that bird-like neck. "This is the key to success. Once Spears is lured to New York, it will be rather easy to make it look like he committed the murder."

There was a long pause as Bishop processed Tony's plan. Strangely enough, it wasn't ill-conceived. On the contrary, it had merit; the markings reminiscent to some of Bishops own handiwork. He…they… could kill two birds with one stone, killing one, while pointing the blame at the other. Then, like a package neatly finished off with colorful bough, they could kill Tom Spears.

Bishop met Tony Manatone's dark eyes. "No plan is without risk, but in this scenario, you would be correct about the blame."

"Yes," Tony agreed, breathing a sigh of relief. "If well-conceived, no one would be the wiser." A thin smile crossed his lips. "So you'll do it?"

"Yes," he replied, "but the price from here forward is one million dollars. It's nonnegotiable, and I want half down right away. The remaining balance will be paid when Spears becomes the scapegoat and then killed. Do we have a deal?"

"Yes!" Tony replied enthusiastically, holding out his hand before pulling it back down.

"When I receive half-payment, I'll get Spears here." He turned to leave when Tony blurted one last request. "I want to be there! I want my father to know who killed him!"

Considering what Bishop already knew about Tony Manatone, this wasn't a huge surprise. "That's an extra hundred grand, and also in advance." He glared at the ambitious young heir. "Never contact me through unsecured means again. Do you understand?"

Tony acknowledged with a quick nod of his head.

As Bishop exited the building and slipped behind the wheel of his luxurious Cadillac CTS, his thoughts drifted to Tanya Spears. Albeit unexpectedly, his plan was coming along nicely. Once Frank Manatone was dead, the ramifications of letting her live would become nonexistent. After starting the car, he turned Mozart's rendition of *Ave Verum* back on, and left the alleyway. The sun had already set, so he turned on his headlights. His next stop was to check on Tanya. Once she was fed, he would place the first call to Tom Spears and give him some direction. Then while he waited, he could conceive a plan for Frank Manatone's demise.

Chapter 5

Tom Spears leaned against the stairwell's cement wall, while cautiously glancing around the corner. He was on the second floor of the Red Hook Grain Terminal. It was one of only two lower levels that allowed access to the entire length of building. Above him, set two abreast and side by side in long rows, were the bases of the circular silos. Fifty-four in all, they were so huge, their combined capacity was well over two million bushels. But those days were long gone. It had been more than fifty years since a freighter had pulled up to its pier; the grain mechanically hoisted from the holds of ships, elevated to the top of the terminal, and dropped into vertical storage bins through a series of moveable spouts.

His eyes strained to penetrate the gloom. So far he hadn't seen any cameras or security measures, much less anything to make him believe anyone was here…or had been here in quite a while. After crossing the soccer fields, he had arrived at the fence only to find someone, perhaps kids, had long ago cut a small hole in the wire. So he had dropped the floor mat he was planning to use to circumvent the razor wire, and slipped through on his hands and knees. From the north end, near the deteriorating parking area, he was able to gain access to the interior through an unlocked steel door. This had put him on the first floor where he had reconnoitered before moving up a set of rusty metal stairs to his present position.

At night without lights, it was impossible to see beyond his immediate surroundings, not to mention seeing past the multiple cement columns that ran the length of the building. Looking like an ancient Roman cathedral, these once white supports—set row upon row—were the strength of the building. But now, with the effects of time, that strength was beginning to diminish, if not waver all together. Like an aging body, several close-by were cracked, the chipped cement pockmarked, and much like the exterior walls, covered in black surface mold.

This didn't bode well for being structurally sound, and holding even less promise, was the rest of the building.

To his left, the lower levels of the exterior staircase, including its outer wall, had collapsed into the basin. Left in its wake, was an impenetrable forest of rusted, twisted steel; all entwined and its combined weight further pulling at the side of the building. Even the once sturdy support girders, having been torn free or bent angrily downward, had given way to the heavy burden, which now draped down and disappeared below the surface of the darkened waters below.

Formulating a search plan, he already knew there were three separate basement storage areas located at each end of the building, with another at the center near the elevator tower. Originally built to safely house expensive spare parts away from the corrosiveness of the nearby saltwater, these once heated vault-like rooms were made of cement and sealed with durable steel doors. Dry and secure, they would even keep the intrusive rats out. So if Tanya was here, and given the lack of cellphone service, this was more than likely where she was being held. Now he just needed to find her.

Satisfied no one was around, he turned his flashlight back on, went back down the stairs, past the first floor landing, and stopped at the base of the stairs. In the shifting light, he followed a short hallway to a single door. It was half-off its hinges and leaning to one side. He leaned in, sweeping the flashlight across the fourteen by fourteen foot room. It was empty, smelled of dampness, and hadn't been used in decades. Not wasting any time, he returned to the stairwell, took the stairs two at a time, and turned his flashlight off when he arrived back at the second floor.

As Tom's gaze floated over the darkened area once again, he tried to recall the layout. He remembered there were only three routes to the far side of the building, as well as only three ways to access the upper levels. To get to the other side, he would have to take either the first, second, or uppermost floor. He decided the second level would be best. It offered the path of least resistance, whereas getting to the top floor—excluding the nonfunctioning elevator at the center of the building—meant taking one of the two near-vertical one-hundred and forty-foot staircases at each end of the terminal. This would also mean walking through a decaying building that was dangerous enough during the day, much less in the dark of night. He also eliminated the first floor in much the same way. Rife with treacherous footing, he remembered how bad the crumbling and deteriorating surface used to be, and that was years ago. He could only imagine how bad it was now.

As he readied himself to cross the expansive and open level, he stole one more look around. To his right, beyond the columns on the far side of the building, he could see the tops of trees in the park, and even the darkened shadow of his car in the distance. That meant using the flashlight was out of the question. If he could see out, someone could see in, and that was a risk he couldn't afford. Fortunately, the ambient lighting, dull but reflective, from the bulk oil storage facility across the Henry Street Basin, shimmered in spectral light across the polished-glass surface and past the columns.

As he waited for his eyes to adjust, his thoughts went back to the decaying building, and what he remembered from years ago. Without question, the first floor had been bad, but the second level wasn't much better. On the contrary, there were some holes big enough to drop a truck through. But it was the smaller, more subtle openings in the crumbling floor that concerned him most. A misstep could mean death, or at the very least severe injury and this said nothing of being able to help Tanya.

He moved forward. Gauging each step, he methodically traversed over and around the pipes, mounds of sharp rusty metal and fallen debris. Halfway across, he stopped abruptly. Before him was a round hole in the floor, five feet in circumference with exposed rebar, bent and twisted, sticking out of the concrete edges like angry claws. He leaned forward. It was at least a twenty foot drop to the cement floor below, where the fallen cement piece could be seen; it's reciprocal of torn rebar bent upward like Vietnamese punji sticks, waiting for an unwary victim. Now even more mindful of his step, he moved around the hole and continued forward.

With his eyes warily sweeping back and forth in front of him, he stopped near a moveable spout which angled down from the ceiling. Gravity fed, it came from the base of a silo and appeared to be the only one with a chute still attached—a four-foot-diameter pipe that once delivered grain to barges from the individual overhead silos. Dormant and long forgotten, the rust covered pipe sloped downward, past the tracks once used for rail carts, and extended beyond the side of the building; its opening twenty feet over the Henry Street Basin.

Beyond the leaning apparatus, he made out a graffiti covered wall. This was part of the elevator-tower that rose up from the center of the building. Inside, aside from the elevator, was another staircase that would lead into a basement storage area. He moved close to the steel rails to limit the chances of falling through the floor. To access the broad tower, he followed the tracks along its side until he found an access door. Already opened, he turned on his flashlight and followed a short hall to the elevator.

After locating the nearby basement door, his disappointment was apparent. It had been welded shut, and sealed long ago. Flipping off his flashlight again, he move back to the tracks.

A light breeze wafted in between the columns, filling the second floor with the fresh scent of the sea. He paused a moment, cocking his head. In the distance, muffled but constant, was a humming sound. His heart quickened. A generator! He stepped back against the wall and listened to the barely audible sound. After confirming it was coming from the far end of the building, he moved forward again.

Following the tracks, Tom crossed the next open portion of the second level.

Once on the far side, he located the stairs. Much like the other side of the building, it was an open stairwell and the main thoroughfare that connected the first, second, and basement floors, as well as the uppermost level and the roof. He followed the stairs down to the first level, tracking the humming sound to an enclosed room. The door was locked, but he leaned into it, and after the second time the wood frame splintered and gave way. Inside, dim and flickering, a light was on. It was an old maintenance room, and against the far wall, was a running generator. Gas operated, it was boxed in on four sides with acoustic insulation for soundproofing. This not only explained why it was so quiet, but also confirmed he was on the right track. After stepping inside, he closed the door. A ceiling vent fan was on over his head to neutralize the buildup of heat from the running motor. Another obstacle to overcome with a gas engine was the exhaust. So a pipe had been cleverly fashioned and run through the side wall.

He stooped and looked closer at the purring Honda generator. At only 3500 watts, it would have limited power output, but more than enough to run lights and electronics to several rooms. Along the back wall were ten breaker boxes lined up horizontally. Under each was an emergency transfer plugin specifically designed for generators in case of electrical power loss. He followed the generator's output cord to the right, where it was plugged in under the third breaker box. Opening the faded grey metal door, there were only three breakers that remained on.

One was for this room, marked "Maint. Shop", another was "hallway", and the last "storage room 1". He closed the door stepping back to the generator. On the far side was a five gallon red gas can. He picked it up and set it back down. It was half full. Next he checked the fuel in the tank. It had less than a quarter of a tank left. That meant her captors would be returning soon to refill the tank.

Turning out the overhead light, he exited the maintenance room and closed the door. Holding his Glock before him, he went back to the staircase to check the basement. He was about to descend the stairs, when a sweeping light, swift and fleeting, glinted off the interior columns. He ducked instinctively. A car was pulling up to this end of the building. His thoughts went to Tanya, and he descended the stairs to the basement. When he got to the landing, and unlike the other staircase, there was a door. He checked the knob. It was locked, but he could see light coming from the hallway under it. That's when he saw the leather flats on the last step. The shoes belonged to his wife. Eagerness, swift and overwhelming, enveloped him. It pulsed at his temples making his heart race with anticipation. Up to now he had been holding any optimism in check, focusing instead on the who, what, where, and why; not wanting to think about whether she was all right, if she was hurt, or even if he was on the right track in finding her.

Unable to contain himself any further, his foot lashed out, shattering both the evening silence as well as the door's frame. Inside was a well-lit cement hallway with broken lightbulbs scattered all over the floor.

A sign of imprisonment, he thought, glancing up and down the hall. There were still no cameras, and he took a measured breath. The air here was heavy with dampness, and the sound of crunching glass echoed in the small corridor as he stepped in front of the first of two doors. Above it was the number '1'. Regardless of expectations, unbearable or not, he would soon have answers and know the truth.

With his heart racing, he reverently touched the cool steel of the faded grey door, and leaned in close. Fear of the unknown now was as crippling as it was suffocating. Swallowing hard, his words became hesitant, and filled with both uncertainty and cold dread. "Tanya, you there?"

*****

The ceiling-light faded and surged again. In the extreme silence of her current realm, Tanya was finally able to pick out the audible sound of a distant generator; the vacillating engine mimicking the power to the light. She found comfort in the sound. Without it, the silence, physiological and unnerving, left her emotions on pins and needles.

Doubt crept in once again. Like slow moving ripples bumping at her resolve, they came at her measured and limited at first. But then those doubts grew, hitting her in steady waves and swamping all rational thought. Uncertain and frightened, she stared at the light again. What if it went out, and remained out? Worse yet, what if Bishop never returned? Would this become her tomb, her sarcophagus? She took a shuddering breath. How many hours had it been since Bishop was last here? Her stomach grumbled and she looked at the empty bag that had held the burger and fries. She would ration the food in the future…if there was a future. She was also getting thirsty…

The crashing sound of the hallway door made her jump, and she rose from the bed. Footsteps on broken glass followed, stopping just outside her door. Then unnerving silence again. Someone was standing on the other side of the door. She could scarcely breathe, and backed to the rear wall. The only sound came from her fast beating heart, pounding like a drum in her chest. Her crossed arms began to shake, and she swallowed hard.

Then her heart surged when she heard the familiar voice of her husband, "Tanya, you there?" Soft-spoken and reassuring, his words almost made her knees buckle from emotional relief. He was here! A shuddering breath took her first words, and she ran to the door. "I'm… here!" she shrieked, through a spasmed breath. "Tom…I'm here!"

"Step back!"

She did and the door exploded inward. Upon seeing him, that dam— those emotions she'd been able to hold in check for all these days— finally burst. As she rushed into his arms, a continuous flow of tears had already begun, and, like a scared puppy, she trembled uncontrollably. "I got you," he said, holding her tight. "I got you."

She released her vice-like grip to look at him. Tears were coming down his dirt-covered cheeks, and the emotional torment of the last week was seen on his face. He looked fatigued. His skin was pale, his face gaunt, like he hadn't slept in days, and his brown eyes were bagged and ringed purple.

She took another shuddering breath, thinking about Bishops words…"Both in strength and weakness, you're his undying love, his eternal flame." Without question he couldn't have been more correct. She also now understood what he meant about *taking Tom from his violent world, and healing the wounds*. It shone now in his hurt, his despair, his very demeanor, and through this vulnerable state, he couldn't have looked more beautiful to her. She cupped his face. "I knew you'd come…" she began, but he interrupted, gripping her shoulders intently.

"Damn straight, but we don't have a lot of time," he replied with conviction, and moved back down the hall to the steps to retrieve her shoes. Returning, he gave them to her. "I need you to remain here. At least temporarily. Someone just pulled up to the building, and I can't risk you being in peril until I've neutralized the threat."

"It's Bishop…his name is Bishop Styles!" she announced. "All this has to do with you killing a man named Teeds." She grabbed the front of his windbreaker. "He plans to kill you. This is all about killing you!"

He looked over his shoulder toward the stairs, and his eyes narrowed. When he turned back to her, the anguish she had seen in his face was gone, replaced instead with a look that was lean, hard, and as cold as a winter wind. He nodded. "It only highlights the fact I need you to remain here a little longer."

"He'll know you're coming," she blurted out with concern. "He said the complex had cameras…" she pointed at the glass on the floor. "And there are glass-breaks."

He kissed her hard on the lips, and followed it, by kissing her forehead. "He lied. This is an abandoned grain terminal. It was only a ploy to keep you here…to take away all hope." Turning, he ran back down the hall and spoke again before disappearing up the stairs. "I'll be back shortly." His words were both confident and reassuring.

Left alone, she stood frozen in the doorway, listening to his footsteps; the sound like a hope lifeline. Then the quiet enveloped her, and she was alone again.

She bent over and slipped on her shoes. The red wool blanket—once comforting—now only represented days of confinement and she shook it from her shoulders, letting it drop to the floor. Then she stared, wide-eyed, at the staircase, willing Tom to return so they could leave this wretched place. Anxiety built swiftly, and each passing second only added to both her uncertainty and dread. Her eyes flicked both ways along the short hallway. Not hearing any sounds, and with fear blossoming once again, she moved toward the staircase, tip-toeing through the crunching glass as much as possible.

She stopped at the hall door, peering around the shattered frame. Two minutes had passed. Looking up the staircase, she was just stepping onto the first step when an explosion ripped through the floor above, making the building shudder. A grey chalky dust floated down the stairwell, and she took a step back.

Gunshots, rapid and deafening, soon followed.

Chapter 6

AFTER LEAVING THE QUEENS ATHLETIC Club, Bishop Styles, alias The Duke, took Interstate 495 west, connected to Highway 278, and later took the exit that wound him around and under the Brooklyn Bridge. Traffic at this time of night had been almost non-existent, and the normally forty-five minute drive during the day had only taken twenty minutes. He had then followed Cadman Plaza west, where it turned into Court Street, which, after five miles, would dead-end at the abandoned Red Hook Grain Terminal. Before getting there, he had pulled into a Jack in the Box drive-through. Open for twenty fours, he ordered an ultimate cheeseburger, minus pickles and onions, with extra ketchup. It was one of her favorites. He also ordered a large side of french-fries, with a Pepsi and extra water.

Nearing the terminal, he pulled off to the shoulder of the quiet two-lane road, and removed a throw away cellphone from its packaging. After opening the yellow file on the passenger seat, he entered the appropriate phone number. As he suspected, it went right to voice mail. It not only gave Tom deniability in never getting the message, but also took the power of control away from her captors. After all, it was difficult to capitulate with a recording, much less argue about unreasonable demands.

He smirked when he heard Tom's voice, and left a short message: "Your wife is alive, but that won't remain the case. You are to come to Lower Manhattan in New York. You have two days to get here. I will call this number again at exactly ten o'clock Friday night. If you don't answer…if you aren't here…if you bring the authorities…it all ends the same." He disconnected, turned the phone off, and removed the battery.

In the distance he could see the roof of the Red Hook Terminal silhouetted by Staten Island's city lights further west. It had been years since he'd used the derelict building. In fact, when he was looking for the appropriate killing ground—a place that would give him every advantage in dealing with Spears—it was Frank Manatone who had suggested it. He couldn't have been more correct. It afforded him both offensive and defensive positions as well as the privacy needed to kill and dispose of the body.

He thought about Tom again, his specialties, his pros and cons. Long before the surveillance and taking his wife, he had already been studying him. It only made sense considering they were rivals in the same deadly trade. And that said nothing of the man's even deadlier reputation. Back in the day, he was quietly known as the Shadow. His specialty was accidental deaths, or at least the illusion of one. Frank Teeds had been the perfect example of this. As the police report goes—supplied by a Manatone informant at the NYPD—Tom had entered Savory Spa as a maintenance man prior to Frank Teeds arrival from… as luck would have it…a doctor's appointment for heart trouble. The strategy had been flawless. Prior to Teeds getting a rubdown, Tom had laced the hot-messaging-oil with concentrated nicotine. After administered, this would raise the blood pressure significantly. Then to guarantee an inevitable heart attack, Tom had also rigged the thermostat of the sauna in conjunction with disabling the lock.

Bishop grinned with respect.

Even this had been thought out, using a chunk of wax in the locking mechanism; the wax slowly melting away leaving no evidence of foul play. In the end it was so well-orchestrated the police had never looked twice. But, as it turns out in this business, you can never prepare for everything. The plans' only pitfall occurred when years later an observant detective spotted Tom—the maintenance man—on a surveillance video after Savory Spa had been permanently shut down for human trafficking. And by sheer coincidence, it was during that same spa-shut-down that Tom's face had been all over the news after rescuing captive children from a sinking freighter. Now curious, and unfortunate for Tom, this detective decided to do some digging, and the more he dug, the more curious he became. In tracing Tom's more than colorful life, he learned there was much more to Tom Spears than met the eye. Legally speaking, his real name was Allen Wittman and he had once lived in Oregon; a family man, studying to be a lawyer no less. Illegally speaking, there was mounting circumstantial evidence, linking, if not incriminating him, as a hired assassin. This included the mysterious deaths of two men responsible for killing his previous wife and child in a DUI case. Then the wheels had truly came off, and the clever ruse in

Savory Spa revealed, when that same detective had Frank Teeds body exhumed. A short time later, Frank Manatone had been notified that his nephew had been murdered. Frank, of course, had been outraged, and then told the detective to bury it, telling him the syndicate would handle it themselves. And now they were.

Bishop continued on his way to the Red Hook Granary Terminal, and a short drive later, turned onto the entry road to the Bay Terminal—a multi-user industrial facility that included a private bus storage lot filled with full-sized coaches, and a gravel pit. After passing the bus lot, he pulled up to the well-lit gravel pit security gate. Two grim-faced men came out of a small guard shack. They were in blue security uniforms and wearing police style utility belts with holstered pistols at their hips.

A perk of the mob-owned facility was to not ask questions and the taller of the two men with unkempt brown hair pushed the chain-link gate open and waved Bishop through. Once past the guardhouse, Bishop passed several large gravel piles on his left. Highlighted in the headlight beams in front of him was a rock crushing machine, a backhoe, and a large excavating cat. He skirted them and the pier to his right where two small freighters, a barge, and a tugboat were tied. Once in back, he turned left, facing the Red Hook Terminal. He pulled up to the south end of the building. After turning off his Cadillac CTS, he popped the trunk and exited, throwing the cellphone he'd just used into the nearby water.

Now that Tom Spears was on his way, it was time to prepare. Inside the trunk were two medium sized hard-covered suitcases. One was black, the other silver. He removed the black case, and opened the other. Inside, set in rows and surrounded by polyurethane black foam, were twenty four of the United States military's newest line of M67 grenades, and two flashbangs. Checking the pins of each, he carefully removed eight grenades, and one flashbang, clipping them to a military nylon web belt and settling it over a shoulder. Then he returned the case to the trunk. His plan was simple. After Spears showed up in Lower Manhattan, he would run Tom through a gauntlet of drops and counter measures to not only confirm he was alone, but to further get inside his head. Then when Bishop was satisfied, he would lure him here to this prepared site. But only when he was completely satisfied. It was the main reason he had only allowed Tom two days to get here. Any more, and Tom would've arrived early to start investigating, and the first people he'd call would be known acquaintances. This Bishop couldn't allow. His whole plan was predicated on the element of surprise…and thus not allowing Tom to prepare. If Tom found out that the Manatones were the culpable party, he would change his predictability and form a strategy…an unexpected strategy. Bishop knew this for certain because it's what he'd do. So right now he needed to keep Tom off balance. Underestimating him…the Shadow—especially after killing his longtime friends Micky Trevor and Mike Rauls, and now the taking of his wife—meant certain death. No one understood this more than Bishop Styles. It was one thing to catch Spears unsuspecting, and quite another to catch him in a calculating state of revenge. No, it was imperative he kill the man right away, at the first opportunity. With the killing of Manatone Senior already set in motion, the stage was set. Now the orchestration of the Shadow's arrival became that much more important…with the key being…not to underestimate him and his deadly capabilities.

He closed the trunk, picked up the black case in one hand, and put the Jack in the Box bag in the other. The entry door was located along the front of the building, and after unlocking it, he stepped inside but alertly stopped. On the other side of the floor, beyond the maintenance/generator room, there was a light spilling onto the first floor. It was coming from the basement staircase, which was out of sight beyond a short wall. Then he heard the abrupt and decisive sound of a door being kicked open. His heart quickened.

A stranger…a vagrant coming to her rescue?

He quickly dismissed the idea due to the security that patrolled the area.

No, there was only one person it could be. Spears! He wasn't sure how he'd managed it, but Bishop knew without question it was him, and oddly, he relished the thought.

Cool, collected, and unshaken, the professional killer known as The Duke of assassins emerged. Setting the case and bag of food down, he removed a penlight from his pocket, and turned it on. Holding it with his teeth, he hooked the grenade belt around his waist, and stripped off his windbreaker. Inside the black case was a Kimber Aegis II 9mm pistol with fluted rosewood grips. He picked it up, and checked the magazine. In his capable hands the stylish hand gun was as deadly accurate as it was a striking. A long breeched, perfectly balanced weapon, its black steel slide, and satin silver frame glinted in the beam of the penlight. After removing the Berretta from his shoulder holster and placing it in the case, he holstered the Kimber, and then removed his Colt .38 from the case as well. After rolling through the cylinder to make sure it was loaded, he slid it into the ankle holster under his pant leg.

He picked up the barrel suppressor for the 9mm from the case, but put it back. Using the hand grenades would effectively eliminate any clandestine operations. Lastly, he removed the military grade Pulsar Edge GS night vision goggles and slipped the headset over his head. Durable and weatherproof, it offered the newest line of five-lens optics, a CF-Super Image Intensifier Tube for image enhancement, and thermal imaging capabilities.

Swiveling the binocular-style lenses up, he was as ready as he could be considering the changing circumstances. His plan before this very moment had been to stage the various floors with ammo caches. Dress rehearsals had also been planned to further familiarize himself with the building, its decaying floors, piles of debris, and more importantly, to ensure he knew where to find cover. But all that had changed, including the use of his M16 rifle for extra fire power. He took it in stride, though. After all, he too, had pros and cons, and one of his many strengths was his ability to digest a changing playing field, and adapt to it.

Holding the Kimber Aegis in a two handed grip, he slowly stepped away from the entry toward the generator room. Now all the surveillance, in-depth study, and knowledge Bishop had accrued about the Shadow, would come into play.

Chapter 7

THE PANGS FROM SEPARATING FROM Tanya had struck Tom as he climbed the steps. After finally locating her, it had been a difficult decision to leave her behind, even for a minute. But he told himself it was only temporary. When he reached the first floor, he realized his first mistake. By leaving the basement door opened, light, in an otherwise dark building, not only confirmed his presence but also spilled past him and left his silhouetted shadow on the two closest columns.

He cursed.

In thinking of the reunion with his wife, and her safety, his judgment had been clouded. A twinge of panic touched him. He thought about going back down to shut the door but there was no longer time. With his back to the stairwell wall, he crouched and peeked around the corner. To his right, and in-between the grey chipped columns, was the distant fuel storage facility and the shimmering waters of the Henry Street Basin. In front of him was only darkness, the bright light affecting his night vision. He had to move, so he committed to getting to the generator-room-wall around the corner to his left. Staying low, he made it in ten quick strides. After squatting in the corner, he closed his eyes to let his eyes adjust, while also listening for movement. The only sound was that of his thumping heart and the purring generator. A full minute later, he opened his eyes and blinked several times. His vision had already improved. In the distance, in front of him, was the silhouette of a debris pile at the center of the floor. He moved to the front corner of the maintenance room and peered around the side. Again nothing. He was about to move around the next corner when he heard another presence above the humming generator. It was a metallic sound, like a foot stepping on a piece of metal. Eyes narrowing, he tracked the sound to somewhere along the far wall near an entry door.

Was it Bishop?

He already knew the answer.

Calculating his next move, he figured Bishop hadn't seen him or he would've opened fire. That deduction however changed a heartbeat later, when something skittered across the floor, striking the front of the generator room and settling not ten feet from his current position. Fortunately, Tom was around the corner, and instincts, nurtured and augmented through years as a hired killer, took over. He recoiled, rolling backward and didn't stop until he hit the stairwell wall. A violent explosion followed, renting the air; the concussive wave numbing his senses, and showering him in cement fragments and grey dust. He lurched to his feet. The front corner of the maintenance room was gone, leaving only torn and jagged cement and a pile of rubble on the nearby floor. Beyond it, through the dust filled air, a shadow appeared, running toward the debris pile at the center of the room. Without hesitating, Tom pointed and fired a quick three round burst from his Glock. Then the shadow was gone, safely hidden once again. Tom however, was now fully exposed. In anticipation of the attackers next move, he dove to his right as a flurry of bullets peppered the portion of the wall he'd just vacated. After rolling once, he sprung to his feet, and ran for the protection of the stairwell. As he rounded the corner to safety, another grenade bounced against the wall. He ducked low. The explosion made the building shudder, filling the air with more grey dust. Then two more blasts followed.

Someone grabbed his shoulder. Without thinking, he reacted, dipping his shoulder, spinning, and leveling the Glock. Before him was his wife's terrified face. She had come up from the basement, and held her hands up defensively. With his ears ringing from the deafening explosions, he hadn't heard her approach. He grabbed her arm and pointed up the staircase. "Go up! Move…move…move!"

After she climbed the first flight and disappeared around corner, Tom crouched and moved to the end of the wall, stealing a glance he saw someone closing fast on his position. The attacker was exposed, so Tom leaned out and raised the Glock.

Just as Tom fired, there was an explosion near his feet, and his world went bright white; the concussive wave disorienting him. He lost all sense of direction, and recoiled in pain. Like daggers to his corneas, he covered his burning eyes as he tried to process what had just happened. The fact he was still standing meant it hadn't been a grenade. Then it occurred to him. Flashbang!

To keep the attacker at bay, he stuck the pistol around the corner, and fired three random shots. Then he followed the wall, stumbling blindly up the first flight of stairs before slamming headlong into the wall at the next landing. Half-deaf, and now blind he knew he was in trouble.

From out of nowhere, hands from above his position grabbed him, and pulled him up the stairs. Tanya had returned, and she was dragging him along. He heard her screaming something as she jerked at his arm, encouraging him up the stairs. But going up wasn't the direction he wanted to go. It meant not only dealing with the buildings unknown and deteriorating condition, but also the possibility of being trapped. He stopped to get his bearings, grabbing her arm. The burning white in his eyes was fading. After blinking rapidly he looked down the stairwell. They were well past the second floor, and a shadow of movement confirmed going back down would be out of the question. The good news by going up, he rationalized, the attacker couldn't use any more grenades or flashbangs for fear of the weapons bouncing back in his direction. He glanced upward. They would have to climb the one hundred and forty feet to the top, and hope they could get across either the upper floor, or the roof.

"Tom?" Tanya asked, her questioning grey eyes fearful. "Can you hear me?"

"Yes, it's better," he answered, encouraging her once again up the stairs. "We'll have to go all the way up."

Sweat gleamed on his forehead, and both their chests heaved when they finally reached the upper level and exited through a door onto another landing. Here the residual lighting from the basement was nonexistent, so he turned on his flashlight. Above and to their left was another flight of stairs and in front of them another door. He opened it slightly. This was the floor just below the roof. The walled-in interior was pitch black but in the sweeping beam of the flashlight he could see the tops of two silos and a catwalk along the right wall. This he knew would go past all the silos to the other side of the building. But it was long, and they would be exposed the entire way…and this said nothing of its treacherous condition. Not wanting to take the risk, they continued up the stairs.

At the top of the next flight, they exited a door onto the roof. A light breeze, cool and clean, touched Tom's cheek, and he surveyed their surroundings. The moon was high in the sky, bright and full, which helped illuminate the black tarred roof. They were standing at the base of a tower that went up another four levels. This is where the conveyed wheat would come up from the barges. Then it passed through a web of pipes and chutes and carried across a horizontally enclosed conveyer belt. Set high over the roof, and running the length of the building, this was the main artery where the grain could be dispersed and fed into the individual silos by numerous pipes.

Tom looked up. Long gone was the conveyer belt and piping, with the only evidence they had ever existed being the huge square hole in the upper tower wall, and several pipes, rusty and bent, still attached to some caps along the roof. He swept the beam over the roof. It was wide open, with little cover. In getting to the other side they would be completely exposed; the moonlight not helping. A closing door alerted Tom they were out of time. It was from the level below them. The same door he had checked before coming up to the roof. He spun back to the tower they had exited. The steel door began to open. Tom closed the gap in three strides kicking the door abruptly back into the attacker, and stepped aside. There was a crashing sound from someone hitting the stair railing, followed by thundering gun shots as bullets passed through the door.

Tom rolled to his left, spun, and returned fire, emptying his remaining six rounds into the door. As he backed away, he ejected the magazine, slid another in place, and smoothly pulled the slide back to snap another round in the chamber. "In a second we're going to make a run for the far side," he said to Tanya, backing to her side, while remaining focused on the pockmarked door. "Get ready."

Continuing to back up, he raised the pistol again and emptied another full magazine, sending fifteen rounds in rapid succession in the door and along the siding to the right of it. Now more than fifty paces away, and while quickly switching magazines again, he turned to his wife. "Now, Tanya! Run!"

She did as she was told, and sprinted toward a door at the base of a smaller tower on other side of the building. It wouldn't be without hazard. At more than three hundred feet away, they were running over a dark surface, and at night. Making it worse, they needed the darkness for cover, which meant they would be running without the benefit of a flashlight.

After snapping another round in the chamber, he followed close behind her while keeping his body between her and any potential shots fired in their direction. Running blindly, they were half way across the roof, when Tanya suddenly dropped through the roof, followed by a sickening sound when her head struck something solid. Only three feet behind her, Tom dropped the gun and dove to catch her as she disappeared into the blackness. Groping blindly with both hands, he desperately latched onto the thin fabric of her shirt, along with a handful of her hair; the shirt already giving way.

He landed hard, sliding forward on the slick tarred roof. When he came to a stop, he was on the edge of a darkened hole, up to his armpits, with his wife hanging precariously below him. He looked down. Past his outstretched arms, it was blacker than black—no light at all; his wife a darkened shadow.

"Tanya…" he grunted having difficulty holding his grip, "grab my arms…" There was no response, no movement. Her body was limp. "Tanya…" he pleaded.

Panicked, his eyes flicked left and right. She had fallen into a four-foot-wide uncapped silo opening, and if she fell, only a one-hundred-and-forty foot drop…and death…remained. The situation grew more dire. Without any purchase, her weight was dragging him over the edge, too. Now up to his waist, and bent into the hole, he was forced to release her hair and swing his right arm up onto the roof to gain leverage. Now she was only being held by the blouse hooked under her arms. "Tanya!" he pleaded again. "Pleas…"

Then it happened.

The buttons on her thin blouse tore free, and from his precipice atop the huge silo, he felt the shift in weight as her arms rose up, slipping free, and just like that she was gone. A deafening silence followed as he continued clutching her blouse helplessly. Far below, the brutality of her fall was finalized by the bone crushing sound of her body impacting the base of the silo. A hideous, echoing sound, it was followed by a watery splash somewhere below in the darkness. Then silence.

In shock, he rolled onto his back, still clutching her shirt. He couldn't breathe, like steel bands ever tightening around his throat. He swallowed hard.

It should've been…him…not her. Dear God, not her!

As anguished tears streamed across his face, he took a shuddering breath and pressed the blouse to his face, breathing her in. A moonlit glint caught his attention. Hooked in his hand was the locket, its golden chain wrapped in his fingers. He held it up—the gift given to her with the single requirement that she never take it off. She never did, and only then did the true shock of what just happened set in. In a daze, he stared up at the moon beyond the locket. His loss was complete. He was beaten, with no fight left in him. Nothing mattered anymore…he didn't care. He waited for Bishop to come…

Chapter 8

Bishop Styles lay on a gurney staring up at the white ceiling. Not helping his already foul demeanor, the small surgical room he was in was less than sanitary, and now reeked of antiseptic from his treated wounds. But that wasn't the real source of his torment. He was furious with himself for allowing Tom Spears to get the better of him. Even being outmatched in firepower, the Shadow had not only managed to find Tanya before Bishop was ready, but even succeeded in rescuing her. Then to top it off, Bishop had allowed himself to be shot. Not once, but twice. Twice! Something that only happened once in his entire thirty-year span had just happened twice in one night! Looking for answers, he went over the debacle at the Red Hook Terminal again in his head.

*****

Once alerted to the intruder, Bishop had armed himself, but remained on the far side of the building. In the darkness, he hid behind one of the huge cement pillars closest to the door he'd entered through. From there, using his night vision goggles—in conjunction with the heat signature software—he was garnered a sweeping view of the floor.

Patience was the key, so he took a deep breath and waited.

The quiet interior was filled with the aromatic smell of the sea, washed in by a cool breeze. It was also in shambles. Debris, from paper to piping and rusted metal, was either littering the floor or put long-ago into sporadic piles. Also highlighted in an eerie glow of green, and widespread throughout, were the six rows of support columns. He looked past the outer row. In the distance, light filtered in from the fuel containment depot across the waterway. Reflective and refractive, it was the only other source of light.

Nothing seemed out of place so he switched to thermal. The optic green phosphors of the screen switched to black and white. In this mode there was far less detail to the surrounding areas, but any heat signature would stand out in a white glow as clearly as the soft illumination of a lightbulb in a darkened room.

He scanned the floor again. With the exception of having an outside wall that stopped halfway down the building, this side of the floor was built much the same as the other side. Not seeing any threats, he moved to the next closest cement column. Then to the second. From here the angle to the far stairwell wall was better.

Movement caught his eye. Quick and fleeting, someone crouched had moved from around the stairwell wall and disappeared on the other side of the maintenance room. He leveled his Kimber Aegis II 9mm and waited. It didn't take long before a head appeared in the middle of the screen before disappearing again. Even in a ghostly-glow of white, Bishop recognized the face. It was indeed Tom Spears! Again, the question of 'how' flashed in his brain. It was infuriating. Bishop had made every effort to not underestimate Spears, and yet he'd done just that. How could this be? It was one thing if Tom had been given any clues, much less time. But he had neither. Not dwelling on it further, he waited for Tom to stick his head out one more time, but as he shifted his feet, his foot bumped a piece of scrap metal lying on the floor. Loud and distinctive, it all but gave away any element of surprise, if not giving away his position. Reacting instinctively, he grabbed a grenade from his belt, pulled the pin, and in one fluid motion threw it toward the corner where Tom had just been. But his throw was off the mark. Short-arming it, it bounced off the floor, hit the maintenance room's front wall, and stopped short of the corner. An ear shattering explosion followed, showering the area with fragmenting cement from the wall.

Even before the dust settled, Bishop was on the move again. This time to a pile of shoulder-high debris in-between his position and the next column. From there he would have a direct line of sight to the corner where Tom was hiding. Halfway across, and six strides short, the Shadow unexpectedly returned fire. The first two shots had been hurried, missing wide behind him. But the third had been spot on, only missing Bishop by happenstance when the bullet struck a thick piece of steel protruding from the pile just as he dove for cover.

The Duke rolled once, stood, and snapped off four shots of his own. But Spears had anticipated this, and the shots narrowly missed as he dove clear. Bishop cursed, raised the night vision goggles, and hurled another grenade just as Tom sprinted back behind the stairwell wall. The explosion was deafening, but did little else beyond pitting the wall and floor. He tossed two more for good measure, but they were about as effective as the last two.

Tom reappeared a split second later. Leaning out, the Shadow fired two random shots in Bishops direction; the shots ricocheting off more steel debris. After ducking, the Duke removed the flashbang from his belt, counted to three in anticipation of Tom's reemergence, pulled the pin, and threw it to the left of the wall.

Used in the military and law enforcement, the typical flashbang is a non-lethal stun grenade but very effective. Bishop knew this. That's why he had purchased a set at a premium years before. They were perfect weapons in confined confrontations, and immeasurable at night; especially inside a darkened building. By producing a blinding flash of light, and an intensely loud "bang" of greater than one-hundred and seventy decibels, it was designed to temporarily disorient an enemy's senses. But the key word here being temporary; as in only lasting a few short seconds. So with timing being the key, The Duke sprinted forward shortly after letting it fly. Mindful to not flashbang himself, he shielded his eyes with his left hand, and looked down as he ran. Half way there, Tom reappeared again, raised his weapon and fired just as the flashbang went off.

Glimpsing the movement, Bishop ducked and rolled once again, but this time the bullet found its mark, passing through the meat of his right shoulder. It wasn't a debilitating shot, but it effectively countered his offensive attack, and had him on the defensive, rolling to the protection of wall. It also cost him a tactical advantage when he lost the night vision goggles in the unplanned dramatic roll. Grateful to still be breathing, he focused on the end of the wall, looking and listening. He saw nothing, and the high frequency blast from the flashbang had his ears ringing. That meant, short of a trumpet-playing-quartet next to him, he wouldn't be able to hear shit…at least temporarily.

Then Tom's pistol reappeared again from the end of the wall, followed by three more shots. Defensive in nature, they were pointed in the direction Bishop had just come from. This told Bishop, with absolute certainty, that Tom was blinded. Getting to his feet, he tried to raise the pistol in his right hand, but pain exploded through his injured shoulder. Proficient with both hands, he switched to his left, and moved forward along the wall. Once at the end, he became very cautious again. Fifteen seconds had already passed, and any lingering effects from the flashbang would be almost gone; his own ears no longer ringing. He stole a quick look. Satisfied there was no one there, he moved to the stairs and paused to listen. The footfalls of two people running up the steel steps could be heard echoing above him.

Now in the light—emanating up from the basement—he holstered his weapon and examined the shoulder wound further. The bullet had missed the bone, but passed through the nerve cluster near the collarbone. It left a nasty inch-deep cleft; the oozing blood already saturating his long-sleeved cotton shirt, and dripping off the end of his numbing fingers. He remained calm, but worked fast. To stop the bleeding, he ripped the sleeve off, and covered the wound by wrapping the bloodied-cloth over his shoulder and under his pit several times. When snug, he used both his teeth and good hand to cinch it down tight. He examined his handiwork. It wasn't pretty, but for now, the blood flow would at least be slowed. Not wasting any more time, he wiped the blood off his good hand, removed the pistol, and once again resumed the chase.

Three minutes later he was at the top of the staircase in front of another door. Stepping through, he found himself on another landing, with additional flight of stairs to his left, and another door in front of him. This was the level just below the flat roof. Opening the spring-loaded door ajar, he cautiously peered inside. The floor was pitch black.

Had they gone this way? If they had, Bishop would be vulnerable without the benefit of his night-vision goggles, much less a flashlight. He also didn't hear the sound of running feet.

A noise from above had him breathing a sigh of relief, and he released the door, letting it shut, and followed the stairs to the roof door. Winded, with sweat beading across his brow, he cautiously approached and put his ear against the cold steel. Hearing nothing, he held the pistol up near his left ear and pressed open the horizontal swing-bar with his hip. When the door opened ten inches, he was about to step through when it crashed back into his left shoulder. He sailed back, bouncing off the rail, and landing on his backside with his head wedged against the far wall. On instinct, he leveled his Kimber Aegis 9mm and fired randomly at the door. With each shot, a quarter-sized hole appeared, expanding to half-dollar-sized holes as the hollow-point rounds exited the other side.

When the gun was empty, he smoothly released the magazine with the same hand in preparation to reload. It was a process he knew by heart and could normally do in less than three seconds. But that wasn't the case with only one good arm. In fact, he'd no sooner pulled out an extra magazine with his good hand when a barrage of bullets came back through the door in his direction.

Remaining down, he scooched to his left and into the corner. The door was now pockmarked like Swiss cheese, but after six rounds there was a reprieve and silence once more. It didn't last long though, and once again before he could reload, the bullets came fast and furious. This time they were coming through both the hole-riddled door and also the wood siding at the side. One bullet cratered the grey cement above his head, and yet another hit the wall to his left. He cursed and rolled for the safety of the stairwell, throwing himself over and down. But before he could draw his legs clear a bullet passed through his calf, throwing his leg sideways. Halfway down the flight of stairs, he came to a stop in a bloody heap. Feeling dizzy, he lifted his head. He was on his back, pointed downward, and now bleeding from both his shoulder and a leg.

There was no initial pain, but he knew that would change rapidly when the shock wore off. Already the shoulder wound had transitioned from numbness to pulsating and blossoming pain, and the roll down the stairs hadn't helped. But right now it was blood loss that was his first concern. If left unchecked, symptoms included nauseousness, lightheadedness, and eventual unconsciousness and death. His mind was already sluggish as he rotated himself upright on the blood slick stair. Out of shape from smoking two packs of cigarettes a day, he felt exhausted, bone weary, from both the climb, and also the blood loss. A bead of sweat rolled off his forhead and stung his eye. Blinking rapidly, he swallowed hard, and put his back against the wall. His eyes flicked up at the door, and then down at the landing below where his pistol now lay. If the Shadow attacked now, Bishop was finished. He groped for the .38 in his boot, cocked the revolver, and waited. But the assassin never showed. So after ten minutes, and a huge effort, he used his belt as a tourniquet for his leg, hobbled down the stairs, and made it to the doctor an hour later.

There was a gentle tap on the door and the physician reentered. He was grey-haired, short and burly, with a gruff manner. His name was Fredrick Ramous. At age sixty two, he was legally retired, but that was only legally. Illegally speaking, he ran a private clinic from the back room of his house for the Manatone family; his sole client.

"As I suspected, the x-rays show no permanent damage," he said stepping to the bedside to take one more look at the leg. It was white-wrapped in bandage from the ankle to just below the knee. "Fortunately for you, both wounds were through and through, and clean, without hitting bone or arteries." He lifted Bishops injured leg off the bed, and rotated it so his patient could sit up. "It's almost five o'clock. The sun will be coming up soon, and you need to be on your way."

After attaching a sling to support Bishop's injured arm, the doctor handed him two pill containers. "I've given you forty Valium for the pain, and forty antibiotics. If you need more come back next week and I'll take care of it." He handed Bishop a pair of crutches and helped him from the room. Once out the back door, Bishop pulled out a handful of hundred dollar bills and handed them to Ramous. The doctor nodded. "You were never here."

"But he is here," a voice snarled from the darkened side of the house.

Bishop turned in surprise. In front of him, arm extended, and holding a silenced Glock pistol was Tom Spears.

Chapter 9

Tom stood before Bishop Styles in the basement of the doctor's home. It had been two days since the Red Hook Granary, and using medical tape Tom had scrounged up, The Duke was laying spread-eagle on the cement floor with his arms and legs pulled taut and tied to four ten-inch-thick support columns.

To find the assassin had been easy. Thirty minutes after Tanya's deadly fall, Tom had risen from the rooftop, and gone back to the stairwell where he'd found the trail of blood down the stairs. With Bishop shot, the process had been that much easier. After all, to get treated quietly and anonymously for a gunshot wound was a specialized field. In fact it was so specialized that Tom only knew of four people that were capable…and willing…statewide. Of course, he had no way of knowing if their circumstances had changed over the years, but, if there was one constant in the cruel life of the underworld, it was the need of a good surgeon with corrupt ethics. So the few there were, were well compensated for their troubles. Knowing this, Tom had been able to narrow that number down further. In fact there were only two that were exclusively operated by the Manatones. Then it had been as simple as picking the closest doctor, which was Fredrick Ramous. But before he could track the assassin, arrangements for Tanya's retrieval had been needed. First and foremost on his mind, she wouldn't be left there for any longer than necessary. So he had called the police using a throw away cellphone, giving basic information on where she could be found without giving any names, including hers.

That had taken care of the recovery. Funeral arrangements were another matter. The problem was, he remained hunted. That meant, as much as he had wanted to take care of it personally, he knew it wasn't going to be possible. After all, the process would be slow, both in finding her and dealing with the police. That also meant if he was to survive, and still find those responsible, he had to set aside his grief and remain elusive. Of course, this did little to appease his troubled conscience. Rational or not, the decision to not be there for her now was a huge weight bearing down on his already tortured soul. Nevertheless, the reasoning was sound, and once Bishop was secure, he had been less worried about being tracked, and put the battery and sim card back into his phone. It had been the first time in days and there were several messages: two from the Port Angeles Police Department, wanting to ask more questions about Tanya's disappearance as well as the security guard that had been shot when she was abducted. Nine were from Reed Davenport who was worried, and wanted an update on Tanya's possible location, and the last had been from Bishop Styles himself.

Tom's only returned call had been to Reed Davenport. One of the few people Tom could rely on and trust completely, Reed was not only his and Tanya's employer, but also their friend—a friend who would have a bevy of questions, including how he could help. But fortunately for Tom—due to the different time zones—the early morning call to

Washington State had gone right to voice mail. His message had been long and profound, detailing where he was, the Red Hook terminal, and what tragedy had befallen Tanya.

During the call, he had confirmed he didn't need any help. Of course that had been far from the truth, but he couldn't risk anyone else being involved with the war he was planning to wage on the Manatones. So to limit any retaliatory response from the vindictive New York mob, Tom had restricted Reed's involvement to one lone request. Heartfelt and excruciatingly painful, this was the recovery of Tanya's body from the bottom of the silo, and making funeral arrangements. It was a task, Tom knew full well, the Crude Technologies man would take care of personally, and probably in a few hours. When he finally hung up, he was once again grateful it had been a recording—the probable questions too much to bear. The only certainty he knew at the time, was his need for vengeance. Even now, it was the only thing filling the vast and insufferable void in his heart.

Bishop moaned. He wasn't looking good. Blood had pooled on the cement floor under him, and since he hadn't been allowed to move, the room was growing dank with the smell of sweat and urine. But there was no pity in Tom's eyes. On the contrary, since tying him up, Tom had been relentless—even cruel—in acquiring relevant information on who was responsible. Not that the cruelty bothered him in the least. Under the circumstances, he was willing to deliver as much agony as possible.

It was a small pittance compared to his own pain. In fact, in those first few minutes he hadn't been able to control his anger and had viciously kicked the assassin into unconsciousness. When he came to, Tom had ripped off the bandages from Bishop's shoulder and calf, and reopened the sutures with a probing screwdriver. Nothing was off the table in delivering pain, and nothing seemed more important than dealing justice to the man responsible for his immeasurable grief.

At first Bishop had been combative and unwilling to answer questions. But that changed once he'd seen the lengths Tom was willing to go through to find answers. It was obvious, regardless of his answers, he wouldn't be leaving the basement alive. So he slowly began to capitulate, and Tom now knew, just like Tanya had said, the Manatones were responsible, putting out a hit on him for the killing of Frank Teeds—a lowlife that happened to be the mob boss's late brothers son.

Tom opened a folding metal chair he found in the corner, and placed it near Bishops head. After sitting down, he leaned over the Duke's battered face. Covered in sweat and ghostly pale, the assassin's eyes were almost swollen shut, and blood trickled from his nose and split upper lip. "What is the timetable for the contract?" Tom asked coldly. "When is it to be fulfilled?" Bishop didn't answer so Tom put his boot on the injured shoulder and pressed.

Bishop screamed in agony. "I…I was supposed to have completed it by now. Frank…impatient." His words were barely coherent. The blood loss, and going two days without food or water, was taking a toll. Blood was also forming on the corners of his mouth from the internal injuries inflicted by Tom.

"How are you to be paid?"

"Caymans…with the extra job costing double…half up front."

Reaching back over his shoulder, Tom picked up Bishop's laptop off the top of the nearby washing machine. It was one of many surprises Tom had found when he searched Bishops car, including a cache of weapons that would make any small army proud. "What is your Cayman's passcode again?"

Tom still had several international accounts, including the Caymans. So he was very familiar with the elaborate, and sophisticated banking procedures. Unlike most local banks there was no room for error, or grace period, with these highly secure accounts. That meant if the wrong password or passcode got entered, he would be immediately locked out. Then unlocking it meant a phone call and more security questions. If that didn't work, a person had to show up in person. That's why Tom had confirmed the information was correct by asking the question four different times. It was, and after several minutes of transfers, he closed the laptop, and nodded with satisfaction. He knew, of course, that Bishop had even more international accounts, but his interest stopped there. In this account alone, there was more than eight-point-two million, and for what he was planning—in conjunction with his own accounts—it was more than enough solvency.

"A deposit of half-a-million was made four days ago. That means this extra job you mentioned is worth a million. Even by your standards, that's pretty pricey. So what…or who…is it?"

Bishop licked his swollen and cracked lips. "Water please…"

Tom didn't hesitate, and pressed even harder on Bishops shoulder. "This isn't a negotiation! Answer the question!"

Bishop squirmed and grit his teeth. "Tony Manatone wants his father dead."

Tom leaned back in his chair. *So Dad is getting in the way of the young Manatone's ambitions. Interesting!*

Tom remembered the teenaged boy back then—a small kid, an introvert with narrow shoulders who rarely smiled much less spoke. Tom was never keen on him. The kid just seemed off, misplaced, unable to fit into the tough guy image of his father. But he still needed to be protected—if only from himself.

In those days, and as part of Frank Manatone's personal protection detail, this fell under Tom's purview, too. On one such night, Tom had gotten word that the young Manatone had gotten into some trouble. So he, and his two close friends and associates—Micky Trevor, and Mike Rauls—had been sent to deal with it, and if needed, clean it up. It did, in both cases. They arrived at a rundown motel just off Route 6 to find the teenager in a room with a dead woman—a whore named Nicki, whose services both Mike and Micky had used numerous times themselves. Blood was everywhere. Tony claimed it was an accident, which might've accounted for her being strangled, but that did little to explain the twelve knife wounds in her back. No, something was definitely off with him. But they had chalked it up to an argument gone wrong—very wrong— and after injecting her with enough narcotics to bring down a horse, they had thrown her tortured body into the Hudson River. When her remains were found two days later, it didn't even make the front page, just another sad story in the life of a crack-head prostitute gone wrong.

On another occasion, a bully, who continually picked on Tony, had turned up dead. It had happened when the young Manatone was in-between his junior and senior year in high school. Turns out, the bully—a privileged black kid with doctors as parents—had a big party one evening during summer break and Tony had showed up uninvited. Witnesses claimed the black kid was once again verbally antagonizing Tony. Then the following morning the kid had been found stabbed to death, his corpse pushed under the bushes along the driveway where all the kids had parked.

Upon learning the bully had died of multiple stab wounds to the back—Tony's modus operandi—Tom had quickly sought out Manatone Junior that same morning. It was a good thing, too. Tony was still asleep when Tom had entered unannounced. Under verbal protest, Tom had done a quick search, and in no time at all, his suspicions turned into reality. Found, stuffed under the bed, were not only the bloody clothes Tony had worn, but the murder weapon as well; a six-inch hunting knife. Two hours later, and just as the police pulled into the long driveway, all evidence of the crime had been cleaned up. Tying things up further, Tom had also told the police Tony had been with him during the time of the murder, giving the young Manatone a seemingly good alibi. Of course the police hadn't bought any of it, and for the next few months they remained undeterred in their suspicions of Tony's guilt. But proving it was another matter.

Tom's eyes narrowed, his mind drifting to Micky Trevor, and Mike Rauls, who were now missing for more than six weeks. Working as security for the Crude Technologies ships—a job Tom himself had offered them—the two had just come back from a six week excursion at sea, and before boarding a newly christened fleet skimmer for another three week tour, decided to take a three day vacation back to New York and their old stomping grounds. That was the last Tom had heard of them. They had virtually disappeared without a trace. Now, for the first time, Tom suspected why—the coincidence glaring in his mind.

He leaned forward again. "It's a big step for Tony to take out his father. How will he contend with the repercussions when Frank's number two's come after him?"

He coughed, his voice turning raspy. "They won't know…you're the fall guy."

Tom blinked at the changing plot. "You're going to make it look like I killed him?" He shook his head. "So you lured me to New York to be a patsy? Is that it? Then your plan was to kill me."

"No, you were originally lured here to be captured if possible, or killed. The contract for Frank has only recently been added."

"So you're killing two birds with one stone."

"Yes," Bishop answered.

Tom thought for a moment before speaking again, "You killed Micky Trevor, and Mike Rauls, didn't you?"

There was a notable pause. "No, not personally. But I was there." He coughed again, but continued, "In gathering any pertinent information on you, they were supposed to supply plenty, but in the end they either didn't have it, or were unwilling to do so."

"Who went after them?"

"Your old friend, Charley Mack."

Tom glared at him. "That fat fuck has never been my friend…"

Bishop shrugged, wincing from his shoulder. "He picked them up at the airport. They never suspected, or saw it coming until it was too late…" He tried to turn his head and spit the blood from his mouth, but his mouth remained dry, and it clung thickly to his lips and drooled down his chin.

Tom stood and went to the bathroom to his left. The door was shut with an old wooden armchair wedged under the handle. Removing it, he stepped inside, turned the light on, and filled a plastic cup from the counter with water. Like the rest of the basement, the room was unfinished, and also smelled of sweat and urine. He paused to look at the doctor, who was lying in the tub. Much like Bishop, he was also tied up, but his mouth was also taped shut. He looked confused, his scared eyes flicking back and forth. At this point, Tom really wasn't certain what he was going to do with him. That's why the ceiling fan had been left on, so he couldn't hear the conversation going on outside the door. However, when he was done with Bishop, he would definitely cull any usable information from the doctor about the Manatones as well. That would decide his fate. He turned the light back off, closed the door, and wedged the chair under the handle once more. Returning to his seat, Tom let a few drops of water cross Bishop's lips, and then let him have a mouthful before setting the plastic cup down.

Bishop nodded. "For what it's worth…the ugliness of your friends' deaths…wasn't by my hands. Charley and his two buddies, Jimmy and

Tim, did most of the damage. They tortured them for almost three days before Tony showed up."

"Tony was behind this?"

"It was his idea…but I suspected it went much further than wanting information. He had them taken to Queens Athletic Club, and when it was time, he seemed to enjoy killing them."

Tom wasn't surprised. Being gay aside, he was a sociopath through and through, and as spineless as he was pitiless. Never willing to challenge anyone from the front, he always did his bidding from behind, like a snake, slinking around in the shadows. Guilt struck Tom, and he fought back the haunting image of how his friends had undoubtedly died.

Bishop whispered something that was incoherent.

"What?" Tom asked.

Bishop whispered again, but it was a struggle, like he was trying to say the right words. "I've done plenty of bad in my life…so I knew this day was coming. You should know…taking your wife was nothing personal…"

Tom stood, the chair flipping back loudly as anger and guilt struck his core like a supercharged thunderbolt. "But it was personal!" Tom snarled, cutting him off. "In fact, it doesn't get any more personal!"

Bishop swallowed hard. "Maybe so," he retorted, "but I…I treated her with dignity…"

"Dignity?" Tom cut him off again. "You think your words can now ease your plagued conscience? You kidnapped my wife, took her in the dead of night and hauled her—tied up—across the United States. You did all this because you were trying to get me. Well, you got me! How do you like it so far?" He glared at the assassin. "In these last two days I've seen the defiance in you—a defiance that comes from arrogance and leaves you with a burning question of how? How were you bested? How, after all your research into my life, my friends, and my loved ones, you ended up here before me?"

Bishop remained quiet, but Tom could clearly see he wanted… needed…to know. So he continued, "It's simple. You're used to being the wolf—the aggressor, the hunter—and not the rabbit. It requires perspective. The rabbit uses all its senses to survive. Long before danger arrives, it knows an escape avenue. It knows terrain and burrows, and even recognizes certain smells carried in the wind. Why? Because it's hunted! You, Mr. Styles, made me the rabbit. And like a hunted animal, I paid attention—even in retreat—to each detail; from your first grenade, to exiting onto the roof. Then when you fired those first shots through the door I knew exactly where you'd be…because it's where I'd be. And like the rabbit, I reacted with no thinking required, knowing the angles, and more importantly, knowing the exterior wall wasn't made of cement. The rest was blind luck."

Bishop nodded, appearing pacified, and turned away. "She's a remarkable lady. I was never going to harm her…how is she?"

He hadn't told Bishop of what transpired on the rooftop. The assassin had assumed Tom had taken her safely away. He couldn't have been more wrong, and those guilt driven…life shattering moments… on the rooftop replayed again in Tom's mind. Like gunfire, his thoughts converged rapidly, one shot more painful than the last. Now when he saw her once beautiful face in his mind, she appeared more dead than alive. It broke his heart further.

"She's dead!" he snarled, swallowing hard. "You took her knowing she was the key to getting me. You were right. She was my world," he hissed, his face reddening. "She had a light that burned deep in her soul. Bright and flickering, it carried no malice or ill will. Even with her regrettable and unpleasant past, she had an optimistic spirit, good and kind. But try as she may, she never forgot those wrong doings of the past. It was a heavy burden and it constantly threatened to dim that eternal flame." He continued to glare at the assassin, his eyes narrowing. "After all Bishop, a soul can only take so much and she had seen so much already. So yes, I tried to do what must be done, to ensure that flame was never extinguished." He removed Tanya's golden locket and let it dangle from his fingers. "This included keeping that frightened child inside her at bay, by letting her know I would always come for her—always…unquestionably…and no matter the situation. So she would never feel alone again."

Bishop struggled to see past his swollen eyes and finally spoke with understanding, "The locket…you tracked her with the locket…"

Tom's anger was now peaking, coiled and deadly, like a scorpion's tale, and ready to strike without remorse. From his waistband, Tom removed the Kimber Aegis II 9mm he had taken from Bishop, and attached the silencer he'd found in the cache of weapons from the assassins car. "This is a contract you should have never taken," Tom growled, fighting back his rising emotions, "and now the arrogance of the 'Duke of killers' will be washed away like a foul stench in a stiff breeze." He aimed the gun at Bishops head and fired two shots point-blank into his face.

Chapter 10

Bill's Barber Shop was located near the corner of Morgan and Grand Street in the upper east side of Brooklyn. Parked along the curb in front, Charley Mack sat in the driver's seat of the black, four-door, 2017 Lincoln Continental. It was Frank Manatone's vehicle, and he had spared no expense with security upgrades. Short of being the proverbial tank, the high-end luxury car not only had all the comfort options, but it was fully armored, and virtually indestructible with half-inch steel plating along the body, a reinforced chassis, and bulletproof glass. Not that it mattered, the mob world had changed over the last several decades on the streets of New York. Unlike the bloody turf wars of the 1930's and 40's, now-a-days the only bonafide threat came from either the bureaucracy of the IRS, or the various law agencies continually trying to bring Frank Manatone down. This made the armored car almost obsolete in today's world, and more of a show-piece—a sign of stature and power. That is, until recently. With Tom Spears—the Shadow—coming to town, the threat was once again real, and the practicality of the armored car obvious.

Rolling down the passenger window, Charley Mack's eyes settled on the grey-suited man standing guard in front the barber shop. His name was George Grevo. Of Russian descent, he was medium height, physically fit, with an aquiline nose that sat above a firm mouth and a square chin, and his eyes—a piercing gray—seemed to dissect everything around him, human and otherwise. "How much longer ya think?" Charley asked with a heavy Jamaican accent.

George shrugged with a grin. "You got somewhere else you need to be?"

"Nah, mon," Charley replied in frustration, while tugging at his tie, "I just want to get out of this thing."

Mandated by Frank Manatone himself, the new dress code required all protection personnel to be in a suit and tie, and this included the three hundred and ninety pound Jamaican.

George smoothed his own lapel. "I'm diggin it. Gives us a classy… sheik look."

"Speak for yourself, mon. It's tight and I'm restricted everywhere."

"I was speaking for myself, you fat fuck," George replied. "And 'being restricted everywhere' has little to do with the suit in this case." He had a friendly grin, but there was no hiding the condescending tone.

Charley's eyes narrowed, his irritation flowering. He didn't like the twenty-six year old, or his brown-nosing manner around the boss. Not that George wasn't good at his job. Oh, he was that; even to the point of being excessive. The smug prick made it a rule to get Frank's daily itinerary and recon each and every stop. Every stop! Even the barber shop Frank visited religiously every two weeks! To Charley this was overkill and more about appearance than any potential threat.

Charley put on the best smile he could muster, his gold tooth glinting in the late afternoon sun that filtered in through the windshield. "Take a look mon, does he look about done?"

George shrugged, and glanced over his shoulder through the big picture window. "Brushing him off now."

Charley nodded and rolled up the tinted window to hide his contempt. Already in a foul mood with having to wear the pimp-suit, the lack of respect from George only added fuel to the fire. "Four years," he mumbled to himself in agitation. That's how long this kid had worked for the Manatones. A college kid no less, having come directly from graduation to being on the payroll. And yet what experience did he have in this type of work? Answer…none! In fact the only reason he had the job in the first place was because he was the son of Mike Grevo—one of Frank's number two men in the syndicate.

The thought was galling, considering Charley had worked for the crime family for more than twenty years, and had climbed the ranks from the very bottom, earning, finally, the coveted *protection* position after Tom Spears, Mike Rauls, and Micky Trevor, had departed for greener pastures. What had George earned, and more importantly why did he have Frank's ear? After all, this new dress code nonsense had indeed been George's idea.

Feeling like Buda in shrunken clothes, he looked down at his grey pinstriped suit and sighed heavily. The coat was unbuttoned and his big belly—pressed hard against the steering wheel—was threatening to burst the buttons of his white cotton shirt, and this said nothing of the jacket sleeves which were bunched, and well short of his wrists. He loosened the black-streaked tie in frustration.

Movement had him looking to his right.

Past the passenger window, Frank Manatone was just leaving the barber shop. Wearing a black Armani suit, he paused to talk with George. Charley had to admit, if there was a prototype of what a crime boss should look like, it was Frank Manatone. He had a commanding presence, an aura of power and invulnerability, and this said nothing of his good looks. Even at the age of seventy-two, he was a handsome man with a grey, close-cropped, beard and matching grey hair. His bright blue eyes were keen and intelligent, and he moved with a graceful swagger—a walk that was both confident and intimidating.

The two approached the rear door and George obediently opened it, allowing Frank to slide in the back seat. Charley smiled, putting on his best face once again. "Looking good, boss."

"Thank you, Charley," he acknowledged without making eye contact. "Any news from Tony?"

"No," he lied. In fact he had talked to him only an hour before. But Frank wanted answers, and Tony had none, so the young Manatone was deliberately avoiding his father for that reason. Making it worse, not only didn't he have anything to report on Tom Spears, but now Bishop Styles was missing too…something Frank appeared to be unaware of. The only thing he and everyone else knew, was a battle had taken place at the Red Hook facility two days ago. By the guards' account at the gate that night, they had heard both gunfire and explosions and as they came to investigate they saw Bishop drive by in an apparent hurry. No one had seen or heard from him since.

"If he hasn't called in by the end of the day, I want you and George to locate him," he said. "Until we get some answers, this Spears thing has me uneasy."

Charley nodded. "Will do, boss."

Frank's eyes narrowed. "Have you tried his protection detail? Jimmy and Tim?"

Not anticipating the obvious question, or wanting to be caught in a lie, Charley turned back forward, swallowing hard. "Nah, but I'll try them shortly after we get back." Fortunately the crime boss seemed distracted, even withdrawn, and didn't pursue the matter any further.

After a moment Frank asked, "I've been told the police will soon be given legal access to the property. Has it been cleaned?" His concern was apparent. The site had been used in more killings than one could count, and now added to this was the blood trail from the stairs to the parking area, the bullet holes throughout the building, and the explosive-footprints from hand grenades. Curiously though, no bodies had been found, which might imply Spears was dead and that Bishop had removed the body. But if that was the case, where was the assassin? And more importantly, who was the mysterious female—a body—the police were looking for?

"Yeah boss, spic'n span. I looked it over myself." It was a partial lie. Yes, he had visually inspected the bullet holes—the slugs having been removed and each hole obliterated further by sledgehammers—and the explosion marks had been hidden under large piles of debris. Where the lie came in was the stairs; there was no way he was climbing fifteen stories. "They won't find anything, I assure you."

"Good," he acknowledged as George slid in the front seat. "Has anyone shown up at any of the local doctors yet?"

"No, there's been nothing. We talked to Fredrick Ramous twice, and as recently as yesterday. He hasn't seen nor heard of anyone with gunshot wounds." After a moment's silence, Charley glanced at his watch. It was after four pm. "Where to now, boss? Back to the office?"

"Yeah, but let's stop and pick up dinner to go from Tripoly's."

The steakhouse was music to Charley's ears, and just like that his mood had swung back from the dark side and into the light. He nodded to George. "What'cha waitin for? Call it in, mon." Then he put his turn signal on and merged into traffic.

Chapter 11

SWEAT GLEAMED ON TOM'S FOREHEAD as he awoke with a start. Temporarily confused, he lifted his head. He was lying in a bed in a darkened room, and it took a moment before he remembered he was at a motel; a seedy place in a rundown area of Queens. He looked at the clock on the nightstand. It was three in the afternoon, the thick drapes pulled tight to keep the light out. Six hours had passed since leaving the doctor's basement, and he'd slept for the last three.

Leaning on an elbow, he yawned, and ran a hand over his unshaven face. Still bone weary, his thoughts were fractured and vaguely disjointed like a mirage over the desert sands. After spending more than a week living in his car, taking a hot shower and sleeping in a bed was long overdue. He let his head settle back to the pillow, his thoughts drifting back to the doctor, Fredrick Ramous. In talking to him, Tom had decided not to kill him. It had been an easy decision. He had been very cooperative, and in the end, once Tom released him, they had come to an understanding: the doctor was to keep his mouth shut about Tom and Bishop having ever been there, and in return, Tom gave him twenty-thousand in cash. Of course there was a risk the doctor might talk anyway, but that was small, considering he knew little about Tom or his plans. Another mitigating factor, it was in his best interest to do so, or as Tom had put it, he would definitely come back and finish the job. Soon it wouldn't matter anyway. Tom only needed three or four days of secrecy to maintain an element of surprise. Right now the Manatones—both father and son—had no idea where Bishop was, and Tom was certain, they would be desperate for information—any information on Tom's location, and, in Tony's case, when his father would be assassinated.

When Tom was satisfied Fredrick Ramous wouldn't talk, he had backed Bishop's car into the garage, loaded the assassin's body into the trunk, and cleaned up all evidence of the incident from the basement. That left the biggest task, and coincidentally what the syndicate did best, which was making a body disappear. It's why they were so successful at circumventing the police and the law. Simply put, if there was no body, there usually was no case. So Tom's first stop had been to a mortuary he was familiar with from the past. It was ironic, considering it was syndicate owned and used almost exclusively for cremating those same bodies; some taken care of personally by Tom when he worked for them.

As Tom had suspected, even on a late Thursday morning, the building had been closed. And of course knowing the layout had made it that much easier. An hour after breaking in through the rear door, Tom had reemerged carrying a cheap brown urn he had found in a storage room. In it were the ashes of Bishop Styles. Tom had also covered his tracks by ransacking the interior of the mortuary, and stealing a lap top to make it look like kids had broken in.

His first stop had been along a deserted side street where he had lifted a manhole cover and dumped both the laptop and the ashes of Bishop Styles into the sewer. It seemed fitting—even poetic justice—that the final resting place for the assassin known as The Duke was in a river of shit.

The next issue was switching vehicles. For what he had planned, he didn't want any future movements linked to him in any way. That meant using Bishop Styles Cadillac, and parking his Honda SUV for a few days. With options limited, he went back to the doctor's house, switched cars and took his to the airport, paying for long term parking. This would serve two purposes: first the vehicle would be safe, and second, if things went sideways and he didn't return, he'd left a hand written phone number for Reed Davenport at Crude Technologies on the registration. Then he had taken a taxi back from the airport, and driven Bishop's Cadillac to Queens.

Up to that point, he had been able to fight back his grief and overwhelming fatigue, but that battle had finally been lost. After days on the road, the loss of his wife, dealing with Bishop, and learning the Syndicate was involved, he was spent, both emotionally, and physically. If he had continued, it would've been reckless; a death sentence. He knew this better than anyone. Fatigue was his number one enemy, and directly proportionate to living or dying—the all-important line between judgments and rational thought compromised, or in this case, so trodden to be virtually unrecognizable. Recuperating was a must, if he was going to come up with reasonable plan. The Sunbelt Hotel was perfect for his needs. The low-key shithole was less about the accommodations, and more about the prostitutes on every nearby corner. Before settling in though, he had made one more pit stop at a corner liquor store, picking up a bottle of Pendleton Whisky. With everything that had happened, he hadn't had any time to grieve, and although a whisky bottle and one night certainly weren't the cure, it was all he could allow at the moment.

Now staring at the ceiling, he felt the anguished squeeze of loss once again; ever tightening around his broken heart. Dressed only in boxers, he rotated upright, placing his bare feet on the worn shag carpet. Before lying down, he had taken a quick shower, and his long, disheveled hair was spread ungainly across both bare shoulders.

He reached for the unopened fifth of Pendleton off the night stand, uncapped it, and took two long pulls, swirling each around in his mouth before allowing the richly flavored liquid to ease its way down his throat. He grimaced as the heated vapors exited through his nostrils.

With the warming of his stomach, a crack formed in his emotional fortress, and the mighty wall began to crumble. To think that he would never see his loving wife again was now allowed to fully sink in, and his eyes welled with sorrow. A shuddering breath followed, and he took another drink.

Over the next hour, the tears flowed down his cheeks as he reflected back on their happy marriage, replaying her smile, her laughter, her quick wit, and her natural grace. She had captivated him from the very beginning. Her charm could be described as a beautiful flower, but even that wasn't entirely accurate. To him, she was more like a field of those same flowers, vibrant in colors of reds and yellows that danced under the sun with the slightest breeze, alive and full of wonder, that's what defined her—the most beautiful woman in the world.

As time slowly ticked by, he saw her smiling face over and over in his brain. With half the fifth gone, his mind began to swim, and his lips cracked into a tearful smirk. For the life of him, he couldn't remember ever having fought with her, not once. It was a sobering thought, and the shame of not being there for her burial followed, rising like acid in his throat. Then anger set in, and his lips formed a thin line. There was only one responsible party for this…all of this; the Manatones. He glanced over at the other double bed. On it, even in the dim lighting, he could see a virtual arsenal of weaponry laid across the floral green comforter. There were hand grenades, a flashbang, a World War II style M1 semi-automatic carbine, a disassembled M16 rifle, a snub-nosed .38, a 9mm Berretta, and a Kimber Aegis with silencer. And this said nothing of the stacked ammo boxes, or the weaponry Tom had brought, including two Glocks, and a set of throwing knives.

He nodded with satisfaction, but that inevitable war would have to wait. Today, and tonight, it was about Tanya, his loss, and the life they once had. He took another swallow, set the bottle back on the nightstand, and laid down again, letting his head settle into the thin pillow. Then he closed his tired eyes, nodded off, and dreamt of his wife…

*****

After sleeping the rest of Thursday, and into early Friday, Tom awoke a little after three in the morning. The night had been long and filled with fits of despair but it was to be expected. To get his mind clear in only a single night wasn't possible, but the cleansing of his soul—at least minutely—had started.

When he sat up, an alcohol related pain, dull and throbbing, manifested in his forehead. He sighed heavily, blinked back the pain, and got out of bed. Grabbing the empty whisky bottle off the nightstand, he dropped it into the trashcan, picked up his small traveling case, and made his way to the bathroom. Predictably, it was small, the shower curtain stained, and the linoleum, much like the cracked and faded yellow wall tiles, looked like it hadn't been replaced since it was installed; perhaps in the seventies. He set his bag on the back of the small sink, opened it, and removed a bottle of aspirin. Dry swallowing four, he put the lid back on, and replaced the bottle.

He stared at his reflection in the small mirror. A plan, in-between bouts of sleep, had come to him in the middle of the night, and he looked himself over with a critical eye.

Starting with his beard, he examined its growth, especially along the jawline. Next, it was the length and condition of his hair, first pulling it forward then back, and even roughening it up along the sides with the palms of his hands. And with each examination, he looked from different angles, tilting his head forward and back, and from side to side, gauging the most deceptive profile versus the most glaring.

When he had a good idea of what he wanted, he relieved himself in the toilet, and stepped into the shower. Turning the hot water on as high as his skin would allow, he let the stinging heat penetrate his chest, then his skull as he tilted his head forward. Through the tiredness and disillusion, he was aware, for the first time in almost two weeks, of the underlying strength which he had begun to doubt was still there. After all, he had been out of the harsh, unforgiving, and even covert world of an assassin for four years; the syndicate more than a decade. But that lingering doubt had been entwined with thoughts of his missing wife. His every move, every decision, and every questionable doubt was all about finding her, to save her. Now he could plan without having to consider the implications, or even the repercussions of worrying about anyone else. Not that it would make the coming days any less difficult, but it would ease his conscience knowing it was only his life on the line.

He lathered without cleaning his hair, rinsed, and when he was ready, turned the faucet off.

Stepping from the shower in a cloud of steam, he dried and slipped his boxers back on. He felt rejuvenated, even invigorated, but for his plan to work, it would be his last shower for a while.

Back in front of the mirror, he removed a roll of gauze, several cotton balls, and a tiny makeup bag from inside his case. Then he wiped off the mirror, and with the Manatones first and foremost on his mind, went to work on his plan.

Chapter 12

Tony Manatone sat in the back seat of the four door Jaguar XJR, looking out the window as his driver drove through the slow moving New York traffic. Outside, heavy clouds masked the sun, and the morning was gray and cool. His cellphone rang. It was his dad, but he didn't pick up. Having finally talked to him after a nine day hiatus, he was going to the office to take part in the monthly meeting, and no doubt, a discussion about Tom Spears.

He glanced at his cellphone again. Eight days had passed since the last time he had talked to Bishop Styles. Eight days! And even though Tony had been warned about contacting him through normal channels, he had hesitantly left a voicemail last night. But still nothing. So where did this leave the assassination of his father? Could the assassin be dead; the blood at the granary his? If so, then what had happened to Tom Spears, and more importantly, what did he know? Did he know who was behind the taking of his wife, Mike, and Micky? He wiped a sweaty palm on his pant leg. What was he going to do if the Shadow came after him? The thought made him even more nervous.

Just as the car pulled up to the curb in front of his father's building, his phone chimed from a text. A surge of relief swept through him when he saw the series of numbers: 1.12M.AC. It was a coded message from Bishop…"1" meant today, "12M" at Midnight, "AC" Athletic Club'.

He nodded with optimism, glancing outside again. Already the wide sidewalk in front of the twenty-four-story Westinghouse Building was bustling with people, but he barely noticed, focusing instead on the rest of his day. "I'll be in the meeting for a couple hours," Tony said to both Tim Barns who was driving, and Jimmy Matt in the passenger seat. The two men had been his body guards for more than four years, but in that time, there had been no tenser situation, or higher security risk, than the threat currently from Tom Spears. Sleep had been minimal, friendships frayed, and tempers short. "After we go upstairs, you can get some breakfast but be back here no later than ten o'clock." Both men nodded and got out, with Jimmy promptly opening Tony's door. Once on the sidewalk, Tony took a moment to smooth the wrinkles from his khaki Dockers, and button his black sport coat. The air was heavy and smelled of dampness.

He looked up past the tall skyscraper. The clouds were grey and darkening with rain.

Someone cursed, and Tony turned to his right. A man in a hurry had tripped over the extended legs of a homeless man on the sidewalk. For a moment the passerby hurled even more obscenities at the beggar before disappearing once again into the flow of bodies. Tony looked closer at the beggar. Sitting against the wall to the right of the main entrance, he wore a filthy beanie over long and greasy hair, his clothes were threadbare, and even his shoes were held together with silver duct tape. On the ground next to him was an empty vodka bottle, and if his lolling head was any indication, he was drunk. Tony frowned, and shook his head in disgust. How long had the man been there? He vaguely remembered seeing…maybe seeing…someone there four days ago. Or did he? He couldn't be sure. The homeless in this part of town seemed to be at an all-time high. But most people, even the homeless, knew better than to panhandle in front of a Manatone building.

Tony leaned in close to Tim Barns ear. "I'm surprised my father has allowed that vermin to remain in front of our building. See that it's taken care of, and don't be kind. In fact, make an example of him. We need to send a message that this portion of sidewalk isn't their personal pissing zone."

A malevolent gleam appeared in Tim's dark eyes. "I'll take care of it. But to do it right, I'll have to wait until tonight when there are less witnesses."

"Just see that it's done," Tony replied coolly, now thinking about his father. "Let's consider this the first of many changes yet to come."

As they entered the building, they were greeted by Henry the doorman, before stepping onto elevator to go to the 24th floor. When the doors opened they exited into a crowded hallway. Anyone of importance in the Manatone business empire was here, and that included their bodyguards, who would be waiting patiently until the meeting concluded. Frank's security detail was no different. Charley Mack and George Grevo were against the far wall with styrofoam coffee cups in their hands. Pausing a moment, Tony made eye contact with Charley Mack, and a barely discernible nod followed between them.

"Remember, two hours," Tony said to Tim and Jimmy as he continued on alone, working his way through the milling throng and down the hallway toward the conference room. Several people acknowledged him along the way with nods or greetings, but Tony ignored them.

No weapons were allowed inside the conference room, so a metal detecting station—operated by four grim-faced men—was set up just outside the double mahogany doors. The added security also countered any eaves dropping or recording equipment from being brought in. Cellphones were banned too, either left with their personal bodyguards, or put on the secured table in the hall.

After turning over his iPhone, Tony stood for a moment just inside the doorway. The room was spacious, brightly lit, and filled with the smell of coffee, cigarettes, and bad cologne. At its center was a huge walnut conference table where more than thirty people were seated. Most were chatting freely, including his father, who was at the head of the table and having an in-depth conversation with Michelle Averton, the company lawyer.

Tony made his way to where Frank sat, and pulled out a chair to his father's immediate left. Once seated, he gazed outside past the wall of glass. As he suspected, rain was already coming down; the droplets streaking down the windows, and the low hazy ceiling obscuring the New York skyline.

With the meeting close to being started, Michelle Averton stood. Due to any illegal activities, she couldn't be present during the meeting for deniability reasons. She and Frank exchanged parting words, and as she turned to leave, nodded a greeting to Tony.

Only then did his father acknowledge him. "Good to see you. I was beginning to worry."

Keeping silent, Tony just gritted his teeth, believing there was no sincerity is those words.

Frank held up his hands for quiet. Then he gestured for the double oak doors to be closed so they could begin. "Good morning to all of you. Let's get right to it. We have a lot of ground to cover."

Gambling, prostitution, and drugs had always been very profitable for the syndicate. They were the mainstays, the three pinnacles of success that would never change because they greased the illegitimate—and tax free—wheels which continually lined their pockets with cash.

This was the topic of conversation for the first forty minutes, which included solving problems, and talking about profits. Everyone liked the topic of earnings. It meant bigger portions in their profit-sharing system that Frank himself had set up. But what really made Frank Manatone successful was his willingness to adapt, legally or illegally, to changing markets and venture into new areas. This included expanding from their online gambling network and tapping into the six billion dollar computer gaming industry—the *legal* computer gaming industry—with their own online game, which was fittingly called 'A Pirates World.' It hadn't been an easy transition, nor had it been cheap; the cost of servers, building an entertaining site from scratch, dealing with programmers, software, and firewalls, easily exceeding $700,000.00. And that wasn't all. Even though Frank had the ultimate say, and believed in the project wholeheartedly, most conversations at the time had included a great deal of skepticism. After all, it was a huge transition—a proverbial leap—for hardened criminals with backgrounds in murder and larceny to think of computer gaming as anything but profitable; the 'legal' concept difficult to comprehend. But now after a full year of operation, they were reaping the rewards of their investment, and there wasn't one negative word raised. In fact, they spent a full hour on that subject alone, talking enthusiastically over the pros and cons of eventually adding two more online games by the end of next year. But that was on the legal side of their business.

Another topic of conversation, and equally lucrative, were the hidden grow fields in the northern part of New York State. For more than three decades the mob had been growing a good portion of its own product, which included marijuana, hallucinogenic mushrooms, opium poppy fields, and even the processing of hashish. Continually evolving, it had become a sophisticated network of not only growing, but also marketing and distribution; a billion dollar a year industry if run properly. But this, unlike computer gaming, had a staggering overhead cost which included a fully armed security force on each site 24/7, low profile housing, camouflage netting to neutralize being seen by aircraft or satellites, and a network of hidden service trails for both bringing product out, and food supplies in. Adding to the monumental task was the rugged location of these sites. Eight in all, and more than two hundred and twenty acres combined, they were spread out from the rugged Debar Mountain Range to the Canadian border; the heavily forested land, inhospitable, rural, and very private. Therefore access to the sites was limited to hiking, horseback, or all-terrain vehicles. And if maintaining and accessing these sites wasn't difficult enough, word had spread that some of the security teams were pilfering product.

"Do we know who the guilty party is?" Tony asked.

Frank shook his head. "Not exactly, but we'll know more in a couple days. It also appears teams from other sites are colluding." The room filled with agitated mutterings and all eyes turned to Rick Motese sitting near the middle of the table. Of Spanish heritage, he was middle-aged with short black hair parted down the middle with a waxy sheen, and a handlebar mustache that was twisted up proudly at the ends. He was also the person solely in charge of the hidden…and very illegal… fields, which included coordinating the supplies in and out, the men, the product, and the living conditions.

"Hold on here," Rick Motese said defensively, "this is the first I've been told about this."

Frank glared at him. "It's hard to say if that is good or bad."

Rick cleared his throat but remained relatively calm. "Without daily monitoring of the sites, much less monthly," he said with upturned palms, "how am I supposed to know what goes on in that fucking forest?"

To remain out of sight from the federal government—much less the few people that lived out there, or even the occasional hunter—their success was dependent on keeping a low profile, and eliminating as much nonessential traffic-flow in and out of the properties as possible. This meant not only were the scheduled pickups and deliveries done at night, and down to the minute, but the workers on site were forced to remain there year round. For most, this amounted to a two year plan, but there were several that had been there for more than fifteen years. Cellphones were also banned, with the only way of communication being a two-way radio system with rotating frequencies to avoid any potential tracking or monitoring. These rules were strictly enforced, or so they were supposed to be.

"Because it's your job!" Steve Johnnson retorted from across the table. He was a tall, slender man, with deep set brown eyes and a thin mouth, partly hidden by a thick goatee. Known for both his witty personality as well as an ugly demeanor, Steve was considered one of Frank's number two's, and in charge of most of the prostitution rings throughout the city and much of the state.

"I don't like your tone!" Rick snapped back, pointing a finger. "Shipments are up, and they've been consistent over the last ten years.

To further that, we haven't had one incident with law enforcement in that time. Not one."

"One could say," countered Steve, "that's only because of the large amounts of money we spend to pay off those same 'law enforcements' you're talking about. That is, the few there are in that remote area." He smirked. "What's the number? Two?"

Rick ignored him and turned back to Frank. "Who made this allegation? The numbers don't lie."

"We'll know soon enough if it's true," Frank responded, without answering his question. "So you're telling me, you haven't heard anything out of the ordinary?"

Rick shrugged. "No. The pickups and deliveries are staggered from eleven at night to five in the morning, and every three weeks during harvesting season. Two months, in the off-season."

Growing illegal crops, much like farming, was seasonal. But during winter months in this case, the hashish manufacturing kicked into full gear. This was another process that had been refined over the last decade. Made from stored marijuana resin, it used to take several days, but the perfected method, quick and simple, reduced the time to a few hours; a process easily managed in several of the half-buried buildings they used as refineries.

"Like I said," Rick continued, "the quantities of shipments have remained consistent. There haven't been any red flags." He looked at everyone begrudgingly. "If this is about pilfering for personal use, how could I possibly know such small quantities were missing?"

The room got notably quiet for a moment, before Frank countered, "Like I said, it's not an isolated case, nor does it appear to be small amounts."

"I think we all know it's not going to be pilfering for personal use if—like you say—there are multiple parties involved," Mike Grevo said flatly from the other end of the long table. Also one of Frank's number two men, he was a short man, with wide shoulders and a thick neck. His deep-set sapphire eyes were fierce, his lean face hard, his expressions unyielding. Mike was responsible for the bulk of the gambling revenues brought in, and his son was on protection duty for Frank himself.

"Yes, it is," Frank agreed. "In cutting these people off from the rest of the world, we have also cut ourselves off from them, and this appears to be the by-product of that." He looked at Rick Motese. "You and I have known each other for the better part of twenty years, but something is off here. My source was unexpected—if not unorthodox—but seems reliable, and if what I'm hearing is true, the guilty party will be taken care of."

Tony was listening avidly. When his father said "the guilty party will be taken care of," he meant they would be exterminated—violently exterminated. And Frank was right, of course. Theft wasn't to be tolerated. Period. He looked over at Rick Motese, trying to read the man. Tony also found it hard to believe, even monitoring from afar, he wasn't aware of everything that was going on in those fields. He turned to his father. "Give me what you have and let me take care of this."

"Done," Frank said without looking at him. He stood. "We have one other issue to discuss. As most of you are aware, I've put out a contract on Tom Spears for his part in the killing of my nephew." Several people nodded and he continued, "With the debacle at the Red Hook Granary, I believe he's here in New York. Get the word out. He is your top priority, I want him found, and if he isn't already dead, make it so."

Tony saw the immediate reaction around the room.

Like teasing a pack of wolves with a piece of meat, people began talking excitedly. There were even a few chuckles; the multiple conversations sounding flippant. A few of these people though, the ones that had been with the Manatones for more than a few years, weren't taking the conversation as lightly. Their looks were more cautious and calculating. One of these men was Steve Johnnson. Raising his hand to get people's attention, he spoke up again, his words stern. "I look around this table right now and I don't like what I see. Am I actually seeing excitement on some of your faces as you chatter like arrogant children?" He shook his head, his brown eyes mocking. "You're actually excited about *attempting* to tangle with one of the deadliest men the syndicate has ever produced. A man as naturally gifted and deadly as any predator in the wild. A man who has killed more than thirty people before going off to work for himself."

"Thirty four to be exact," Mike Grevo added, his look just as serious.

Steve nodded and continued without pause, "Is this the man you're excited about? A man who never missed a mark. Not once that I'm aware of. A man once known as the Shadow because he was rarely ever seen; his kills cleverly disguised as accidents or of natural causes."

His eyes respectfully met Frank Mantone's. "The same method that made us believe Frank's nephew died of natural causes. But there wasn't anything natural about it." The muscles along his jawline flexed as he spoke. "With this cock-sure attitude I'm seeing right now, you've obviously forgotten who the fuck you're dealing with, so let me remind you." He leaned on the table to make his point, and before speaking again, he glared at each and every man around the table. "If you underestimate this man you're already dead. He was one of us, so this I know to be a fact. A deadlier man you won't find. I once sent him to kill a man. You remember Lynchpin? That sociopath who was killing my prostitutes a ways back? The guy who, literally thought he and his gang could *carve* their way into our prostitution ring?" No one answered, and the room became deathly quiet. "The Shadow not only killed the psychopath, but also his two bodyguards, and six others on the same floor." He stood, still leaning on the table. "It was the entire gang, and you remember how they were killed?" Again he glared at the people around him. "They weren't shot, oh no, that would have brought the police in right away, and that was something I didn't want. So the stipulation I gave him was…make it look like a terrible accident. He did. Killed each of them with either his bare hands or a knife, then broke the gas lines, and set the warehouse on fire. It burned for three days!" He shook his head again slowly. "So I guarantee giddy isn't the proper response from you." Taking a moment, he let his head sag forward, chin on his chest. "What makes Tom Spears even more dangerous is the code he lives by…his particular trait when it comes to picking contracts. You remember what that was?" Again, no one answered. "Well, let me remind you. He only killed people that—according to him—needed killing. Not house-wives, cheating spouses, or any other petty reason for someone with money to want someone dead. No, he was very selective, even obsessively so. These contracts were for murderers, cut throats, liars, cheats; the worst of the worst. Now I want you to look around this room. That characteristic alone should make everyone in here wary…very wary." He sat back down, his reddened-face remaining stern. "And not acting like this is going to be an easy task…child's play…a cake walk."

Mike Grevo nodded in agreement. "Like Steve said, chirping about killing Tom Spears, and actually killing him are going to be two different matters. For most of you," he said with a sweeping hand gesture, "that have been here long enough, you already know this to be true. But as for the rest of you, if he is indeed here, I wouldn't be so excited to make his acquaintance, especially under these circumstances."

Tony fidgeted in his chair. No one in the room actually knew the depth of what those circumstances were except him, Charley Mack, his own body guards, Bishop Styles, and of course, Tom Spears. His father only knew a battle had taken place at the Red Hook Granary between Bishop Styles and the Shadow. Beyond that, Tony had kept him in the dark, about everything, including the abduction of Tom Spears wife.

He thought about filling them in to get everyone on the same page, and the danger it posed, but changed his mind. He had been put in charge of dealing with Spears, and to say it hadn't gone well would be an understatement. It meant his decisions would be put under a microscope, and with his lack of success, also his abilities. Repercussions would then follow. There were always repercussions.

His eyes flicked to Frank Manatone.

Getting his dad's appreciation, his praise, or even his approval had been nonexistent throughout his entire life. No, he wasn't going to say anything until he talked to Bishop Styles at midnight tonight to find out what the fuck was going on. He needed answers about not only Spears, but also a timeframe for dealing with his father.

Chapter 13

SITTING AT THE BASE OF the twenty-four-story Westinghouse Building, the gentle looking man in the rumpled trench coat and dirty high necked cotton sweater, thanked the passerby for the quarter pitched into the open violin case between his knees.

Beyond the occasional money dropped in, most people barely slowed, and not only did no one give him a second look, but he was about as non-memorable as anyone could be. Wearing a dirty grey-knit beanie on his head, and even dirtier military-green surplus pants, he blended unceremoniously into the ubiquitous city life. In fact, to all that walked past his sidewalk home, he was featureless, and indescribable; his unkempt hair—long, ratted, and flowing forward—all but guaranteed it. Not that it mattered to the multitude of bodies that continually walked the sidewalks. To them he was merely an obstacle, and like a rock in a stream, they just flowed around him and continued on their way.

Becoming a chameleon was by design though. Tom had learned years ago that sometimes the best way to change his appearance was usually the simplest. Hair for example, could be dyed, lengthened with wigs, cut short, or even removed altogether. For this current charade, and the illusion of greasy disheveled hair, Tom had first applied a light coat of baby oil, then ratted it all along the sides. The trick had worked to perfection, looking like it hadn't been washed in weeks.

Physical attributes, and/or the deficiencies also played a huge roll with perception, and that all-important first impression. In this case does the physical appearance compliment the disguise? Is he age appropriate? Does he need a disability? If he answered all these correctly, most onlookers would only give him a fleeting glance, and later, wouldn't even recall if he was black or white, much less a physical description. To accomplish this was also somewhat easy. In a pinch, and far better than cosmetics, capturing infirmity or altering his apparent age was done by adjusting the muscles of the face and body. The trick was to set the muscles in the desired position of abnormal stress, then go about a regular routine, fighting the discomfort like fighting old age, or even cripples and their deformities. With practice and the right technique, a twenty-four year old could transform into an arthritic eighty year old man who was barely able to walk and knocking on death's door. In fact, Tom had become proficient at any number of ailments connected to old age, including imitating respiratory problems by slouching his shoulders and using shaky, erratic, breaths. Even dementia wasn't out of the question, replicating it with a slight tilt of the head, shuffling feet, and a wayward look.

For today though, Tom concentrated on substance abuse, which also meant wearing the appropriate attire. This he had accomplished in a homeless population two blocks over, including a filthy beanie. As it turned out though, getting clothes that fit his broad-shouldered, six-foot-four, two-hundred-and-forty pound frame became the most difficult part of the plan. But after an hour, he had found several 'full-bodied' vagrants willing to part with their threadbare clothing for cash. Finishing off the ensemble, and to the delight of one the vagrants, were the worn out shoes Tom also purchased. With them, he used duct tape both out of necessity—wrapping the shoes to keep the hard soles from separating further—and also for added theatrics; drawing more attention away from his face. Another theatrical prop to keep focus elsewhere—its implication obvious—was the empty vodka bottle; its lid off, and laying on its side near his leg.

A middle-aged woman in a white skirt, and expensive black leather coat, politely stopped in front of him and stooped. She was going to say some heart felt words but then abruptly stood, dropped five dollars into the case, and briskly walked away without a word. Tom didn't look up, but fought the urge to smirk. The fact was he stunk. In keeping with the realism of an alcoholic living on the streets, he'd urinated all over the clothes after purchasing them. Filthy and foul-smelling before, this added the words rancid and overbearing to the colorful adjectives. It was yet another detail that perpetuated the deception, and more importantly, all but eliminated the fresh scent baby oil while also keeping people out of close proximity.

Once he was satisfied, he had left the Cadillac parked on the street a block over and made his way here to the front of the Manatone building. Arriving before sunrise, Tom had already gotten a heartbeat on the goings-on of the building. For instance, Henry, the talkative doorman, was approaching his sixtieth birthday, a widower, and single. He was also lactose intolerant, a recovering alcoholic, and had a dog name Beau. As to how much of this information was useful, only time would tell. After all, most of these conversations had only been with the tenants who either worked in the building or lived in the high-end apartments. Renovated from old office spaces long ago, these took up most of the floors in the twenty-four-story building. In fact, there were only two that weren't for residential use. But this wasn't anything new to Tom. He already knew the basement was for storage, and the uppermost floor was exclusively for Frank Manatone himself…or at least it had been before Tom's departure. Now though, evidently that had changed. According to the 'chatty-patty' doorman—while taking a smoke-break and talking to a building supervisor over Tom's shoulder—the new company lawyer had also taken up office space on the floor. Her name was Michelle Averton. This had been news to Tom, and definitely useful information.

That was ten minutes ago.

A horn honked and Tom watched a yellow cab cut through traffic and stop in front of the building. The back door flew open, and a leggy blond in heels and a short tan skirt exited. Bending over, she paid the driver through the passenger window, smoothed her skirt and approached the doorman. "Hi Henry."

"Hi Miss Averton," Henry replied.

Upon seeing her, it had been easy to see why she had been the topic of conversation between the hired help. The single, thirty-six-year-old attorney was striking, and this was telling in itself as to why she was also on the upper floor. First and foremost, the gangster had an infinite attraction to blonds, and it was easy to deduce this went beyond a professional relationship.

"Has Frank been in yet?" she asked. "The monthly meeting is today and I wanted to get in early."

"No ma'am," he replied holding the big glass door open, and letting her pass by. "You're the first."

Tom couldn't believe the stroke of luck. The meeting, held monthly for all the syndicate executives, was being held on this very morning! Participation was mandatory, so anyone that was anyone in the syndicate's New York territory would be here, including both the mighty Frank Manatone, and also his son. That means everyone responsible for Tanya's death would be here…

And they would walk right by him.

His wife's face came back to him in an anguished rush and he replayed the roof scene again for the hundredth time, and him telling her to run…the fall in the hole…and then she was gone forever. The questions followed, repetitive and merciless, without reprieve. *Could he have done anything different? Could he have saved her? Would things have turned out differently had he taken her out of that room right away…NO!* In his heart he knew it was the right decision. Bishop had to be neutralized.

He pushed the haunting memory aside, focusing on the now, and the meeting.

Contemplating the fortunate turn of events, he tilted his head forward, chin to chest, and looked across the street. Through the glass window of the coffee house, Tom could see the clock on the wall. It was approaching seven in the morning, and people were already filling sidewalks on both sides, readying themselves for the Friday work day.

A black luxury car pulled up to the curb in front of the building, and Tom's heartbeat quickened. Not just any luxury car, it was a fully armored, four-door, 2017 Lincoln Continental; the type only Frank Manatone himself would own. Tom fought the urge to reach for the Kimber 9mm located under his trench coat, and conveniently resting against his inner thigh.

Both the driver and the passenger exited. Dressed identically in grey pinstriped suits and black ties, they cautiously surveyed the crowd on both sides of the street.

Tom studied their movements with a professional, calculating eye.

The man from the passenger side seemed familiar, but he couldn't quite place him. He was solidly built, in his early twenties, with brown hair trimmed short on the sides. He was also focused, his body language purposeful, and emanating confidence. This man, Tom knew right away, was a professional. Even as his grey eyes scrutinized the surroundings—settling briefly on Tom—his hand never strayed far the bulge under his coat where, no doubt, a shoulder-holstered-weapon hung.

Tom would have to use caution around this man, or give him a wide birth when possible.

The large black driver on the other hand, seemed far less concerned as he came around the car. Tom's eyes narrowed. Upon seeing who it was, he wasn't surprised by his nonchalant work ethic. Notoriously lazy, and with a gait more like that of a slow waddling duck, his name was

Charley Mack, and the big Jamaican seemed even more enormous than Tom remembered.

At close to four hundred pounds, the stitching on his ill-fitting suit was stretched to the very limits and threatened to burst at any moment. In fact, he was so overweight and out of shape, sweat gleamed on his bald plate just to get to, and over, the curb. Breathing heavily, he stepped to the back door and opened it.

Frank Manatone exited and paused on the sidewalk to hang his full-length cashmere overcoat loosely over his narrow shoulders. From what Tom could see, not much had changed with the notorious crime boss, other than his short-cropped hair and beard were now completely grey. He still looked physically fit, and his bright blue eyes, keen and intelligent, didn't reflect a man over the age of seventy. On the surface, he was stoic; the embodiment of class, and elegance, befitting the rich and famous. But Tom knew better. Frank Manatone thrived on power and the aura of invulnerability. It was his trademark. In spreading fear, he became untouchable. On one hand he was as canny and determined as Donald Trump in any construction seminar, and yet on the other, he was as deadly as any viper. This, Tom could vouch for personally, both working for the man and now the recent turn of events with Tanya.

At only ten feet away, Tom heard him say something to the younger man whom he addressed as George. It was broken up, the words fragmented, due to the passersby, but Tom did hear Tony's name mentioned. Then Frank headed to the front door, his walk both confident and intimidating; the surrounding foot traffic parting easily for him.

Henry held it open with a smile and nodded. "Good morning, Mr. Manatone."

"Morning," Frank replied, passing through the entryway with George following close behind.

Charley got back behind the wheel, and as soon as he pulled away to go park, more cars began showing up. Lots more cars. All chauffeur driven, they came in a fluid line, one right after another, and like children being dropped off in front of school, the rear doors briefly opened, someone got out, and as the car quickly moved on, the men were escorted immediately inside by a bodyguard. Several of the people Tom recognized, but no one gave him a second glance. Even as they stepped around his outstretched legs, he remained nondescript and unnoticed. Then two of these suited men stopped no more than six feet away. After a short exchange of good-morning well-wishes between one another,

Tom overheard some useful information, such as: the time and length of the meeting, who would be present, and even one of the subjects to be covered. In fact, they mentioned his name, and he swallowed hard. He found it sobering. It was one thing to assume the entire New York syndicate was looking for him, and quite another to have it reaffirmed. Another topic touched on had something to do with the northern New York grow fields. Of course Tom was familiar with these sites, after all the syndicate had been growing a large portion of its product for decades. So Tom didn't think much of it. The monthly meeting would cover a broad range of important topics and that...one of them.

The flow of cars pulling to the curb lessened and then stopped all together. Tom looked across the street at the clock again. It was almost eight, the meeting to start in a few minutes. Then one last car pulled up, and again Tom tensed. It was a blue four-door Jaguar XJR, and the tinted windows were halfway down. Tony Manatone had finally arrived. He was sitting in the backseat, and Tom watched him closely as the young heir casually leaned over and glanced up at the sky. The man known as Lil Mouse had changed much since the last time Tom had seen him. He still had a long birdlike neck, but his jet black hair, once parted along the side, was now slicked back, and the pubescent look of youth—characteristically with him long into his teens—was no longer there. It was just as well, too. A representation of soft and frail hadn't boded well for him in this particular environment. Also added were the sideburns, tapered and trimmed close. It injected an element of maturity, and even his dark eyes, once fearful and uncertain, now radiated with both conviction and power.

Keeping his movements measured, Tom fumbled for the throwaway cellphone located in the front, side-pocket, of his trench coat. Using the code phrases he had pried away from Bishop—the same code phrases the assassin used when contacting his clients—Tom sent a pre-typed text to the young Manatone.

A split second later, Tom watched his reaction upon receiving the text. As suspected, there was no missing Tony's relief at thinking Bishop was contacting him. Tom smirked with satisfaction. It was possible that the killer of Mike and Micky, and the facilitator in his wife's death, would no longer be breathing later this evening. The thought appeased his aching heart...at least a little.

Tom took notice of the two bodyguards in the front seat and his eyes narrowed. Bishop had said the two men responsible for beating

Mike and Micky—aside from Charley Mack—were on Tony's security team. He also stated they were easily identified: one was blond and always wore a Yankees hat, and the other had a hideous scar on his forehead. Right now, neither man wore a hat, but Tom noticed the driver did have blond shaggy hair.

He got out of the car first.

Tom judged him to be in his mid-twenties. He had narrow shoulders, not physically imposing, and much like most of the security teams Tom had already seen this morning, wore a grey suit and tie. The man in the passenger seat exited next. Dressed similarly, and about the same age, he was tall and muscular, his dark hair cut close to the skull, and most telling—and like Bishop had described—was an angry scar that zig-zagged up his forehead. This, Tom now knew, was Jimmy Matt. That meant the driver was probably Tim Barns, minus the Yankees hat. Tom also took note of their injuries. Jimmy Matt had two black eyes from a recent broken nose, while Tim Barns's walk was stiff, like from a pulled muscle or a sore chest.

Tom couldn't help but wonder if the injuries related to the confrontation with Mike and Micky.

Jimmy opened the door and Tony stepped out. After a quick look at the bustling people on the sidewalk, he smoothed his khaki pants, and buttoned his tweed sport coat. A man cursed, and he turned in Toms' direction.

Foot traffic along the sidewalk had picked up, and a man had tripped over Tom's outstretched legs. He obviously wasn't happy, and after righting himself, he continued the berating in a threatening manner. But Tom wasn't fazed, overtly or covertly, by the man's lingering…and obnoxious…presence.

Pretending to be comatose and unaware, the Shadow kept his head down, while his keen eyes—hidden behind the bangs of flowing hair— remained focused on Tony Manatone as the young heir leaned right and then left to see through the flowing traffic of bodies. Then his eyes locked onto Tom just as the abusive stranger continued on his way.

In all reality, Tom would have been more than happy just to pull his gun—now gripped under his coat—and kill the man who had caused him so much grief. It was a temptation almost too hard to resist. Quick and easy, he could fire a shot in the air to clear the sidewalk, and before the two surprised bodyguards could clear their weapons, he could kill them almost effortlessly, saving Lil Mouse for last.

Tempting indeed.

As the three men stared in his direction, Tom paid very close attention to their body language, but there was no indication he had been recognized, nor any telltale sign of concern. Their demeanor was more of curiosity, so Tom let it play out, watching as Tony leaned in and spoke to Tim Barns. The bodyguard's reaction, more importantly his malevolent smile, was all Tom needed to see. In all the years Tom had worked for the Manatones, panhandling in front the syndicate's main building was never tolerated. This was a rule by Frank Manatone himself and it was strictly enforced; usually without police involvement, and by whatever means necessary. To him, the homeless were filth, and like rats, the scourge of the city.

That's what now shone in the bodyguard's eyes, more so the 'by whatever means necessary' part. But Tom had already anticipated this. In fact, he was counting on it, because he knew if there was a squatter, someone would eventually come to take care of the problem. Of course, Tom couldn't have been more pleased at who was being sent to deal with this particular problem.

Chapter 14

A N HOUR AFTER THE MEETING, and long after everyone had left, Frank Manatone was still in the conference room and listening to Michelle Averton. "According to my sources in the police department, the search warrant for the Red Hook facility will be served tomorrow morning. I managed to drag it out as much as possible, but it should be routine. As you well know, with any calls to the police about bodies, they're obligated to investigate." Frank nodded, his expression neutral, as she continued. "That being said, without any evidence of a crime having ever been committed, it will be very limited and look something like this." The lawyer slid a two page document in front of Frank. "It's the most generic warrant a judge can sign. In other words Frank, they're looking for a body. That means they can open doors and do a general walkthrough of the whole property, every room, every grain silo, and even the waterway surrounding it. But here's the thing, it's limited to only what they can see, nothing hidden under anything, nothing under the water, or buried." She paused a moment to make sure he understood what she had said, before continuing. "However, that all changes if they find evidence of a crime. In that case, the building would be closed off and the warrant immediately expanded to a criminal investigation. Then there is nothing off-limits and they will tear into everything, including the walls, what's behind them… and in them. It would mean cadaver dogs, underground radar, divers, and even whiffers."

Whiffers were the newest tool in criminology investigations. Capable of smelling for gunpowder residue, the backpack and wand looked more like something from a Ghostbusters movie than an investigative tool. The revolutionary concept bypassed the standard and archaic swabbing practices of the past. Using a hollow wand, air is drawn into a microcomputer in the backpack, where it's then filtered and processed. So sensitive is this filtering software that it can pick up the lingering scent-particles of burn gunpowder even days later. This made it a game changer for both criminals and criminologists alike. Now with less need for visual proof, uncovering a potential crime scene became a whole lot easier. Not only could invisible trace evidence be found on walls and floors in close proximity of the discharging weapon, but also in the surrounding air. And this said nothing of the substantial amount of ground the apparatus could cover in little to no time versus swabbing techniques.

Michelle watched the subtle change in his expression change. As Frank's lawyer, there were aspects of the Manatone syndicate she was aware of, but that was on the legal side, like land use laws, tax laws, and their internet businesses. But that's not to say she was naive or ignorant about the illegal operations. On the contrary, she had represented the syndicate on varying fields of illegal activities such as prostitution, drugs—including both trafficking and smuggling—as well as laundering charges filed by the federal government. Then there was the body—the presumptive body—at the Red Hook Granary. Considering Frank had vehemently fought the police from going anywhere near the property, her gut told her, regardless of whether they found a body or not, the syndicate had killed someone. This was further confirmed by how many times she'd heard the word 'cleanup' in the same sentence as the granary; most of which from people here in Frank's building. As the attorney of record in the case, and setting aside her gut feeling, she had done her best to learn who had made the call to the police in the first place. After all, legally speaking, this could very well just be a prank call, or an embittered employee. At least that's what she had argued to the judge. But, after listening to the 911 call to police, he hadn't bought their plea. Even though the call had been anonymous, the man seemed very convincing in telling police exactly where the body could be found, which was at the bottom of one of the silos. Michelle had listened to it too, and although she argued against it, the man indeed sounded credible, especially when he said it was the body of a woman. At that point, and prior to hanging up, his words became shaky, implying emotional duress. Could the caller be the killer? More than likely he was, but finding him had turned into a dead-end; the call made from a burner phone.

That wasn't all. It was in that same timeframe, and through more bits of information she'd picked up from office gossip, that the body at the granary was only part of the problem. Causing an even bigger stir was a name that kept popping up, and oddly enough, also as frequent as the word 'cleanup'. His name was Tom Spears, and he seemed to be at the core of whatever had happened at the granary.

"That can't happen," Frank responded, his eyes turning cold. "That warrant mustn't be allowed to expand. You will see to it, and that's nonnegotiable."

She swallowed hard, and her pulse quickened. "I understand that," she said. "I'll do what I can…"

He put his hand over hers on the table, stopping her words. "You don't understand because you're not listening, Michelle." He leaned forward with a malevolent gleam in his dark eyes; his face no more than a few inches from hers. "This is why you're here, and make no mistake about what I'll do to you if you fail."

Fear, real fear, swept through her for the first time in their relationship. But even at that, she didn't…couldn't…pull away; her reaction beyond abnormal. What was it about the man that could stir so much fear, and yet, supercharge her desires? Even under the threat of violence, her heart beat faster in erotic splendor. It was an ongoing theme, and the hold he had over her even early on, not easily dismissed.

The first time they had met was when she'd worked for another law firm, and he needed representation in a drug smuggling conspiracy charge. That had been four years earlier, and in winning the case, Frank had showed his appreciation by setting her up with her own firm here on the same floor as him. But, thinking back, her accepting the job at the time hadn't just been about her ambitions. In fact, during the court case, she had been fascinated by being so close to such a dangerous man—a man considered pure evil by most.

At first she had fought the unusual feelings, but even with the huge age difference, this fascination had blossomed from a professional working acquaintance to a growing attraction—a forbidden temptation— and then to fantasy. But, so she'd thought at the time, that's all it was, an urge, a fantasy; her sexual thoughts veiled and kept to herself. Then he had caught her in the elevator that day, and in taking her—without any form of seduction, much less her consent—right then and there, she had learned a hidden, yet undeniable, secret she never knew existed about herself. Vulnerable and defenseless, it was the unexpected pleasure of being controlled sexually without mercy or inhibitions. Of course, her first impulse had been to refuse; to contest his rough hands that were touching and probing at will. But that soon changed, her capitulation coming with the realization of how badly he'd wanted her, and how much she was enjoying the power of him violating her. The experience had been not only daring, and intoxicating, but fresh, filling her with an unexpected lustful splendor. Never before had she felt such a wanting from a man—much less such a powerful man. So she had succumbed, and like the petals of a flower on a warm sunny day, opened herself to his will; even obliging his every wanton need. Now she was at his beck and call, which meant anytime, anywhere, and no matter the circumstances. In fact, even now under the veil of threats and intimidation, she couldn't fight her arousal, and felt as helpless as a fawn in front of the big bad wolf.

"I'll…take care of it," she said, the tremor in her voice not totally from fear. "Honest Frank, you have...."

"I know you will," he interrupted, lifting her hand to his lips. "You are mine until you're not." He turned her in the chair so she was facing him. Without taking his eyes off her, he let his hands move up her tanned legs to the base of her tight fitting skirt.

Accepting of his touch, her body trembled with anticipation. Then he stopped, grabbed her by the shoulders, and forced her to her knees in front of him. "I'm tired of your words, so before you do what I'm paying you quite handsomely to do…" He unzipped his fly and exposed his growing arousal. "Let's make that mouth of yours more useful." He let his head roll back against the chair, and repeated his words more tersely, "remember, you are mine until I say you're not."

She knew it was true, and did as she was told, letting him feel her heated breath.

Chapter 15

THE RAIN WAS COMING DOWN hard and heavy when the meeting let out two hours later. Most people who exited the building were in a hurry and running to their waiting cars. But not all. Two men whom Tom recognized, stepped outside and huddled against the wall of the building. They were near Tom's position, so he kept his head lolled forward, but tilted to the side to watch them.

The short man, with his back to Tom, was Mike Grevo. A wide shouldered man with a thick neck, he was responsible for the bulk of the gambling revenues brought in. He was also a major player, and probably next in the line of succession behind Tony Manatone as crime boss.

Upon seeing his face, Tom realized who the familiar bodyguard had been with Frank earlier. It was his son, George, all grown up. Meeting him on more than one occasion while working for the Mantones, Tom remembered the bright eyed twelve-year-old as a decent kid, with good grades, and even at that young age, already preparing for college. But more than anything, what Tom remembered most was how close the father and son were.

Mike flipped open his lighter, cupped a cigarette, and lit it. Drawing in the smoke, he handed the lighter to the tall, thin man, standing next to him and facing Tom. He was well dressed, with short blond hair, and intense brown eyes. His name was Steve Johnnson. Another major player, he was in charge of most of the prostitution rings throughout the city and much of the state.

Tom had to admit, it was good to see them again. Both of them. In his years working for the crime family, Tom had worked side by side with each of these men. They were intelligent, respectful, and professional, using Tom on multiple occasions as either a facilitator in money owed to the syndicate, or to have someone killed. Tom had done both, and usually without question. In those days, Tom had a job to do and in retrospect considered both of these men allies…not friends…but allies.

It was a big difference in this particular business. Friends were people you hung out with socially, either drinking a beer together after work or at a weekend barbecue, and allies were people you could trust. Tom had trusted both these men with his life on more than a few occasions. Now as he watched them, it seemed strange they were no longer allies. But he accepted it. They were indeed adversaries, so like a fly on the wall, he listened avidly as they discussed the meeting amongst themselves.

"Good news about the website, huh?" Steve Johnnson asked.

"Yeah, I never saw that coming. Big money," Mike Grevo responded, looking around to make sure they were alone. Then he asked, "So what do you make of Motese?"

"If the anonymous tip is true, I don't believe for a second he didn't know what the fuck was going on," Steve answered.

Tom remembered the name. They were talking about Rick Motese; the man in charge of all the growing fields up north. This was interesting. In a span of a few short hours, the topic of the fields was brought up again. Now Tom wasn't so quick to dismiss it.

Mike nodded. "Agreed."

Both men took long drags from their cigarettes, before Steve asked, "You think Tony is up to the task?"

Mike grunted his dissatisfaction. "What do you think? The old man is sending a flaming sperm-burper to get answers." He shook his head. "Seriously, how many answers is he going to find?"

Steve chuckled at Mike's description of Tony. "Guess we'll know soon enough." He sighed heavily, and his eyes flicked along the block before he followed up with his own question. "Spears is going to be a problem, isn't he?"

"You can count on it," Mike answered flatly.

Damn straight. Tom thought. *And may the two of you not get in my way.*

Chapter 16

I T WAS EARLY AFTERNOON BY the time Tony stepped out in front of the Manatone building again. And although the rain was still coming down, it did little to alter his good mood. The meeting had gone far better than expected. To prove his worthiness in a leadership role, he had stepped up in the northern fields matter. Now he needed to solve the problem—if indeed there was a problem.

His thoughts went to Rick Motese. Shortly after the meeting, Tony had gone right to work figuring out what was happening in the hidden fields. First, he had gone to his father to learn what he knew. This was very little, all started with a call from an unknown informant. Not trusting anyone, the caller had been insistent about only talking to Frank Manatone himself. And when finally put through, she—sounding like a kid no less—had told him that the security teams from several fields were collaborating in duping the syndicate by continually skimming product. The call had been brief, and then abruptly cut off before Frank could get any details. Then Tony had gone to Rick Motese, probing into what he knew, or was willing to elaborate on. This was outwardly very little, but in fact Tony had learned a great deal from him. First was his nervousness. It seemed the longer the interview went, the more nervous he got, and this was from a normally cool and collected…if not arrogant…man. So this begged the question, was it because he didn't have any answers, or because he was hiding something? Tony thought the latter because the more he'd pressed, the less convincing Rick had gotten.

No, he confirmed to himself, *Mr. Motese was definitely hiding something.* To confirm this, and starting tomorrow, he would begin the long trek to the fields himself. Then, if his suspicions were correct, he would be the one to deal with Motese personally; again showing his value.

As he waited for his car to be brought around, he breathed in the damp air. It tasted clean and sweet. Making the day even better, tonight he would meet with Bishop, and learn what had happened at the granary. Then—regardless of whether Tom Spears was alive or dead—he would insist that his father be killed with no further delay. This would help their plan two fold. First and foremost, Tony was tired of waiting, and second, with him having to drive the two hundred and forty miles to the northern fields, it offered him the perfect alibi. After all, it wasn't a big secret that Tony despised his father, and he needed the transition in becoming the crime boss to go as smoothly as possible.

"Crime boss," he mumbled with satisfaction. "It has a nice ring to it."

He grinned. It was the beginning of a new day—a new time in his life. Soon his father would be dead, and no longer would Tony be looked at with pity…as a weakling…unworthy…and never again would he hear the name Lil Mouse mumbled behind his back. All that would be behind him.

A new day indeed.

Tony's Jaguar XJR appeared around the corner. Tim Barns was behind the wheel, and pulled up to the curb. As it came to a stop, Jimmy Matt moved from Tony's side and opened the back door. But before the young heir slipped into the back seat, he stopped, and looked back over his left shoulder. With the rain, the pedestrian traffic had become nonexistent, and his gaze settled on the vagrant, who was still there, and looking like he had never moved.

His good mood began to fade, and as he slipped in the back seat, he turned to Tim Barns. "Get that piece of shit away from the front of my building," he said harshly.

"Soon, after nightfall boss," Tim responded with confidence.

*****

With the long day behind him, and approaching early evening, Frank Manatone was finally getting his appetite back. "How does dinner down the street at Deangelo's sound?" Frank asked Charley Mack and George Grevo as they descended in the private elevator from the uppermost floor. Both men nodded with grins of approval.

When they exited onto the first level, the doorman opened the front door. "Thanks Henry," Frank said, handing him a ten dollar bill.

"Thank you, Mr. Manatone," Henry replied. "Always a pleasure."

Frank exited and stopped on the now-deserted sidewalk. The heavy rain earlier had turned into a light drizzle. He buttoned up his cashmere overcoat, and glanced up. Light was fading, and the dark rain-heavy clouds hung low over the tall buildings.

It was going to be a very wet night.

Flipping his collar up, he turned left with his two bodyguards trailing two steps behind. A beggar, sitting against the wall with an open violin case between his legs, caught his attention. He was destitute, with long greasy hair, clothes that were filthy and thread bare, and shoes held together with grey duct tape. Frank stopped and gazed down at the man; his temper and disgust rising equally. Every once in a while one of these…individuals…would show up in front of his building. But that had been months ago. He shook his head. They were like filthy rats, eating from dumpsters, pissing and shitting in alleyways and sunken entryways. And if one was allowed to stay, it would only encourage more and more of them to show up; their garbage and drug paraphernalia littering the sidewalk. He sighed heavily. How many times over the past decade had he warned the homeless about being on this particular block? How many times had he been forced to prove his point by beating or even killing one of them?

Obviously, it was time to make his point clear again.

The man's head was tilted forward like he was sleeping, and in the wet violin case was no more than ten dollars in loose change.

Not completely heartless, Frank peeled off a twenty dollar bill from the roll in his pocket. Bending over, he dropped the money in the case. "What's your name, son?"

"Bill," came a whispered, detached, voice.

"Do you know who I am, Bill?"

"No," he answered, without moving.

Frank nodded. "Then because of your ignorance, consider this a courtesy. The building you're leaning against, and the sidewalk you're now sitting on, belong to me. That means you're trespassing." He smelled the pungent odor of urine and stood. "Go get yourself something to eat Bill, but don't be here tomorrow. If you are, I'll assume you've mistaken my courtesy for leniency, and that would be very disrespectful. In which case, I'll see that both your legs are broken, plus interest. That means also a broken arm. Do you understand, Bill?"

There was a long pause, then a barely audible, "Yes…thank you… kind sir…"

"Good. We have an understanding then. So in good faith…" he peeled off another twenty and dropped it into the case, "get yourself some shoes, too." Turning to leave, he gave the vagrant a final warning. "Don't ever be on my block again, Bill."

Six minutes later, and just as the three were being seated at the famous restaurant, Frank received a text. "Well, it's about fucking time," he said out loud. The text was from Bishop Styles, and he wanted to finalize the contract tonight at the old spa in Queens. That meant, Tom Spears was officially dead, and it was time to celebrate. After flagging down a waiter, he ordered a six-thousand-dollar bottle of Armand de Brignac Brut Gold champagne to get the evening started.

*****

Just as the darkness of night settled over the city and the street lights flickered to life, Tom heard a distant whistling drawing closer. It came from the alleyway along the side of the Manatone building; the sound merry and confident. A shadowed figure wearing jeans, a hooded blue sweatshirt, and a Yankees baseball cap, emerged onto the sidewalk a minute later. It was Tim Barns, and he paused to scan the empty block before continuing toward Tom's position.

Uncertain of whether the syndicate-man would launch an attack while Tom sat on the sidewalk, the Shadow levered himself to his feet, and as he rose up, grabbed the pistol from between his legs, sticking it in his waistband with his hidden hand. Leaving the violin case behind, he gave the illusion of being drunk, staggering toward the syndicate-man. Then as Tim Barns drew close, Tom leaned heavily into the building for apparent support. Tim, not recognizing any threat to himself, reached out to assist the panhandler by hooking an arm around the waist. "Easy there, homeless dude. Let me help you," he said guiding Tom around the corner and into the alley. Satisfied they were out of any prying eyes, he abruptly pushed Tom against the wall. "You picked the wrong wall to piss on, you worthless piece of shit. Now I'm going to teach you a lesson you'll never forget."

Tom was also satisfied that no one else was around, and hissed back in kind, "Not today, and not by the likes of you." His anger seemed to crackle like electricity. No longer lethargic, his threatening words were crisp, his eyes unwavering as he looked the assailant square in the eyes.

Surprised, Tim recoiled just as the heel of Tom's hand lashed out, sending a lightning-fast chop to Tim's neck. Quick and decisive, the carefully placed blow was debilitating and not meant to kill, striking below the Adams apple. Incapacitated, the shocked syndicate-man dropped the bat, and staggered back, clutching his throat with both hands. As he fell to his knees and struggled to breathe, his face turned sheet white, his eyes bulged, and his mouth flew open in a frozen look of horror.

Tom removed the beanie from his head, pushed his disheveled hair back off his face, and settled it back onto his head. "Now you and I are going to get acquainted."

Tom heaved him to his feet, picked up the bat from where it had fallen, and threw Tim against the wall between two nearby dumpsters. As the paralyzing effect of the blow lessened, the color returned to Tim's face, and the guttural noises from his injured throat were replaced by shuddering breaths.

"You know who I am now?" Tom asked, while searching him for weapons. He had none.

Still struggling to breathe, Tim nodded with apprehension, while continuing to clutch his throat.

"You have a chance of walking out of this alley alive," Tom lied, keeping him pinned to the wall by the front of his sweatshirt, "if you answer my questions truthfully." Confirming he indeed had a rib injury, Tom pressed hard against Tim's chest. The reaction was immediate with Tim taking a shuddering breath, and grabbing Tom's wrist defensively with one hand.

"Break some bones, did we?" Tom glared.

Tim tried to speak, but was still unable, and drool ran from the corner of his mouth with the effort.

Tom gave him a moment. The effectiveness of the blow had eliminated any form of retaliatory response, and yet, would eventually allow him to speak. Otherwise, if Tom had had a mind to, he could've killed him instantly by crushing his larynx. But he needed him alive and able to talk. Walking however, was another matter. To keep Tim vulnerable, and further lessen the possibility of any confrontation, Tom lifted the bat over his shoulder and then sent the cutoff-Louisville-Slugger into the side of Tim Barns knee. The solid strike sent a bone-popping echo down the alley and Tim dropped like a sack of rocks, screaming and writhing in pain.

Tom took a quick look both ways down the alley to confirm no one was around and then ducked between the dumpsters. "Now let's get to those questions we talked about, and then…we'll have a discussion about what you did to my friends: Mike and Micky. You remember them?" Hearing the names, Tim's immediate pain seemed less important and genuine fear shone in his dark bulging eyes.

Minutes later Tim Barns was dead, beaten over the head with his own bat, and then thrown into the dumpster and covered in trash. Much like Bishop's final resting place, it seemed fitting, and if Tom was lucky, the body would end up at the landfill and never discovered. But if it was, and the police got involved, Tom had carefully cleaned the scene, taking the bat with him. Then later he would dispose of it properly, along with the clothes he was wearing.

As he walked back towards his car, his thoughts were on both the useful information Tim had supplied, and also the meeting later tonight at the Queens Athletic Club. If all went well, soon everyone responsible for the deaths of Tanya, Micky and Mike, would all be in one location.

Chapter 17
Worlds Collide

THE SHADOW ARRIVED AT THE Queen's Athletic Club two hours before the first scheduled meet-time with the Manatones. Having gotten the spare key from Bishop Styles, he was sitting on a bench seat in the locker room. Before him, and resting in a claw foot tub, were the decomposing remains of Mike, and Micky. His friends were well beyond recognition, but there was little doubt it was them considering what Bishop had told him. Even their hands and feet were still bound to the legs of the tub. It was a dreadful sight, and Tom could only imagine the brutality of their deaths. He tried not to dwell on it, but that was easier said than done when his world was continually being shaken; the pain tumbling like dice from a cup of chance.

How had his life come to this, where people he loved could die just because they were close to him?

The grief of Tanya's death was one thing, hitting him in continuous waves like twisting daggers to his heart. But now seeing the viciousness first hand, was unconscionable. Brought here by deception, they were betrayed by the syndicate—a family they had served faithfully for more than twenty years. Then they were tied up, and tortured; all in an effort to find Tom Spears, alias the Shadow.

"The Shadow," Tom mumbled. He was aware of the moniker. Who had started it, he wasn't sure, nor cared. In his mind it wasn't flattering. How could it be? It was a term associated with years of killing; the name emerging after rarely being seen much less caught. Then as his success grew, so did the legend. But in name only. Tom didn't consider himself a legend. On the contrary, he felt completely the opposite. He had never killed for the lust of killing like the name implied. So to be likened to a nightmarish boogeyman who lurks and prowls the night, he found both disheartening and disturbing. He was merely a man, not some unstoppable force, and implied legend or not, he could be put down like anyone else by a well-placed bullet.

His thoughts went to the Manatones, and his face became a mask of anger. If a bullet was indeed his destiny, then so be it. He didn't care. His only real desire was to kill Charley Mack, Jimmy Matt, and the Manatones; both father and son. Of course the optimal plan initially would be to take them alive.

He rose from the bench, adjusted his shoulder-holstered Glock, and zipped up his dark blue windbreaker. He still needed a shower, but at least now he wore clean clothes. After leaving the Manatone building, Tom had driven under the Brooklyn Bridge, located an empty fifty-five-gallon drum used by the homeless for warming fires, and deposited the bat and his rancid wardrobe into the burning coals. Catching fire almost immediately, any evidence of his involvement in the death of Tim Barns was then gone.

Focused again, he left the locker room to familiarize himself with every square foot of the building, and begin preparations for his guests.

*****

Frank Manatone got to the Queens Athletic Club fifteen minutes early. He was delighted, even glib, that this Tom Spears issue was finally behind him. But that's not to say he was any less cautious. Dealing with any assassin, much less the likes of Bishop, you could never be too careful when it came to the possibility of being double-crossed. So aside from his normal security detail of Charley Mack and George Grevo, Frank also brought along two extra men. Their names were Sid Kemper, and Jason Sanders. Sitting on each side of him in the back seat, they were young and inexperienced, but much like most employees in the syndicate, would more than hold their weight in a fight.

Charley Mack pulled up to the back door in the alleyway. Parking under a fading and flickering overhead light, all five men exited Frank's armored Lincoln Continental.

The building's steel door was closed, but unlocked. Charley entered first. The interior was pitch black beyond the iridescent glow of the single outside light. He tried the wall switch but nothing happened.

"Hello? You here?" Charley asked, looking down the hallway to his left.

There was no response. He glanced back at the men huddled around the entry, and cautiously removed his Colt .45 from the holster on his belt. The other three bodyguards followed suit.

Charley tried calling out once more but again there was no response. He shrugged and moved forward, but after only a few steps ran into the side of a set-of-four steel lockers against the wall. They were tall and narrow, typical of gyms and high school hallways.

The two new men, Sid and Jason, snickered with delight as Charley stepped back in surprise. "Funny, but I don't remember seeing these before," the big Jamaican said, while pulling out his cellphone and turning it on flashlight mode. Holding it in front of him, he stepped around the lockers and continued forward. At the end of the short hallway they came to a large room. This is where the workout equipment used to be, but now, all that remained was a rubbish pile at the center of the room from the stripped interior walls.

Frank brought up the rear, noticing right away, the stale and stagnant air had turned more sinister and foul smelling, even rancid. He didn't know what to make of it, but his earlier jubilance turned to unease as his eyes floated over the eerie scene. It had been at least ten years since he had been to this building. But there really hadn't been a need. Its purpose, and the reason it remained on the books, was much like the Red Hook Granary. Simply put, it was a quiet place to take care of business transactions quietly, which included killing; the thought not lost on him now.

"Look over there," George said, pointing down the short hallway beyond the front desk. "It's a light."

"Yeah, very dim," Charley added, "coming from the men's locker room."

Frank moved to the front, stepping past the two new guys. "Bishop, you here?" he shouted with a hint of concern.

There was no response, the interior remaining deathly quiet.

Charley began to move forward again.

"Wait," George cautioned. "I'm not liking this." He turned to Frank. "I think we should get back to the alley, regroup, and maybe just two of us come back and check it out."

Frank nodded in agreement. Bodyguards or not, something wasn't right.

With Sid Kemper and Jason Sanders leading the way—their guns held loosely down at their sides—they picked up the pace and reentered the entry hall; now dimly lit at the end from the exterior lighting that spilled in through the open door.

Frank swallowed hard, his eyes flicking left and right. With the darkness and rotting smell, the atmosphere, cold and dank, had become tomblike, and the sound of their shuffling feet seismic, echoing off the corridor walls in ghostly fashion. Then, just short of the oddly placed lockers again, Frank's heart skipped a beat when his cellphone rang. They stopped, and all eyes turned to him as he dug it out of his coat pocket. At that moment—their distraction complete—two of the doors from the steel lockers burst open and Tom Spears stepped into sight from the expanded interior. At no more than six feet away, it was easy to see his face, as well as the silenced pistol in his upraised right hand.

A spitting sound followed as the Shadow fired in rapid succession. The first shot caught the closest man, Sid Kemper, in the side as he turned to face him, and the next went to his forehead. As he flew backward, two more shots followed, hitting Jason Sanders with one shot to the chest and one also to the forehead.

Fear touched Frank for the first time in years, and he stepped back in shock and disbelief. Fluid and agile, Tom Spears moved with uncanny efficiency. Even as the assassin fired the four shots, his left hand came forward, lobbing something down the corridor. Then he was gone as fast as he'd appeared, ducking out the entry door to the alley. Less than three seconds had gone by. A precision attack, the deadly shots had been unwavering and accurate, leaving two of his men dead—execution style—long before ever hitting the floor.

Charley and George returned fire with their large bore weapons. The sound was deafening, and the close proximity of the concussive blasts was felt as well as heard. But it was only a retaliatory response, and much too late; the wooden door frame taking the brunt of it, exploding and splintering under the barrage of bullets.

Meanwhile, the object Tom Spears had thrown, bounced off the wall, hit the floor, and rolled against Frank's foot. He looked down just as it exploded. Blinding white light seared his retinas and the concussive wave threw him from his feet onto his backside. Stunned and unable to see, he lost all sense of direction, and recoiled in pain as his hands flew to his eyes. Chaos and confusion reigned. More shots filled the air, and a bullet struck the side wall near Frank's head. He ducked down, covering his head with his arms. Charley screamed, but after a deadened sound—like being struck in the head—his anguished cry was cut off. Then George was next. His frustrated cursing stymied in mid-sentence.

An eerie silence befell them and Frank quit moving, trying to listen past his pounding heart and ringing ears. Footsteps! He heard footsteps, slow and grating, over the debris covered cement floor. They came close and stopped. Blinking rapidly to clear the pain and blindness in his watery eyes, he saw someone stoop over him. A shadow, mirage-like, leaned close.

The crime boss took a shuddering breath.

"Frank Manatone," Tom said, his tone cold as a winter wind. "In your arrogance, you made a huge error in coming after me…"

Frank heard another noise…distant footsteps…and in a hurry. Then more thunderous shots followed. Tom dove over him, rolled once, and moved back into the building's interior. Frank's vision finally cleared. With relief he saw Tony and Jimmy Matt standing inside the doorway, they were shooting round after round into the back corner where Spears had apparently disappeared.

To stay out of the shooting lanes, Frank rolled to the opposite wall, stood on wobbly legs, and surveyed the scene. George remained down and bleeding from head injuries sustained by Tom. He was alive but not moving. Meanwhile, Charley had gotten to his hands and knees, and was crawling back toward the entryway; a bleeding gash atop his bald head. But the tide was turning.

Frank looked back over his shoulder toward where Spears had disappeared. There was still no return fire or sign of the assassin, and with the changing circumstances, Frank's fear turned to confidence. If Bishop Styles couldn't take care of this problem, he and his men would. He waved Jimmy and his son forward.

*****

The flashlight and cellphone distractions, combined with the flashbang, and the revamped and hollowed out lockers, had worked far better than Tom could've imagined. But that had been the good news— the portion of the scheme that went well. As with most hastily contrived plans there are always setbacks—those unforeseen events that can derail any good plan. It was the nature of the beast, and something Tom knew all too well. In this case, and what Tom hadn't accounted for—when giving himself a full hour in between the two meetings in the first place—was Tony's obvious enthusiasm at wanting his father killed and showing up forty minutes earlier than scheduled. But eagerness or not, this wasn't Tom's first rodeo. He had learned long ago that being able to adapt to changing scenarios was as advantageous as setbacks were detrimental. Now crouched around the corner, he calmly let the half-full magazine drop from the handle of the silenced Kimber Aegis II 9mm and replaced it with a fresh one. He also removed the added bulk of the silencer, and slipped it into his coat pocket.

He took a deep reassuring breath. The smell of cordite filled the air and the interior now sounded like a war zone. To his left, no more than three feet away, the corner wall was disintegrating by the peppering spray of the bullets. Exploding like popcorn, the chunks of white sheetrock flew through the dust-filled air and scattered across the cement floor; its chalky cloud swirling in the dim lighting. It was as intense as it was sobering, but Tom wasn't concerned. After securing the only emergency exit earlier, he knew there was only one way in or out, and this was it—a choke point, and as he had already proved, a perfect killing field. Another mitigating factor was the lighting: it was dark where he was, and they were silhouetted by the light—although minimal—from the open door.

He forced himself to be patient, waiting for the precise moment, and letting the continuous suppression fire play right into hands. Getting ready, he stood, removed his Glock from the shoulder holster, and checked the chamber. Then, while holding the pistols upward in each hand, he waited for the two panicked, overconfident men, to reload. It didn't take long, and when they did, Tom reappeared around the corner, while calculating the immediate threats in a millisecond. The closest man, Frank, was no threat. He was unarmed and standing statuesque against the far wall, and both Charley and George were still down—with Charley crawling away toward the door.

As expected, both Jimmy Matt, and Tony Manatone were looking down, distracted, while reloading their weapons. Tom ignored Tony, who was fumbling with his magazine, and focused on Jimmy Matt. Much more efficient at reloading, he was already bringing his weapon up. Tom didn't hesitate. His first two shots—one from each gun—thundered into Jimmy's chest and head simultaneously. Devastatingly effective, the impact of the hollow-point-rounds not only lifted him off the ground but drove him backward, where he bounced off the lockers, and fell unmoving to the floor; his blood and brain matter blossoming like a roadkill skid-mark along the sidewall.

Tom kept firing, the alternating guns now pointed at Charley Mack After crawling to the back of the hall, the big Jamaican rose from the floor and ducked behind the lockers, but not before one bullet passed through the meat of his shoulder, and yet another misplaced round grazed his cheek; the ugly trough gushing blood, and his scream of pain drowned out by the deafening gunfire.

As Charley took the hits, Tony eagerly retreated, cowering back into the alley to finish reloading.

George Grevo struggled to his feet, and a round from his gun whizzed by Tom's ear. The Shadow dived to his right, firing randomly as he rolled to the far wall. Frank ducked. In-between the two men now, the crime boss broke like a flushed quail for the door. But his escape was a fraction too late, and one of Tom's rounds struck him high in the shoulder, pirouetting him into George. Their heads smacked together, the impact harsh, and both men went over like bowling pins with George landing hard on his backside, and Frank on top of him.

Tom scooched up against one of Frank's dead bodyguards. Using the corpse for cover, he stole a quick look. Tending his wounds, Charley Mack's gun had gone silent. This was good news. If Tom could take the fat Jamaican alive, he would. He turned his attention to Frank.

Panicked now, with obvious thoughts of self-preservation, the crime boss ignored the pain in his shoulder and crawled over George on his hands and knees, trying once again to make it to the safety of the door. But safety, in regards to Tony, was a loose term, and as the young Manatone peeked around the corner of the door frame, his dark eyes narrowed with a glint of triumph at seeing his dad's vulnerability.

At that moment, Tom knew—Bishop or no Bishop—what was coming next. So instead of shooting Frank, he pointed his weapon at the doorway; anticipating Tony's next move.

Standing between his father and that proverbial safety, Tony waited for Frank to approach, then stepped out and brought his pistol down viciously into the top of his father's exposed head. The surprised and unsuspecting crime boss flattened like a deflated balloon.

Tom fired, but misjudged where Tony would appear, narrowly missing; the doorjamb above the young mobsters head splintering. He fired once more, but it was too late. Tony recoiled after the first round and retreated to safety once again. Remaining undeterred, and knowing that Tom had a bead on his position, he crouched, reached in, grabbed his father by the hair, and yanked him closer to the entry. Now with only a portion of his hand exposed, he lifted his father's head. Tom heard a guttural plea from Frank, and some snarling words from Tony. It was brief and moot because Tony didn't hesitate, putting the barrel of his gun into his father's eye socket and pulling the trigger; the bullet bursting Frank Manatone's head like an over ripened watermelon.

And just like that, there was a new crime boss; the torch passed—taken in this case—and the coup launched.

Tom wasn't surprised, considering what Bishop had told him, but what happened next was indeed unexpected. For several more seconds there was no shooting, but George Grevo was in trouble. The two blows to the head—first by Tom after the flashbang, and now the head-butt from Frank—clearly left him dazed and disoriented. Dropping his gun, he began to crawl away much like Frank had done. He got as far as Charley's feet, then collapsed, and rolled onto his back. His eye was swollen shut and he was bleeding from the brow.

The reception wasn't what George had expected though. Cold and traitorous, Charley said something derogative, pointed his pistol, and shot him between the eyes; the large caliber bullet cleaving and vaporizing the upper skull in an explosion of grisly red spray.

Not that Tom much cared either way, but it was obvious that George hadn't been part of Tony's plan. Prearranged and deliberate, it was an assassination just like Frank.

Tom reloaded as Charley settled once again in back of the lockers. The cover was inadequate to hide his huge frame, but that wasn't what got Tom's attention. It was the sound of a car door being shut in the alley.

Tony was running!

Tom pushed himself to his feet. Taking careful aim, he fired two rounds into Charley's exposed belly. The raking impact was violent, the hollow-points bullets carving through the fatty flesh like hot knife through soft butter, and spinning him away from the locker. He hit the back wall with a grunt, dropped his gun, and collapsed in the corner.

Hearing a car start, Tom charged forward, and out the open doorway. Upon seeing Tony behind the wheel of his father's car, he fired repeatedly at the driver's side glass with Tony recoiling after each thunderous impact. But aside from leaving white pockmarks in the bulletproof glass, the rounds had little effect.

Their eyes met.

The initial fear in Tony's blanched face faded. Only confidence remained, and he slammed the car in drive, and punched the accelerator.

As the car lurched forward, anger swelled inside Tom at the thought of this little weasel escaping. Running alongside, he tried the door, but it was locked. In desperation he fired several rounds into the front tires and then the back as it sped past. Again, it was futile. Aside from blasting away several chunks of outer rubber, the lightweight, reinforced, polymer-liner was unaffected and the tires remained inflated.

Not giving up, he continued running and firing, and when his guns were empty, he dropped the Glock, expelled the empty magazine from the Kimber 9mm, and jammed another home. Then he stopped, snapped a shell in the chamber, and emptied the gun once more into the car—the discharged brass casings arcing gracefully from the breach and scattering across the pavement like rolling dice before Tony sped from the darkened alley and around the corner. Again, the bullets did little damage aside from pockmarks and chipped paint.

Disappointed, and breathing in ragged breaths, he bent over, leaning heavily on his knees; the pistol's open breach venting smoke from the heated barrel. Just the thought of Tony escaping sickened him. An opportunity had been missed but the reality was he had no time to dwell on it further. Remaining pragmatic, he straightened.

"A minor setback," he reassured himself, "it only means a change in plans."

Already thinking about the changing ramifications, he walked back down the alley. Soon, Tony would have the entire syndicate converging on this location from every direction. That meant Tom only had a few minutes. He picked up his gun and empty magazine, and headed back to the athletic club.

The interrogation of Charley Mack now became mandatory, and once back at the entryway, he looked at the mortally wounded Jamaican. It was a ghastly sight. Blood oozed from both the gouge on top of his head as well as from his opened cheek and the open shoulder wound. But this was nothing compared to the belly wound. Now in the seated position, he was moaning and trying to cover the flayed flesh with his hands. But it was little help. The blood was free-flowing between his fingers, and a portion of his intestines had already spilled onto the floor between his legs; a crimson pool forming under him.

Tom ignored him for a moment, stepping inside the doorway to remove the small camera he had stuck on the back wall. One of four, they were wireless, and cellphone compatible for monitoring, which he'd done from inside the lockers. This had been the key to his success, eliminating any unforeseen surprises. Not only had he known the exact number of men when he had finally stepped into the hall, but also their location.

He stuck it in his pocket, and cleared a path down the hall, using his foot to move the multiple dead bodies out of the way. Standing over George's body, Tom was touched with a sense of regret from the pain this would bring to his father; Mike Grevo. The two had been close, and Mike's wrath would be swift, his need for vengeance unequivocal. He would be looking for accountability, and there wasn't anything Tom could do about who the 'perceived' villain would be in all this.

With Tony now in charge, they would come after him—the Shadow—with everything they had, using every resource, from police, to thousands of syndicate employees, and even to prostitutes. On every corner, from Long Island north to the Canadian border, and west from Pittsburgh to as far east as Boston, there would be no place to hide. All eyes would be searching for him, and the bounty for his head beyond extreme.

He grabbed George by his arms and dragged him out the door and across the alleyway, laying him reverently along the wall next to the dumpster and covering his mutilated head with Tom's jacket. It was out of respect for Mike Grevo, and the least he could do for his one-time ally.

Satisfied, he went back inside. After recovering the other three cameras, it was time to deal with Charley Mack. Grabbing him by his legs, Tom dragged all four-hundred-pounds of him unsympathetically toward the men's locker room, and the remains of Mike and Micky. He couldn't be there when his friends died, but they would be there when Charley did.

As Tom worked, his scorn bubbled to the surface again like molten lava, spitting and hissing, and once Charley was tied to the claw foot tub with the same bindings used to tie Mike and Micky, Tom shot him in both knee caps. "That's for each of my friends, you fat fuck," Tom said, squatting in front of him. "Now let's get to the questions."

Nine minutes later, Tom exited the building as the whoosh of spreading flames could be heard coming from the interior. To ensure the fat Jamaican died in immeasurable pain, he hadn't poured any gasoline in the men's locker room, giving Charley plenty of time to contemplate his impending death.

A gruesome demise to be sure.

This Tom knew from hearing the grim story of Sam Cadet, a friend of Reed Davenport's and DEA national director at the time, who had been tied up, his wife killed in front of him, and the house set afire all around him. The damage to his body had been horrific; the pain unimaginable, before eventually succumbing to it in the hospital and dying.

It was the least Tom could do for the traitorous Charley Mack.

After closing the door, he locked it once again. The flames would be unstoppable by the time the firemen finally arrived.

Chapter 18

A HALF BLOCK AWAY, MIKE GREVO stood on a rain soaked sidewalk, staring at what remained of the Queens Athletic Club. The entire building was ablaze, an inferno, with flames now boiling through portions of the roof. In fact, the five-alarm fire was so intense, the entire block had been cordoned off, and engines from every firehouse in the area were here. Even now, he could hear more sirens drawing closer, and soon more beacons, bright and illuminated, would join the virtual cornucopia of spinning red and blue lights.

All around the building, the focused firemen scurried to and from their duties, and firehoses arced water high onto the flames. It was a grandiose effort, but futile. The building was consumed, the immense heat in the interior drawing the fire through the roof and launching it into the air—the glowing fireballs, translucent and swirling, lifted high in orange and red, before dissipating quickly in ghostly fashion.

Tony's car, which had been left in the alley, exploded, and Mike watched the firefighters fall back. It was a chaotic scene. Then their tactics seemed to change, aiming their hoses at only the surrounding buildings to at least save the rest of the block. That meant any further recovery of bodies would have to wait until then.

Mike sighed heavily. His son—the only body found so far—had been discovered in the alleyway. After making the grim identification, he learned from police and firefighters that the body had been dragged from the building before the fire was set. Obviously staged, they said there were bloody drag marks, and a coat had been placed over his head. Then there were his hands, which were placed reverently on his chest.

This was confusing to Mike. Was the staging a sign of remorse or was this a form of taunting? In either case, the loss was like a huge weight across his chest, making it difficult to breathe. He looked to his left. A gurney with George's body was being loaded into the back of an ambulance. Covered by a crisp white sheet, it seemed surreal; the bloody image of his son's head etched into his brain for all eternity. Although grateful George hadn't been devoured by flames like the others, he was no less angry that his one and only son was dead.

"I'm sorry, Mike," Tony said, standing at his side. "Like I said, it happened very fast."

Upon getting a frantic call from Tony, Mike had met him in the underground garage across from the Manatone's building. That's when he had been told the news about Frank's assassination and George's death. According to Tony, the Shadow had been merciless, killing all who entered the building except Tony.

The news had been nothing if not shocking, and even though Mike despised Tony Manatone, and trusted him even less, there was no reason to doubt him after seeing the damage done to Frank's armored car, not to mention the blood spray on both his hands and face. Of course, he couldn't be completely sure either way, considering it was coming from Tony; an underhanded, underachieving, self-adulating, lying, little prick.

Mike nodded, but before speaking, he cautiously took a quick look around. They were well away from the growing throng of bystanders across the street—stacked three deep along the police tape—with no one in their immediate area. Satisfied, he spoke evenly, "I appreciate that, but I would like to know why Tom Spears is even here." He turned and faced Tony.

Coming directly from the underground garage, the young Manatone hadn't changed clothes yet, so his fancy suit was soiled, and a coat-sleeve torn at the elbow. But at least the blood on his hands and face had been wiped away so as not to draw undo attention. "My boy is dead, and I want to know why. To further that, I've worked for the syndicate for more than thirty years so I recognize when there's more to a story than what's being told. What is it? I mean, even with a contract out on him, Tom Spears is...and always has been...idealistic and selective. He doesn't kill seven or eight people unless there's a reason, and/or he's provoked." He shook his head, glaring at Tony. "So which one is it? What happened and what's the real reason the Shadow is back in New York?"

Tony's dark eyes seemed distant, like he was processing a question that should've been answered right away. But in hesitating, it only confirmed Mike's suspicions.

"I'm not sure," Tony finally answered. "It was Bishop's operation, and he didn't confide in me."

"Funny, your dad told me you were in charge of dealing with Spears."

Tony's demeanor flashed in an instant. "I told you what I know," he snarled, "and evidently you need to be reminded of who's in charge now." He stepped in close, his eyes unwavering. "That's me. Like it or not, I'm the man now, and regardless of the differences with my father, this is my show." His eyes narrowed. "Now it's time to avenge him and your son. Do I make myself clear, or do I need to replace you?"

To be replaced, meant killed, and Mike didn't take well to the veiled threat. His face turned red, and he had to choke off the retort that almost flew unchecked out of his mouth. Instead, he gritted his teeth, and answered the question in an agreeable, copacetic, tone, "We both want the same thing, which is Spears in the ground."

Tony nodded. "Good. Spread the word, I'm putting a ten million dollar bounty on Tom Spear's head. I want him dead sooner than later. You can also contact the heads, and let them know we're having an emergency meeting first thing tomorrow morning—say nine o'clock. In the meantime, let's get every contact we have looking for Tom Spears. The more eyes the better in case he gets past our initial net." He gestured to the immediate area. "I've already contacted our man in the police department to start searching from his end. You get word to your dealers and whores to keep a close look out for him. He can't get far." He turned with no further words, and walked back to his waiting car—a replacement to the car left behind in the alley.

Mike watched him go. "*Can't get far*, isn't accurate, you mean he *won't* go far," he mumbled. Regardless of what Tony told him, he knew there was much more to this than just a spiteful man killing people. Spears was acting vengeful, his determination obvious. The total number of dead so far was six, and with the recent discovery of Tim Barns found in the alley alongside the Manatone building, that number had climbed to seven. And what of Bishop Styles? If he was dead, which Mike suspected he was, that meant the current number was at eight—a figure that would surely rise before this was all said and done.

The rain got heavy again, pitter-pattering off his dark colored overcoat, and soaking his short-cropped grey hair. He looked up above the towering blaze. With the downpour, the thick black smoke was no longer rising high, but swirling and creeping through the surrounding buildings like a ghostly apparition.

His thoughts went back to his son and a growing ache in his chest. Why was he found in the alley with a coat over his head? It didn't make sense, especially in light of what Tony had said about the Spears attack. Why would the Shadow even take the time?

He pulled out his cellphone. Regardless of Tom Spears's apparent reasons, Mike would make sure the full weight of the syndicate landed right on top of him.

Chapter 19

OM STOOD IN FRONT OF Essics Technology, his back against the red brick wall. It had been more than forty-eight hours since leaving the Queens Athletic Club, and night had fallen once more. To remain hidden, and off the syndicate's radar for the day, Tom had been left with few options. So after escaping the immediate area—and long before the syndicate could implement a grid search—he'd found a quiet residential neighborhood in the suburbs of Long Island, parked along the curb, and slept in the back seat until dark. This he had done two days in a row. It had been far from comfortable, but if they couldn't see him, they couldn't find him. And if they couldn't find him, they couldn't defend him.

He glanced at his watch. It was approaching midnight. The rain had stopped, but even in the darkness the wet sidewalks and street still gleamed from the on and off showers throughout the day

The three story, windowless, building he was leaning against was located on the corner of Metropolitan and Diggs Avenues in Queens, and approximately fifteen minutes east of the Manatone's main headquarters. It was also where the main server station could be found for the syndicate's online gambling and gaming network. In fact, according to Charley Mack, this was the central nervous system, and to take it out would completely cripple their computer network.

His thoughts drifted back to Charley. In the end, after Tom had tied him up to the base of the claw foot tub that held Mike and Micky's remains, and before torching the place, the fat Jamaican—crying like a baby in both pain and fear—had willingly told Tom everything he wanted to know. This included both where Tony Manatone would run, and also this building—a financially coveted, high value target. Not that Tom had any interest in damaging their financial interests, but it came down to semantics. With the entire Manatone organization searching for him, he needed a worthy distraction to draw them away from his real purpose, which was dealing with Lil Mouse.

He took one more look down the block. It was dimly lit and deserted except for an old couple crossing the street under a distant street light; a translucent mist, gentle and swirling, hanging just above the illumination.

He focused again on the entry door thirty feet to his left. According to Charley the upper floor was vacant, and there were always no less than eight security personnel in the building, plus one technician to monitor the two hundred and forty servers in the basement.

The plan was simple. Now that Tom knew the layout, he would enter, kill whoever stood in his way, and destroy the servers. Helping matters, the building was syndicate owned. It meant he wouldn't have to worry about police involvement. Killings or not, there was no way the syndicate would want the police snooping into their online businesses; legitimate or otherwise. So he was certain it would be handled in-house. He was also certain—once alerted—they would swarm into the area like angry bees.

He removed the silenced Kimber Aegis II 9mm from his waistband, and stepped to the steel door. After firing a single bullet into the overhead camera, and two more into the doors locking mechanism, he lashed out with his foot, splintering the frame and sending the heavy door into an interior side wall.

Sitting behind a steel desk in the hall, two uniformed men were monitoring a computer screen. They stood while attempting to draw their weapons. But they never stood a chance. Tom shot both of them in succession with bullets first to the chest and then the head.

As both crumpled to the floor, Tom paused a moment to look and listen.

The shadowed interior reeked of cigarettes but it was quiet; the hallway to his left and in front of him empty.

He stepped to the desk and checked the monitor. According to the split screen there were only two cameras: the one he'd disabled outside, and another in the interior—over the door he'd just come through. He turned and fired his weapon once more; the camera lens exploding, its body left swinging back and forth on a single remaining wire.

He replaced his magazine.

With the interior camera monitoring the door and also this station, meant there was another security post, and more importantly, another team now knew he was here. He entered the stairwell to his right, following the cement stairs downward. Someone shouted an alert from behind, then more anxious voices could be heard, including radio chatter, coming from the staircase above him; their quickened footfalls echoing off the surrounding cement walls.

Just as Tom reached the basement landing, the door in front of him burst open. A blond haired man appeared no more than three feet away. Tom stepped in, blocked the man's pistol from coming up with his left hand, and fired his own weapon point blank into his chest. The guard flew back, and as he bounced off the back wall, Tom shot him in the head; the blood bursting like an exploding water balloon onto the wall. Another man came around the far corner of the hall to his left and fired his pistol, the missed shot striking the back cement wall and ricocheting into the tiled ceiling. Tom dove forward, rolled once, and snapped off two shots just as he came up to a knee. The first shot was misaligned but effective, striking the guard in the kneecap, and spinning him to the ground. The second bullet passed through the back of the syndicate-mans exposed neck, bursting through the windpipe in an explosion of blood. He died instantly, his skull cracking hard against the iron gray cement floor.

Tom heard fast approaching footfalls coming down the staircase behind him. Ejecting the magazine, he snapped another in place, and stepped back to the doorway. The spring-loaded door had closed again so he waited. A radio in the waistband of the blond haired guard at Tom's feet crackled to life. They wanted an update, and when they didn't get one, they opened the door. When it was pulled open a crack, Tom stepped forward and kicked the heavy door as hard as he could. It crashed into the first unsuspecting man, the weight driving him backward and into the other man. Stepping forward, Tom shot the first guard as he tumbled to the floor, and the second while he lay on the ground. Again, his shots were efficient with a bullet to each of their chests and heads.

Tom ran down the narrow hall, and around the corner, locating the server room through the first door on the right. Inside, there were four aisles that separated twenty-four ten-foot-tall black-colored columns. And stacked inside each of them—with a multitude of red and blue blinking lights—were ten, two-foot-wide, servers.

Not sure how he was going to disable them, he started to move down an aisle toward the back but stopped. To his right, along the front wall, he saw a man in a blue lab coat hiding in the corner behind the only desk.

"You the technician?" Tom asked, looking at the computer screen showing a diagnostic page like the man had been working.

The technician nodded. He had a bald head, narrow shoulders, with a pair of wire-rimmed reading glasses still on his nose. "How do I shut these down?" Tom asked with a wave of his hand.

The man gave him a curious look, so Tom repeated himself, "How do I shut these down?" He pointed his gun at him. "And don't make me ask again."

Another security man appeared next to the technician. He was standing in the farthest aisle, and leaning around the end of a row of servers. In his upraised hand was a Glock, and he fired twice, narrowly missing Tom as he ducked down the center aisle. Both bullets struck the server close to where Tom's head had been; the thunderous shots deafening in the confines of the cement-walled room. Electrical sparks followed, and all the lights in the column flickered, and then went out.

Remaining unfazed, Tom never slowed, making it to the end of the aisle in four quick strides. Of the complement of guards Charley had told him about, at least two were left and probably here in the room with him. At least that was the theory he was going with. That meant they would try to flank him as fast as possible, coming from two directions. He was right. Just as he got to the end of the servers, a pistol wielding hand appeared before him. Without hesitating, Tom grabbed the man's wrist with his left hand, pushing it down and away, while at the same time thrusting the man's elbow up with his right. The hyperextended arm broke at the joint, and Tom flung him face-first into the nearby servers. Stunned and now screaming in pain, the man dropped the gun, and as he plummeted to his knees Tom silenced him with a shot to the back of the head.

Again, the Shadow never slowed, his movement's fluid—choreographed from years in the field—as he continued boldly forward to the last aisle. Peering around the corner, Tom saw the last man. His back was to him.

"Live or die?" Tom announced, holding his pistol out, aimed, and ready.

The man chose wrongly and tried to turn. Tom fired once, the bullet entering the side of the man's head, and driving him over the nearby desk where he careened off the wall and crumpled to the floor.

The technician, watching wide-eyed and still in the corner, had seen enough and broke for the door. Tom let him go, hearing the door crash open, and his fading footfalls back down the hall. "And tell them this is just the beginning," Tom yelled after him, "no building will be safe!" It was an empty threat. He had no interest in any of their buildings, but they didn't know that.

A respite followed and Tom took a moment to reconnoiter, his thoughts going back to the problem of how to disable the servers in the shortest amount of time. In a perfect scenario, he could've used explosives, but on short notice he had none, and he certainly didn't have sufficient bullets to get the job done. Oddly enough, it was the stifling heat in the room from the warming electronics that gave him an idea. He looked up and grinned. Mounted to the white tiled ceiling were several rows of fire suppression sprinklers. In this vast array of electronics the only thing worse than an explosion, fire, or an electromagnet charge, would be water. He went to the desk, rummaged through several drawers, and found a lighter.

Chapter 20

I T WAS FOUR IN THE morning, and Mike Grevo stood outside the darkened server chamber. At his feet, a gentle flow of water ran out and into the hallway, and inside the room a constant dripping sound could be heard from the ceiling tiles and sprinklers.

Steve Johnson stood next to him in jeans and a hastily thrown on trench coat. Looking like he'd just woken up—which he had—his blond hair was unkempt, and his normally bright brown eyes were dull and bagged purple. "It's a total loss," he said with disgust.

Mike had to agree. Inside the room the circuit breakers had been kicked from the short-circuiting servers, and the technicians sweeping flashlight beam could be seen gleaming across the wet walls and servers. And if one needed further confirmation of the loss, there was also the faint odor of fried electronics hanging ominously in the air. Mike shook his head. "He knew where to hit us, and I can tell you, this is only going to get worse before it gets better."

"I heard our technician was the only person to survive," Steve said. "Any news on where Spears will strike next?"

"Well, if you believe his words to our only witness to be true, it could be any number of targets, including the one hundred and fifty servers in the Briggs Building." Although Essics Technology had held the bulk of their servers, there were still two other buildings at their disposal that carried a combined three-hundred more as they worked to expand their gaming network.

"You don't believe it? You think the tech is lying?"

"He's not lying," Mike answered, "but no, I don't believe attacking more of our buildings is in the Shadow's plan."

The server specialist finished his evaluation and came out of the darkness. He was still in his blue lab coat, splattered on the shoulders from the dripping water, and looking bone weary. He ran a hand over his balding head to remove the water drops. "The fire was started in a waste can which was then held up to a sprinkler. The resulting heat triggered the system." He shrugged, and continued. "As for the damage, I won't know for certain how bad it really is until we dry out the room and go through each individual server before adding power. But it doesn't look good. At the very least, multiple circuit boards and processors will be fried. At the very worst, we lost more than half of the servers when it's all said and done."

"You'll get whatever you need," Mike reassured him. "Do what you can."

The technician nodded and disappeared back into the room again.

Mike looked back down the hall where two of his men were dragging away another dead security man. As he suspected right from the start, the Shadow was proving to be a formidable force. With the eight here tonight, that brought the death toll to more than sixteen, including his son, Frank Manatone himself, and even Bishop Styles.

"How is the cleanup coming?" he asked Steve.

"The bodies are being disposed of quietly, and much like the remains of Tim Barns, the police aren't involved," Steve answered, and gestured toward the server room. "We even managed to keep the fire department away after they were electronically notified of the sprinklers turning on. We told them everything was fine and that there was a glitch in the system. That will hold them for the time being."

"Good."

There was a notable pause before Steve spoke again, "Has Tony been notified?"

Mike thought about the mandated emergency meeting yesterday morning. Tony Manatone, sitting at the head of the table, had said all the right words, filling people in on the loss of his dad. He had used words like, "he'll be missed," and "we'll have to proceed without him." But Mike, and most of the people in the room, knew it was just a charade. Not that the tension between the father and son mattered anymore, the main thing Tony had confirmed was it would be business as usual. This was good. It needed to be said to calm fears as the transition of power occurred. Then of course, the topic of how to proceed with Spears had come up. In this there were two things Mike gleaned from the conversation: one, there were no more glib remarks from his colleagues about the man known as the Shadow. In fact, now that they had been reminded of what the assassin was capable of they'd been professional and respectful, if not stoic. And two, was the fear in Tony Manatone himself. No matter how hard the new heir tried not to show it, those dark flickering eyes said it all. It also spoke volumes about his new armed security detail of six men, who remained at his side during the entire meeting—something unheard of until now. Then there was his willingness—his eagerness—to get out of the city and hole-up at his father's mansion in Bonnie Briar Country Club. Of course, he didn't use the words "hole-up". Instead he used the words "current problem in the growing fields" as an excuse, saying he would be better off monitoring the situation from either the mansion or the ranch. This of course, wasn't that farfetched in regards to the M-Ranch, considering it was located along the Debar Mountains—the same mountain range as the growing fields. It was the primary reason Frank had purchased the property over twenty-five years ago. With more than two hundred acres spread out along the Titusville State Forest, the horse ranch was a perfect waypoint for supplies and for accessing the rugged terrain.

But that had little to do with the current situation. Of this Mike was certain. Tony Manatone was now holed up, and probably shitting himself. Mike just didn't know the real reason why.

"Mike? Hello?" Steve queried, leaning in front of him.

Lost in thought Mike hadn't heard him talking. "Yeah, sorry."

"So has Tony been notified?" Steve asked again.

Mike nodded. "I already left a message on his cellphone, and the hardline at the mansion. But I can't be bothered with him right now. The problem is, I don't know what Spears is up to, and although I don't believe his goal is to hit us in the wallet, I can't rule it out either. So I've already upgraded our man-power at every building that's of financial importance, including the Briggs and Theater buildings to cover our remaining servers."

"That's a lot of man-power." Steve shook his head. "And not near enough to cover other vulnerable areas."

"Yeah, I know. The best scenario is for us to find him. If we can locate him, we can isolate him, and then we can kill him. Any word from your girls?" Mike asked, referring to the statewide prostitution rings Steve was in charge of.

"Nothing yet, it's like…" he stopped like he didn't want to say it.

"It's like he's a ghost…a shadow…is that what you wanted to say?"

"It is," Steve answered flatly. "And I don't mean to sound frustrated, but I am."

Mike turned to his friend. "We'll get him. It's just going to take longer than we're used to."

Chapter 21

Tony Manatone paced back and forth over the thick shag carpet in his second floor bedroom. He couldn't shake how close he had come to being killed by Tom Spears. At first when he'd escaped in his father's Lincoln down the alley, he felt exuberant, even cocky, at having outsmarted the assassin. But that euphoric feeling had since faded, and after the meeting with Mike Grevo a short time later, he had actually thrown up. Even now, being secure at his father's two hundred acre M-Ranch, he didn't feel much better. Before leaving town he had considered, even planned, to hide out at the Bonnie Briar mansion. After all it was a proverbial fortress. Much like Mike's estate in the upscale, yet isolated, area outside of Ridgefield, New York, it had a ten foot wall, and numerous security features, including multiple cameras both on the grounds as well as around the buildings. And this said nothing of the dogs, and armed patrols. But in the end, he had come here.

He stepped to the large bay window. The early afternoon sky was dull and carpeted grey, and beyond the huge red barn and green pastures, he could see the majestic Debar Mountain Range—its peaks obscured like they were reaching into the heavens.

So why hadn't he gone to the mansion? In hindsight, was it the right decision?

He took a calming breath. His growing apprehension was only leading to doubts and speculation. The answer, and the reason he was here, had been simple. He needed the space—the separation—from where Spears would obviously look. Out here, beyond the broad security-net the syndicate now had in place around the city, there was little doubt that Tony was beyond Tom Spears's grasp. But the same couldn't be said of the Bonnie Briar estate. It was where Tony grew up, and one of the first places Spears would look. Worse yet, there was little doubt in Tony's mind that the assassin could breach any and all security measures. After all, how many times had Tom been there over the years?

Too numerous to count was the answer, and most of those visits, if not all of them, had to do with that same security. So after the meeting with all the heads of the cartel, notifying them of Frank's demise, and taking the seat at the head of the table, he had come here.

"No, this was the right decision," he mumbled. *Wall or no wall, Tom could—would—easily counter any and all security measures at the Bonnie Briar estate.*

His gaze floated around the room. In all the years Tom had worked for Frank, the assassin had never been to his father's ranch—at least that he was aware of. This was a huge advantage.

He nodded with satisfaction, the uneasiness lifting away like a feather in a warm breeze.

Did Spears even know about the ranch? It was possible, but not certain. But even if he did figure out Tony was here, could he escape the city without being seen by the huge contingent of people looking for him?

Not likely. Confident again, he drew a sigh of relief, and a thin smile appeared on his face. *The fact was he had outsmarted the Shadow again!*

Now pleased with himself, he crossed his arms in defiance. "The Shadow," he repeated out loud with distaste. "Who is he, compared to me…the new crime boss?"

His father's upturned face flashed in his brain. In those final moments, before putting a bullet in his head, Tony saw the shock in his blue eyes. Then it had turned to fear when he realized his own son was going to kill him. Never before had Tony wielded such power over him. It was always vice versa, and he found the experience to be both intoxicating and liberating at the same time.

He took a deep refreshing breath. His dad was finally dead. How many times since being a youth had he envisioned, even fantasized, about killing him. Now it was done, and it seemed the weight of the world had lifted from his shoulders. With his death, Tony could start a new life. One in which he was in control of his own destiny, and more importantly, without ridicule.

There was a tap on the door. "Excuse me, sir," said Myra, the house servant. She had worked for Frank as long as Tony could remember. "There's an important call for you on the house phone."

He stepped to the door and opened it.

Myra Coolage stood in-between the four armed guards stationed outside his room. She was in her late fifties, plump, with short grey hair, and wearing her customary blue and white maid uniform. "It's Mike Grevo," she said politely and handed him a cordless phone. "He didn't know you were here. He's been trying to reach you at Bonnie Briar and also on your cellphone." She turned away, heading back down the carpeted hall toward the staircase to continue her duties.

In his haste to leave the city, Tony had forgotten to let Mike know the change of plans in coming here. He had also forgotten the cell service, or the complete lack of it, at the ranch.

"Mike?" he answered, closing the door.

"Yes. I've been trying to reach you." There was a notable pause, before Mike continued. "Spears attacked the Essics building, destroyed the servers, and killed several men."

And just like that, the weight of the world was back on Tony's shoulders. As he listened to the details, he stepped to the window once again; his confidence all but gone, his eyes flicking back and forth, looking expectantly for an unwelcome shadow.

Chapter 22
Compounded Trouble

AFTER LEAVING THE SERVER ROOM, and Essics Technology, Tom had been torn about going after Tony. The fact of the matter was, he had been lucky so far. The odds were tipped unfavorably and unrealistically against him. Eventually, he was going to be spotted, and then it was over. The syndicate had too much manpower and too many resources at their disposal. So he altered his plan—such as it was—to see if he could turn an enemy into an ally. But to pull it off, he would have to continue to do what they didn't expect.

That led him here, to an isolated area outside of Ridgefield, New York, and up a tree near the top of a ten-foot-tall cement wall. In the distance through more trees, was a well-lit mansion—Mike Grevo's mansion. The good news was Tom had been there many times when he worked for the syndicate, and the property was set up much like Frank Manatone's. In fact, thanks to the late boss's detail to security for both he and Mike, it was almost an exact replica of the Bonnie Briar Estate. The bad news was Tom hadn't been here in more than ten years. Another problem, now with Frank's assassination, was the heightened security around all the syndicate's top heads, and more importantly, Mike Grevo. But then again, that was why Tom had come directly here from the Essics Building.

In disabling the servers, word would be sent to all the prominent heads. And because of its value, Tom knew…or at least hoped…Mike Grevo himself would want to go investigate. True to form, and forty-five minutes after Tom arrived, he had watched the syndicate's number two man pass through the gate in his chauffeur-driven Mercedes S 550, and like Tom suspected, security was tight. Escorting the elegant Town Car were no less than two dark-colored Chevy Suburban's—front and back—with at least four men in each. A presidential candidate couldn't have appeared more secure. But looks can be deceiving when one only gazes forward and not back, reacting instead of anticipating.

Stealing one more glance around, he took a deep breath, tensed his muscles, and leaped forward off the branch with his left foot, propelling himself over the wall. He fell to the ground, rolling to break his fall. Now inside the compound, he got to his knees and listened for any signs of alert. There were none, so he rose to his feet and started threading his way through the dense woods toward the central area of the property. When he saw the lights from the main house filtering through the trees, and the beginning of a large expanse of lawn, he paused and looked up, examining the tree trunks until he located one of the cameras. If memory served him, there were eight covering the grounds, and eight more mounted to the house. But Tom also remembered the blind spots. In every system the optimal plan was blanket coverage, but there were always dead spots, which is why Tom had chosen this particular route. In this case the camera he was looking at was pointed at the house, and also right at a huge fir tree. As Tom had hoped, the camera's location had been overlooked and not moved as the tree got bigger. This meant, once on the other side of the big fir, he could cross the open lawn unseen.

He crawled on his belly to the edge of the manicured lawn, a good forty paces from the building. Now safely in the camera's blind spot behind the huge tree trunk, he studied the surroundings. The house appeared bigger at night, imposing but not ostentatious. Square built, it had a sloping red tile roof and boasted no ornate columns, no frescoes, or paint-work beyond the stylish grey color, and white trim.

Seeing no one, he looked to his right. A winding driveway could be seen going past a huge brick carriage house—ivy covered with no fewer than five garages fronting an enormous concrete parking area— and ending at an elegant roundabout in the front of the huge house. At the center of this roundabout, and lit up, was a water feature—a white marble statue of Neptune with water flowing out of his upturned hand.

That's where Tom spotted three suited men. The only foot patrol he had seen so far, they were chatting together between the statue and the front steps. With Mike Grevo gone, along with a large contingent of his security force, it was as Tom had hoped. A dog barked, and Tom's eyes alertly flicked to his left and the rear of the property.

He removed his silenced Kimber 9mm from his shoulder holster. Up to now, he hadn't seen any dogs, but he knew they were used on the grounds. This again was both good news and bad. The good news was they were usually accompanied by the guards with leashes, and rarely allowed to run free. The bad news was Tom couldn't be sure if that routine had changed, and the thought of four ninety-pound German Pinscher's suddenly appearing next to him, snarling, with exposed teeth, wasn't a pleasant thought. For several seconds he held his breath, listening for movement through the screen of bushes. There were none and after a moment he relaxed, figuring the bark had come from the outdoor pens located along the very back wall and out of his line of sight.

Ready to move forward again, he studied the area along the side of the house. Here the lighting was limited and his eyes strained to penetrate the shadows. Making it worse, the interior lights beyond a sliding glass door—which overlooked a small garden patio—were off.

To the right of the door and near the front corner, there was also a blackened, recessed portion of wall. If anyone was there, they would be all but impossible to see, so Tom gave it another two minutes just to be safe. He started to rise, then froze. The silhouette of a man separated himself from the shadows. He had indeed been standing in the blackened recess of the building, probably relieving himself, or even trying to relax away from prying eyes.

Tom lowered back down. If he was going to turn an enemy into a friend, it was crucial to not get off on the wrong foot. That meant not killing anyone on the grounds unless absolutely necessary. He watched the guard step around the corner. Dressed in a suit and much like the men in front, he wasn't carrying an obvious weapon, but there was little doubt he was armed.

Once in the light, the other three men acknowledged him as he walked their way. Words were said, but Tom couldn't hear, nor cared. With the bright light at the front of the house, it would be virtually impossible for the men to see Tom along the darkened side of the building. So he rose and sprinted over the grass to the recessed area the guard had just vacated. Confirming he hadn't been seen, he stole one quick glance around the corner.

Satisfied, he walked over to the sliding glass door and peered inside to see if there was a security brace installed on the back of the door. There wasn't. This was good for what he had planned. Even if the door was wired to a security system, sliding glass entries had one glaring vulnerability, and Tom was about to expose it. He removed one of his six diamond-shaped throwing knives from a leg holster wrapped around his thigh. Careful to avoid the razor sharp edges, he bent down and used the blade to lift the slider off its tracks. Then after a bump on the rear frame with the heel of his hand, it separated and he pivoted the back open enough for him to slip through. The process took less than two minutes, and with the door remaining locked at the other end, any security system was bypassed, too.

After entering, he pushed it back in place, and stepped around the drawn curtains, replacing the throwing knife in his hand with the silenced Kimber.

*****

It was nearing four in the morning, and a light rain was coming down when Mike Grevo's Mercedes and his two car entourage appeared once again in the driveway. Stopping in the turnaround, a guard opened his door and Mike exited, heading up the stairs and going inside.

The large entrance hall was well lit, the walls covered with numerous Renaissance oil paintings; the colors vivid and dramatic under the pinpoint spotlights. They extended along a wide curved staircase made of Italian marble and polished oak. Overhead, hanging from the vaulted ceiling, was an elegant chandelier—its dangling crystal's glowing like diamonds and glinting off the polished floor's surface.

A broad shouldered guard with a receding hairline and an Ebenezer chin followed Mike inside, but remained by the entryway. His name was Allen Tempy and Mike liked him. Courteous and soft spoken, he was a consummate professional.

"You good for a few hours, Allen?" Mike asked, hanging his trench coat on the rack and heading for the stairs. "I need to catch at least a little shut eye."

Allen nodded. "I'm good, Mr. Grevo." He sat in his chair near the door. This was customary because it was a house rule that only one guard be inside at any one time, and, unless needed, he remain by the doorway. The rule was strictly enforced too by Lucile herself, Mike's wife of twenty-five years. More to do with privacy than anything else, another enforced directive was not having more than one guard in the house when Mike wasn't home. Even one was too much for her, and he wasn't surprised to see no one else inside.

Mike understood, though. The interior was her domain. Outside however, was a different matter. He and the security could…would…do whatever was necessary to secure the grounds, and in doing so, would keep any potential intruder from ever making it inside the house. At least that was the theory, and it had worked without incident for more than two decades.

Mike stopped, and turned to the guard. "You've known me for more than ten years Allen, please quit calling me Mr. Grevo."

"Yes, Mr. Grevo…sorry…" he grinned, "Mike."

Mike nodded, then noticed a light was on in the cigar room; the door cracked open. Thinking Lucile had left the light on, he sighed, and crossed the marble floor, leaning in the doorway to make sure she wasn't in there. As his head came around the door, the barrel of a silenced gun was pressed into his temple. He froze, turning. Tom Spears stood in front of him with a finger to his lips for quiet.

Chapter 23

MIKE STARED DOWN THE BARREL of the silenced pistol. His first thought was how Tom had gotten past his men and into his house undetected. He was about to say something, but Tom again encouraged him to be quiet while waving him inside the room. Once inside Tom closed the door behind him, stepped in close, and whispered, "Curse out loud."

Unsure, Mike's brow furrowed, "What…"

On the nearby rosewood desk, and sitting on a silver tray, was a half-full crystal decanter of brandy along with two glasses. Using the barrel of the silenced pistol, Tom pushed the tray onto the floor; the loud sound of breaking glass soon followed.

"I said curse!" Tom growled into his ear.

"God damn it!" Mike finally said out loud.

Tom stepped back behind the door just as someone spoke from the other side. "Sir…Mr. Grevo…I mean, Mike…are you okay?" came Allen Tempy's excited voice.

Tom nodded, so Mike answered, "I'm good Allen, just a little clumsy…" Tom gestured to invite him in. "I could use some help though," Mike added.

As an experienced bodyguard, Allen opened the door cautiously with the Glock in his hand leading the way. Tom waited until he was almost through the doorway before bringing his own pistol down hard on Allen's exposed wrist. A crack of bone could be heard, and the gun flew from his hand. Bending over in pain, the surprised man was about to scream a warning when Tom fluidly stepped in and delivered a vicious elbow to Allen's cheek, snapping his head back into the doorframe. Then Tom spun and smoothly brought the butt of the pistol down hard into bodyguard's temple, catching him as he fell.

Tom laid the unconscious man down on the marble floor and closed and locked the door, before speaking to Mike. "No one has been seriously hurt on the grounds yet, but that could change. It's up to you."

After picking up Allen Tempy's pistol and sticking it in his waistband, Tom faced Mike, who remained standing next to the front of the desk. "Are you armed?" Tom pointed the gun once again at his midsection.

Mike put both hands up and answered flatly, "No."

To confirm it, Tom crossed the room in two quick strides, and while jamming the barrel hard into Mike's chest, patted him down from head to toe. Once satisfied, Tom ushered him to one of the two upholstered chairs facing a brick fireplace; the remnants of charred wood along with several cigar butts lay in the grey ashes. "You and I are going to have a little talk."

Mike grit his teeth as Tom Spears forced him to sit. In all reality, he expected to die. In fact, he was surprised he was still breathing. The man before him had already killed more than sixteen men that he knew of…including his son. Anger touched him then. "Get it over with," he spat. "It won't make any difference in the long run because in the end we'll find you." He defiantly glared as Tom sat in the other chair, turning it towards him. "I assure you, you will need to kill me. After killing my boy, there's no place you can hide and nothing in this world that will stop me from coming for you."

"That's exactly what I thought, and the reason why I'm here." Tom leaned in close, no more than two feet away, the gun still leveled at Mike's belly. "It's what I would do if someone attacked and killed a member of my family—a loved one."

Not really listening, and still not understanding why Tom hadn't killed him yet, Mike thought fast, looking for an advantage….any advantage "Two more of my men are upstairs…"

Tom cut him off. "No, they're not. If I know one thing about your wife—even after a decade—there's still one firm rule in this house that hasn't changed, and that's only one guard is allowed inside." A slight smirk altered Tom's otherwise neutral expression. "How is Lucile?"

At hearing his wife's name, Mike started to lift from his chair defensively. "If you've hurt her…"

Again Tom cut him off pointing the pistol at Mike's face. "Sit your ass down!" Tom snarled. "I don't have time for this. If you do like I say, you and your wife, who is sleeping comfortably upstairs I might add, won't be harmed."

Mike sat back down, staring into Tom's eyes. He was looking for deceit but found none. "If you're not here to kill me, then why are you here?"

"Like I said, I want to have a brief conversation."

Still defiant, Mike asked, "What about?"

"Do you know why I'm in New York? Why…" Tom paused momentarily; a flicker of emotion showing in his brown eyes. "Why I came out of retirement to reenter this vile life?"

Mike decided to play along and see where this was going. "I know you killed Frank's nephew, and I've been told you're retaliating now because we're looking for you."

"Part right," Tom said, without hesitation. "Did you know about Bishop Styles?"

"Only after the granary incident," Mike responded.

"Is that what you're calling it…an incident?" snapped Tom, his face now red and that earlier flickering of emotion in Tom's eyes now flared, turning menacing and volatile. "Let's review, shall we? First Bishop Styles, under orders from Frank and his son, kidnapped Mike and Micky." Tom's jaw muscles swelled as he spoke. "You remember Mike Rauls and Micky Trevor? They worked for you and this family for more than twenty years." Tom didn't wait for an answer. "Tony had them tortured and killed. For what? They knew nothing…absolutely nothing."

Mike was listening now. He only recently had found out that Bishop Styles was involved, but that wasn't unusual considering the syndicate had used him on several occasions. He could only assume now, regardless of what Tom said, there had to be a good reason, and killing the man known as the Shadow definitely would warrant it. But the torture of Mike Rauls and Micky Trevor was news to him. As Tom said, he did know them. In fact, much like Tom, both of them had been here at his house on numerous occasions. "I only heard about Bishop recently, and as far as Mike and Micky, this is the first I'm hearing about it. But I find it hard to believe Frank would go after them without reason or provocation," Mike said doubtfully while maintaining eye contact.

"I agree. No, he wouldn't have, unless someone put a bug in his ear. The Frank I knew was short tempered, but focused. He would have come after me hard, but nothing beyond retaliation…and not for some sick fucking pleasure." Tom drew a deep breath. "Were you aware Tony,

Bishop, and as far as I know, Frank, colluded in coming after my wife, taking her hostage from Washington State before bringing her here?"

Mike leaned back. Suddenly things clicked in his head. With the half-truths spoken by both Frank and Tony, the pieces now made more sense. All along he knew there was more to this than just endless killing. "If what you're saying is true…"

"It is," Tom cut in flatly, his brown eyes as cold as tombstones.

Mike studied him for a moment as they sat in uneasy silence. Dressed in jeans, and a dark blue windbreaker over a black sweatshirt, Mike could see Tom looked tired. Even with the hood pulled over his head, he looked worn and frayed, like he hadn't slept in a week, but—as he had already witnessed—his movements remained confident, agile, and crisp; his demeanor controlled but angry. Around one thigh, he also noticed, was a harness for six knives; each in its own sleeve for easy retrieval.

The knives, Mike thought, flashing back to Lynchpin's gang, who had tried to move into the syndicate's prostitution ring. *That's how the Shadow had killed nine men without shooting them. He had used throwing knives!* It only confirmed how deadly the man was before him. So why hadn't Tom killed him yet?

He continued to study him, but once again Mike could see no sign of treachery in his words. He shook his head. "I swear on my son's grave I didn't know anything about them taking your wife, and you killing me right now won't change that."

Tom stood. "As I've told you already, I'm not here to kill you. But I do believe you. So now I need to tell you, I came here because I plan to right a wrong, just like what you told me about avenging your son."

"Yes, my son." Mike said in an accusing tone, and stood slowly. "He was only twenty-four-years-old…"

"I didn't kill him. In fact, I didn't kill Frank either. It was a plot hatched by Tony and Bishop. They would kill Frank and blame me, killing two birds with one stone. It would've worked too, had I not survived."

"That's insane," Mike countered. "You expect me to believe this?"

"Yes, I do." Tom flipped him a flash drive he pulled out of his pocket. "All is not as it appears. I had a camera at the athletic club, and I removed that video from my phone. You won't like what you see." Tom's brow furrowed. "Remember what I said about someone planting a bug in Frank's ear? I suspect the same thing happened here with you. But I'll let you be the judge of what the truth is or isn't."

Mike's eyes narrowed. "What makes you think I will trust you? Up till this very moment I believed…knew…you had killed George." Saying his sons name, brought an unbearable ache to his chest.

"Deeds, Mike. That's where the truth is found…where it's always found. Deeds can't be misinterpreted as lies. Words can. So I came here on my own volition." Tom nodded at the unconscious man on the floor. "And again, no one here has been killed tonight."

Removing Allen Tempy's pistol from his waistband, Tom ejected the magazine, and using his thumb, emptied all but two shells from it; the brass casings glinting in the overhead lighting and bouncing high off the marble floor like dice on a craps table. He reinstalled the magazine, leaving the one shell in the chamber. "Now comes the moment of truth. How will you make your next move? Will it be on some lying words— an emotional response for being wronged—or will it be tempered until all the facts are known?" Tom moved to the sliding door. Using his forefinger, he carefully moved the large mauve curtain and peered outside.

No longer feeling threatened, Mike watched him closely, gauging and analyzing, with a calculating eye. There was no reason not to believe him, but like Tom said, he would make the final judgement himself. "Your wife, what happened to her?"

Still facing the curtain, Tom's head sagged slightly and his body seemed to deflate. "She's dead, Mike. Now the only person left alive to deal with is Tony Manatone." The Shadow turned, his eyes narrowing again, his demeanor chilling. "Mob related or not, I won't deny that I killed Frank's nephew. Nor will I apologize for it. He was a sick, arrogant, fuck; the reason just." Tom paused before continuing. "In all the years we worked together, you were always square with me. Never once did I ever have a reason to not trust you. But make no mistake Mike, it will be me that kills him, and if you or anyone else gets in my way…you do so at your own peril." Again there was an uneasy calm, before Tom spoke again. "I'll need you to stay seated, and give my best to Lucile. You'll also need to apologize to her for waking her up."

"What…" Mike began. Then he watched Tom unlock and open the slider, flick the wall light switch off, and stick his arm outside, firing the last three shells in Allen Tempy's pistol into the dark sky.

Chapter 24

SLEEP HAD BEEN PITIFUL, AND when Tom heard the distant sound of a tractor trailer, his eyes flicked open. Bone weary, he was stretched out as much as possible in the back seat of Bishop's Cadillac.

Two days had passed since his impromptu meeting with Mike Grevo.

Leaving the estate had been relatively easy. Once he had fired the three shots in the air, the guards had converged on the west side of the house as expected. Meanwhile, Tom had passed through the interior to the east wing, exiting through a side door near the large garage. From there it was a quick jog to the tree line and the wall, having gotten over it just as the barking dogs—now released—converged on his position.

Then the real uncertainty began.

It had been a huge risk to meet Mike and give away his location, knowing the manpower and resources available to the syndicate. His only hope at the time, was that Mike would be the reasonable, clear headed man, he remembered. So far that had been the case. In fact, it was Mike who had told Tom where to find Tony later the next day. This happened after Tom had spent a full day staking out the Bonnie Briar Estate. With no luck in finding Tony Manatone, Tom had finally called Mike from an untraceable cellphone he had purchased while fueling at a 7-Eleven store. The call had been brief, with no courtesies. And as it turned out, this had happened shortly after Mike had organized another emergency meeting with the heads of the syndicate.

Mike said he had seen the flash-drive-video of Charley Mack killing George, and in conjunction with the execution of Frank Manatone by Tony's own hand, it was easy to see that Tom had spoken the truth. Not that it changed the fact that the syndicate was still after him, but at least the lie had been exposed and it would change their focus. Now Tony Manatone—the killer of the Godfather himself—would draw the mob's ire, and according to Mike, become their top priority. This was helpful, and in theory, meant less men looking for Tom—at least for the moment.

But that was the good news.

Mike's anger, though, had gotten the better of him. Wanting… needing…to confront the killer of his son, and blinded by rage, he had called the traitorous young heir to let him know his treachery had been exposed. But in doing so, he had warned him.

Although Tom understood his motives more than anybody, it definitely changed the scenario. Like dominoes going the wrong direction, this had unwittingly given the young Manatone the upper hand and complicated matters. Without cell service at the ranch, the only form of communication was by landline, so when the grieving father had called back to warn Tony's security detail, it was too late. Another fifteen minutes of calling went by before a female voice came on the line. It was the house custodian, Mrs. Myra Coolage. Hysterical and screaming, she had told Mike that Mr. Manatone had gone berserk, killing his unsuspecting bodyguards before running out of the house.

Now Tony was on the run.

Sitting up, Tom stepped out the passenger door, and stretched his aching back. Still dark out, the damp early morning air was cool and refreshing. Surrounded by tall fir trees, he was parked at the end of a grass-covered, seldom used road. In the distance he could hear the rush of water from a nearby creek. An owl above him hooted, then the fluttering of wings could be heard carrying it away into the night.

He ran a hand over his unshaven face just as his stomach growled. How long had it been since his last meal? Aside from a bag of potato chips—the crumpled bag now on the passenger side floorboard—he couldn't even remember. But it would have to wait a little while longer.

After relieving himself, he slid behind the wheel and started the car. He figured he was no more than twenty five miles from the ranch. Having driven through the night, the trip had taken more than ten hours to get here. Then the lack of sleep had gotten the best of him, and he had been forced to pull over.

He glanced at his watch. The luminous green hands showed it was almost five in the morning. This was good, the sun wouldn't be up for another two hours, and he would have time to case the ranch before it did. His mind drifted to Tony Manatone. What was he thinking now? The world as he knew it was destroyed, so where would he run? Tom put his money on Canada. It was no more than one hundred and fifty miles north, and even driving through the mountainous region, he could be there in a few hours. But had he left yet? Tom figured it would take time to gather some belongings, and prepare to be on the road for a while. And what of Mike Grevo? He was the next in succession to become Godfather, and the fact he'd told Tom where to find Tony wasn't lost on him. Was it a trap? By all means. Simply put, Mike wanted both Tony and him dead. Period. So by telling him, Mike gained everything. At the very least, he would now have both his targets at the same location, and undoubtedly had a large force already heading this way. It was the smart play, and an ideal place to close the net. But it would take some time for them to get here. Tom figured he had a head start of at least another five hours—seven on the outside. He also knew he would need every minute considering he'd never been to the ranch before.

He flipped the headlights on, turned around, and reentered Highway 3 heading west. There was no traffic on the unlit two-lane-road, and after a quarter mile, he came to Route 26 and headed north. Turning the dome light on, he set the folded street map on his thigh, and glanced down at the hand written "X" marking the ranch's position. It was located on the eastern edge of the Debar Mountain range, and to get there, the ribbon of road went through the foothills, and then past a waterway called Loon Lake. Four miles after that, he would turn right on the narrow, barely discernible, dotted line known as rural Route 27. This is where the pavement ended, and three miles later at the tiny town of Porcaville, the road to the farm seemed to disappear altogether; no longer visible. Tom knew, that's where the real challenge would lay, which was finding the ranch's unmarked, mile-long, driveway, which snaked through the surrounding forest.

An hour and fifteen minutes later, Tom was belly down at the edge of a tree line. In front of him, across a fenced-in sweeping green pasture, was the M-Ranch—its interior lights aglow in the predawn light. Finding it hadn't been near as challenging as he had assumed.

After passing through Porcaville, he had followed the bumpy, washed-out, and seemingly unused road for another three miles where it ended and a driveway began. A sure sign he was in the right place had been the aluminum gate, which was secured by a thick logging chain and the three signs—"Keep Out", "Private Property" and "No trespassing"—hanging from it.

Using his bolt cutters, he had negotiated the chain with ease and after opening the gate he'd stooped and carefully examined the dirt along the driveway, looking for indications of vehicles recently passing through. There were none. Satisfied Grevo's men hadn't arrived before him, Tom had driven through, not bothering to close the gate. There was no point. Anyone passing through behind him already knew he was coming here. In fact, they were counting on it. A mile later Tom had followed the winding driveway into a flat plateau surrounded on three sides by rearing mountains, and located at the far end—hunkered into the side of the mountain—was the M-Ranch.

The setting was as rural as it was quiet, and he could see how the ranch and grow fields had been so successful over the last decades. The seclusion could be seen in the mountainous terrain, and felt in the sibilant sounds of the surrounding wilderness. His eyes narrowed trying to penetrate the gloom. He could see no movement other than the shadowed appearance of six horses milling along the far fence line. Beyond them and to the left of the two-story house was a large red barn; its high-pitched roof to accommodate both the loft and the heavy snowfall during the winter months.

The barn's front twin doors were open so he could see the interior was dimly lit with no sign of security. He looked up to the sky. It was still dark but predawn light was drawing close and if he planned to get to the house unnoticed, he would have to go now. Rising to his feet, he followed the three-boarded white fence to the right until he reached the corner. Satisfied he hadn't been seen, he continued following it left to the barn.

He stepped inside, pulling his silenced weapon from his waistband. The interior smelled of hay and horses, and on both sides of the wide corridor were rows of stalls. In them, with heads turned toward him over the wooden gates, were several horses.

As his eyes gazed over the interior, he noticed something was off right away. Three saddles, normally draped in a neat row along a wooden rail with other tack gear, had been thrown haphazardly to the hay-covered ground. He also noted that two stalls, including the barn's twin back doors, had been left open as if someone had been in a hurry.

He made his way to the first open stall and peered around the corner. Inside was a dead horse, shot once in the chest and once more in the throat. Blood soaked the ground near it, turning the yellow hay dark and tinted red. Tom stepped in and laid a hand on its shoulder. The body was cold and stiff, the death not recent.

The next stall was empty, but beyond the back double-doors of the barn, Tom found the body of a man sprawled face down on the ground. It appeared he had been shot in the back while running away. Tom used his boot to roll him over. The man was black with greying hair in his beard. Tom judged him to be his late fifties. He also wore worker overalls like maybe a caretaker for either the house or horse's. Tom stooped and touched his shoulder. Again the body was cold and stiff.

He made his way to the back of the house and looked through a kitchen window. A golden retriever—shot in the head—was dead on the floor and much like the barn, the spacious kitchen was in disarray with cupboard doors open and various food stores spread across the floor. Even the island countertop—inlaid with farm-style tiles of white and flowering yellows—was littered with debris.

The back door was open so Tom cautiously stepped inside. As he made his way around the kitchen island, cereal crunched under his boots from an opened box of Wheat Chex thrown on the floor. He stopped and raised his gun when a middle-aged woman stood up on the other side of the island.

She jumped back in surprise, raising her hands to her face, "No!" she screamed. "Please!"

Of Mexican heritage, she was short and squat, dark skinned, and dressed in a blue short-sleeved button-down top and matching skirt that resembled a maid's uniform. Her shoulder-length black hair was streaked grey and her fearful eyes were still wet from tears.

Tom assessed the woman. She seemed dazed, in shock, and just going through the motions…of all things…cleaning. "Who are you?"

"I work here," she answered, with a slight Spanish accent. "I take care of the place." Her eyes narrowed, and she lowered her hands. "Who are you? Did Frank send you?"

Tom avoided the question. "Is there anyone else here?"

"No," she answered, "everyone is dead."

Tom lowered his gun and spoke in a reassuring tone. "I'm only here for Tony Manatone."

Given they probably got few guests out here who didn't work for the syndicate, she appeared to relax. "He's not here," she said, taking a moment to gather herself. After wiping her face with the back of her hand, she straightened and smoothed her bloodstained uniform. "He left hours ago." Tom could tell right away, this was a woman who had been around the divisive environment of the mob for a while. In working for the Manatones, she had seen many things, good and bad. And it was in the swiftness of her regained composure—after the threat of being killed, dead people, and guns pointed at her—Tom could tell there had been plenty of bad.

"Does Frank know what happened here? Is that why you're here?" she asked, her tone turning angry, if not confrontational. "Did he know this was going to happen?"

Tom didn't answer. Cut off from the outside world, there was no way for her to know Frank was dead unless someone called her on the house telephone or Tony had told her, which he obviously hadn't.

She glanced over at the dead dog. "If you wanted to catch him, you needed to be here six hours ago when he killed…began killing…everyone…and everything." She crossed her arms in front of her and her eyes became distant. "It started with a late call from Mr. Grevo, and then Tony came out of his room firing his gun, killing four of his body guards in the hall. Then he killed the last two as they came up the stairs to his aid." She swallowed hard, while fighting back her emotions. "I happened to be in the dining room and witnessed the killing. So I ran down the hall and locked myself in my bathroom and prayed I wasn't next."

Tom stepped to the kitchen's swinging double doors. Using the silenced barrel of his pistol, he pushed one side open and half-stepped through. He was standing in a large dining area. A chandelier, hung from an open beam in the vaulted ceiling, was lit over a ten-place oak dining table. Beyond it and through the front window, the first light of dawn was sweeping across the mountains and he could see the darkened woods he'd just come from.

He turned to the staircase on his left. Blood spray was along the wall and two bodies were on the stairs in a crumpled heap. Having been shot from above, their heads were pointed down the steps, and one of their legs hung ominously between the wood balusters below the railing. On the floor below them were their pistols, left where they had fallen.

Tom turned back to the lady. "What's your name?"

"Myra… Myra Coolage," she answered. "I've worked for Frank more than thirty years, and never seen anything like this."

Tom was put in an awkward position. He didn't want to care. He only wanted to find the killer of his wife and friends, but this became more difficult with each passing second. After all, Tony Manatone had once again killed without regard to anyone else, and Tom could relate. He pointed at the blood on her uniform. "Were you injured?"

"I'm not hurt." Her words became shaky and she gestured out back. "Tony also killed Abe, our caretaker. When I found him, I tried to help but it was too late."

"I'm sorry for your loss Myra, but I haven't much time," he said, while stepping back to the open back door. "Do you know where Tony went?"

"Yes…well…he took a horse and supplies and headed toward the fields," she answered. "It's the only other direction to go from here, other than leaving out the driveway…" She stopped. A thought appeared to strike her and she looked at Tom, studying his unshaven face, his hulking form, and the long ponytail now hanging forward over his right shoulder. Her eyes narrowed. "You don't work for the Family." It was a statement, not a question, and recognition now shown on her face. When Tom didn't respond right away, one of her hands came up and covered her mouth as if in shock. "You're him…oh my God, you're actually him."

Tom's brow furrowed and he recoiled, looking puzzled. He had no idea what 'him' meant or what she was talking about. "Listen, I mean you no harm…"

"I'm not afraid of you," she interrupted meekly, her hand remaining over her mouth. "Why would I fear you?"

Tom was speechless. He didn't know if it was meant as a complement or derogatory. He took it as the latter. "You know me?"

A calmness seemed to settle over her. "No. I know *of* you." She shrugged. "It's mostly gossip, but at my age, I've heard the stories… learned the sobering tales. And when they've been repeated multiple times by multiple people I know they carry at least some value of truth."

"Listen, I don't know what this is about," he said, turning to leave, "but all I really need from you is to point me in the right direction."

She let him get to the door before speaking again, only this time with conviction, "This is what I know…or believe to be true," she blurted out. "They call you the Shadow."

There was a pause between them—the silence deafening. To him it was shock and to her it was confirmation. She took a step back. Not in fear, but in almost religious awe. "It is you! So you've returned—the rumors are true." She paused again before speaking. "Living in these hills for decades, I've heard the stories. Most were carried up here by the syndicate's men from the city but you never really believed them to be true." She half smiled, her eyes sparkling. "Yes, I know of you, and those with the syndicate who live out here know the stories too. You're the rescuer of children, the protector of prostitutes, and the assassin of evil. This is what I've heard, and even now you wage war on the Family itself."

Half in and half out of the door, Tom glared at her. She knew nothing but abstracts of the truth. Yes, it was true he had saved several children from the sinking container ship, *San Paulo*. But Tom looked at it differently. The bigger picture wasn't about the children he saved, but more so the ones he couldn't save—and should have. This was the real truth and to this day the guilt ripped at his soul like flaming talons, burning deep and painful. There was also another little tidbit conveniently left out, but just as important in this particular story. The fact was, he had been paid to be there. Granted, by a distraught father looking for his daughter, but paid no less. So to sensationalize what he had done as some grand gesture or even as heroic was delusional. The same could be said of the prostitute incident in which a Russian gang was carving up the syndicate's prostitutes.

A shortsighted plan at best, the Russians had underestimated the retaliatory consequences in their attempt to move into the syndicate's lucrative prostitution racket. This had been a huge mistake, and the family's response had been swift and without mercy.

In fact, it was Mike Grevo and the mob—the same mob now chasing him—who had come to Tom about sending an even stronger message. Tom had, and a short time later the gang was dead—all nine exterminated. And as for the "assassin of evil"…that was preposterous.

His eyes narrowed, and his words came out colder than intended. "You know nothing of who I am, yet you paint me to be some type of idealist," he sneered. "You misunderstand. I'm no martyr. I didn't come here to save you, your dog, or even your friend on the ground." He stepped onto the back porch and turned once again. "You got the last part right, though," he clarified flatly, "it's definitely going to be a war."

Chapter 25
Climbing Mountains

TOM PUT HIS FOOT INTO the stirrup, pulled himself up, and settled onto the saddle. It had been years, no decades, since he had last been on or even near a horse. In fact, the last time he had ridden horseback had been on a small farm outside of St. Louis that belonged to his previous wife's mother and father.

His thoughts drifted back to his ex-wife, Mellany, who had been killed—along with their infant daughter, Sally—by a drunk driver. Before their deaths, they had visited the parents' farm on multiple occasions, and Tom had even planned to buy their own place out in the country when he got out of law school. "The perfect environment to raise a child," Mellany had said at the time. But that all changed with their deaths, and now it was just a distant memory.

Tom patted the gelding's neck. It was a beautiful bay with a black mane, tail, and stockings. Even the edges of the ears were trimmed raccoon-like in black.

"His name is Jessy," Myra said coming over and adding six bags of dried fruit to Tom's saddlebag. "He's not much of runner, but he's a powerful climber." Myra was all business and patted the animal's reddish-brown-coat along its flanks. "That's what you'll need where you're going, and he knows the trails, having made the trip to the fields many times over the years. So if you're uncertain of where to go just give him free rein. He'll get you there." She handed him a sheet of paper. "For obvious reasons, there are no maps to the fields but I've hand written this."

Tom held it up. It was very basic, with markings for east, south, north and west, a crude drawing of a valley, a lake, and rough distances to the first X which marked the beginning of the fields. At the northern edge of the paper, beyond three upside-down V's for mountains, was the Canadian border.

"It's not much considering where you're going but I suspect anything will help." She handed him the reins to the trailing horse—a bay mare; all brown with white stockings. "This is Molly. She's another climber, and she works well with Jessy." She hugged the mare's neck. "When on the trail it's always better having two horses that get along rather than the type that constantly snap at each other." On the mare's back was another saddle, but draped over both sides was a fully-loaded canvas saddlebag.

Tom watched Myra as she came around the side of the mare. After their talk in the kitchen, Tom had dragged Abe's body inside the barn and then looked for an appropriate horse to saddle. Unsure, he had just entered the closest horse's stall with a saddle when Myra came out and joined him. First she had thanked Tom for taking care of her friend, and then she stopped him from taking the wrong horse for the job.

He had quickly learned she was a horse woman through and through, and under her tutelage, Tom grabbed the appropriate tack, too. The surprise from their previous conversation remained unsettling, but during this time, he had apologized for being so cold with her. He had also informed her about Frank and how Tony had been responsible for his death. She had been taken back initially but rebounded swiftly again. When they were finished, Tom had walked back to where he'd left the Cadillac, driven it to the barn, and unloaded anything he might be able to use, including clothes, a sleeping bag, and his arsenal of weapons from the trunk.

In dealing with the mountainous climate, he had also changed into a fresh pair of jeans, a flannel shirt, and his leather hiking boots. Myra had also supplied him with an insulated parka for warmth, and a long, double-shouldered leather rain coat, which was now tied down in back of the saddle and over his saddlebags. Under his leg, in the scabbard along the saddle, he had slipped an M1 military style rifle that Bishop Styles had had in his trunk. In the other horse's scabbard was a Myra-supplied Weathersby Mark V 240 magnum hunting rifle with a scope. Due to the added weight, he only grabbed two of Bishop's hand grenades and decided to leave the disassembled M16 behind too.

"You have enough food for a week," Myra said, patting one of the canvas saddlebags. "Water is a different story. It's heavy and a burden on the animals when you start to climb, so you only have enough for about three days." She gestured toward the tree line. "But finding water isn't a problem up there. Mountain streams are plentiful this time of year. Caring for the animals is also straight forward and simple. Just remember to wipe them down at night. I've also included grain sacks, but they will fend for themselves if you hobble them near grass." She checked the cinch strap on Molly. "The only real threat to them up there is wolves. If you run into a pack, it will be at night." She moved to the side of the gelding and looked up at Tom. "When…or if…you have no more need of the horses, just put the reins over the pommel and release them. They will find their way back in a day or two."

"Thank you, Myra," Tom said. "You've gone above and beyond." He was near the open double doors of the barn and pointed toward his vehicle parked on the other side. "The car doesn't belong to me, and the owner will never be able to claim it, so do as you see fit."

She nodded. "I'll let them take care of that."

"Speaking of which," he glanced at his watch; it had taken an hour and a half to prepare the horses. "I'd guess they'll be here soon. Just tell them…"

"You don't fret over me, Tom Spears," she interrupted. "I've worked at the ranch for more than thirty years, and I've seen evil here. The faces change, but evil it is. So I knew one day the hunter of men would come here. It was only a matter of time." Her brow furrowed. "You might take an old woman's words as malarkey, and just as easily discard them, but you are a crusader, a champion against evil. And whether you like it or not, this enigma known as the Shadow has taken on a life of its own. I have seen it...witnessed it. You generate hope in people and yet fear in others." She shrugged. "For some reason this unsettles you…but I suppose we all have our demons." Her eyes averted, and she paused, biting her lower lip as if she was thinking. "I've heard the rumors about the Red Hook Granary, and also what happened to your wife…" She turned and headed back to the house, talking over her shoulder as she went. "So there's no thanks necessary. Even as a child, Tony wasn't right in the head. Find him and kill the son-of-a-bitch."

Tom slipped the cowboy hat Myra had supplied on his head and tapped the flanks of the horse with his heels. "You can count on it."

Chapter 26
On the Run

TONY MANATONE LED HIS HORSE up a steep rocky rise. Once at the top, he bent over, his chest heaving. Since leaving the ranch at one in the morning, it had taken no less than six hours to get here. He drew an arm across his sweaty brow.

At least now the sun was up, he thought.

Not that he had had much of a choice, but riding at night carried immeasurable risk, and this said nothing of the slow pace and loss of time. Fortunately for him, he had been riding in this area most of his life, and he knew the trails well. He was also comfortable around horses. In fact, more so than people; the farm a form of escape. It was the primary reason he had volunteered to find out what was going on in the fields. It meant being back at the farm, and the feeling of being free—free from his dad, and free of people.

The farm. Would he ever see it again? *No, he wouldn't.* Anger surged through him with thoughts of Tom Spears. Because of him he was now being hunted—hunted by the very people who were supposed to protect him. Who could've guessed the shootout at the athletic club had been recorded? It had changed everything, leaving Tony with no way of denying the assassinations.

Yes, assassinations. He had no problem with it, and other than the running part, he had no regrets. Even the killing of George hadn't bothered him. He actually felt worse about killing Rogue, his preferred horse, in the barn. But the animal was agitated from hearing the shot that had killed old Abe, and wouldn't cooperate. So he had killed the horse out of anger.

He thought about the old caretaker. *Why had he killed Abe?* Again he felt no remorse, and the only answer he could come up with was it just felt right. After killing everyone in the house, including that fucking dog, adrenaline had taken over. He also had to admit he enjoyed it. The old man had hidden in the barn and when Tony had entered, he'd made a run for it.

Tony grinned. "You didn't get far though, did ya Abe? Took that bullet in the back like a man, you did."

The horse snorted and shook its long black mane. Its name was Jake. Young and unseasoned, the big black gelding was already showing signs of being tired. On its back, and stuffed full of both canned goods and bottled water, were canvas saddlebags—saddlebags typically used for the packhorses. In a perfect world Tony would've taken the time to bring another horse…to distribute the burden.

But it wasn't a perfect world, was it?

Agitated, he snapped the reins taut when Jake tried to reach a clump of grass growing near the rocks. "You'll eat when I eat," he said, mounting up again, "and that isn't now."

He glanced up. The early morning clouds were darkening with the threat of rain. Below him, and settled between two mountain ranges, was a long valley filled with tall fir, spruce, and pine trees. It was green as far as he could see, and he knew, less than a day's ride ahead and hidden under camouflaged nets was the first grow field—the first stop en route to Canada.

Chapter 27
Children of the Woods

ARIA KAYLOR CAUTIOUSLY ROLLED FROM the mattress that was set on the floor, picked up the revolver, and went to the glassless window. She blinked several times to clear her sleepy vision. Out front, and left there long ago, was a small woodpile with a weathered axe protruding from a log.

She looked beyond the pile.

Dawn was just breaking and two armed men were approaching cautiously through the shadow-filled woods in front of the small cabin. The fourteen-year-old moved swiftly to the other four sleeping children, waking them, and ushering them out the back door.

Once in the woods she picked up little Tara, the youngest of the bunch at only five-years-old, and started to run. "I got you, little one," Maria said, bringing up the rear and hurrying them forward. "We need to get to the stream." Her heart was racing, and she cursed herself for spending an extra night at the cabin. But the children had begged to stay and she hadn't argued.

She knew better!

She ducked under a branch and looked forward. Jeffery was leading the way through the thick underbrush and on course for the river. He was eight, the only boy and the fastest of the five. After him was seven-year-old Jody, and Kate, who was six. Suddenly Jeffery went down when his foot slipped off a moss-covered log. He landed hard and she heard his arm snap. Rolling to his knees, he shrieked in pain. The group huddled around him, helping him to his feet as he cradled his arm. It was broken just above the wrist.

A distant voice came from behind them.

"They're coming," Maria said. "We need to hurry." Still holding Tara, she took the lead. In the distance, the river's rushing water was growing closer.

"I'm getting tired," Jody said from behind, her words shaky. Next to her and running hard was Kate who began to cry.

They were in trouble, and Maria knew it. She stole a look over her shoulder. Jeffery had fallen back. In enormous pain and afraid of falling again on the injured arm, he was barely at a fast walk. Maria stove off her rising panic and stopped. She set Tara down, and gathered the other two girls together. Winded, she swallowed hard before speaking. "Jody, I need you to take them to the river, then head to the cave."

Tears welled in Jody's green eyes. "Where are you going? I'm scared and I don't want to lead."

"You can do this," Maria said, and gently grabbed the seven-year-old by the shoulders. "You have to do this…you're the oldest. Look, it's very simple. I want all of you to hold hands." Maria put Jody's hand in Kate's, and Tara grabbed Kate's other hand. "Good. Now take them to the river!" Tears were now free flowing over Jody's dirty cheeks, but she led them away. "And after you get to the river, remember, go to the cave above the bend. Don't stop, and I'll meet you there later."

She turned to see Jeffery no more than thirty paces away. She was about to go to him when a man holding a pistol appeared on the trail behind him. Her heart sank and she ducked behind the trunk of a large fir tree. Then came the gunshot—the thundering sound making her jump. At that moment terror struck her to her very core, and like the rabbit before the wolf, her whole body began to shake. Biting her lip to keep her emotions in check, she pulled the old revolver from her belt and stole a look around the tree. Fear was replaced by anger at what she saw. The man had killed Jeffery, and he was looming over his twitching form. Maria raised the pistol in her shaky hand and stepped around the tree. His back was to her, so he didn't see her approach until it was too late.

She pulled the trigger, and didn't stop firing until she heard the metallic sound of the hammer landing on empty cylinders. All three bullets had found their mark, and after the first shot pitched him forward to the ground, the second and third went into his chest as he rolled over. She stood over him for a moment, as blood oozed through his coat from the wounds to his chest. She felt no pity for him. It wasn't the first time she had killed, and it probably wouldn't be the last. He tried to say something, blinked several times, then died; his eyes remaining open and staring up at the forest canopy. She didn't know his name but she recognized his black shaggy hair and unshaven face. He was one of the pigs from the cartel—the Mexican cartel. Disgusted, she spat on him.

Another voice, in Spanish, came from the direction of the cabin behind her. "Reko, you there?"

The second man!

She lowered to her knees. Dropping the empty revolver, she picked up the attackers pistol. Fear once again surged through her when she glanced at Jeffrey's still form, and the hole in the center of his back. She gritted her teeth. At the moment, there was nothing she could do for him, so she levered herself to her feet, and ran as fast as she could in the direction of the river. Later though, just like so many times before, she and the children would come back and bury him.

Chapter 28

THE HOOF PRINTS MADE BY Tony's horse had been easy to follow, and Tom had picked up the trail shortly after leaving the farm. For four hours he had ridden through the hazard-filled foothills, only stopping to either relieve himself or to help the horses over the rugged terrain.

He arched his aching back for the hundredth time. It was approaching noon, and after not riding for more than twenty years, his body was rebelling. The pain that had started in his spine, had moved into his lower back, blossoming from a dull ache into a knifing agony. And this said nothing of his inner thighs. The seldom used muscles had turned angry with each sway, jostle, and bump, in the saddle. Making it worse, the fatigue over the last couple weeks was now flogging his mind into submission. Twice he had nodded off, swayed in the saddle, and almost tumbled from his lofty perch.

He blinked several times to clear his tired eyes, and leaned forward in the saddle, scrutinizing the pockmarked hoof prints in the soft soil. It looked to be an easy stride, with no splattering of dirt to indicate the horse had been running. This was good news. It meant Tony wasn't pressing his horse and Tom was pacing him. But that was at the very least. In fact, Tom was more optimistic. He guessed he had closed the gap significantly, considering Tony had been forced to ride at a cautious pace at night. Narrowing the distance further, Tom had run his mounts whenever possible, and Tony was riding an overloaded horse.

But gaining or not, Tom's body needed rest, and he contemplated stopping for at least a few hours—arguing with himself over the pros and cons: close the distance, or allow Tony to get further ahead. The argument came down to whether Tony—an experienced horseman—would ever stop to rest. Tom had to believe…wanted to believe…he would. The only reason he wouldn't was if he knew Tom was right on his heels. And Tom was sure he didn't.

Decision made, Tom decided. He would stop and rest at the next suitable place.

At the top of a ridge, he pulled rein and surveyed the area through the tall trees. Below him and running north, was a long, forest covered, valley that separated two mountain ranges; their tall peaks hidden in the grey clouds. He checked the map Myra had given him. The surroundings matched her drawings and confirmed Tony was heading for the fields. He put the map back in the breast pocket of his parka and turned in the saddle to look at Molly. The big mare was staring at him, eyes and ears alert. Once again, Tom was grateful to Myra. The two horses were indeed used to each other and knew the routine. They seemed to move as one with the mare mirroring the gelding's movements. He was also grateful for the smoked salmon she supplied, which he finished not long after leaving the farm.

He continued on, following the tracks through the trees along the slope. At the northern end, the valley narrowed and he guided the gelding onto some flat ground at the base of a towering cliff face. There, trickling down the iron grey surface, he found a collection of water pooling in a rock basin. As the horses drank their fill, he surveyed the site. Screened in by tall trees and brush, it would make as good a spot to rest as any. He could even build a campfire without the worry of being seen. Dismounting, he walked the horses to a fallen log, and tied them off. After setting the saddles and supplies on the ground near the log, he wiped the horses down with a supplied brush, removed their bitless bridles and, as Myra had instructed, tied them to a tree with plenty of surrounding meadow grass. Then he went to work, creating a circular barrier with rocks, and rounding up both firewood and dry tinder. Thirty minutes later he was satisfied. The fire would be later, and primarily used for hot food. Right now, he needed sleep. So he unstrapped his sleeping bag from the saddle, unrolled it, and laid down. Within minutes he was in a dreamless sleep.

He woke to the sound of a crow squawking in the tree overhead. He blinked several times, lifting to his elbows. The sun was still up, but long shadows now filled the valley below him. He looked at his watch. It was just after five. He had slept for the better part of four hours. Rolling to his knees, he stood and looked over at the horses. Both seemed content, with heads down and cropping bundles of grass that grew in abundance on the forest floor.

He took a step toward the makeshift fire pit and stopped. If exhaustion wasn't bad enough, the pain along his inner thighs had turned excruciating. He took a moment to widen his stance, and stretch his quads. The initial pain was disheartening, but soon the muscles relaxed enough for him to get on his hands and knees to start the fire.

Holding the lighter close to the base of a twig-pyramid, he ignited the wad of paper underneath. Two sticks caught, and he crouched low, blowing gently and coaxing the flame to life. Once the fragile blaze had taken, he gathered thicker branches and sat beside the fire, feeding it until the heat drove him back. Then he pulled off his coat, laid it over a nearby rock, and removed a slab of salt-cured bacon from the saddlebag.

While the thick slices cooked in a small frying pan, he took stock of the food Myra had supplied. Most of it was dried food from peaches to beef jerky, and even more smoked salmon. He also had twenty packages of military rations and another fifteen of chicken soup. Once again, he was grateful to Myra. All the food was lightweight to lessen the burden on the horses. Taking one of the chicken soup packages, he poured it into a small pot, added a bottled water, and put it next to the fire too. Then he picked up the two grain sacks and walked over to where the horses were foraging. They seemed to anticipate getting fed and came over to meet him. He rubbed their necks and then dumped two equal piles on the ground.

By this time, the bacon was sizzling and popping; the sweet aroma making his taste buds water.

After eating, Tom slept again, deciding to get as much rest as he could before pressing forward again. Waking to darkness, he slipped his arms under his head, listening to the wind over the trees, and watching the stars as the broken clouds glided by. He thought about Tony, where he was, and what his plan might be.

The grow fields were isolated and, by design, out of immediate contact from even the syndicate. So the small working security force there would have no idea about the killings in the city until the first of the month. This is when the new supplies would arrive, and the accumulated drug resources brought back. That was in another week—a date Tom was sure, much like the imposed communications ban, had never changed. It's what made the growing fields so successful. That meant Tony would be made comfortable, and with the added security, the young Manatone might relax. At least that's what Tom was counting on to close the gap and finally catch up.

Tom thought about the grow field's security forces. There was no way Tony would divulge the true reason for this unscheduled trip. He would stick to his original plan, which was—according to Mike Grevo and Steve Johnnson when Tom was eavesdropping in front of the Manatone building—to find out what…if anything…was going on in the fields.

"An anonymous tip," Steve Johnnson had said. They also believed Rick Motese—the man in charge of the field operations—might be behind the theft of product.

Once again, Tom's mind drifted back to the security forces placed at each of the fields. Having never been there, there was no way of knowing the number of men he might have to contend with, but he figured— given the ability to remain hidden and off the federal governments radar for so long—the security details couldn't be too big.

Seven per field at most, with four being more likely, he thought objectively. But that number increased when he did the math for eight different fields. "Somewhere between fifty-six and thirty-two armed men," he mumbled out loud. In totality, it was a large number, but the good news was they were separated by miles of wilderness; each on a secluded island with limited communication. That was his advantage… and of course that they didn't know he was coming.

He closed his eyes and slept again, deep and long. Two hours before dawn he woke up fresh and invigorated, and broke camp.

Chapter 29

ARIA KAYLOR BROKE FROM COVER. The pursuit had been relentless. After reaching the river she had turned toward the bend to follow the children, but halfway there, both Jody and Kate had come running back her direction along the trail.

"Where is Tara?" Maria asked, kneeling in front of Jody, and holding her by her trembling shoulders. The seven-year-old had tears streaming down her face, and she was hyperventilating so badly, she could barely speak. "I got scared…"

"It's okay, Jody. Just tell me what happened."

"We…we…were almost to the bend," she answered, taking a shuddering breath. "Then a man appeared…and we ran."

Kate tucked into Jody's backside. "Tara fell...and then I heard her scream," she said, while glancing over her shoulder with fear in her young eyes.

Feeling sick to her stomach, Maria stood and looked along the trail. No one was coming…at least not yet. What had happened to Tara? She hadn't heard a shot and there was always a shot. Her eyes, filled with anxiety, flicked left and right. Like a constricting avalanche, her hope wavered, leaving her with no time to breathe. Unsure of what to do next, she listened for a moment, but the only sound came from the fast moving river and her beating heart.

Calm down and think!

With men on two sides, they were almost boxed in. She looked at the river only a few feet away. It wasn't very wide or deep, but with two young children it might have been a mile across and bottomless. She grabbed each girl by the hand. There was only one direction to go. "Come!" Maria said in panic, heading into the thick brambles between the two forces converging on them.

Brush raked at her unprotected face, and a low tree branch struck her forehead but she continued forward, running blind. Her only thought was to get away, to save the children. Then they broke into a clearing. A sinking feeling washed over her and she stopped. They were to the left of the cabin—the same cabin they had started from. She heard snapping branches coming from behind them.

Oh no! They are getting close!

Both Jody and Kate were now in convulsive sobs with trembling arms wrapped around Maria's waist in a vise-like grip. Panicked, Maria was about to run for the wooded area in front of the cabin when a short man, wearing camouflaged clothing appeared. He was grinning. Maria picked up Kate, and grabbed Jody's hand again, running across the backyard in the direction of the dense trees beyond. They didn't make it. The smiling man from the front now came from the side of the cabin, stepping in their path.

Maria set Kate down and drew the pistol that she'd taken from the man she'd killed. "Stop!" she yelled, pointing the weapon at the man with a shaky hand.

He stopped, his smile fading at seeing her armed, and his hand drifted down to his own pistol at his side.

"Don't!" Maria growled. Unlike the man she had killed moments before, Maria didn't recognize this one. He was short and bald with thick arms and a wide chest. His deep-set dark eyes were fierce, his lean face hard, his expressions unyielding.

Another man appeared from the trail she had just come from, and yet another appeared from the path they had originally taken. Both had pistols raised. One spoke angrily to the man in camouflaged clothing. "We got one, but the little bitch killed Reko."

The camouflaged man nodded, but his eyes never left Maria. "There is no place for you to run." He took out his pistol and pointed it threateningly. "This stops today."

Like a cornered animal, Maria's body was shaking uncontrollably as she backed to the rear wall of the cabin, jerking her weapon unsteadily toward each man. Jody and Kate—clinging desperately to Maria with their faces buried into her sides—had now quieted.

The three men moved in until they were cupped around her. Now there was no place they could go, no place to run, they were cut off. She accidentally knocked over an old shovel leaning against the wall; the sound seismic in her panicked mind.

"Get back, you fuckers," she snarled. But she knew she couldn't fire. If she did, they were dead. She might get one but that would be all.

She protectively hugged the girls with her left hand, and sweat rolled down the side of her face.

"Listen, Maria," the camouflaged man began. "Just tell us if there are any more children running around out here."

Maria blinked at hearing her name. She had been on the run so long with the children, without adults, it was almost shocking to hear her name spoken by anyone over the age of ten.

"My name is Rodrigues," he said, while gesturing to the men to lower their weapons. "Just answer the question and we can work something out." He half-smiled. "Is there anyone else?"

It was a lie, but what could she do? Her mind spun to grasp a solution, but there wasn't any. These vicious men had been hunting them ever since the Mexicans—unbeknownst to the mob in New York—had quietly taken over the grow fields. They had killed everyone except for the traitors, including the women. Whores mostly, they had been smuggled in for the men's needs long before the Mexican's arrived. At first this had been an occasional visit, but when no one from the Mantone family found out, a more permanent arrangement had been reached. Then came the unplanned pregnancies. Offspring soon followed. Maria, the two girls clinging to her, Tara, Ricky and Bridget, were all that remained of those children. Born out here, Maria had never been anywhere beyond these woods.

At one time their numbers had been nine, including her.

Nine! She thought with distain.

Now they were six—if Tara was okay. Anger began to replace her fear again. She was at her best when she was angry. Her arm stopped shaking, and instead of moving her pistol to each man, she settled on the man in charge. If she killed one man today, it would be him. "Where is Tara?" she snapped, "and don't lie to me, or I swear, I'll kill you."

Rodrigues just raised his shoulders and gave her a malevolent smile.

Anger overshadowed all reasoning and she pulled the trigger. But nothing happened. Panicked, she looked at the gun and tried again. Only a clicking sound followed. The gun was empty! Forced to run after retrieving it from the dead man, she never thought to check it. Her heart sank.

Rodrigues's face turned crimson. "Kill them," he roared. "Kill them now!"

She dropped the pistol, and bent over, squeezing the children closer so they wouldn't see what was about to happen.

"Not so fast!" came a snarling voice in back of Rodrigues.

Maria turned to see a stranger appear from around the corner of cabin. He was a big man, unshaven, with lips drawn into an angry line. He wore a blue down parka, jeans, and a cowboy hat. His brown hair was long and pulled back into a ponytail. But it was his brown eyes, intense and cold, that got her attention.

With the three men bunched together, he stepped forward with focus. In his hand he carried the wooden-handled axe from the woodpile in the front. Holding it by each end across his chest, he wasted little time, snapping the wooden haft forward into Rodrigues's mouth just as he turned. His teeth sheered, and as his head snapped back, the stranger sent the steel head viciously into Rodrigues's temple. He was dead before hitting the ground but the stranger never slowed.

Even as the man to his left raised his pistol, he stepped forward, the axe becoming a blur as he smoothly switched to a baseball grip and, in one fluid motion, brought the sharp edge down on the man's pistol bearing arm, spun, and then drove the weighted end into the face of the last man; the blow so violent the rotted end of the haft snapped, sending the head of the axe pirouetting into the tree line. Both men were down in seconds; one squirming on the ground with a severed arm, and the other dead with a staved in head.

Confused and in shock, Maria just stared. Blood was everywhere. The stranger's movements, even for a big man, had been lithe and controlled. Where had he come from? Who was he, and more importantly, what was his plan for her, Kate, and Jody? The thought spurred her into action and she picked up the shovel at her feet.

She watched him turn and step to the man curled on the ground. The injured man was holding his bleeding stub and screaming in pain, but there was no reprieve, no pity from the stranger, and the haft hissed through the air once more, ending with the deadened crack of wood against the man's forehead. The screaming abruptly stopped, the axe handle embedded into the man's fractured and bloodied skull.

With his back to her, she stepped forward, swinging the rusted spade high over her head as hard as she could muster. It struck the back of the unsuspecting stranger's skull with a loud clank.

For a moment nothing happened. Then the big man dropped to his knees where he swayed briefly. She was about to swing again, but then, like a giant felled tree, he fell face first to the ground.

Chapter 30

Tom's eyes fluttered open and he rolled to his back. He hadn't been out long, but it took a moment to gather his senses and when he did he quickly sat up. Seeing the children were gone, thoughts of being robbed came to mind. He checked his pistol in the shoulder holster and then the other at his waist. They were still there. He unzipped his front coat pocket and breathed a sigh of relief to find Tanya's gold locket was also still there.

The horses!

He levered himself to his feet, picked up his hat, and walked around to the front of the cabin. When he saw the two animals tied up where he had left them, he relaxed and probed the back of his head. A good sized knot was forming, but beyond a probable concussion and a very bad headache, he would live.

Putting the hat back on his head, he walked behind the cabin again, and searched the pockets of the three dead men. Not surprising, there wasn't much of value to Tom other than a handful of ammunition and a hand-held two-way radio clipped to Rodrigues's waist. He put the walkie-talkie in his pocket and stood over him. The camo uniform seemed out of place considering the clothes on the other two were worn, dirty, and much more of what he'd expect from the security force out here. Letting the thought drop, he remembered something they had mentioned in their conversation with the girl they called Maria. He looked in the direction of the river. The man with the severed arm had said the girl had killed Reko.

Tom picked up the three pistols from the fallen men, stuck them in his belt, and then followed the nearby trail until he came to two bodies. One was obviously Reko, and the other...a child. After picking up another gun—this one an old .38 revolver on the ground near Reko—Tom stood over the youth. It was a boy. He was sprawled face down with a hole in the middle of his back.

For what reason would a person do this…what possible excuse? A sorrowful ache grew in his chest, as he stooped and gently rolled the boy over. His innocent brown eyes were still open and Tom judged him to be no more than eight. He had a fine boned face and his straight black hair was parted at the side.

Tom used his finger to brush away the dirt that stuck to the coagulating blood running down both sides of the boy's mouth, and closed the eyes with his hand. Then he assessed the child. It was a disturbing sight. He was gaunt, unhealthy, with sunken black rings under his eyes, his cheeks hollow. It reminded Tom of an extreme version of a homeless person. Adding to this was the boy's exposed and tortured skin, which was covered in bug bites, cuts and scrapes—old and new—and caked with ground-in dirt as if he hadn't bathed in weeks. And then there was his clothing. It was threadbare and several sizes too big; the shirt sleeves and pants legs cut off and held up around his narrow waist by a piece of rope. Tom also noticed one of the boy's arms had been recently broken, and he appeared to be cradling it when he landed face down in the dirt.

Exanimating him further, Tom picked up the uninjured limb and looked at the small hand. Showing more signs of malnutrition, the filth covered nails were abnormally split, and even worse, the fingers showed scarring from frostbite. Tom had seen this before. While working for the Manatones, he had met a couple of Russian immigrants with similar scars which were acquired while working in subfreezing temperatures at the mines outside Soyinka.

This implied the boy had been out here, surviving in the wilderness, for at least a winter, probably more. To confirm this Tom only had to lift the boy's shirt. What he saw reminded him of an emaciated cow he had seen when younger—its bones barely hidden under the thin hide. The boy was no different. Skeletally thin, his stomach was withdrawn and his bony ribcage showed just below the taut skin. Encapsulating the grizzly scene further, was the angry exit wound from where the bullet had passed through his skeletal frame. The damage had been horrific.

Anger began to swell deep within him, rising to a crescendo with each beat of his heart, and settling between his throbbing temples. Malnourishment aside, it appeared as if the boy had lived like an animal, and then hunted and killed.

Scooping the boy up, Tom took him back to the front of the cabin and laid him down by the horses. His thoughts went to the other children. What were they doing out here, and again, why were they being hunted?

He looked at the cabin. Roughhewn, with a flat roof, it looked like it hadn't been used in years, but for desperate children, it would serve as a good place of refuge. He walked to the entry to seek some answers.

There was no front door so he peered inside. The interior smelled of mildew and the wood floor was covered in filth from both animal waste and garbage. He stepped inside. The only furniture was a wooden chair. Placed in front of the window, it was next to an old stained mattress on the floor. On it, next to two worn blankets, was a small brown teddy bear with a missing eye and three Hershey's chocolate wrappers. Tom took the bedding and the bear and returned to the horses. He couldn't be certain of the direction they had gone, but he was sure they wouldn't return here again. After rolling the boy into one of the blankets, and securing his small body to the saddle of the mare, he rolled the teddy bear into the other blanket and secured it to his own saddle.

Once more he stared at the cabin but his mind was elsewhere. The girl—Maria—who had struck him with the shovel, couldn't have been more than fifteen and the other two less than seven.

There was another girl, too.

He thought for a moment before remembering her name: Tara. She was missing or, according to Maria, taken by the men. Then there was Rodrigues. He had said "this stops today."

"What stops today?" Tom mumbled. It implied *this*—whatever *this* was—had been going on for a while. Not having any answers, he shook his head. He was just grateful that he had come along when he did or it could've been much worse. In fact, it was only dumb luck that he had come along at all.

Shortly after saddling before dawn, he had followed the valley past the two mountain ranges into a heavily forested area. This, according to Myra's map, put him less than three miles from the first grow field. It was at that time he had heard the first shot, then three more shots in quick succession. That had brought him to the cabin. The axe in the woodpile had only been a weapon of opportunity and used out of necessity.

Tom shook the thought from his brain. Solving the world's injustices or its tragedies wasn't his to bear. He was only here for Tony Manatone—Tanya's killer—and tracking down unknown children, through unknown woods, for unknown reasons, wasn't part of that scenario.

Stepping into the saddle, he pointed the horse north again, toward the first grow field.

Chapter 31

MARIA MOVED CAREFULLY INTO THE dense woods below the cliff face. High on a slope, it would give her a good sightline to the valley below, and the rocky ground would leave no tracks.

She was hungry and tired but pushed on. Behind her and following in single file were Jody and Kate. They had been holding each other's hands since leaving the cabin. Maria still questioned whether or not she should've hit the stranger with the shovel, but fear and adrenaline had gotten the best of her.

Who was he?

He was obviously uninvited. In fact, the hunters had been just as surprised. So whose side was he on? Was he sent by the mob in New York? It was possible. Even so—and not that she wasn't grateful—it seemed odd that he had come to their aid.

Parting the bushes, they came to a wide ledge, and a high fissure in the towering rock face. Maria entered it, walking up a steep slope within. Light filtered down from high above them and glittered on the surface of a deep cave pool to her left. Here the walls narrowed, and water from above moved down the slime covered rock, dripping into the center of the pool.

They sidestepped it and entered a cave at the end of the fissure. "Ricky, you here?" she asked as she stepped into the darkness. A tired voice answered with a yawn. "Yeah, I'm here…did you bring food? We're really hungry."

Maria's eyes adjusted quickly to the darkness as she moved to the back wall. On a two-foot-tall boulder with a wide smooth flat top, she found Ricky wrapped in a blanket. He was six years old, rail thin, with light wavy hair.

He sat up.

Sleeping next to him, and also wrapped in a blanket, was a girl. Her name was Bridget, and she barely stirred.

Maria sat on the rock and handed him a small canvas bag. "Its mushrooms and tubers tonight. I was going to get some wild onions and blackberries but we ran into some trouble."

Sitting up, Ricky smiled with delight, having only heard she had food.

Jody and Kate joined them, jumping on the rock next to Maria.

"How's Bridg doing?" Maria asked. For three days now the seven-year-old had been sick, and she only seemed to be getting worse.

Ricky shrugged, wiping the sleep from his eyes, and brushing the dirt from his cheek. "I don't know. I kept the blanket on her, but she hasn't moved since last night."

Reaching over, Maria pushed Bridget's damp matted hair off her face and placed a hand on her forehead. "Her fever has worsened, she's cold but sweating. We need medicine." Her eyes averted from the children's faces. "I'll have to risk sneaking into the camp."

Just the mention of *the camp* put everyone on edge and there was a chorus of "No" from Ricky, Jody and Kate. "You can't go!" said Jody, with fear in her voice.

Kate started to cry. "Please, don't go…"

Maria wrapped her arm around Kate's shoulders and squeezed her reassuringly. "Not tonight. Let me think on it, but maybe tomorrow."

Now realizing something was amiss, Ricky looked right and left. "Where's Jeffery and Tara?"

Maria bit her lower lip. In her mind she saw Jeffery again…heard the thunderous shot…and the twitching of his body afterwards. "They're gone," she answered flatly, not meeting his eyes. There was no sense in saying anything beyond that. Jeffery was dead, and in all likelihood so was Tara. But if she had survived and escaped, the five-year-old would know to get back to the cave.

Maria got off the rock, stooped, and picked up a metal bowl. "Jody, I need you to get some water for Bridg." Maria handed her the bowl. "And Ricky, please get some firewood so we can make mushroom soup."

"But what about Jeffery and Tara?" Ricky persisted.

"I said do it!" she snapped.

He slid from the rock, and stormed from the cave with Jody right behind him.

"And watch for the hunters when you gather the wood," Maria warned over her shoulder. The cautious words, she knew, weren't needed. All of them had become accustomed to being vigilant of their surroundings. It was part of their everyday life, but the words made her feel better after the death of Jeffery. She didn't want to lose…couldn't lose…another friend.

"Where's Teddy?" Kate asked with a shuddering breath and an extended lower lip. "Can we get Teddy?"

Maria sighed heavily and flipped Ricky's unused blanket over Bridget. "I'm sorry little one, but Teddy is gone just like Jeffery and Tara. We can never go back to the cabin. It's too dangerous." She leaned on the rock and looked into Kate's tear-filled eyes. "You think you could help me build a fire? You're so good at it."

Without another word, Kate nodded, slipped off the rock, and went to the fire pit near the cave entrance. Maria watched her go with pride. Even though their numbers continued to dwindle, she and the rest of the children, had become very resourceful over the last four years.

Four years. Had it had been that long? She glanced at the old windup Timex watch on her wrist. It was the only way to keep track of time and days. The month and year however, were figured by the passing seasons and more of a guess.

She cringed with the thought of the coming winter. In that first year of living in the woods, the snow had been deep, and it cost two children their lives. Then another the next year. She roused herself and shook the thought away. By her calculations, they still had a few months to prepare.

She went to help Kate with the fire. Today they would have a hot meal; the first in five days. She didn't like the risk of someone seeing the smoke, but they needed…Bridget needed…the heat and a warm meal.

If the fever didn't break by tonight, she decided, *she would make for the camp while the children slept.*

She needed to get medicine or Bridg might not survive.

Chapter 32
The Grow Fields

THREE HOURS AFTER LEAVING THE cabin, Tom was leaning over in the saddle, following Tony's tracks once again. A breeze touched his cheek and he looked up. Above him, the clouds were growing dark and angry. A storm was coming, he could smell the dampness in the air. As the gelding continued forward, he took off his down parka. Reaching behind the saddle, he untied the double-shouldered long-coat Myra had supplied, and after putting it on, secured the parka.

The land rose sharply, becoming thickly wooded with towering pine. The gelding was tired and stumbled twice so Tom stepped down and led both horses up and into the trees. They came to a crest on the mountainside, and Tom gazed down to the next plateau. He had arrived. Before him was a sprawling canopy made of camo netting, which dipped and teepeed across the valley trees like a massive circus tent. The coverage was awe-inspiring; at least thirty acres.

After remounting, he moved down the slope and back into the trees, stopping at the leading edge of the net. It was more than thirty feet overhead, the intricate webbing laced around the trunks of taller trees. Tom could see why it had gone undetected from overhead for as long as it had. The netting wasn't laid over the tops of trees, but attached halfway up. This left the bulk of the tall trees exposed and natural, making it almost impossible to differentiate from what was real and what wasn't.

Noticing it was much warmer under the netting, he curiously reached up and grabbed the draping edge that stopped just above his head. Thin cables were interwoven into the netting, which wasn't unusual, but it also had a plastic liner for a greenhouse effect, and perforations to allow the wind and rain through. Tom was impressed. It was an engineering marvel; all designed to get healthy plants and maximize product.

He took a slow, deep breath. With the temperature remaining constant and airflow limited, the sweet smell of marijuana plants permeated the air. Uniquely fragrant, the young plants were set row upon row as far as he could see through the forest floor.

He didn't know much about growing these types of plants, but he could plainly see that they were meticulously cared for. Rising from the verdant, dark, soil, each stalk was tied to a stake two feet off the ground. Then each stem was secured to a horizontal string so, as the buds grew bigger and heavier, they could dangle like grapes without the worry of breakage.

A distant clap of thunder rumbled through the valley, and the first raindrops could be heard landing on the overhead netting.

He continued on, following a row through the trees to the top of another rise. He stopped. In the distance, he could see two tents pitched along a winding creek. He twisted in the saddle, making a 360 degree sweep of the area. Up to now he hadn't seen a soul, but with the smoke rising from a small smokestack protruding from the top of one of the tents, that was about to change.

This was the moment of truth. Tom had no way of knowing what the security teams knew and didn't know about what had happened in New York. He could only assume Tony would try to bluff his way through, leaving out his traitorous activities in an attempt to get to the Canadian border. Would he say anything about pursuit? After all, he knew the mob was coming for him. How would he handle that? What lies would he spin? Tom couldn't know, but he still had to believe Tony was unaware that Tom was close behind.

Deciding on a bold approach, he tapped the flanks of the horse with his heels, and made his way to the biggest tent. The smell of cooking food was wafting out the closed tent flaps as he approached. After dismounting, he tethered the horses to a support post for the netting, and stepped inside the canvas doorway. The interior was lantern lit, and five men were in conversation and eating at one of two large folding tables. Another man, large-boned and well-fleshed, stood behind a large pot on a woodstove, the smokestack running up through the ceiling. All eyes turned to Tom and all conversations stopped when Tom entered. Along the wall of the tent, and behind the five men at one table, was a girl no more than five years old. She had long brown, ratted hair, and she was sitting on the ground with her knees pulled up tight to her chest. She looked up at him as he entered. Her brown eyes were fearful and blinking away the tears that left troughs down her filthy cheeks. In front of her was a piece of bread that had been carelessly thrown in the dirt.

Keeping a hidden hand wrapped around the handle of his Kimber 9mm pistol in the pocket of his coat, Tom nodded to the men politely, stepped over to the other folding table, picked up a paper bowl and plastic spoon from the utensil pile, and moved to where the cook stood. Still saying nothing, Tom leaned over the pot, and smelled the contents. The aroma of chicken soup made his mouth water. Satisfied, he used the stainless steel ladle hooked on the side of the pot and put two scoops into the bowl. Then he grabbed a piece of black bread from a tray, returned to the utensil table, and sat facing the other men. Two of them stood but they were still unsure what to make of him, their eyes flicking back and forth to each other.

Tom eyed them carefully, but remained detached, appearing untroubled. Using his free hand, he dipped the bread into the soup and took a bite. The soup was watery but remarkably good.

A third man stood.

With a quick flip of his thumb, Tom removed the safety to his hidden pistol which was now pointed at the men through his coat from under the table.

Tom took note of their clothing. Much like the men at the cabin, one man was wearing military camo-fatigues, and the other three an assortment of jeans and flannel shirts. All were of Mexican descent with black hair and dark skin. The only weapons Tom could see were the holstered pistols at their hips, but curiously, none had gone for them yet.

Tom took another bite, letting it play out. The man remaining seated was in the camo clothing, and seemed to be in charge. He was middle-aged with a hatchet-face and a long nose, his narrow eyes confident. "Who exactly are you?" he finally asked with a Spanish accent.

Tom shrugged. "Just passing through. I was hungry." He took the last of the bread and stuffed it into his mouth

The leader leaned forward, resting his crossed arms on the table. "This is private property, and you are trespassing."

Tom nodded, lifted the bowl to his lips, and drained the contents. Setting it back down, he sighed heavily. "Well, then I'll be on my way." He made to get up, then sat back down. "First though…I have two questions for you."

Camo-man seemed to get perturbed. "I don't think you realize the danger you're in right now."

Tom didn't back down, or even blink. "Actually, you don't seem to realize the danger you're in right now. So I'd suggest you answer my questions," he argued. "Let's start with Tony Manatone. Where is he?"

The interior of tent went deathly quiet.

Outside, a torrent of rain began to fall, pelting the canvas ceiling through the overhead netting and creating a hollow pitter-patting sound on the tent.

Two of the three men started to move their hands toward their pistols, but the leader stopped them with a wave of his hand. "If, in fact, I did know who it is you're talking about, what is your business with him?"

"Like you said, it's my business," Tom answered flatly with his own show of annoyance. "Now where is he?" He rose from the table. Upon seeing the little girl on the floor when he walked in, his anger had been swelling like an over-ripened melon and about ready to burst.

The man held up his forefinger as if he was in charge of the room. "Before this gets out of hand…"

"It's already out of hand," Tom interrupted, while casually picking up a fresh paper bowl and spoon, and stepping over to the soup pot again. "And I haven't even asked my second question yet." As Tom filled the bowl with two scoops again, the cook, looking unsure, backed away.

Camo-man's face turned red and he stood. "And what question might that be?"

Keeping them further off balance, Tom boldly carried the full bowl of soup around the right side of the men's table, and stopped near the little girl. Again they looked at each other, not knowing what to make of the stranger's brazen self-confidence.

This played right into Tom's plans. With their indecision, and not dealing with him right after he had walked in, they had unknowingly given him the advantage. That was their first mistake. The second was allowing him to get within a few feet of them. Now they were bunched together, without weapons in their hands, and their only benefit of having more men had been unwittingly lost.

With his eyes warily on the men, Tom handed the steaming soup to Tara—at least he assumed she was Tara. She took it, tipped it to her lips and drank greedily. When Tom stood again, his silenced pistol was no longer hidden. It was at his side, and pointed down. He had also swept back the left side of his double-shouldered long-coat, revealing the set of throwing knives which were in a scabbard strapped around his thigh;

one hand already gripping a handle. "Now, where is Tony Manatone?" he asked again, not hiding his contempt. "And for what reason would men willingly hunt and kill children?"

The men saw the gun, and now realized a fight was imminent. Their hands went for guns, but it was much too late. In a blur of movement, Tom's left hand swept up, releasing the handle of the knife with a flick of his wrist. As is sailed across the table, embedding itself into the neck of the closest man to the left and pitching him backward, Tom leveled the pistol in his other hand. The first shot punched the next man from his feet, and backward over his folding chair. The next two men went down in quick succession with shots to their skulls; the back of their heads flowering like a scarlet bloom.

The last was Camo-man, and just as he leveled his own gun, Tom stepped forward, and shot him from point-blank range in the chest, followed by a shot to the head; the impact sending him bouncing off the tent wall before hitting the ground in a crumpled heap. All four were dead in seconds, having never fired a shot.

Tom continued forward, and stepped behind the cooking table to confront the cook, who was crouched and cowering in the back corner. Grabbing him by the lapel of his apron, Tom hauled him to his feet. "Where is Tony Manatone?"

"They took him to field two for questioning," the cook replied without hesitation.

"To question?"

"Yes, he's under guard."

Tom frowned. "So you know about what happened in New York?"

The cook gave him a blank stare. "I don't know what you're talking about…but I only prepare the food."

Tom put the pistol to the man's head. "How many more men are here?"

"Four…only four! I don't know where they are," he pleaded, pointing at the dead men. "That's what they were talking about. They didn't know either."

The three men he'd killed at the cabin, plus the one he didn't, Tom thought.

He glanced back at the front entrance. He wanted to press the cook for more information, but, on the chance of someone else unexpectedly showing up, didn't want to overstay his welcome. Tom patted him down for a weapon and then hauled him to where the little girl sat. She hadn't moved, and stared up at Tom with those big brown wet eyes. Seeing all the killing, her arms were trembling, and she looked to be in shock.

Tom lamented over her sad state.

Reminiscent of the boy he had found dead, she was skeletally thin, with hollowed cheeks indicative of hunger and starvation. Her clothing, much like his, was threadbare and also several sizes too big.

Tom rounded on the cook. "You want to live?"

The man nodded smartly.

"Then we have an agreement, until we don't." Tom gestured toward the small shelving unit near the cook stove. "Those thermoses over there. Fill them with soup, and I want all that bread on the tray put in a bag. You understand?"

The man nodded again.

Fifteen minutes later, Tom had the dead men stripped of their guns and ammunition, and the horses loaded with the cook's food. He had also taken the liberty of going inside the second tent. Inside he had found a boon of supplies, filled with an assortment of goods from blankets and freeze dried food, to clothing and medicine. He had also found a crate of 9mm ammunition, but settled for only two thirty-round boxes so as to not add more burden to the horses.

Tom brought the cook outside the cook tent.

Tara had yet to say a word. She now sat in the saddle, wearing an oversized parka Tom had scrounged up, and gripping the pommel tightly. Atop the big animal, she looked tiny and fragile, and her wide-eyed expression only confirmed she'd never ridden before.

What had he gotten into?

He turned to the cook. The rain was falling hard now, rolling off the brim of Tom's hat, and he had to speak over its drumming sound as it hit the overhead netting and puddled the ground at his feet. "You can tell your friends I only want Tony Manatone," Tom said. "Nobody else has to die. But let me be very clear, I'm not leaving without him." He glared at the cook. "When can you expect them?"

"When they don't hear from Miguel…" he gestured inside the tent, "they will send someone tomorrow…probably Ramon Ramirez."

Tom had appropriated another walkie-talkie from Camo-man in the tent. He held it up. "Have them…Ramon Ramirez …contact me no later than tomorrow night. Channel twenty. If I don't hear anything, I'll have my answer. Then I'll be retrieving Tony Manatone by force."

Tom untied the horses and stepped in the saddle behind Tara.

He turned to the cook once more, the treatment of the child still unsettling. "My business here, much like the agreement to let you live, has concluded. In the future I'd suggest you give me a wide berth." Tom spun the gelding and headed out the direction he'd come; the fully-loaded mare trailing close behind.

Chapter 33

MARIA AWOKE FROM A DREAMLESS sleep. She flipped the blanket off, sat up, and looked at her watch. It was ten o'clock. She had been asleep for only three hours. Her thoughts went to the grow field camp and getting medicine. It was at least a two and a half hour walk, and that was in the daytime. That meant if she was going to get there, have enough time to search for medication, and then get away before daylight, she would have to leave now.

She looked toward the cave entrance. The faintest glow from the dying fire could be seen, the empty cooking bowl lying near it. Her stomach growled. The cooked mushrooms and tubers had been tasty but not near enough to feed five hungry mouths. A distant clap of thunder sounded, confirming the weather remained inhospitable. Another indication of the rain was the water basin outside the cave entrance where the slow dripping sound had turned into the rumblings of a fast flowing water fall—its deepening sound echoing like drumming hoof beats in the confines of the cave's interior.

"It's going to be a long wet walk," she mumbled with trepidation.

Above her and sleeping on the rock, she heard Ricky talk in his sleep.

She forced herself to her feet. On the boulder, Bridget, Ricky, Kate, and Jody slept side-by-side. Maria felt Bridget's forehead. Her skin was cold…too cold…and Maria's heart fluttered. Leaning in, she put a hand close to her mouth. Bridget was breathing, but it was faint, labored, and slow. Any doubt about not going to the camp was swept away like a leaf in a stream.

Before leaving the cave, she put on the only parka they had with a hood. Over that, she pulled on a Hefty plastic bag with holes for her head, and arms. It wasn't much, but it was the closest thing they had to a raincoat. Standing at the entrance, she took one more look at the sleeping forms on the rock. If she was lucky, she could get to the camp and be back before anyone woke up. The risks were substantial though, and she cursed herself for not picking up one of the pistols off the ground before leaving the cabin. But in her defense she had been petrified.

She grabbed the thick walking stick leaning against the wall. It wasn't much—a fallen oak branch stripped of its bark—but at least she felt better having something in her hands.

She flipped her hood up.

In the dim light to her right, the waterfall was growing deafening, the deluge overflowing the rock basin and creating a creek that now ran through the fissure. She looked at the fast flowing water, the frothing swirling bubbles glowing in the darkness. The once dry path was now ankle deep, and it meant she wasn't going to be leaving without wet feet.

She crouched and tightened her boot laces, and when she stood she reared back. There before her, standing in the darkened fissure entrance, was a hatted man in a long coat, his silhouette highlighted by a flash of lightening.

They'd been found!

She stepped back, and threw a hand to her mouth to stifle her scream.

Chapter 34

ANOTHER CHILL RAN THROUGH TOM and he shifted in the saddle. He would have to stop soon. His clothes, even with the long leather rain coat, were soaked. He had to think about Tara, too. Sitting in front of him, and now wearing his hat, she remained quiet, but he hoped it was only temporary. If he had any chance of locating where the other children had gotten to, he would need her to point them in the right direction. In the meantime, he headed for the last place the children had been seen, which was the cabin.

He looked up. Since leaving the grow field camp, the falling rain had been continuous, and more heavy black clouds loomed over the mountains. Lightening forked across the sky, and a rumble of thunder followed almost immediately. In front of him the forest floor, damp with a woodsy smell of rotting debris, grew darker as the sun settled behind the obscured horizon. Not helping, the woods were thicker here, the overhead canopy of trees heavier.

"I need to go," came the little girl's soft voice.

Tom was startled at Tara's first words. He pulled rein, stopping the gelding. "What was that?" he asked, trying to hear her above the falling rain.

There was a long pause, as if she was scared to speak again.

"What was that…Tara?" Tom repeated. "Is that your name?"

She nodded and whispered her words again, "I need to go to the bathroom."

Tom dismounted, and secured the horses to a nearby log. With his mind going over the uncertain problems of the day, which included security forces, missing children, and trying to locate shelter, he had forgotten about the child's physical needs. He helped her from the saddle, and then waited as she stood there for a moment.

"I'm scared," she said, on the brink of tears.

The words broke Tom's heart. Her young life—or the tale of it—had been tragic. In his brief time knowing her, he had learned she was homeless, living in the woods, hunted, taken for whatever reason, and then forced to watch men being killed around her. Worse yet, she was now in a darkened forest, riding her first horse, with the stranger responsible for killing them. And this said nothing of living on the verge of starvation. So he couldn't blame her. Under the circumstances, scared probably wasn't even close to being accurate.

Petrified was more like it, he thought.

He pushed the hat back, which was much too big for her small head. There was sadness in her big brown eyes, and fear seen on her quivering lower lip. "You have no reason to fear me," Tom reassured. "My only goal is to see you reunited with your friends."

"Maria?" she asked hesitantly, blinking the tears from her welling eyes.

"Yes, Maria."

With her obvious fear of strangers, Tom fought the urge to lift her in his arms and give her a reassuring hug. Instead, he brushed a strand of her brown wet hair off her cheek and pointed to a nearby tree. "If you need to go, I'll be right here. Okay?"

She turned, looking unsure. Then she stepped to the tree. The sight of her walking was almost comical considering Tom's hat was so big that she had to keep her head tilted back to see, and this said nothing of the coat which was so big it dragged on the ground, and she had to lift it to walk.

Tom turned away when he saw her crouch. A heartbeat later, her scream rent the air. He spun to see two large animals' no more than ten paces away, their sleek and well-muscled bodies iron grey with patches of black on the face and shoulders. But it was the eyes that got his attention. Eerie and haunting, they glowed demon-like, the reflective surface behind their retinas shifting back and forth from red to clear in the dimming light.

Wolves!

He remembered Myra's words. "The only real threat to the horses is wolves. If you run into a pack, it will be at night." She was right on both counts, and now one faced Tom, while the other stared down Tara who had backed to the tree.

Pulling his Glock from his hip holster with one hand, he stepped forward while waving the other hand high over his head. "Hey!" he yelled. "Back off!"

The closest wolf did so, snarling and moving parallel with the other. It was big, a hundred-pound animal, and its demeanor was sourly, showing exposed fangs inside snapping jaws. How long had they been stalking them? Tom couldn't be sure. With the noise from the falling rain and thunder, they had approached undetected, and could've been trailing for hours.

Tom stepped in front of Tara and pointed the gun. Due to noise and for the sake of the animals, he didn't want to shoot unless absolutely necessary. Behind him, the horses had become aware of the two snarling predators. As they grunted and jerked on the reins, they stared unsteadily at the threat, while stomping and raking their front hooves in agitation.

Reed Davenport's words flashed in Tom's mind. "When confronted by a threatening animal," he had warned, "it's a game of cat and mouse, and all about intimidation. So don't give up ground unless absolutely necessary, and never…ever… run." Tom now took heed of that warning and stepped aggressively forward. "Get! Be gone with you!"

Looking uncertain, both animals growled with ears flat against their skulls, but backed further into the brush. Now only their wet, black-spotted heads, and exposed fangs, could be seen. Tom took two more quick steps forward and yelled once more. Then the wolves broke and disappeared…at least temporarily…into the darkness.

Holstering his weapon, he spun on a heel, picked up Tara, and returned to the frightened horses. After putting her back in the saddle, he calmed the frightened animals by rubbing their necks, but continued to survey the scene. He didn't see anything but that didn't mean they weren't there. With the darkness worsening by the second, it was impossible to see beyond a twenty foot radius.

Was it a pack, or just the two?

In either case, it wasn't a pleasant thought in the growing darkness, and he found it hard to believe they had moved very far away. In fact, they were probably lurking closeby, and working up the courage to return.

He stepped to the big canvas saddlebag on the mare, and lifted the protective covering that kept everything dry. Inside, he removed one of the beef jerky bags and tore it open, throwing the large chunks of tender meat into the woods where the wolves were last seen. He hoped it would serve as a distraction, keeping the predators busy long enough for them to get far enough away. He remounted, grabbed the reins to the mare, and headed in the direction of the cabin at more of a brisk pace.

A couple hours passed before Tom heard the distant sound of a fast flowing river above the lashing rain. He was getting close to the cabin. Not that it helped in any capacity, the forest was pitch black, shadows inside of darker shadows, with a potential wolf—real or imaginative—behind every tree. He ducked under a low sweeping branch, and leaned into Tara. "I don't suppose you know where we're at?"

She pointed to the right. "We need to go to the cave."

"Good girl." He swung the horse onto the new bearing, and after another hour, the trees thinned and the gradient steepened. Climbing at night on horseback was one thing, but the situation became much more precarious with the slashing rain, which drenched the ground and made the slope treacherously slippery. His gelding snorted and half reared. Tom patted its sleek neck, then stepped from the saddle. "Steady now," he said, keeping his voice soft and soothing.

He looked up at Tara. "Hold on tight."

She did as she was told, and Tom, with reins to both animals in each hand, guided the caravan up the slope. Twice Tom fell to his knees, but continued on.

The rain began to slacken, and Tom could see the darkened silhouette of the cliff face looming before him. To his left, a shallow creek ran down the slope. He stepped through a screen of bushes onto a wide ledge. Breathing heavily, he put his hands on his knees and looked up. He was standing to the right of a giant fissure that split the towering rock face like a jagged tear; the darkened interior like an angry scar.

After looping both horse's reins around a rocky outcrop, he helped Tara down, and followed her to the mouth of the fissure. She stopped, looking unsure at the water flowing from the entrance.

"Wait there," Tom said, moving past her. "I'll carry you, but let me have a look first."

He cautiously checked his footing in the ankle-deep water, then stood for a moment, staring into the darkened depths of the large crevasse. From here, he could hear the rumbling of a waterfall, and see the frothing white bubbles swirl past his ankles. A flash of lightening lit up the night. Bright and clear, it branched across the sky like skeletal a tree, lighting up both the mountainside, and the interior of the fissure as well.

To his surprise, Maria stood before him, silhouetted in the soft glow of a simmering fire behind her. She was standing near the base of the waterfall where the water frothed and pooled.

She saw him and stepped back in fear. In her hands she held a large stick, which she lifted defiantly.

Not wanting to scare her further, Tom leaned over, picked up Tara, and entered the darkened lair. Tara saw her. "Maria!" she screamed with joy, writhing from Tom's grasp just as he made dry land.

"Tara?" Maria acknowledged, stepping forward with outstretched hands to meet her. But the excitement got the better of Tara, After taking only two steps, she stumbled on her oversized coat and Tom's hat came off as she fell.

Maria shot forward, dropping the stick and picking her up. "You're here," she said with a trembling voice. "You found your way back!" The two happily embraced, talking over each other with excited voices for the next moment.

"He helped me…" Tara said, turning to see Tom reentering the fissure with both horses.

"Hope you don't mind," he said stepping past them. "I'd like to get these animals and my gear out of the rain." Once past the fire, Tom went up a slope and entered a deep cave. As his vision acclimated to the darkness, he saw he was standing in a cavernous area twenty feet wide, by thirty feet deep, with smooth walls and a tall domed ceiling.

He unsaddled the horses.

After stacking the tack gear along the wall, he brushed the animals down, watered them, and gave them grain at the back of the cave. Then he removed both the 240 magnum Weatherby with scope, and the M1 military rifle from Bishop Styles from the scabbards and wiped them down. When satisfied, he checked the rest of the supplies under the protective canvas covering.

Surprisingly, everything remained dry.

Nearing eleven o'clock, he finally changed into some dry clothes, removed his sleeping bag from a protective liner, unrolled it, and stretched out on the cave floor.

By that time, Maria and Tara had gotten caught up on the day's events and were staring at him from a large boulder along the far wall. On it, Tom could see more sleeping forms. Again, he wondered what he had gotten into, but decided it would have to wait until tomorrow. Too tired for words, he put his wet hat over his face and finally closed his eyes, falling instantly into a deep sleep.

He awoke to the sound of whispering. Lifting his hat, he saw that it was daylight, and at the top of the large boulder to his right were three small heads—a boy and two girls—peeking down at him. All three cowered back, with one of the girls—a child with soft curled black hair—sweeping her head under her blanket with a shriek.

Tom looked back over his shoulder. Next to the horses were Tara and Maria. They were squatting and feeding the animals handfuls of handpicked grass.

Tom rolled from his blanket, stood, and stretched. Tara joined him as he began to unload the packs. "Good morning," she said without the bashfulness of the previous day. "I've fed the horses."

"Thank you," Tom said, while removing the teddy bear from the rolled blanket behind the saddle, and handing it to her. "I don't suppose you know who this belongs to?"

Tara shrieked with delight, and ran it over to the boulder, where she gave it to the black haired girl that had hidden under the blanket. "Kate! Look. Teddy's back!"

The little girl reemerged, took it shyly, and disappeared again. "Thank you, Tara," she whispered.

Tara ambled back over to Tom. "Thanks," he said, "and this is your reward." He handed her the sack of black bread from the camp. Her eyes lit up when she looked inside, grabbing a slice and holding it up for the others to see. "Food!"

That single word from her shocked Tom, and only confirmed it wasn't used often.

The others flocked to her, including Maria who held out her hand to Tom. "I'm Maria," she announced boldly.

Tom nodded, and took her hand. "I'm Tom."

"I know," she said with a broad grin.

Tom didn't know what to make of that. She had no way of knowing who he was. He let the subject rest, assuming she knew his name because Tara had told her.

He had told Tara…hadn't he?

He watched the children.

Even as Tara tore a big chunk of bread off with her teeth, she held the bag open for the others. It was an amazing interaction to watch. They were starving, cherishing every scrap of food, and yet they didn't squabble, and shared equally. Even Kate, who lingered cautiously behind everyone else, with big blue eyes focused on Tom, was given her share. Soon the full bag was empty, and all their cheeks were puffed out like chipmunks. Laughter followed as they lifted their shirts and compared big bellies.

Maria took the last two slices to the boulder, and the other children joined her.

Wrapped in a blanket, Tom noticed an unmoving form.

"You need to eat," Maria said.

Tom heard a soft murmur from under the blanket, and joined them at the boulder. It was a girl, lying on her back, no more than seven, and Maria was stroking her black matted hair. "Please Bridget, eat," Maria pleaded.

Tom put a hand on her forehead, the skin was cold and clammy. "How long has she been sick?"

"Three days ago it started," Maria answered, "and she hasn't eaten in two. I was on my way to the camp last night to look for medicine when you arrived."

Tom pulled the blanket back and lifted her filthy shirt to reveal her stomach and chest. He swallowed hard. She was skeletally thin, and her rib cage could be seen under the pale dirty skin. He walked over to his big canvas saddlebag, sifted through it, and came back with two white metal boxes. The bigger one, coming with its own tight-fitting canvas backpack, was labeled Emergency Medical Kit, and the other Medications. Both had been acquired from the storage tent at the camp.

"She has a fever and she's dehydrated. We also need to get some food in her before her system shuts down." Tom handed Maria the medication box. "But we'll take one problem at a time. I want you to find anything labeled antibiotics."

Nodding, she set it on the boulder, unlatched the lid, and began looking at the labels of the plastic containers inside.

Tom pulled out his medical kit from the backpack. He opened the lid, and was happy to see that it was quite extensive, including several disposable IV kits. He unrolled one, and as he attached the narrow surgical tubing to the bottom, he pointed at the canvas saddlebags. "Tara, I need you to get me two water bottles please." She nodded and scampered over to the row of tack gear.

"I got it," Maria said, holding up a small white bottle. "Antibiotics."

Tom glanced at the label. "Good. Amoxicillin. Take two out, and when Tara returns with the water, lift Bridget's head, and give her a drink to get them swallowed."

Tom focused on the inside of Bridget's arm. Opening a small bottle of alcohol, he poured a small amount onto a gauze pad, and cleaned an area over a vein. Then he inserted an IV needle, securing it with medical tape.

Tara returned with the water bottles, giving one each to Tom and Maria.

Opening his, Tom poured the water into the plastic IV bag. When it was full, he resealed the bag, attached the IV tubing to the needle in her arm, and released the crimp on the line.

Maria put two pills into Bridget's mouth, and with one of the girls lifting her head, Maria tilted the water bottle and forced the cool liquid between her lips. Bridget coughed but drank. This, Maria did several times. Then to confirm the pills had been swallowed, she visually inspected the inside of Bridget's mouth. "Good," Maria announced, "she swallowed them."

Holding the IV bag high, Tom had watched the process, and Bridget's eyes never opened once. This wasn't a good sign. Feverish and comatose, she had no idea what was going on around her. Tom leaned close to the wide-eyed boy standing near Maria. "What's your name?"

"Ricky," he replied.

"Okay, Ricky, I want you to jump up here." Tom patted the boulder above Bridget's head.

Ricky did as he was told, and once he was seated, Tom handed him the IV bag. "This needs to be held high so the water will drip into her system. Can you do that?"

"Yes," he replied, eager to help.

"Good. We'll figure out a more permanent solution in a minute." He turned to Maria. "We're almost done. Now we need to get some food in her." He went back over to his supplies and returned with a military ration packet, opened it, and removed two of the six toothpaste-like tubes from inside.

"What is that?" Ricky asked

Tom read the labels, and held one up. "Well, this one is mashed potatoes…and this other one is…roast beef." He handed them to Maria. "Just squeeze them into her mouth. She doesn't even have to chew."

Ricky frowned. "Is that really mashed potatoes? It looks like toothpaste."

"You don't believe me?" He took out another tube. "I can't say how good it is, but you want to try one?" He held the tube up to read. "This is macaroni and cheese."

Ricky nodded, his brown eyes gleaming.

Tom took the cap off and handed it to him. Using his free hand, Ricky was cautious at first but soon he was squeezing the tube vigorously into his mouth with slurping sounds, and murmurs of joy. Tom stood, and set the last three tubes on the boulder for the others. Then he walked to the cave entrance to get some air.

Standing in the fissure, he looked up. The rain had stopped and so had the flow of the waterfall, which was now down to a slow dribble. Two hundred feet above him, through a narrow opening in the rock face, he could see open sky. It was the oddest sensation; like a narrow eye, bright and gleaming, looking down at him. And reminiscent of tears, he could see trickling water coming down from one corner of the eye and landing in the middle of the pool.

He removed his hat, and stepped over to the standing water. It was crystal clear, and at least four feet deep; the rock bowl more than twelve feet in diameter. Leaning over, he saw his reflection, which only confirmed the difficulty of the last three weeks. Tired and haggard, his deep-set eyes were red and ringed purple, and with a full beard, he didn't recognize the image looking back at him.

Three weeks, he repeated to himself. *Three weeks since his wife was taken*. It wasn't a great deal of time, but the emotional burden, heavy and taxing, felt like years. His hand snaked out, disturbing the water.

Soon, it would be over.

He cupped his hands, scooped some water, and drank. It was refreshing, sweet and cool. Looking up again, he surmised this had once been a raging river, and over the centuries, the waterfall had carved out both the fissure, and the cave itself.

He put his hat back on.

The creek was no longer present, and he followed the muddy trail outside the fissure's entrance onto the wide flat ledge. He stopped near the edge. The air tasted damp and mountain fresh. A shadow passed overhead and he looked up. A bald eagle floated on the air currents above him, its large white head shifting back forth looking for prey, its dark wings standing out against the grey clouds.

He looked out over a tree covered valley. In the distance, stretching right and left, was a ring of mountains that reared up like a jagged black crown, their snowcapped peaks reaching up and disappearing into the overcast sky. A prettier sight, he couldn't imagine.

Maria came out and stood beside him. "I gave Bridg the tubes of food," she said. "At first she fought me, but then she ate."

"Good."

"I've never seen food in tubes before," she said inquisitively.

Tom nodded. "They're called military rations. It's not gourmet by any stretch, but it will do in a pinch."

"Well…" she began with a hint of guilt, "the other three tubes are now gone too. Sorry, but we couldn't help ourselves…even me," she admitted shyly.

"Not to worry, there's plenty more."

"Will she be okay?" she asked.

Tom studied her for a moment. Her skin was pale, with dirty cheeks, and her thick blond hair—shortened to her shoulders—was cut ragged like she'd done it herself, either with an inadequate pair of shears, or even a knife. Like the other children, she was thin, looked unhealthy, and her clothes were threadbare. In fact, the flannel shirt she wore was in tatters, with more holes and tears on the sleeves than thread count. But beneath the clothing and rugged, haunted exterior, she had the glow of youth and her blue eyes were bright.

"I won't lie to you. Today will be a pivotal day for your friend, Bridget. You can feed her two tubes every two hours, and we'll monitor the IV bag, refilling it as necessary. As for the antibiotics, give her two… three times a day." His brow furrowed. "How old are you, Maria?"

"I'm fourteen, or close to it. I'm the oldest." She thought for a moment, and continued, her words brimming with pride as she spoke of her friends. "Jody and Bridget are next. They're seven. Then Ricky and Kate at six." She smiled, and the hardships of her young life seemed to melt away like a spring thaw. "Tara brings up the rear at five years old."

Like a proud parent, her words were spoken with love. These kids were obviously her family, and she had taken on the role of surrogate mother. She was also the protector. That's what impressed Tom the most. She wore her determination like a cloak.

She turned to him. "How's your head?" she asked unabashed. "I am sorry for hitting you."

Tom took off his hat, and rubbed the bump on the back of his head. "I'm okay. But let's not do that again," he said flatly.

She grinned. "Why have you come here?"

Not mincing words, Tom replied without hesitation. "I'm here to find a man…to kill him…because he needs killing." He turned to her. "Someone has to do it, and I'd prefer it be me."

"Tony Manatone?"

Tom stared at her in disbelief. "How could you possibly know that?" He thought about the conversation in the tent before he killed the men. "From Tara?"

She giggled, the sound rich, like she no longer had a care in the world. "Yes and no. I didn't know the who or why, I just knew you would come….one day…you would come."

Another odd statement. "Who would come?"

She didn't answer him, and after a moment Tom asked, "Why are those men hunting you and the children?"

She sighed, and began her harrowing tale. "Years ago, the fields were syndicate owned, and from what I've heard, very profitable. But ownership has changed, and the people in New York don't even know it."

Tom remembered the conversation he had heard outside the Manatone building between Mike Grevo and Steve Johnnson. They had mentioned Rick Motese—the person in charge of the grow fields—and a problem. Then there was Charley Mack, who also had brought up the growing fields…and *a problem*.

Tom now knew what that problem was: someone had moved into the cartels turf, and through an anonymous tip, Tony was sent to investigate.

Tom nodded as she continued. "Before the takeover, the men here had brought in women…prostitutes. At first one or two, but that number grew to more than twenty throughout the different fields, and many of these women became permanent residents. Pregnancies followed. My mother was one of them." She nodded toward the fissure. "Just like their mothers."

Tom's eyes narrowed. "I don't understand. What happened to them?"

"They're dead." Her voice cracked with emotion. "It happened when the new owners took over. They killed everyone who didn't agree to work for them, including witnesses."

"Witnesses to what?" He motioned her to a nearby boulder, where they sat.

"I've learned the takeover was secret, and right under the noses of the Manatone family. One week they ran the business, and the next someone else did."

"Who…who are the new owners?" Tom asked.

"The Mexican cartel. Before attacking, they knew everything about the fields, even delivery schedule and the quantities of product that's sent out. So to New York, it was business as usual. Meanwhile, the Mexican cartel expanded the growing operations here, added two more fields for higher profits for themselves, and even bought out the few surrounding farms to guarantee privacy."

Tom ran a hand over his unshaven face. If what Maria was saying was true, and there was no reason to believe it wasn't, the takeover had been incredibly ballsy. The Manatones had learned decades ago, by growing product here in the United States, they didn't have to contend with smuggling product across the border. It streamlined everything, and it appeared the Mexican cartel wanted in on the action, especially if they could keep the Manatones in the dark. "How long ago did this happen?"

"Four seasons. One night, they just came into camp and killed everyone. The only reason many of the children weren't killed was cause of camp night."

"Camp night?"

"Yeah, one night a month, the children were gathered and sent to an outlying cabin so the adults could have *camp night*."

Tom didn't need any more details to figure out what "camp night" meant. "Go on," he said.

"We were too far away to hear the shots," she continued. "Then one of the adults, Manny Gomez, showed up at the cabin. He had been shot twice, and he was bleeding badly." As she relived the moment, her head lowered and she traced the ground back and forth with the toe of her boot. "He told us what had happened, and died after that."

Tom tried to put himself in their shoes. The story was hard to even imagine. One minute they were kids, on a camp out, and the next they were hunted. "How many children were with you then?"

"Including me, there were fourteen, but we had no idea what was coming next. A day later, they came for us too. It was chaos. That was our first day of running, with the older kids carrying the youngest like Tara, and everyone else in the cave right now. Shots came from everywhere.

We were so scared, and everyone scattered. Later that day the survivors gathered near the river. There were nine of us then. We've been together ever since...the ones still alive. Now there are only six of us."

Tom now understood. The children couldn't be allowed to escape the area to talk to anyone. It would put the Mexican cartel's operation in jeopardy. If the information came to light, it would mean an all-out bloody war between the two factions.

Knowing that, he could assume "camp night" had been an oversight—a miscue—in the Mexican cartel's coup. That's what made the children's saga so incredible. They had survived against both the environment and also armed men. Tom leaned forward, resting his arms on his knees. The enormity of what they had accomplished boggled the imagination. Maria's knowledge seemed uncanny—beyond her years. "How did you survive without food and clothing? Where did you get the know-how?"

"Mostly from Webster." She stood briefly, removed a pocket-sized-book from the back of her jeans, and sat again. "This is what we read."

She handed it to Tom. The cover had been ripped in half with only the upper portion remaining. On it, worn and almost unreadable, was a single word "Webster". Tom fanned the pages, most were smudged, with previous water damage, and like the cover, almost unreadable. But its wear could be seen in its use, with most of the upper pages bent at the corners to mark a spot. "This is what you read...to the children...to gather knowledge... a dictionary?"

"Yes, mostly. I also have two old magazines," she said simply. "I was the only one who could read. So I teach when I can." She shrugged and continued without further thought on the matter. "Surviving the first month...and then that first winter was the worst. We weren't ready. We had to learn to steal food from the camps, or find it in the woods. This amounted to tubers, wild onions, the occasional squirrel or rabbit, and mushrooms." She gestured down the shadowed slope where a crop of various colored mushrooms grew. Sprouting overnight from the inclement weather, some were all white, but most were vibrant reds, oranges, and yellows—a cornucopia of colors.

Tom held up a hand. He was in awe of this young girl's intelligence, his respect apparent. "You learned what to eat and not eat...what's poisonous and what's not...through the dictionary?"

"Me and my mother used to walk in the woods. She had a favorite saying; 'All mushrooms are edible, but some only once.' She taught me what she knew, and the rest I learned in Webster."

"In the winter, there are no mushrooms."

"Yes, and nobody could have prepared us for that first snow." She pointed at the fissure. "We didn't know about the cave then. So we huddled together under lean-to's or in one of the deserted cabins." She shook her head. "But that was rare because the patrols were always checking them, looking for us, and if they found our tracks…" She stopped talking for a moment, then continued, "I'll never forget how cold we were that first winter. Two of my friends, John and Cindy, died after the first heavy snow. Then the next year we lost Adam. Last year was the first winter that no one died, because by then, we learned to sneak into the camps late at night, when the watchmen were asleep, and to steal what we needed, including coats and clothing."

Tom remembered the frostbite scarring on the hands of the boy he'd found at the cabin.

The boy, he thought. He had forgotten about the boy.

He glanced over his shoulder and stood. "I'm sorry about everything you've gone through," he said, as he walked over to a bundle lying at the base of the cliff face. It was wrapped in a green tarp and bound together by rope. "But I think this boy was your friend."

Maria joined him, stooping, and touching the polyurethane tarp reverently.

Tom sighed heavily. "I found him on a trail near the cabin, lying next to a dead man. I put him here last night."

Sounding unsurprised, even cordial, she said, "Thank you for finding him. I will take the children and we will bury him with the others." Her head dipped forward in sadness. "I wanted to go back for him…I did…but I was scared." She paused a moment before continuing. "His name was Jeffery. He was only eight and I watched him get shot."

"So *you killed* the man then?"

"Yes," she answered, repeating Tom's own words. "He needed killing." Her blue eyes narrowed. "So I did it. Someone had to."

*****

Jody came out of the fissure. "The bad man is talking on the radio," she said to Tom.

Maria sat down on the boulder again, but she couldn't take her eyes off Tom as he followed Jody back inside. She couldn't believe it. *Tom Spears was here. He was actually here!* Only after talking to Tara last night did she know for sure. Her tale of rescue from the tent—one man against five—left little doubt. And then the wolves. What kind of man holds his ground against a pack of wolves? No man she knew, much less one willing to risk his life to save a child—their Tara—to do it. Then, of course, there was the killing of the three men at the cabin.

It was definitely him!

She thought about Myra, a woman she'd never met, who, she knew, worked at the farm and occasionally had sent treats for the children hidden in the bimonthly supplies. That wasn't all though. Also brought in, were the stories by the delivery men; the goings-on with the syndicate outside the mountain range. A recurring topic, and conversed openly, had been the name Tom Spears. Known as the killer of men, his reputation over the years had grown into folklore around the camps, and each time a new tale was spun, his name seemed to not only grow mystically but take on a whole new meaning.

The Shadow, they called him. A man who couldn't be seen. A man who fought evil, killed without mercy. A man who can't be killed. He was indestructible…immortal. These were the stories passed on through word-of-mouth from the woman she knew only as Myra—the same stories Maria had told the children numerous times, even embellishing when needed. How many times during the years of being hunted, hiding in the shadows with little to eat, or huddled together under a single blanket in the snow, had she told the stories of Tom Spears? Fifty? A hundred? She smirked. At one point she even had him riding a white stallion down into the valley, his guns blazing, to rescue other children caught by the Mexican cartel. Not that she didn't believe he existed. Oh, she did. Myra had all but said so. But the children needed hope. They needed to know someone out there cared, and he would come to protect them. In her embellishments, she even began to refer to him as "the Protector of Children."

She glanced back at the rock face. It had served as another protector. Her home. The children's home. It had been a saving grace. Without it…

Tom reappeared, looking agitated. He walked to the edge of the ledge, held the radio high to get a signal, and then paced back and forth. "Say again. I didn't get that."

"I said," came a voice over the radio with a Spanish accent, "we will meet today, later, before nightfall."

Maria recognized the voice and a chill ran down her spine. His name was Ramirez. The cartel's main man here, who controlled all the fields, the people, and the hunting parties who had been chasing the children now for years. Twice she had escaped as he and his men closed in, and twice she had heard him scream obscenities after them.

"Not likely," Tom responded. "If Tony Manatone isn't with you, there is no reason to meet."

"You don't tell me what to do…or not do," Ramirez said angrily. "You're in no position to negotiate. We meet today. Here! Before nightfall!"

Tom's words were straight forward and unwavering. "Will Tony Manatone be there?"

There was a long pause, and when Ramirez spoke again, he was almost stammering. "Yes…he'll be with me," he capitulated.

"One more thing, I'm not going into your camp. We'll meet at the center of the grassy plateau a mile north of the grow field, and come alone, with Tony in plain sight."

Again there was a long pause. "I look forward to it."

Tom switched the radio off. "As do I." The words cracked like thunder, his meaning clear, and his brown eyes became distant, unyielding, and cold as a winter wind.

Maria watched him as he stood next to her. Tom Spears was an imposing man. At six foot four and more than two hundred and forty pounds, he was solid looking, with broad shoulders and a wide chest. His face was unshaven but there was no missing the conviction and determination along his swelling jawline. Then there was his long brown pony tail, which added to his mystique. Like a proud Indian brave, it hung down the center of his back, and swayed to his movements. Even his stance seemed purposeful, righteous and charismatic.

He was oblivious now to anyone else being around, and she noticed the change in him. Focused and unwavering, this was not the same man she had conversed with only minutes before. Fear touched her. Stories aside, she was sitting next to the killer of men…the Shadow…and by that emotionless look on his face, he was plotting to kill even more.

Chapter 35
Mexican Cartel

RAMON JUAN RAMIREZ TURNED OFF his radio with a snap of his wrist. He was agitated. Not only did the grow field operation remain in jeopardy from the children roaming free, but now Tom Spears was here! In the middle of nowhere, he was here!

He went back inside the tent. Before him sat Tony Manatone, his head tilted forward. He was naked, tied to a chair, and to ensure he wasn't going anyplace, each foot had been encased in a five gallon bucket of cement. Not that he was really going anywhere. Ramon had already taken the broken ax handle and shattered Tony's knee cap; now swollen, purplish blue, and as big as a ripened cantaloupe.

Ramon grinned with the memory. It had happened after Tony's arrival—when he expected to see his men in charge of the fields. *Big surprise!*

But what Ramon found more surprising is what he had garnered from interrogating Tony over the next three days. Turns out Tony was very talkative under torture, and in no time at all—while crying and screaming like a little girl—had answered each and every question asked of him; and that had been the first day alone. By the second, he had pissed and shit himself.

The name Little Mouse seemed fitting, he thought, looking at him now. It was almost hard to believe that this little bitch had assassinated New York's notorious crime boss, Frank Manatone.

Although it was good news, the killing left other problems in its wake which affected operations here. One was the fact that Tony was here at all. It meant New York would send people to find him, and bring him back…if not kill him on the spot. Tom Spears was the perfect example of this. Not that Spears didn't have an ulterior motive.

Talk about making enemies, Ramon thought. Aside from Tony killing his own father, Ramon had learned that he had also killed the assassin's wife, and even his two closest friends. Not that any of this mattered to Ramon. His only goal was to keep the coup in the fields quiet, while also keeping business as usual. But how to accomplish this?

According to Tony, Spears was also wanted by the New York syndicate. It seems the assassin had gone on a major killing spree while looking for the men responsible for his wife's death…and now that number was down to one. That was why Spears had been so adamant about wanting Tony Manatone, who, Ramon had also learned, was on his way to Canada.

Had been.

Ramon shook his head, thinking about what had sparked all the confrontations and killing in the first place. Tony had told him, Tom Spears, the Shadow, had killed a relative of Frank Manatone some years back. Ramon chuckled. "If every cartel in Mexico retaliated simply because a relative had been killed, it would be a never ending cycle, and no work would ever get done," he mumbled. "It's just business. Nothing personal—a means to an end."

The Shadow, Ramon thought. He had heard of him and his deadly skills long ago. Although he himself had never attempted to acquire his services, the reality was, Tom Spears wouldn't have accepted anyway. Yes, he had heard about the killer's reputation, and his absurd criteria for accepting contracts; kills he alone did or didn't deem necessary. And according to the stories, the only acceptable agreements were for the killing of the unsavory…the less than righteous.

What kind of assassin doesn't kill…anyone…anywhere…for the right price?

But one thing was certain, he wouldn't underestimate the man.

He thought about the conversation with Spears. In a perfect world, the assassin wouldn't have come into camp and killed his men. Then they could have worked something out. Hell, he would have given Tony to him. But not now. The death of his men couldn't…wouldn't…be overlooked. Too bad, too. There was little doubt the assassin would've approved of Tony's present condition.

So now the question remained what to do with Tom Spears and Tony Manatone without drawing any more attention to the fields? There was only one logical answer that came to mind, but it would have to be done soon, before the next two days, which was when the men from New York would arrive—a bit of information Ramon had already learned from Rick Motese. He was the Mexican cartels inside man, and according to him, ten men were en route. He also said they were coming for both Tom Spears, and Tony Manatone.

He checked his watch. It was just after ten in the morning. From his current position at field number two, it would take him two hours by quad to arrive at field one, which wasn't bad. However, they only had four quads, plus Tony's horse. That meant the rest of his men would have to hike, including the teams even further north.

Six hours to get all thirty three men there, he calculated. *Most of the day*. That's why he had insisted the meeting take place just before nightfall. It would give Ramon time to prepare, and hopefully by the time the sun set, Tom Spears would be sitting in a chair much like this one…bleeding and getting ready to die.

Given the numbers against one man, he reasoned, *it was the only viable outcome*. He smiled with the thought. Only an arrogant man would boldly kill and then have the audacity to challenge a superior force…like he held all the cards. Which he didn't!

Anger bubbled to the surface again.

He stared at Tony Manatone. The killing of the crime boss had been a stroke of luck. It would leave the New York syndicate in shock, and disarray, and the grow fields a low priority. At least that's what he hoped. According to the latest sat phone call from Rick Motese, a woman had tipped New York off on what was going on the fields—an anonymous call.

At first this had seemed odd to Ramon. After all, there were no women left out here. All of them had been killed, wiped out, and then buried in shallow graves. There was also no cell service out here. None, for miles and miles. His first thought had been the woman at Frank's ranch—the same place that sent the supplies every two months. Her name was Myra. But two days later he had learned who the culprit had been. Her name was Maria, one of the children he was hunting, and she had stolen a cellphone from the troop tent.

Then, he surmised, she had climbed one of the tallest peaks, probably back to the south toward the Manatone farm, and picked up an intermittent cell signal. Once through, she had talked her way up the chain of command until she had talked to Frank Manatone himself. It alone had been quite the feat.

Ramon shook his head, and glanced at his watch again. There was still plenty of time before he needed to be on his way to field one.

He picked up the axe handle once again. Even without the sharpened steel head, the hard wood was weighted, the handle worn smooth and comfortable in his hands. He tilted it up. At the business end—splintered like the base of a fallen tree—were specks of blood. He put it under Tony's chin, lifting the young Manatone's head.

Tony had taken a massive beating. One eye was swollen shut and bleeding, and his front teeth were broken stubs, leaving his lips flayed open and bleeding down his chin and chest. More blood flowed from his broken nose and cheekbone, where the skin had burst like a ripe tomato. His body hadn't fared much better. Along with a broken arm and crushed knee cap, his two nipple rings had been removed in ghastly fashion, leaving craterous, red, oozing, wounds.

"Please...don't hit me...again..." Tony begged from a semiconscious, delusional state.

"I'm going to do much more than that." It was true. Ramon liked dealing pain. Actually enjoyed it. He learned this at the tender age of ten, while living in the streets of Cuernavaca, Mexico. A man had approached him once in an alley, looking for sex, and willing to pay. This had disgusted Ramon, but he played along knowing the man had money. Turns out, lots of money, which he had waved around to make a point. So Ramon had lured him to the back of the alley, and in between dumpsters, dropped to his knees like he was going to capitulate. But that wasn't going to happen, and as soon as the man revealed himself, Ramon had produced a knife and castrated him on the spot.

The pervert had bled out in seconds, and Ramon watched each one of those seconds tick by in morbid fashion. He found himself intrigued, if not fascinated, watching him die. It had been his first kill, and the money and jewelry he had stolen from the man had kept him living well above his means for the next two months.

A short time later, he had learned the identity of the man he had killed. Turns out he was a member of the Sanchez cartel—a small syndicate that operated in the southern portion of Mexico. They were also warring rivals with the deadly Tapito drug cartel. This had been good news for Ramon. In a country where a fearsome reputation is everything, Ramon had approached the Tapito syndicate for employment. Even at his young age, they had hired him on the spot, and after working his way up the ranks over the next decade, he had become a lieutenant in the most ruthless and lethal cartel in all of Mexico. From drugs to prostitution, to kidnapping and gambling, if it was in Mexico, odds were it was related to the Tapito syndicate.

Now at the age of twenty four, killing had become a way of life for Ramon, and as much as he would have liked to kill this perverted queer in front of him, he would have to wait. To draw out Tom Spears, he would have to keep Tony Manatone alive, and take him to the meeting place. Then he could kill Tony when Spears was located. So for now, the queer would live, but that said nothing of his condition.

"So you like men?" he asked chuckling, as he separated each of the cement buckets further with a foot, and set the shattered end of the axe handle on Tony's exposed genitals.

Feeling his legs forced further apart, and the prickling of pain of the splintered wood, Tony's one eye flared open when he realized what was about to happen. He began to squirm. "Please!" Tony begged with a shuddering breath. "I have bank accounts…money…lots of money…"

"You haven't near enough, Little Mouse," Ramon replied coolly. "Now hold still and don't look down. I wouldn't want to split your head open too soon." Ramon took a slow, sweeping, practice swing, finishing once again by setting the end on his genitals.

Tony jumped at the touch. He was beside himself now, and bloody drool flowed across his mutilated lower lip as he begged further. But Ramon wasn't listening as he focused on the next swing. Not near as slow as the first, he quickly swept the handle back in a counter-clock-wise motion, letting the end drop low and past his own legs, before smoothly arcing it over his head. Then he brought it down with two hands, swinging with all his considerable strength; the whipping handle making a whooshing sound as it picked up speed.

Outside the tent the guards heard a solid thud, followed by a shrieking…ear-piercing scream.

Chapter 36
Common ground

LYING PRONE ON A RIDGE, Tom used the binoculars to scan the plain below for signs of movement, but there was nothing suspicious. It was quiet, no people, alarmed birds, or manmade sounds carried in the gentle breeze. Above him, through the umbrella of trees, heavy clouds masked the sun, and the day was gray and cool.

After his talk with Ramon, Tom had saddled the gelding, and made the trek to the grassy plateau a mile north of grow field one to case out the meeting place. From this vantage point he had a clear sightline to the center of the grassy field, and if he decided, it would make a good sniper position with the Weathersby. But that was if he decided to. After all, there was zero chance Ramon was going to stick to his end of the bargain and show up with Tony by himself. On the contrary, if his angry words were any indication, Tom was counting on him bringing backup. Plenty of backup.

He slipped back from the edge so he wouldn't be silhouetted on the ridgeline, and stood. Then he remounted the gelding, and headed down the backside of the rocky slope. His next stop was to get another look at the field one camp before all the reinforcements arrived from the other grow fields. He would need to know layouts, structures, and potential escape routes.

When he finally arrived back at the cave, it was approaching noon. As he approached, he saw the green tarp that had been used to hold the boy's body. It was folded next to a shovel leaning against the rock face.

The aroma of cooking bacon wafted out of the fissure.

Before leaving that morning, Tom had piled the large stocks of food he'd brought with him from both the farm and also the storage tent in the camp, and told Maria and the children to help themselves. Upon entering, he found Maria squatting near the fire with two pots set on warming rocks, and the last of the salt-cured bacon sizzling in a frypan.

"I made some bacon and chicken soup," she said with a grin. "We already ate, so I was keeping it warm for you."

"Thank you." He paused at the pool to let the gelding drink, and then headed to the back of the cave to unsaddle him. Before passing Bridget, he ran a hand over her forehead. The fever was gone. She was no longer sweating, and her skin had restored its color. He looked at the half-full IV bag, now hooked on the top of Maria's walking stick above the girl's head.

Jody, Tara, and Kate sat with her, talking to Ricky, who grinned when he saw Tom look at the contrived IV holder. "I made it myself," he said confidently, "and I've refilled the bag twice with water."

The whispering and untrusting environment Tom had witnessed when he first arrived had disappeared, evolving into something else. Now there was a common bond. Tom felt the change in them. Although he wasn't a father anymore, he knew most children inherently wanted to feel needed, worthy, and loved. These kids were no different. Through accomplishments, they gained praise, and with praise, they aspired to be better and responded like flowers under the rays of the sun.

"She's also eating," Jody added. "I've fed her four tubes already today."

"Yeah, while eating two yourself," Ricky snickered.

"It was one," Jody argued, brushing her straight brown hair off her face, and slapping him on the shoulder. "I was hungry and Tom said we could."

"I did," Tom agreed. "Good job to both of you. She looks much better, and I think we can remove the IV…"

Bridget's eyes fluttered opened, then flared upon seeing the stranger hovering over her. Tom stepped back to give her space.

"Bridget's eyes are open!" Ricky announced triumphantly.

"Maria, come and look," Jody yelled, with joy. "She's awake!"

Tom nodded and took the gelding to the back of the cave near the mare, and unsaddled him.

Not wanting to be left out of Tom's approval, Tara and Kate approached him as he wiped the gelding down. "I made more fire starter," Tara said, "and Kate helped."

With Teddy Bear clutched tightly, Kate nodded bashfully.

Tom grinned as the two piled more handpicked grass for the horses. Before leaving with the gelding, he and Tara had had a brief discussion on horse poop, its smell, and who was going to clean it up. Tom had told her the horse droppings—when dried—made good fire starter. Problem solved. Now she had enlisted help and was taking it to heart.

When he was finished, he went back outside and gathered more firewood. Then he ate the last of the soup and bacon, and refilled the two pots with water, setting them by the fire once more. Not since the rundown motel in Queens, had Tom had a bath, and he was long overdue. Using some rope, he tied up a screening blanket near the pond for privacy, took the bar of soap from his saddlebag, and stripped behind the blanket.

All eyes, except for Bridget, were now gathered near the fire and watching him with keen interest.

The two pots Tom was using for heating water weren't near big enough to do both washing and rinsing, so, using a metal cup, he began by scooping cold water from the nearby pond. It was freezing—taking his breath away—and left his skin covered in goosebumps, but it was marvelously refreshing. When lathered, he held up a soapy hand along the side of the blanket. "Warm water please."

Happy to help, all four children stood, but Tara and Ricky moved quicker and brought the warm water to Tom, setting it at the base of the blanket.

He took the pots and thanked them. The shock, going from mountain fed water to even warm was intense, leaving his skin tingly clean. Once rinsed, he dried with a clean flannel shirt, put on a fresh pair of jeans and stepped around the blanket. "Who's next?" he asked cheerfully, as he finished drying his hair, and then put the shirt on, buttoning it and tucking it into his pants.

There was a quick show of hands, but Maria was already on the move, picking up the two empty pots. She refilled them from the pool, setting them once again near the fire.

"There's a bar of soap on the rock," Tom said, as he pulled his long mane back into a ponytail, and walked to the back of the cave.

He stood over the blanket he had laid out. On it were all his weapons and ammunition. The arsenal was impressive, with two hand grenades, two rifles, his two pistols, plus the seven he'd taken from the men at the cabin and the camp. There was also plenty of ammunition, with the only exception being the old .38 revolver. But even with the weaponry, it wouldn't diminish or solve the real problem, which was numbers. Ramon would have them. Tom had already done the math, figuring four to six men at each of the eight fields. Even though he had already culled the numbers by eight, he would still be going up against twenty-four to forty armed men. It was a staggering number considering his meager force of one. Originally, he had hoped…assumed…he wouldn't have to engage their entire force, taking on, at most, the men at one or two fields. That had changed.

He looked at the children. Maria was done washing, dressed, and drying herself with a blanket. Ricky was now behind the curtain, and Jody and Tara were giggling at his cold water shrieks, while arguing who would be next. The laughter seemed to warm the cold walls, washing away…at least for a moment…the emotional and physical trauma these children had endured.

Tom's face relaxed into a smile, but he couldn't dwell on it. A storm was coming, and they were unaware as to its size or how dangerous it was. Guilt touched him. Somewhere over the course of the last few days, his priorities had changed. He had come here to find the killer of his wife, and if he had failed, then so be it. He would've died trying. But now the consequences of his actions were much more complex. No longer was there the option of putting a bullet through Tony Manatone's head from a distance and then disappearing. The men would scour the mountains looking for him, and how long before they discovered this rocky hideaway? A week? Two weeks? Feeling the increased burden, he drew a deep shuddering breath. As much as he wanted to continue his quest for revenge, he knew he couldn't leave them. His conscience dictated it. Much like Tanya's little girl, he couldn't…wouldn't…make that same mistake twice.

It was a haunting memory—a tormenting picture that ripped at his very soul, and replayed over and over again like a rerun movie on a never-ending loop. In it, he remembered every detail, from the steel container strapped to the deck of the *San Paulo*, to her face that lit up briefly by the flash of lightening as she crouched near him, and of course the *San Paulo*; a doomed ship that would later go to the bottom from a hurricane.

No, he thought. *His only option was to stay and fight.*

But how?

Bridget stirred, and when Tom turned she was sitting up. Her black, matted, hair was disheveled, her green eyes uncertain and blinking in his direction.

Tom went to her, and called out to Maria, who came right away and helped him remove the IV needle from her arm, and replace it with a band aid from the medical kit.

Bridget spoke; her first words soft and tentative. "I need to go to the bathroom," and followed it with, "I'm hungry." It was good news. Bridget would make a full recovery.

Maria helped her off the boulder, and guided her toward the cave entrance.

Tom's thoughts went back to the men, and his lack of a plan. He looked at his watch. It was one o'clock. He still had seven hours to prepare before nightfall. But prepare how? Frustrated, he walked outside their rocky domain. As the girls disappeared to the right of the entrance, he sat on the boulder overlooking the valley again, deep in thought. After a few minutes Maria joined him. "I can help."

"What?" he asked, turning.

She looked like a different person after a bath. Her blond, wet, hair was combed, gleaming, with a hint of soap, and her skin was no longer dirty, taking on a lustrous pink healthy glow. The clothes she wore—a blue sweatshirt and jeans from the extra clothes Tom had found in the storage tent—were still too big, needing the sleeves and pant legs cut or rolled, but they were clean. It was a far cry from the little girl he had first seen outside the cabin.

"I can help," she repeated, "with whatever you have planned."

"That's the problem," Tom replied, "I don't have a plan." He threw a thumb over his shoulder toward the fissure. "Children were never part of *any* plan, and now I feel like a leaf in a storm, a ship without a rudder."

"You will think of something. You're Tom Spears. You're the Shadow," she responded with confidence.

Tom tried not to show his annoyance, but he wasn't surprised by her words, given Myra's statements earlier at the farm. He didn't agree with them, but he wasn't surprised either. "You sound like the woman at the farmhouse."

"Yes, Myra. I've never met her," Maria said with a smile, "but through her, I've heard the stories."

Tom's brow furrowed, his tone hardening. "I know nothing about your imaginative tales of unicorns and white knights. They are born of fiction—fictional characters. I only deal in facts and realities. The fact is my wife was killed, and the reality is I've killed everyone involved, except one. That's why I'm here, not to protect children." The frustrated words flew out before Tom could stop them, coming across much colder than he intended.

The moxie that had served Maria and the children so well—the main reason they were alive today—came bubbling to the surface. Her face flushed as she stood. "We're not children," she snapped. "It's nice that you're here, and thank you for the food, the clothes, and helping Bridget, but we don't need to be coddled, or even cared for. We have survived here in this wilderness together, and all alone. And we'll continue to do so. So don't patronize me or them. You can go. No one has asked you to help, or even stay." She glanced back at the fissure and continued with unbridled tenacity. "If they come after us, we'll run, or I'll kill them!" Her eyes welled, but she remained defiant and repeated the words, "I'll kill them!" It was a temperamental flash fire from having been alone…and the possibility of being alone again. She turned to Tom, her blue eyes angry with obvious disillusionment. "Myra also sent us treats hidden in the resupplies. Are they fictional too?" She crossed her arms defensively. "If you aren't who I think, then who are you?"

Tom listened to the angry words—words that should never be said by a fourteen-year-old girl. She had the backbone of a lioness protecting her young, and make no mistake, the other five children *were her young*. But it didn't change the fact that the words were empty. Her conviction, or spirited moxie, wasn't going to stop bullets, and that's what was coming…bullets.

Unsure of how to answer her question, he ran a hand over his unshaven face before he spoke, and when he did his words were direct, sincere, and to the point. "Killing is like war," he began, "and war is vile. I didn't choose this life, or the image you seem to have of me. It seems it chose me, for I'm not allowed to leave it, although I've tried." He nodded toward the fissure and the children inside. "As with any war, innocent people die along with the guilty. This is inherent to both sides, and also accepted. Not with me. So although I don't choose to be here, in the middle of nowhere, chasing the murderer of my wife, I don't let the lines blur between who is guilty and who is innocent. That defines me. Not war. Not killing. After that, I let the cards fall where they may. It's not in my control. Much like this, with you, and the rest of these children."

He sighed, carefully considering his next words, wanting to explain as well as calm her fears. "Most wars start with hatred, lust, and greed… and occasionally from religious indifference. This is no different. It's greed. The Mexican cartel has a secret they want to keep, and they'll do everything possible to maintain it. But that's just one side. As with any war, there are always two sides…two views. Also with any war, there's always a dominant side; or at least perceived to be dominant." He shrugged. "However, this usually has little bearing on the outcome. In most cases it's decided on much simpler terms: the difference between right and wrong. I'll take one man willing to risk all in a just cause, versus the hundred on the other side that would follow blindly like ignorant sheep." He looked into her angry, unflinching, blue eyes. "Don't be so blinded by your hate, and visions of a perceived hero, to not see a friend…and only a friend. Even outside this world of trees you live in, real friends—along with truthful words—are as rare as snowfall in the desert. I would take one sure friend who would have my back, in contrast to the many that 'say' they would have my back."

There was a long uncomfortable silence before Maria spoke again. "If you want to leave, leave. If you want my help, *I will help*. And those aren't empty words."

She spoke with articulated maturity. It was sharp and to the point, and Tom had to continually remind himself of her age. "Well, I'm not going anywhere." He looked down the slope, past the hooded mushrooms, and the desolate forest beyond. "So now we need a plan…" He abruptly stood…then smiled. "Of course. I should have seen it sooner!" He turned to her, smiling. "I'll be taking you up on that offer to help after all."

They talked for the next few minutes. Then Maria stood with a knowing smirk, and reaffirmed her earlier words. "I knew you would come."

Chapter 37
Fungi

Ary of any counter-measures they might have, Tom crouched in the woods, staring at the distant camp. Where would Ramon have his men placed? Would they consider the possibility that Tom might attack the camp, or would they leave a minimal force, and send the rest to the meeting place?

The latter is what he was counting on. A small patrol, perhaps a sentry. Both? Probably. If he himself were planning a defense—especially that of an unknown gunman—he would have at least three, two-man units on call. The first would be stationed outside the perimeter, patrolling for an approaching party in the likeliest areas. Further back, and inside the perimeter, the other two-man groups would be stationary and in constant contact through radios. Then when contact was made, they would all converge, surrounding the unknown force and cutting off any line of retreat.

Doubt crept in. A plan was only as good as the preparation, and this quickly concocted plan had almost no preparation at all. Granted, under the time constraints, he didn't have much choice.

How many would there be? He turned to Maria at his side. *Was she walking into a trap? Was he sending her to her death?*

She was staring forward, appearing lost in thought.

"How are you feeling?" he asked.

"I can't say," she answered, her blue eyes now flicking left and right. "I'm throwing five kinds of smoke."

"I admire your sand, but you don't have to do it. I could do it myself or find another way."

"And you're impudent," she chided. "I've decided, *I want to have your back*. Not just words. I've also decided I'd rather walk in the dark with a true friend than walk alone in the light."

"You read that didn't you?"

"Yes," she answered straight faced. "In one of my magazines, but I shall call it my own."

They were on the north end of the first grow field. In front of them, under the huge camo-net was one of two sunken cabins with flat roofs. These, according to Maria, were where the hashish from the marijuana plants was processed. She had also gone into great detail about poppy production, opium, and hallucinogenic mushrooms.

It shouldn't have surprised Tom considering her accomplishments so far, but once again it did. She was a paradox, and when it came to the illicit drugs, and the comings and goings of the fields, Maria—much like the dictionary she read—was a world of knowledge, from the manufacturing of various products, to delivery. She knew the best times of year to grow, temperatures, and soil content. She also knew each of the steps...in every product...in the manufacturing process. "For hashish," she had told him, "there are numerous methods. Using a flat screen or a blender to make hash is simple and cheap. Although there are more contaminates than the bubble bag, or drum-machine methods, the flat screen is more practical out here. It's just slow, and requires patience; the process can't be rushed."

She had even gone into THC content, the varieties of marijuana, gland heads, potency, and the stalks, which—except for the making of hash—would normally be thrown away. But what piqued Tom's interest, and the reason they were here, was the value of the product, and flammable nature of this particular process. This was a major key in the diversion he had planned.

He handed Maria one of the two radios he had acquired. "Ramon and his men were on channel seven. I've set ours to 22.2. Remember, don't use it unless absolutely necessary. The call could give away my position, and vice-versa. Do you understand?"

She nodded, putting it in her coat pocket.

He picked up a canvas sack at his side, and handed it to her. "Our whole plan hinges on this. Are you good?"

She stood. "I'm good."

Tom watched her, his concern apparent. "To be safe, I could walk you over there."

Her lips formed a thin line. "I've lived in these woods my entire life, and you…I've noticed…haven't. Sneaking around is nothing new to me. We've been doing this for almost four years. I'll be fine."

Tom had to agree as he watched her sneak off. Compared to her, a woodsman he wasn't, but he was learning. He checked his watch. He would wait twenty minutes for her to get in position. This would also correlate with the time he was supposed to be meeting with Ramon a mile southeast of his present position. He looked up through the trees. The light was already beginning to fade. In another hour, it would be dark.

A cold reality set in.

He was all that stood between life and death for the children, and the tension swept into his body. His concern wasn't about dying, but failing.

He thought about the men he was about to engage, who they were, and their egregious lawlessness against humanity. That was the difference between him and them. He didn't consider himself a hypocrite at being above any perceived laws, but being above evil people and common decency was another matter entirely. There would always be lawless people, but that didn't make them bad. Just because someone cheated on a tax return didn't condemn their souls to purgatory. At least that's what he believed. In fact, when it came to a "higher power" he didn't believe whatsoever. After all, what kind of God would allow the injustices going on around the world such as starvation? Disease? Simple brutality? And if—supposedly—there was a greater good behind some of these tragedies, what greater good came from the loss of his first wife, and infant daughter? And now Tanya?

He swallowed hard, thinking about the two women that had been in his life.

It seemed people mined joy as if it were an endless stream; sifting and throwing away gems at will. Contentment to them was only a word, a moment in time, and not a lifelong ambition. So they remained unsatisfied and always looking for bigger, brighter and more beautiful treasures. Tom, however, had panned that same stream and found gems that would satisfy him for a lifetime.

He looked up, his thoughts drifting to the children…children he would probably have to die for.

"Well, God," Tom spoke softly, "considering we've never had an actual conversation, I thought we might have a chat in case things go south. I've got to be honest. I don't believe in you. But I figure I've got nothing to lose in this conversation. And if, by chance, I'm talking to myself, it won't matter anyway. But if you are there, then maybe you'll listen. I've never once asked you for anything, but these children are about to die. That's probably no big thing to you—people have been dying since the beginning of time, but I want to remind you…they're just children. They don't have an evil bone amongst them." He smirked, his heart stirring with warmth. "In case you haven't been paying attention, Maria is their leader; the protector. She has a gift, an ability, to take on any task responsibly, and she does it well. Jody is the next in line. She's analytical, quiet, but smart, and in any other environment she would become a college graduate, popular and driven. Kate is six. She's the quiet, bashful one. A caring, gentle soul, her blue eyes are inquisitive, and seem to see right through you. The sick one is Bridget, but don't be fooled. You can see her strength and determination in her green eyes, and if I had to guess, she's as fearless as Maria, and half her age.

"The only boy in the bunch is Ricky. He's six, with an optimistic spirit, regardless of the struggles put before him." Tom took a measured breath. "As you are aware, he should be in grade school right now, learning to play baseball and football; not fighting every day for his very survival. Then there's Tara. She's the compassionate one. It's almost magical to watch her strive to help others, even under the constant pressure of starvation." His eyes narrowed. "None of them are deserving of this type of life. They're fighters, and that should mean something. So I'm asking you, for their sake, don't let harm befall them. This is for them, not me. I don't expect, or want anything from you. In fact, I'd forfeit any heavenly posturing I might have left to see them safe. Do as you will with me. For this I'd be immensely grateful. That's all I got to say, God."

Tom removed the Kimber 9mm from his shoulder holster. Twenty minutes had passed and he moved forward. A light smoke was drifting lazily from the chimney pipe of the furthest hashish-processing-cabin. Out front, within the sweeping field, there was no sign of movement, save for a rabbit that darted in front of him, disappearing into the brush to his right. He focused on the furthest cabin. As he approached it, a burly man stepped out the front door. He was short and round shouldered, his black hair unkempt, and he had a black shaggy beard. He wore jeans and a thick coat. On his hip he carried a holstered pistol. He never saw

Tom, and just as he looked up, Tom shot him through the left eye—the booming sound echoing across the wide valley.

Tom cleared both buildings. No one else was inside, so he returned to the first cabin, stepping over the dead man and down a small flight of stairs. The interior was warm, and smelled of both burning wood, from the woodstove along the left wall, and also plants. Fresh and sweet, the pleasant scent reminded him of a florist shop or even fresh cut grass.

He gazed around the room.

The interior was lit by four battery powered lanterns hung in each corner, and like Maria had described, there were several rudimentarily-built screens over catch basins with sheet-metal bottoms. Set end to end in line, these were as tall as a table, three feet by three feet, and shallow; only six inches deep. Tom stepped up to the closest one, lifted the screen, and ran a hand through the fine yellowish powder. The texture was as smooth as flour.

"Trichomes," Maria had called it. Unpressed, this was the beginning of block-formed hash. Next to it was a stack of scuff—marijuana leaf trimmings and stems—to be rubbed over the screens. And on the dirt floor, stacked waist high along the right wall, was a pile of discarded plant debris that had already been screened.

Tom nodded with satisfaction. Fire was the number one worry to any grower, and this place was a tinderbox, a fire-code nightmare that would make any fire inspector salivate. Even the lone fire extinguisher in the corner, was a joke.

The plan was simple. Beyond the booming sound of the shooting, he needed a distraction, and fire was his best option; not a big-bang-explosion, or a fireball that might burn down the entire forest, but a simple fire.

He stepped over to the woodstove. On top of it was a steel box—a homemade version of an oven, complete with a door, and a propane hose exiting out the back which attached to one of two, five gallon propane cans along the wall. This is where the cooking of product took place, but Tom had a different type of cooking in mind. Grabbing a large handful of the dried scuff, he opened the woodstove door, and touched it to the small fire crackling inside. As expected, the flashpoint was high and he had to spin quickly to keep from burning his hand, tossing the now flaming handful of plant debris onto the pile along the wall. It caught immediately, and in seconds a whooshing sound filled the room, with flames leaping and dancing along the wall. Then he went back up the stairs, and exited the cabin.

A pistol shot rang out from his right, the wood door frame splintering near his head. He dove to his left, rolled once, and ducked alongside the cabin just as another gun opened up from the field in front of the cabin, pockmarking the ground at Tom's feet before he could get out of the line of fire.

With his back to the cabin wall, Tom paused a moment, forcing himself to not return fire. Instead he took a controlled breath, listened, and waited. A moment of silence passed. Then running footsteps could be heard and Tom made his move, stepping around the corner with his pistol raised. In front of him, and unsuspecting that Tom was still there, was a tall gangly man with narrow shoulders, no more than fifteen paces away. He tried to stop and evade, but there was no place to go. Tom pulled the trigger twice, double tapping him in the chest, which first pitched him backward and then spun him to the ground; his pistol cartwheeling through the air.

Another man, short and bald, and sucking wind as he ran, appeared on the far side of the cabin. Seeing the demise of his friend, he fired once—the wild shot harmlessly hitting the ground four feet to Tom's left—and tried to veer to the cabin for cover. He was too late. Tom's next shot thundered through the attacker's skull, and he collapsed face first, into the dirt.

Tom waited a moment longer, eyes sweeping along the rows of marijuana plants, and ears listening. Distant shouts came from the northern side of the field. More men were approaching, and if Tom's numbers were correct, that meant at least four to six more men.

So far so good.

He sprinted between the two buildings, heading back to the tree line. Once there and up the slope, he ducked behind the trunk of a large pine tree and looked back at the scene below.

There was more shouting and three men appeared in front of the cabin, the black smoke billowing out the front door. Two carried pistols, and the one who appeared to be in charge, a bolt-action rifle, plus a sidearm at his waist.

That's the man Tom paid close attention to.

He was black haired, wide shouldered, wearing a camo hat and military fatigues. His Mexican heritage could be seen in his dark skin, and neatly trimmed black sideburns hooked forward toward his mouth. On both exposed wrists were tattoos.

Mexican cartel, Tom guessed. Much like the other two uniformed men Tom had killed, he wasn't a grunt. He was a person of authority.

As his eyes flicked around angrily for Tom, he unclipped a two-way radio from his belt, and began speaking into it. The conversation was brief. Tom couldn't hear the words, but there was little doubt the man on the other end was Ramon Ramirez. Then he turned to the other two men, issuing commands. They took off running back in the direction of the cooking tent, while the tattooed man slung the rifle over his shoulder and disappeared into the closest cabin.

Tom watched the two men disappear back down the rows of marijuana plants. He had a good idea of where they were going. While pilfering supplies inside the storage tent the last time he was here, he had seen more than twenty fire extinguishers stacked in a corner. This was the extent of their fire brigade. That, and the generator-run-pumps in the nearby stream that ran the grow-field sprinkler system.

Tom waited and watched. Sending the men back confirmed that more reinforcements weren't readily available to fight the fire. He calculated their return. Even at a dead run, the round trip to the storage tent and back would take at least fifteen minutes, and turning on the sprinkler system another five.

More than enough time.

As the man in charge reemerged carrying a fire extinguisher, Tom moved back down the slope, coming around the back side of the first cabin. Hearing the discharge of the fire extinguisher, Tom peered around the front corner. The man, completely preoccupied, was at the other cabin, shooting fire retardant inside the doorway.

Tom stepped around the corner and shot him in the head, punching him sideways to the ground, the fire extinguisher still in his hands. A hollow, rattling sound had Tom looking to his left. The sprinkler system was coming on line, and the closest four-foot-riser was trembling as air was displaced inside the PVC piping. Then water spurted from the sprinkler head, increasing velocity as the pressure increased. Soon sprinklers swept the sides of the building from four sides.

Tom ran back to his previous position behind the tree trunk on the slope. Smoke billowed from the cabin door, but it wasn't engulfed yet. It would take longer without a wooden floor, and the half-buried walls would limit the spread too. With any luck, the men would contain the fire, and keep them busy at the same time. He turned and headed southwest to meet Maria at the prearranged rendezvous site.

*****

Maria waited patiently for Tom's signal. Finally hearing the gunshot, she flinched, but remained staring at the back of the cook tent. Two men—one tall and the other short and squat—exited through the front, and with guns in hand, ran in Tom's direction. She waited another full minute before picking up the canvas sack, and creeping to the creek that ran along the tent and western edge of the grow field. Using the rocks as stepping stones, she crossed it in four easy strides to the back of the tent. There was no rear entry point, but she knew what to do. Having done it numerous times in the past, she settled to her knees, lifted the bottom edge of the tent wall, and peeked underneath. Not seeing or hearing anyone, she dropped to her belly and lifted it further. It was a tight squeeze, but she squirmed through the narrow gap, pulling the canvas sack through once inside.

The tent was warm, and smelled of soup and cooked bread. Her stomach grumbled. She was already hungry again. She stood and peered beyond the cook stove and tables to the front flap of the tent. No one was here, and as she suspected, neither was the cook. Before dinnertime each evening he disappeared for an hour or so. This had been a routine Maria had taken full advantage of over the years.

More shooting thundered down the valley…multiple shots this time…and she stepped up to the big cooking pot. It was over a propane burner on the cook stove and set on low. She took the lid off, and steam billowed up from the bubbling broth. Her hunger was intense now and her mouth watered, but she fought the urge to take a mouthful, and opened the canvas sack.

She looked inside.

Amanita Phalloides, she thought pleasantly, *the death cap mushroom.*

She felt invigorated. After years on the run, hunted like an animal, her mother killed, and friends slaughtered in front of her, she was going to fight back—a retaliation in the making.

Her hands shook with anticipation.

It had been Tom's idea, but she was the one with the expertise to pick the correct mushrooms, the worst of the worst. That was the poisonous *death cap*, and even better, its color wouldn't be a dead giveaway in soup. Unlike the vibrant colors on most wild varieties—such as the deadly Santa Claus mushroom with its red dome and white sprinkled spots—the *Amanita Phalloides* were most often whitish with shades of brown; at least the most poisonous variety.

No, this one was perfect, she thought. She had even included the stems, the most toxic of all. She ran her fingers through the mashed up goo to break it apart further. Slimy to the touch, and squirting between her fingers like mud, the mushrooms were now in paste form. With more time, dried would have been best. Then she could've ground them to powder, and made them all but invisible in the soup.

A plopping sound followed as she dumped the entire contents of the bag into the heated mixture. After giving the empty sack a quick shake, she stuffed it in her flannel shirt, took the long-handled ladle from the side of the pot, and swirled the broth until the whitish paste disappeared. When satisfied, she hooked the ladle back to the side, and took one more look. She could see some bigger chunks floating at the top, but nothing that would raise suspicion.

She was about to replace the lid when another shot broke the silence. Instinctively, she ducked and almost dropped the metal lid.

Gotta go!

She put the lid back on, but took a moment to lift the towel that had been laid over the bread tray. The fresh baked smell was more than she could handle and she took two slices, jamming one in her mouth, before crawling back through the gap at the back of the tent. That's when the plan went awry. If she had been less concerned about that second slice of bread getting dirty, she might have paid more attention when she exited. As it was, she had just stood up when she heard the generator being started to her immediate left. Two men were standing there no more than thirty paces away. One was near the big insulated box that housed the generator, and the other kneeling by the pipe coming out of the creek. Both their heads were down and, so far, hadn't seen her yet.

She crossed back over the stream and was reentering the woods when one of them yelled.

"Hey!"

She glanced over her shoulder, dropping the bread. The man kneeling by the pipe was looking at her, and stood. But he didn't move right away, looking hesitant about crossing the creek and getting his feet wet.

She bolted for the cover of the tree line, running up the gentle slope. Foot splashes behind her confirmed the men were now in pursuit. "Come back here, you little bitch!" one yelled.

By the time she reached the rise, her legs shook, and her heart felt like it was lodged in her throat. Unable to breathe, she wanted to stop and rest, but one look over her shoulder told her that wasn't possible. The man who had seen her was right behind her and he raised his pistol just as she disappeared from sight, running down the other side of the slope as fast as her tired legs could carry her. When she reached the bottom, she stopped. Bent over and sucking air, she looked back up the tree engulfed slope. She couldn't see the man, but she heard distant talking.

The man had waited for his friend.

She turned right, following a small ravine that had once been a creek bed. Staying low, she worked her way through the thick brush. The terrain was familiar to her. This was a route she had used often in her prior raids of the cooking tent. But this was the first time someone was actually chasing her, and soon she would have to climb the steep slope on her left, or risk being cornered in the dead-end canyon ahead. Not waiting any longer, she turned up the steep slope, dropping to her hands and knees to accommodate the steep incline. She hadn't gotten far when a man yelled.

"There she is!"

Exposed, Maria stopped. She was real scared now, remembering how Jeffery had been shot in the back. Her eyes flicked up the slope, and then down. Climbing was no longer an option, nor could she remain in the creek bed.

A shot rang out, and the bullet lodged into the tree trunk near her shoulder. Panicked, she slid back down the slope on her hind end, and resumed running once again toward the dead end. Another voice, this one very close, made her jump. Then when she heard it again, she realized it was the radio in her pocket.

It was Tom!

"Maria!" she heard him say again. "Answer me!"

She pulled the radio out of her pocket, pushed the button and talked as she ran. "I'm here!" she said.

"I heard a shot. Are they shooting at you?"

"Yes…" Winded, and scared—her tongue tacky from thirst—she found it difficult to talk…to form even the simplest of words. "They… are close…"

"Where are you?" he asked, sounding panicked.

She swallowed hard. "They saw me…leave the camp…creek bed to the…" A branch struck her face, and she went down to all fours.

*****

Tom had already made it back to where they had tied the horse. In fact, he had been waiting for Maria when he heard the first shot. Concern had swamped him, and after repeated attempts to reach her by radio, he had remounted and headed back toward the grow field. Now he was zigzagging through the woods, pushing the gelding hard. He rode up and over the first rolling slope, and then stopped at the crest of the next.

"Maria, answer me please!" he yelled once more into the radio.

Still nothing.

"Maria. Answer me!" He was just getting ready to head down the next slope when she finally responded.

"I'm here!"

"I heard a shot," Tom replied. "Are they shooting *at you*?"

"Yes…" he heard her say. She was breathing heavily. "They are close…"

He could hear the fear in her voice. "Where are you?"

"They saw me…leave the camp…creek bed to the…" then silence.

He kicked the gelding into a run again, down the tree engulfed slope, guiding the horse through the maze of trees, and trying to quell the rising panic in his chest. Halfway up the next rise, another shot boomed. It was close, very close. As he crested the next hill, he stopped again. Way off in the distance to his right, he could make out the grow field, and to his left loomed a wall of rock. He leaned forward in the saddle. Before him was a near vertical incline.

Someone yelled from below. "Shoot her! Shoot the bitch!" Then another shot sounded.

The words and subsequent shot confirmed Tom was out of time, and if he wasn't panicked before, he certainly was now. The chilling words also meant at least two men were chasing her. Cold dread touched him and he spun the nervous horse toward the treacherous incline. At first the gelding fought the reins, throwing its head back in dismay, but Tom urged the animal forward. Then the ride from hell began, going from zero to twenty in a heartbeat.

Standing in the stirrups, and leaning as far back as possible, Tom watched, wide-eyed as the horse plunged headfirst downward, its front legs digging in stiff-legged, and its hindquarters dragging the ground to gain footing. It was a gallant effort by the gelding, but much like trying to stop a freight train with one's foot, it did little to slow the descent as the soft ground beneath them gave way to the fourteen-hundred-pound animal. Picking up speed, they were halfway down, ploughing through the brush, and slipping between two large fir trees, when Tom saw movement ahead of him.

Two men had stood to see the commotion barreling down at them from the hill.

Their pistols started coming up and Tom realized in a flash that if he remained on the incline much longer he was dead. Out of options and without thinking, Tom kicked the tired horse hard in the flanks. The reaction was immediate. The horse leapt forward, and for an instant there was nothing; no sound of brush, or tumbling debris, only the sinking feeling in his stomach as the horse went airborne. Then they dropped like a stone. More than twenty feet they fell, and as the lower part of the slope came up, he readied himself for a hard landing. First to hit were the horse's back legs, followed by the front. This threw both horse and rider forward, and with no way to stop the forward momentum, a hard tumble into the fast approaching creek bed was imminent.

Feeling the horse falter, Tom cleared his right leg from the stirrup, and bailed. He landed hard on his backside, pulling his pistol as he tumbled into the dry creek bed below. The horse followed suit, hitting the dirt with its chest—the impact hard, the sound resonating—before tumbling headfirst, rolling once, and rising on shaky legs; the soft dirt and thick brush cushioning the ungainly fall.

*****

Maria was gassed. Sweat now gleamed on her forehead, the beads rolling down the sides of her face and over the tip of her nose. Her contracting diaphragm muscles ached, and twice she had been forced to stop with the dry heaves. She swallowed hard. If she didn't stop soon, her heart would burst. A bullet slammed into the boulder she had just slipped past. She looked up at the looming outcrop of rock. She was almost to the end of the line. Her chest pounded and she fought back the need to gag again as she continued forward on all fours; the soft dirt giving way to sharp rocks that now dug into her knees and hands.

"No place to run now," a man snarled, sounding winded himself.

Then suddenly there was no place left to go. The creek bed ended where once there had been a pool from a waterfall. Like the rabbit before the wolf, she looked desperately for an avenue of escape. But there was none. She sought refuge behind the last boulder. Peeking around the side, she saw the man who first yelled at her. He was standing in a line of brush forty paces away. Behind him, the other man saw her, pointed and yelled, "Shoot her! Shoot the bitch!"

A bullet struck the rocks to her right, sending fragmented chips into her arm. She recoiled, and screamed. The heated pieces had opened her skin in two places along her forearm, the blood already seeping between her fingers as she hugged the arm close into her chest.

She knew the end was close now, and her whole body trembled with fear.

A strange tumbling noise, loud and intrusive, came from the steep incline to her right. Branches broke, rocks rolled, and the ground resonated with movement. Sounding like an avalanche, she stole a look around the boulder. At first she couldn't believe her eyes. High above the creek bed, a man on horseback was barreling down the near vertical slope. The picture was surreal, a suicidal ride. In a rush of movement, between brush and trees, she glimpsed the horse. Trying to negotiate the impossible angle, the animal's hindquarters dragged the ground, its stiffened legs—desperate for purchase—troughing the earth, and sending dirt flying up along its flanks. Sweat glistened on its brown coat, and its mouth—drawn back deep into its wide chest—frothed from the effort.

Then she saw the rider, and took a shuddering breath. The man was Tom Spears! It was him! Just like her fictional story, told numerous times before, the protector…the Shadow…was here, coming down the slope to her rescue! Never before had she witnessed such an unselfish, gallant, effort…least of all from an adult.

Wide-eyed and awestruck, Maria's spirit soared, then just as swiftly faltered when she saw his looming peril.

Focused and grimacing, Tom was standing on the stirrups, leaning way back, and hauling desperately on the reins to maintain control. A low hanging branch whipped past his face, and then inexplicably, the horse leapt and they were airborne—airborne from halfway up the slope! Thoughts of rescue vanished, and her heart fluttered like a dying sparrow, as man and beast plunged from the sky. Then he was gone, dismounting just before the horse went down, and both disappeared into the brush-filled creek bed. Sounds of tumbling followed, sticks snapping, and something big hitting the ground hard, reverberating the earth.

Two quick shots rang out, and Maria's bloodied hand flew over her mouth.

A man screamed, followed by four more booming rounds. Then all was silent. Maria stared at the bushes, waiting, wide-eyed, and listening…too petrified to move…too petrified of the outcome…

*****

With his gun in his hand, Tom hit the ground hard, and rolled twice before making it to the bottom. Losing his hat, he blinked away the dirt from his eyes just as one of the men appeared in front of him. He had jumped out of the way of the charging horse, and rolled clear no more than ten feet away. Tom snapped off two shots in rapid succession to the man's chest. He was punched from his feet, and sent backward into the brush.

Changing his shooting position, Tom rolled once and pointed his gun in the direction he assumed the other man would be. Two shots rang from the undergrowth, peppering the ground Tom had just vacated. Then a head appeared between two low-lying bushes. Tom fired a single round to the man's forehead, the shot snapping his head back and pitching him backward into the undergrowth.

Unaware of the number of men left, Tom rolled to a knee, and swept his pistol back and forth, waiting for the next attack. None came.

"Tom?" Maria whispered in the distance, with an uncertain quiver in her voice.

"Still here," he said wearily. "You okay?"

She came loping through the brambles. Her face, bloodied and dripping in sweat, was pained in emotional aguish with facial muscles pulled taut in a frozen look of horror. Seeing Tom, she began crying in convulsive gasps and dropped to her knees, clinging to him, and squeezing with all her remaining strength.

Tom hugged her. That strength, that fortitude, that emotional glue, that had held her together for so long, finally took a back seat, and she was once again—even briefly—a vulnerable fourteen year-old-girl.

Overwhelmed, and happy that she was safe, Tom looked up at the heavens. *Thank you.*

Chapter 38

RAMON RAMIREZ STARED AT THE smoldering cabin, the coals shimmering and glowing in the night, and made no effort to conceal his rage to the men putting it out around him. Six of his security force had been killed, including Sanchez, his second in command; shot down while trying to put the fire out.

Questions buzzed in Ramon's brain like swarming bees, the answers few and far between, fleeting, and nagging his ever thought. Why attack a hash station? What was the point? His gaze dropped to Sanchez in front of the cabin, his body lying where he'd fallen, the fire extinguisher still in his hand. Nester, the hash maker was lying next to him. Had this been about killing his force, culling the numbers? Then there were the other two men found in the dry creek bed along the northwest boundary. Was this part of a coordinated attack? Seemed probable. A horse had been used there, and his men had tracked it, losing the trail two miles west along the Trout River. But it had been dark, tracking by flashlight, and he hoped they could pick up the trail again in the morning. He thought about the man responsible.

Spears!

In no time at all, the man had become a thorn in his side. Making it worse, now he was working with the children. At least that's the way it appeared by the small footprints leading from the steam in back of the cooking tent to the creek bed. The thought made him even angrier.

For four years he and his men had been hunting the youngsters, thinning their numbers to just a handful. But still they remained, and it hung over him like a black ominous cloud.

Four years! How is that even possible against armed men in this rugged terrain?

Maria was the key. Had they been able to kill her sooner, none of this would be happening now, no one the wiser as to the change of circumstances in the fields. Whether it was underestimating her, or the lack of general knowledge, it had grown into an assembly of errors. 'Camp night,' four years ago, had been the first. It was a term—a monthly activity to separate the children from adults—nobody on the attacking force had been aware of at the time, including him. That had been a huge mistake. Then, after learning of their blunder, the attack on the children's cabin the very next day had been the second miscue. Instead of wiping them out, all evidence of the fields' takeover removed, Maria had found a way to escape, taking with her the handful of children who they continued to search for to this day.

Maria—the daughter of a whore—leading a band of misfits. It was almost laughable, but he wasn't laughing. Eight grow fields at the time, and eight different cabins with children sent away for camp night, and only one had survivors by the following day. The biggest error however, had occurred a month ago, when Maria had been allowed to sneak into camp—into one of the troop tents no less—to steal an officer's cellphone. That's when the real damage had occurred.

The guile of that little bitch!

A crackdown of all cellphones, regardless of network limitations, had occurred after the incident, but the harm had already been done. He touched the sat phone clipped to his waist. It was the only practical method of communication in the desolate mountainous region, and he carried the only one allowed at any of the fields.

A low ring tone came from it, and he answered it. "Yeah."

"I need an update."

It was Rick Motese, their main man inside the Manatone syndicate. His insight had been a major key in the Tapito cartel's ability to pull off the takeover of the fields. Without him it would never have happened. However, he was merely a pawn, and Ramon took objection to his current tone. "First off, I don't report to you. Mind your place," he snarled. "And so we're clear, that place is under my boot. Now what do you want?"

There was a pause, and a notable tremor in his voice. "I need to know…" A nervous breath followed. "I was hoping, you could tell me of your progress with Spears. Mike Grevo has launched a full blown investigation into my activities. He's trying to keep it quiet but I have friends, and I don't like what I'm hearing."

"The Spears issue," Ramon answered, "will be resolved tomorrow morning; the children soon after that."

"Good. I'm running out of excuses. In fact, I'm planning to get out of town tomorrow."

"Listen to me very clearly, Rick. I don't care if you're pissing yourself or shitting your pants, you aren't going anywhere. This will soon blow over. If you run…and rest assured, they will know you're running…they will come after you. And if that happens, *they* will be the least of your worries. Then you will no longer be of value to us, and I'll personally come for you myself."

A long silence followed, before Ramon continued. "Now what is the progress of the men coming here?"

Rick cleared his throat. "They will arrive by tomorrow night. Ten heavily armed men. They're expecting trouble."

"Of course their expecting trouble," Ramon snapped. "Tony Manatone, the man responsible for killing the New York crime boss, is here, and so is the assassin known as the Shadow. But no matter. Tony and Spears will be found dead by those *heavily armed men* before they get here. Now quit acting like a little bitch, and do what you've been paid handsomely to do!" He disconnected the call.

Taking a slow calming breath, his thoughts returned to Tom Spears and where to go from here.

The loss of six men was only a setback, he told himself. *True, it brought their numbers down to twenty seven, but that was more than enough to deal with the problem.*

His men doused the last of the coals with fire extinguishers. They had been lucky. It could've been much worse, including the burning of the field or the camo net above. Fortunately, the propane tanks to the oven had been empty, and as for the building, the roof was still intact, and aside from the expensive loss of product, only one wall was damaged. But now what? In their search of the creek bed, his men had also found a slice of bread from the cook tent, which was obviously dropped by whoever made the small footprints. Was this about food? How could that be? Spears had raided the supply tent before leaving the first time.

His radio crackled to life. "Ramon, you there?" It was Spears.

Ramon gritted his teeth, and grabbed the radio from his belt. "I thought we had an understanding?"

"Ramon, Ramon, Ramon, I've been to the prearranged meeting place, and I counted more than thirty footprints," Tom Spears replied. "So don't tell me about understandings. I know a snake when I meet one."

"You got that right, Mr. Spears. I am a snake, from a host of snakes, deadly, without forgiveness, and this cat and mouse game you're playing only ends one way."

"Give me Tony Manatone, and the game ends right now. You go your way, and I go mine."

The signal was breaking up, so Ramon could assume he was nowhere in the vicinity. His hand trembled, but he still needed to draw Spears out to kill him. "This is what we're going to do," he began smoothly. "You are going to meet me, like you said, at the meadow south of here tomorrow morning. And let this be a warning to you. If you no-show again, I'm going to have Tony Manatone transported out of here. He'll be taken to a place of my choosing, and surrounded with armed personnel. Then I'll just wait for you to show." He grinned. "And you'll show. Your dead wife guarantees it." The jab gave Ramon pleasure. "Then there's those fucking kids. If you no show, I promise you, I'll bring in an army to find them, and slaughter them one at a time, saving sweet Maria for last." There was a long pause, so Ramon continued the pressure. "Sunrise is at seven. If you're not there by seven-fifteen, everything is off the table." He terminated the connection, not waiting for a response.

Tomorrow this ends! He would take Spears alive, learn where the children were, and then cut him into tiny pieces, a part at a time, saving his heart for last.

Chapter 39

TOM FINISHED SADDLING THE MARE outside the fissure entrance. Riding the gelding was out of the question. The gallant horse was going to need some time to mend. After finding the animal along the creek bed, Tom had carefully gone over its injuries. At first, he hadn't been optimistic. Covered in dirt, the animal was traumatized, shaking, with a bad front leg and bleeding from a gash on its chest. The horse also had a swollen right eye, and these were just the injuries he could see. But at least the animal had been able to walk.

To get away, and stay clear of Ramon's forces returning from the southern meadow, they had headed west in the dark, walking the limping animal two miles to the Trout River. Then they had turned north, using the water to cover their tracks. A half a mile later they had exited the freezing water onto a rocky shoal, which continued upward into a shale ridgeline. Only when they were certain they couldn't be followed, did they finally turn back west, arriving back at the cave at two in the morning.

Now, two hours later, Maria stood behind him with her arms crossed, and there was no hiding the concern in her tired blue eyes. "How will you know if they ate the soup?"

As Tom finished cinching the belly strap, the moon came out from behind the dark clouds, bathing the scene in silver light. "I won't until sunrise. We can only hope."

There was a palpable feeling of tension in the air. It had taken most of the night for Maria's emotional trauma to subside, and she was far from herself even now. "Well, what if it didn't work? What if there are thirty men waiting for you?"

Tom's head dropped, and he leaned on the horse. He wanted to reassure her, but like he said earlier, this was war and there were no assurances in war. "This confrontation was inevitable. Do I wish I had better numbers? Yes. Would it change the outcome? Who knows. Futility is born on 'what ifs', and I can only go with the cards that are dealt me." He picked up the M1 carbine that was leaning on a rock and slid it in the scabbard. "When I left the Manatone farm a week ago to come here, Myra had warned me only trees, valley, and endless wilderness lay ahead of me. But she was wrong. I've learned there was much more. It came in the form of children…special children…with an unbending will to survive." Tom nodded, his gaze remaining down. "You've done yourself proud, little girl."

She turned away as well, her words crackling with emotion. "It's my world. I've learned nothing in this life comes easy. There's wicked men that God don't kill, and there's good men—like you—who die out of their time. But I know that's just life; it don't come with promises. If you want something, then you have to be willing to fight for it. I've also learned you don't give ground, and you don't complain and whine. You take your knocks and get on with living. These are the rules of how we survive."

"You speak of a code?" Tom asked.

"Yes," she replied, turning, "that's it…a code. We don't learn much out here without parents or even a role model—a person to guide us in what is right and wrong, just or unjust. So we make it up as we go. If we are hunted we hide. If they find us we run. If they kill, we…" her voice trailed off.

Tom looked at her over his shoulder. His expression was neutral, but his heart was breaking. He knew all about killing, and the weight was almost too much to bear. And yet, this fourteen-year-old talked about being hunted, running for her life, and killing as if it were an everyday, normal occurrence—the way of the world. Her eyes were pooling and Tom forced himself to look away. She looked sad, but there was more strength in this little girl than in most adults. She had talked earlier of the dead children as failings. But Tom now knew what she had been up against, surviving in the mountains, with little food, without shelter, and hunted by armed men. It boggled the mind and also reaffirmed her inner strength. Then there were the other children. All under ten, and suddenly the survivability was multiplied by a hundred. He also knew it was she who had notified the Manatones about the fields being taken over. How she had managed that monumental feat was anyone's guess, but there was little doubt it had been her.

He nodded with approval, and repeated her words again in his mind. *Yes, I live by a code.* The thought warmed his heart. Whenever possible, he too lived by a code. "Yesterday, you asked who I am." He sighed, his words seldom ever said, but coming easily. "I'm no saint, but I'm not evil either. I don't cheat, lie, or kill, unless it's warranted, which brings us full circle back to what I said earlier about right and wrong. Many don't know the difference between the two or just don't care. Does this make my side the winner in war? Not a chance. Do I have faith in some heavenly power? Again, not a chance. There are too many wrongs in this world for me to be a believer. But I'm not naïve either, and to each their own. I don't happen to need a divine power, or some religious words in a book to stay on the righteous path. Nor do I have to make excuses like the many parents who raised thugs, and criminals, then act all high and mighty when their child is deservedly killed. The fact is, at that point, the only thing they're after is money. But that's a debate for another day." He looked her in the eye. "You're right, when you said you didn't ask for my help. But as you can see, you got me." He nodded. "I'll return later or I won't. But if not, you can know with certainty that I tried." He held out his hand, and she took it. "It's been my honor Maria to have known you."

At the fissure entrance. Jody, Ricky, Tara, Kate, and Bridget were all up, standing there in the early morning darkness. "Is Tom leaving?" Tara asked Jody, her hair disheveled from sleep. They were huddled together, like family, and watching him, wide-eyed with sadness and certain.

Tom looked at them proudly. How far they had come in the last few days. No longer were their clothes threadbare, and their faces smeared in dirt. Nor was there the look of desperation from lack of food. They were children once more with a semblance of normalcy.

He was also reminded that they were the reason he couldn't fail; their destiny and his inevitably linked. It could be no clearer than that. His heart began to ache, and he forced himself to look away. He gazed at Maria. To him, she and the children were a link to his past. They represented both the little brown eyed girl—Tanya's daughter—who he couldn't save, and also the other children—imprisoned in shipping containers—who were swept from the deck of the *San Paulo* in a hurricane. It had plagued his dreams since that fateful day, a tormenting picture that still ripped at his very being. Even now, the graphic images left his soul haunted and his heart filled with pain. And then there was the loss of his infant daughter…

He couldn't save any of them then, he thought, *but now, in some way, he would make things right, or die trying.*

He stepped into the saddle. "If I haven't returned by noon, I won't be returning at all. In that case, I want you to retrieve the mare. She'll be on the west side of the bluff that overlooks the southern meadow where I'm to meet Ramon. Then I want you to load both horses with all the supplies I've left you, and head toward the Manatone's farm." He removed the map that Myra had given him and handed it to her. "Follow this as best you can. Just stick to the valley heading south. It will take a couple days, but if you get lost—as per Myra's own words—just give the horses free rein and they will take you there." He glared at her to make his point clear. "This place…the cave…is no longer safe, Maria. Not even for a day. Leave by tomorrow night. Understand?"

She nodded, biting her lower lip to keep her emotions in check.

"One more thing. I suspect the Manatone's have men coming from the farm that will be here by tonight or, at the very least, the following day. They are coming here for both me and Tony Manatone. Don't engage them. In fact, avoid them. I have no idea what to expect from them in regards to you. Again, you understand?"

She nodded again.

He swung his horse around, and disappeared into the forest.

Chapter 40
Showdown

ORE COMFORTABLE RIDING AT NIGHT, Tom had arrived at the meeting place before six in the morning. After leaving the horse on the other side of the western bluff like he had told Maria, he'd cased the perimeter of the meadow a half-hour later. This was important considering he had lied to Ramon about seeing more than thirty footprints there. In fact, he hadn't come here at all, aside from looking at it through the rifle scope that previous morning—long before Ramon and his men had arrived that evening.

Now sitting on a log at the north end of the grassy field he waited, the M1 leaning nearby. Daybreak had arrived, and the sky was bathed in gold, the few clouds drenched in reds and yellows at the base, and glowing charcoal at the crown. The air was fresh and clean, and a slight breeze whispered along the treetops.

Removing his hat and setting it on the log, he stood and leaned against the trunk of a tall fir tree. The time now was seven-fifteen, and Ramon was running late. He looked through the binoculars hung from his neck. Strategically speaking, the easiest access points were from the north, or through a flat forest of the valley to the east. Any other access points got dicey at best, including the rocky ridgeline behind him and the bluff to his right where he'd been the previous morning. Both would make good perches for long-distance shooting, but almost impossible to descend from. This was both good and bad: good because Ramon's men weren't going to magically appear behind him, but bad if they indeed had a long rifle of their own like Tom's Weatherby, which he doubted. But that was only a guess…a roll of the dice…a crap shoot at best. In the end he was only one man, and could only cover so many variables.

Engine sounds echoed up the valley, coming from across the wide meadow. These were the quads Maria had told him that Ramon used. He scanned the southern slope of the meadow. Up to now, the only sign of life had been a big raccoon that had come to investigate soon after he sat down, and a distant wolf howl that Tom found to be both pleasing and intimidating at the same time.

He took a deep slow breath. Now was the moment of truth. How many of Ramon's men…if any…had been affected by the mushrooms? He would soon find out.

Over the waist-high meadow grass, heads appeared, then four quads, green with winches mounted on the fronts. They stopped a hundred yards away at the southern edge of meadow. Tom counted the men as they turned off their machines, and dismounted. Each ATV carried three armed men, which brought the number to twelve so far. It was a far cry from thirty, but who knew how many men were beyond his field of vision.

A rider on a black steed arrived.

Tony Manatone's horse.

Tom focused on the rider. This would be Ramon. Like he expected, the Mexican cartel man was in camo fatigues and hat. He dismounted and tied the horse to a tree. Where was Tony? Tom refocused on the quads. One man remained sitting in the rear storage rack, his head tilted down and unmoving. He had black hair like Tony Manatone, but Tom didn't have a clear view from this distance.

"Spears," Ramon said over the radio.

Tom didn't respond, but continued watching. Ramon wasn't visible anymore, but his men were obviously looking at him, and none had moved very far…not even to establish a defensive picket line. That was good to see, and told Tom plenty. By staying huddled together, they were either untrained, or believed they were in complete control of the situation, or both. Tom also noticed no one was looking toward the western bluff, or the high ground above Tom's position either. This was good news too, confirming they hadn't sent men around the backside. If they had, they would've been in constant communication, and more than likely, continually looking in that direction…at least that's what Tom reasoned. Another good sign, no more heads appeared—the number remaining at twelve.

"Spears!" Ramon said again, his tone agitated. "You here?"

Tom picked up his radio, but continued to wait and watch. When Ramon appeared at the edge of the grass, Tom finally answered, his words flat and direct. "Tony Manatone. You bring him?"

Tom watched Ramon step over to the black-haired man still on the quad. "He's here. Now come and get him."

This was the part of the plan…where there was no plan. Tom had no way of knowing the strength of Ramon's force. Even twelve was too many without the element of surprise, which he no longer had. He glanced back over his shoulder again, seeking another alternative. There was none. The only way he could potentially survive this was if he remained under cover. If he went into the field he had no chance.

"Bring him to me," Tom countered. "Just you with him."

Ramon laughed in the radio. "I'll deliver him with my men…all of my men. Now where are you?"

Did Ramon just make a slip? He said "all of his men." Was twelve the extent of his force? It bettered the odds, but he still couldn't go out in the open. He thought for a moment before speaking again. "I'm looking at you through the crosshairs of my rifle. Now do like you're told and bring Tony to the middle of the field, or I'll put a bullet through that hatted skull of yours."

Tom watched Ramon shield his eyes and look toward the western bluff, while his men crouched defensively, disappearing from sight. Ramon laughed defiantly again. "You lie. Besides, my shooters would make sure you wouldn't pull the trigger twice. That's not all. The rest of my men have already encircled your position." He chuckled. "Yes, I learned about your pitiful attempt to poison the soup. It was a nice try, and might've worked if Maria hadn't dropped a chunk of bread after leaving the tent. It was Maria right?"

Checkmate, Tom thought. *A lie for a lie.* In a last ditch effort to separate Ramon from his men, kill him, kill Tony Manatone, and then attempt to fight his untrained band while remaining under cover. Of course, he couldn't know what was truth or fiction, but the fact remained, he was still outgunned at least twelve to one, and completely vulnerable if he went into the open field.

"Of course if what you say is true," Ramon continued, raising his other arm in a defenseless gesture, "you could make me a liar and just shoot me. So go ahead! Let's do this. Then we'll kill you, and those wretched children."

At that moment Tom wished he had brought the Weatherby instead of leaving it in the cave. If he had it now, he would've killed the man on the spot, and then taken his chances with the remnants of his force… if it was a remnant force. It was an option he had eliminated earlier, but in a constantly changing scenario, it had been going against thirty men. Out of options, he finally responded. "Bring him to the south end of the field."

"We'll meet in the center," Ramon countered. "Everyone in the open."

"Out in the open it is then."

Tom watched Ramon smile with satisfaction, and then yell at his men to get to their feet. They entered the field in a group, then spread into a line. At the rear was Tony, being brought out on the quad. Tom reaffirmed the number, counting ten men, eleven with the quad driver, and twelve with Ramon, who was at the center.

So this was indeed Ramon's entire force.

The thought didn't give him much solace, but he reminded himself that Ramon probably wanted him alive to learn the location of the children. At least that's what he hoped, otherwise they might shoot him on sight.

Taking the binoculars off, and setting them on the log, Tom rechecked the loads of his pistols, and the extra magazines in the pockets of his long coat. He didn't have many tricks up his sleeve, except one: the two grenades. It was his only tactical advantage. He settled the hat on his head once more, picked up the semiautomatic rifle, and stepped into the field. A light breeze swept across the tall grass like a wave on an ocean, its green blades swaying and rolling as one before stillness set in once again. Above him to his left, the sun broke from the clouds, rising above the tree line, filling the field with bright radiant colors.

Tom glanced up, enjoying the warmth on his face.

Sadness touched him.

Tanya would've loved this, he thought. She loved the spring above all others, with its intrinsic melody of life, and growth, its chorale of birdsong, and richly colored flowers pushing back the winter weather. The air, too, was clean, and a man could drink it in like a sweet wine filling his lungs with the essence of life itself. He felt the claustrophobic tightening of his stomach muscles. It was at that moment, when he looked beyond his own emotional pain, that he knew his personal vow to avenge Tanya was now unattainable. "I'm sorry my love…" his throat constricted, "but it appears I won't be able to uphold my promise to you."

He thought about his words to Maria, and war, about right usually winning out over wrong. But it wasn't entirely true. What he had chosen not to add was that when two groups of men desire the same thing, the strongest will usually take what they want. That is the way of life; strength always decides.

Thinking of his past life, his heart welled with sadness, repeating his own words to himself, "I've learned a man doesn't choose his life, it's chosen for him." When he had said it, he didn't know…couldn't know…for sure it was true, but he did now. "This is who I am, and all I will ever be."

He continued forward, gazing out over the rippling grass. A hawk suddenly flew up to Tom's left. His eyes fastened to it, and as it disappeared over the treetops, he realized he'd instinctively clicked the safety off to his weapon. This brought the grim reality of the situation abruptly to the forefront. Like a sudden slap in the face, the mesmerizing surroundings were beautiful no more. He stopped, and stood defiantly with the rifle casually across his chest, focusing on the line of men who now stopped before him. They were no more than fifty paces away; the long waist high grass swaying in the breeze.

Still alive. So far so good.

"Tell me, Ramon," Tom spoke evenly, "do you believe the romance of life?"

Uncertain, Ramon's lingering smile faded and he gave a blank stare, his eyes flicking to the men at his flanks. But he didn't answer, so Tom continued, "You know, love stories like Guinevere and King Arthur, Tristan and Isolde, or even Romeo and Juliet?" Tom waited for a response. There was none, other than a few smirks. He shrugged. "I never used to believe in it, but I've seen it twice in my life, and unfortunately, both times it was taken from me…ripped from my life by people much like you." Tom could see the man was growing impatient, but Tom held up a finger for quiet and continued, "I tell you this because I have good reason to see each of you dead. You're here for money. Paid by the Mexican mob to keep the drug cash flowing, and kill all that stand in your way."

As Tom spoke, he systematically went down the line of men, sizing them up, including the threat level. Of the twelve before him: all had pistols, two men had bolt action rifles, and two had the M16 rifles. These were the men Tom would have to focus on or this fight would be over long before ever getting started; not that it got any better considering the number of weapons he was up against. By his calculations, to survive the initial onslaught, he would have to avoid at least twelve rounds with the real number being closer to twenty. And that was just at the beginning. The longer the fight, the less chance of survival. The good news was they didn't appear serious about his chances, and much like when he had walked into the tent, not one weapon was trained on him.

Which is good, Tom thought flatly, *or this firefight would have already begun.*

"Men like you are always the same," Tom continued. "Violence. Death. Destruction. It follows you like a plague. You are the political structure of what ails common decency." He casually lifted the M1 from across his chest and pointed it in the air, letting the butt rest against his hip. "Now I'm sure you're wondering how I can stand here in front of twelve armed men." His left hand was already in his left front coat pocket, along with a grenade. Gripping it tightly, he smoothly pulled the pin with his thumb.

He was ready.

Tom's eyes narrowed. "The fact is, someone has to do it, and it might as well be me."

Ramon took a step forward, pointing his finger. "I want those children. You think these are good odds for you?" He chuckled with confidence. "Everywhere I go in this wretched forest I seemed to hear your name. Whispers mainly. They call you the Shadow; the killer of men, the killer of killers." He smiled. "But I only see a man of flesh and blood. A man who can die like everyone else."

"Are you the man to attempt it?" Tom snarled. "Because I only see a rat of a man willing to hunt people…children…over scraps that aren't even his in the first place." He leaned in. "I can assure you of two things. One, I'm no child, and two, you are going to die in the next few seconds."

A shot rang out, booming and echoing through the valley, and Ramon sailed backward and to the left. Tom didn't know who the shooter was—poetic justice or not—but didn't hesitate, lobbing the grenade in the air at the scattering men with one hand, while leveling the M1 with the other. Shots now filled the air.

*****

After Tom left, Maria had gathered with Jody, Bridget, Ricky, Kate, and Tara. Their discussion had been simple and to the point. No one wanted to see Tom go, and although they didn't know if they could help, everyone had agreed they wanted to try. Of course, when Bridget went inside and reappeared carrying Tom's Weatherby, they had a definitive answer as to how they could assist.

Forty minutes later, they were following Tom and heading toward the northern meadow. However, with Jessy on the mend and still limping, they wouldn't have the luxury of a horse, and would have to pack everything in themselves. They had done just that: Maria had shouldered the rifle above her bandaged arm, and pocketed an extra pistol from Tom's arsenal. Tara, after giving Jessy a large pile of grain, had carried the two belts of ammunition for the Weatherby—crisscrossed like a bandito—across her chest. Ricky's job had been to carry the small backpack full of food and water, while Bridget, still weak from being sick, had done her part by carrying another pistol, and extra ammunition. Not to be left out, the soft spoken Kate was responsible for the medical kit, which was on her back; its straps looped over her slender arms. And filling out her responsibilities was carrying Teddy, who she tucked inside her oversized coat.

They had arrived before sunrise, finding Tom's mare, and then getting situated on the bluff between two towering pines. Now all six children were prone on the ground, gazing at the distant meadow. The morning was cool, smelled of pine, and they watched the sun come up, rising above the distant mountain peaks, making the sky glow in shimmering waves, red and orange like windblown coals. Then after a few minutes, a cloud bank moved in, and temporarily masked the radiant colors.

"How far do you think that is?" Kate asked. Lying next to Jody, she was on one end of the row of bodies.

"It's a long way's," Jody replied.

"Where's Tom?" Ricky asked holding up Tom's spare radio. "Maybe we should call him."

"No," Maria replied. "I don't know how he might react to us being here."

Lying to the left of Maria, next to Ricky, Tara asked, "So it's a surprise?"

"Yes, Little Bean," Maria whispered. "We hope to make it a good surprise." She was still familiarizing herself with the rifle, its barrel resting across a narrow log as she looked through the scope. The polished wood stock was cold and smooth against her cheek, the trigger grooved and cupped to align perfectly with the last joint of her index finger. She had never fired a rifle before, and she found it hard to believe a bullet could travel the distance she was looking at now.

"Hear that?" Bridget asked.

In the distance they heard the familiar sound of quads approaching. A chill ran through Maria. It was the sound usually accompanied by one of her friends dying. She rotated the barrel toward the far end of the meadow as the four quads appeared. They stopped along its grassy perimeter. She counted twelve men, including Ramon, who showed up on a black horse.

"Spears?" came Ramon's ominous voice over the radio.

Ricky set the handheld on the ground like it suddenly had leprosy, and all the children, including Maria stared it. Over the last four years, Ramon had become their worst nightmare, and even hearing his voice made Maria's skin crawl.

"Spears!" Ramon repeated, his tone more agitated. "You here?"

"Shoot him," Jody whispered to Maria. "Can you shoot him?"

"Yes, shoot him," Ricky joined in. "He deserves it."

Tom finally answered, but Maria's mind was preoccupied as soon as she looked through the scope again. She was looking at Ramon. He was standing on the edge of field and, almost like she was down there facing him herself, his form filled the lens. She rotated the dial on the scope, magnifying, to see the face that had haunted all their dreams these past years. The clarity was incredible. Never before had she seen the man up close.

Below the bill of his cap, he had a lean, hard face with an unyielding expression, and she could vividly see the scar that ran down his left cheek; chalk-white against the dark hair on his unshaven face. His eyes were sapphire, deep-set, and cruel. His nose was large, and hooked, and his lips formed a thin line as he talked back and forth to Tom.

Bridget now weighed in. "He said to shoot him, and I think you should. You really should."

It's true, Ramon was challenging Tom now with an arm raised.

Maria pulled the bolt back. "Hand me a bullet please." Tara removed one from her bandolier and handed it to her. Maria examined it briefly. Three inches long, the jacket was polished brass and felt smooth in her fingers. The leaded end was a coppery-color too, except for the very tip, which was grey and hollowed. It was the biggest bullet she had ever seen. She slipped it into the rifle and closed the breach.

"You really going to do it?" Ricky asked Maria.

She didn't have an answer. A better question might be, could she shoot him from this distance? She was a little nervous, but it seemed simple enough; put the crosshairs on his chest, hold the rifle tight, and squeeze the trigger.

The sky seemed to open up, and the sun broke through, sending bright rays across the green grass of the meadow, turning the valley a radiant gold.

"They're going into the field," Bridget announced.

"There's Tom," Jody added, pointing as he came out of the tree line; he and the other men looking like ants from this distance.

It was true. Looking through the scope, Tom brazenly walked into sight. He was wearing his hat and long coat, his long ponytail swaying as he walked defiantly through the waist high grass. In his arms, laid across his chest was a rifle. She blinked hard. Unbelieving, and filled with anguished concern, she watched Tom walk out to face twelve armed men. To any other man it was suicidal. "You may not have chosen this life, but it suits you, Tom Spears." Maria's praise was unabashed, her awe, overwhelming and resolute. "You *are* the Protector…the Shadow…a man of infinite courage." Her lower lip quivered with the grim outlook. "You never run, even when you should. It is I who have been honored to know *you*," she said with pride, sweeping the scope across the line of men, and Tom, standing alone against them. "You're a man of mettle…and I'm proud to call you my friend…"

"He's our friend, too," Jody admonished anxiously, lying prone at her side. "Just shoot someone, please!"

"Yes, shoot someone!" Ricky urged. "Or I'll do it."

Bridget giggled. "The gun's bigger than you are, Ricky."

Ricky's brow furrowed. "I'd still do it."

"And don't shoot Tom if you can help it," Tara added from the other side of Maria.

"You wouldn't shoot Tom, would you, Maria?" Kate asked, blinking away the welling in her blue eyes.

I hope not.

She took a slow breath, flipped off the safety, and drew the rifle in tight to her shoulder. Everyone in the meadow had now stopped. Words were said, but they were no longer talking on the radio.

Realizing what was about to happen—her face suddenly a flurry of concern—Tara turned to Maria and spoke in a quick shuddering breath, her words pleading, "Don't let him die, Maria. Please don't let him die." Then her words turned frantic. "Just kill them! Kill them all!"

After everything they had been through, the years on the run, cold and hungry, and men constantly hunting them, those were the first angry words Maria had ever heard Tara say.

She put the crosshairs high on Ramon's chest, and pulled the trigger.

*****

Tom rolled again, this time left. The initial onslaught had been furious, even with the grenade exploding amongst them. After Ramon had gone down, most of the men had dropped to the ground, but not before Tom snapped off two shots with the M1 rifle, killing both men holding the M16's. Another man had died in the exchange of bullets sweeping through the grass as Tom went to the ground and continued to fire. Then the grenade had exploded. At only twenty paces away, he felt the concussive wave down to his very bones. A scream followed, and along with grass and flying debris, Tom watched a man lifted off the ground and cartwheeled through the air.

He still didn't know who the sniper was, but that was a moot point at the moment. Bullets seemed to be everywhere, and the once peaceful meadow had turned into a war zone; the booming gunshots echoing through the valley and to the surrounding mountaintops.

Tom pulled the pin on his last grenade, and threw it in an area of concentrated fire. More screams could be heard after the deafening explosion. When the dust settled, the concentrated fire had changed to a trickle, sporadic at best. The odds had improved significantly. He figured with Ramon dead, the original number of twelve men, had dropped to five. But the bullets continued to whiz by, steady and furious, from at least four positions.

In his will to survive, everything became a blur of movement; his hands aiming the rifle and pulling the trigger, his body continuously rolling left and right. When the rifle was empty, he smoothly ejected the magazine, slid another in place, and snapped the bolt back to reload the chamber; the process taking less than three seconds.

Now lying on his back, head to the ground, he fired blindly as more bullets cropped the grass six inches over his head. Then he recognized the rhythmic sound of the M16. Someone had picked one up, and the three round burst was both frightening and disheartening. Worse yet, it would keep him pinned.

They will come now, he thought with dread.

And they did.

Movement to his left had him rolling to his right, and pain shot through his upraised shoulder as he swept it through the sweeping line of bullets. At the same time, the ground exploded around him when two men charged in, shooting their semi-automatic pistols. Tom rolled twice, a bullet passing through his upper thigh, before coming to an abrupt stop when his side went up against an old log—the vestiges of a fallen tree, decades ago.

The two men came forward in a rush. Screaming and shooting, they were now no more than ten feet away. A bullet struck Tom's left arm, the impact throwing it awkwardly off to the side. Another booming sound came from the sniper, and the first man's shoulder exploded in a grisly manor, the impact corkscrewing him to the ground.

Lifting the M1 with his good arm, Tom fired the rifle's last two remaining bullets at point blank range into the second man. The first bullet struck above the left breast, and the second through his throat, dropping the attacker in a spray of blood.

For a moment, it got noticeably quieter when the M16 operator was forced to reload.

No more than three men left, he thought, dropping the empty M1, and pulling the Kimber 9mm from his shoulder holster. Tom heard the metallic sound of a bolt snapping shut, then the M16 opened up again, and more bullets peppered the rotted log, the damp wood disintegrating under the constant barrage.

Pressing himself into the ground, the half-buried log was a scant three inches above his body—a depth that was being whittled away at an incredible rate. Wood chips exploded, leaping into the air like angry hornets, and the musty smell of rotted timber and cordite filled the air. He turned his head and closed his eyes as flying debris covered his face. A bullet whizzed by his ear, and above the drumming shots in the valley, another thunderous round could be heard from the sniper. But it did little to quell the deadly pulsing sound of the M16.

Wait! he thought, listening for his next chance…his only chance. *Even an extended magazine had to be reloaded at some point.*

The M16 drew closer. Then Tom heard the audible click of a firing pin landing on an empty chamber and the gun went silent again.

Now!

He stole a quick look and saw the man no more than fifteen feet away, his head down, changing the magazine. Tom sat up and fired. The man was punched from his feet, the M16 flying from his hands and pirouetting into the tall grass. A stirring at Tom's feet had him looking at the man with the mutilated shoulder. The attacker was attempting to roll onto his stomach, and Tom shot him in the back of the head.

Levering himself to a knee, Tom blinked away the debris and the warm flow of blood that ran down his forehead and into his eyes. His hat was gone, and using the heel of his gun hand, he wiped his brow. His hand came away smeared red…lots of red. A bullet had creased his head. It was the first time he was cognizant of any injuries. Feeling noticeably dizzy, he looked down. A steady flow of blood ran down the front of his coat, and his left pant leg was saturated from the gaping hole on his outer thigh; the rapid flow already puddling under his left leg.

He was losing a lot of blood.

His instinct was to wrap it, to stem the bleeding, but time became a factor. First and foremost, there were still at least two men left that he had to deal with. So for the moment, any injuries, life threatening or not, would have to wait. At least for now, he could still function; the pain masked behind the shock and numbness associated with sudden injuries. But soon that would wear off, and like multiple rocks thrown into a flat lake, the pain would ripple through his body.

As he rose to his feet, his left knee almost buckled, but the thigh-pain remained dull and disjointed. His injured left arm was no longer of use. It was immobile and straight down at his side with more blood rolling off the end of his numbed fingers.

He focused on his right hand and swept the pistol cautiously before him. All was quiet. In front of him, in the distance was the quad. It was facing forward, and Tony's back was to him, his head remaining down.

Tom's gaze floated over the tall grass. It had become a maze of flattened trails from running and diving men—two of which he knew still remained. But where were they? One man, the driver, had been near the quad when the shooting had started, and considering any cover in a firefight was a commodity in the open field, he focused his attention there.

As he stepped awkwardly over the lifesaving log, he noticed the front side of it was bowled, eaten away, like the work of an enthusiastic beaver, and wood chips littered the ground. He had been lucky. Any longer, and playing hide-n-seek with a barrage of bullets would've ended badly. One more barrage from the M16 was all that was needed to cut it in two.

A man burst from cover to his right, and Tom raised his gun. Like a panicked quail flushed into flight, he ran away as fast as he could, but it wasn't fast enough. Tom fired twice pitching the man forward without further movement.

Tom continued forward, a hobbling gait, a step at a time. As he approached the quad, the last man stood with raised hands, his face a mask of terror. He pitched his pistol to the side like it suddenly scalded him. "Please…" he pleaded.

His plea went unanswered. There would be no compromise, and Tom didn't hesitate, firing a single shot to his forehead. The man's body jerked once and then fell backward like a felled tree.

The killers of children now ceased to exist.

Feeling light headed, Tom stood there for a moment with a startling reality. *All gone, and yet I'm still here.* The thought was almost comical, considering the odds that were stacked against him.

Dizziness threatened to swamp him as he stepped to the rear of the quad. Finally, after weeks of bone weary travel across the country, the lies uncovered, and the continuous killing from New York to here…he could face the killer of his wife and friends.

Strapped to the luggage rack, Tony was sitting in a legless wooden chair. It was the only reason he remained upright. He was wearing what appeared to be a blanket, cut out, pancho-style, with a hole for his head. "I suspected they were in over their heads," Tony mumbled, lifting his battered head. "But considering their hospitality toward me, who was I to warn them." He tried to smile, but there were no teeth, and his bloody engorged lips barely moved beyond a slight crease at the corners of his mouth.

The damage inflicted to his body was horrendous. Nearing death, his skin was pasty white, his eyes swollen, hollowed, and withdrawn. Dried blood covered his face, arms and legs where deep punctures could be seen along both thighs. His left kneecap had been crushed, and both feet were missing, having been crudely lopped away; the legs tied off above both ankles with tourniquets. Excessive dried blood was also on the lower blanket around his crotch area.

All things considered, the sight pleased Tom.

Tony looked nothing like the brash prick he had come to know. Before him now was a beaten person, physically and emotionally; no cockiness left for a man who was once destined to be the next crime boss of the biggest cartel in the United States.

"Torture seems fitting to me," Tom said. "When I learned you were behind the killing of my wife and friends, I wasn't surprised. You've always been a worthless fuck." Tom widened his stance to keep from falling over, and raised his pistol. "This is for Mike and Micky…and my wife."

Tony's head lolled forward, red drool passing his swollen lips. "I didn't kill your wife…"

"I don't want to hear it. You left me with nothing. So I want nothing. I'm content in watching you die."

"You are just as evil," he snarled with one last gasp of contrition.

Tom leaned in close, his forehead resting on Tony's shoulder, and the pistol barrel pressed into Tony's chest over his heart. "I guess that would depend on your definition of evil," Tom responded in a callous tone. "You, however, saw to it that my wife was killed, and that's all that matters. Good bye, Little Mouse." He pulled the trigger, the sound barely audible as Tony's body jerked once, and then stilled.

Tom stepped back. "It is done," he whispered.

His tired heart was palpitating irregularly now, and his eyes fluttered as the pain suddenly came in waves, battering his ability to stay conscious like a boxer before hitting the canvas. With no fight left in him, his vengeance done, and little need to carry on, he dropped to his knees, and let himself go…needing to let himself go. "I'm coming…my wife…" Deliriousness swamped him, and all sense of weight left him, and his mind tumbled like a windblown feather into a darkened storm. Closing his eyes, he swayed twice, then fell forward to the ground. His last passing thought was of Tanya…his wife…

*****

"Good shot!" Ricky exclaimed triumphantly, in boyish wonder. "You got him!"

Maria looked through the scope again. The first booming shot from the rifle had caught everyone by surprise, making them jump and their ears ring. It was a deep echoing sound and, like a kick from a horse, the jolt into her shoulder had been intense. But to her surprise, she had hit Ramon in the chest, throwing him backward where he remained down.

The horrific gunshots followed, multiple booming sounds. There was even a thunderous explosion. At first Maria was frozen, gripped in fear and terror for Tom. Then Tara's screaming voice broke her from of her spell. Fearful for Tom's safety, she was yelling again, "Shoot them! Keep shooting them!" She was no longer at Maria's side. Covering her ears from the booming sound of the rifle, and the rumbling gunfire below, she had moved back to Maria's feet; her tears streaming down her face.

Another explosion, amongst the multitude of gunshots, ripped through the valley.

Bridget was the first to move, grabbing another bullet from Tara's bandolier. She tapped Maria's shoulder. "You heard her," she said unsympathetically, "kill them all."

A wispy puff of smoke lifted from the breach when Maria drew the bolt back, ejecting the empty cartridge and replacing it with the new round. Slamming the bolt back in place, she looked through the scope again, settling the stock against her cheek; the wood no longer cold but heated and slick against her sweaty skin. The scene below was chaotic, and the fresh morning air now filled with the acidic smell of burnt gunpowder. Through the haze that had settled over the field from all the shooting, she could see some men were dead, while others were either shooting from prone positions or cautiously moving in on Tom's location.

Alarm touched her, and dread showed on her tight drawn face.

Tom was down, but she could see his movements in the grass and two men were charging him. Her hands were shaking now as she aimed at the closest man to Tom. Adding to the difficulty, and unlike Ramon, this man was moving. But at least it wasn't left to right. He was coming in her direction; head on. She fired again, the rifle bucking in her hands, and another thunderous blast was sent through the valley. The man went down, and this time she didn't hesitate, ejecting the shell, and taking another cartridge from Bridget, who was already organizing a row of bullets on the ground in front of her.

Ricky punched the air. "Another one down. Good shot, Maria!"

Jody took both Kate and Tara lower on the hill and away from the ear-piecing sound.

Maria reloaded and sighted again. The tall grass had been flattened, and Tom was now visible. Up against a log, he had already killed the second charging attacker. Now he was pinned down by yet another man who had what appeared to be a machinegun—its drumming sound echoing like a sputtering chainsaw. Even from this distance, she could see it was carving Tom's log to pieces. She quickly aimed, and fired, missing behind him as he stepped to her left and forward toward Tom.

"You missed," Ricky shrieked, "Reload, reload, hurry up…reload!"

The beat of the machinegun stopped, and after Maria's panicked hands reloaded, she looked through the scope in time to see Tom pop up and shoot the man.

Then the field went eerily quiet, and Maria felt the first twinge of optimism…of hope.

"Are there any left?" Jody asked, laying back down near Maria. "Is Tom okay?"

Maria swept the meadow with the scope, looking for targets.

A shot rang out.

Anxiety turned to relief, when she refocused on Tom, who had just killed a man at his feet. Leaning heavily on the log, she watched him stand and step over it. His back was to her but he seemed unsteady, his movements awkward.

As he moved forward, a man appeared and Tom shot him in the back as he tried to run away. Another man died seconds later when he stood near the quad. Again, the meadow went silent.

He continued his ungainly stride to the back of the quad, and turned toward her, facing the man sitting in the luggage rack. Then, like the constricting anxiety of an avalanche, her hope wavered, leaving her with no time to breathe. She swallowed hard, a stabbing pain in her heart. For the first time, she glimpsed Tom's injuries. Blood! Lots of blood! It flowed down his face, and down the front of his long coat; the dark crimson shimmering under the morning sun.

No. Please, no!

Tom Spears…her friend…was in dire trouble, and any previous optimism vanished like warmth in a winter gale. His face was sheet white, and blood poured from the top of his head, saturating his hair and down his neck. Two more wounds were visible along his left arm: one at the shoulder, and another below the elbow. More injuries were hidden under his coat that was shredded with multiple holes in it.

Keeping her composure, she turned to Kate, who still had the medical kit strapped to her back. "You're up little one. We need to get that medical kit down there right now." She got everyone up and moving.

Time was a factor. So after sending Kate, Jody, Bridget, and Tara back to get the horse, Maria and Ricky took the medical kit, traversed the front of the bluff, and entered the meadow below. But even at a dead run, getting to Tom had taken the better part of fifteen minutes. When they arrived, their chests were heaving, and sweat gleamed from their brows.

The meadow was a gruesome sight, with dead men and blood everywhere. But they ignored the grisly scene and moved to Tom's side. He was face down in the grass and unmoving. She took the medical kit off her back and handed it to Ricky. "Open this, while I roll him over." As Maria knelt by Tom, she prayed like never before, hoping he wasn't dead. Rolling him over, her heart sank. He looked more dead than alive—his injuries worse up close.

"Is he dead?" Ricky blurted out, choking back his tears in his big brown unblinking eyes.

She didn't know, but it didn't look good. The front of his coat was now open, and besides the wound to his head and the two to his left arm, two separate bullets had grazed his sides—one below the ribcage, and another near the hip—with yet another hole in his upper left thigh.

She tried not to get overwhelmed with panic. First she needed to know if he was actually alive. Leaning over him, she put a hand over his heart, and a cheek near his lips. "He's alive!"

"Don't let him be dead, Maria," Ricky pleaded.

"I'll do my best," she answered. "But I'm going to need your help. Okay?" She pointed at the medical kit. "You remember what Tom did for Bridget? We are going to clean the wounds with alcohol and wrap them. Then…" She took a deep shuddering breath, her heart fluttering with apprehension. "If he's still alive, I think we need to counter the blood loss with an IV. It's the only thing I can think of without doing some sort of transfusion…" *Which she had no idea how to do.* "You understand?"

He already had the med-kit open. "Yes, I'm not a child."

Maria smirked. "No, you're not. Thank you. We'll start with the shoulder and thigh first. They're bleeding the worst."

By the time Kate, Jody, Bridget, and Tara showed up with the horse, both the shoulder and thigh had been cleaned and wrapped, and Maria was cleaning the head wound, while Ricky finished wrapping Tom's lower arm.

"He's alive," she said as the four gathered around, "but we have to work to keep him that way." To limit the ensuing questions she knew she couldn't answer, she barked out orders. "Bridget take out your pistol and keep lookout for us. We don't know how many are left. If anything moves, flip the safety off and shoot!"

Taking out the pistol from her coat pocket, Bridget nodded, stepped a few feet away, and cautiously swept the weapon left and right in front of her.

"Jody, we're almost out of gauze, so I want you, Tara, and Kate to start stripping Tom's coat for bandages." She pointed at the scissors in the medical kit. "You can use those."

For the next few minutes no one spoke, each in anguished torment, and Maria completely understood. The man on the ground before them had stepped into their lives from out of nowhere. A caring, courageous man, who had helped them when no one else would, and never asked once for anything in return. He was man without pause, even to fight the evil that had hounded her and the children for several years. Now he was hurt real bad. Would he die? She couldn't know, but she did know that each of them were asking that very same question right now.

She finished cleaning the three-inch-long bullet wound across the top of Tom's skull. The trough wasn't very deep, running sideways, ear to ear, but she still had to stitch it. While she did, she glanced at Tara. The five-year-old had been particularly smitten with Tom, and continuous tears streaked down her cheeks. Kate, sitting next her, wasn't much better, her lower lip quivered, and her sniffles reminded everyone what was at stake. Even Ricky and Bridget weren't immune in their affection toward him. In fact, there wasn't a dry eye amongst them, even Maria, who had been crying the entire time.

Finished with the sutures, she dried her cheeks with a bloody sleeve, and went to work on the injuries to his sides, while Ricky took care of the IV all by himself. Thirty minutes later, she finished cleaning, stitching, and applying the compress bandages to his sides. "That's it." She looked at her handiwork. It wasn't pretty, but all the bleeding had been stopped, and Ricky held the IV bag full of water. More importantly, Tom was still alive.

Maria looked at Kate curiously.

Having Tom's flannel shirt open, and his bare chest exposed, Kate was leaning over him with a furrowed brow, touching an old wound—a cratered scar just above one of his compress bandages. "He gets shot a lot, doesn't he?" Although her words were sad, and she couldn't have been more sincere, it lightened the atmosphere and everyone laughed, long and hard, out loud, and as a group. A warm feeling washed over them, and their anguished, forlorn, spell was broken, washed away like a cleansing rain.

"You all look like Indians," Bridget said with a grin, standing over them and looking at their blood painted faces. "Laughing Indians."

Another round of laughter followed. It was good for Maria to see, and even the blood on everyone but Bridget, seemed less scary. Maria's gaze swept past them at the vast field. Not even the morbid reality surrounding them, the death they had seen this day, and days past, mattered. Was it possible they no longer needed to run? Was it over, their daily lives less daunting—less intimidating?

Tom moved slightly, and just like that, they went from happy laughter to happy tears.

Maria got serious. "All right, this is what needs to happen today. Tom said men from the Manatone's farm will be here by tonight. That means we need to get moving. We can't know what to expect from them, but they will kill Tom, so I think it's best that we avoid them. Agreed?"

They all nodded.

"So that means," she continued, "we have the rest of the day to get Tom loaded, get to the cave, and get out of here before they arrive." She pointed to the man she assumed was Tony Manatone. He was still on the chair in the luggage rack of the ATV. It was a grisly sight, but they had seen plenty of that over the years, and no one even flinched. "I think we should untie that man, put Tom in the chair instead, and make use of their quads."

"Yeah, heck yeah," Ricky said with a boyish grin. "I want one all by myself."

An hour later, they were on the move with Maria on the first quad and Tom strapped to the chair. Ricky was second, Jody third with Kate sitting in front of her and Tara in the luggage rack, and bringing up the rear was Bridget with Tom's mare and the black horse trailing—their reins tied to the rear luggage rack.

Chapter 41
Peace of Mind

Tom's eyes fluttered open. His head throbbed, and he blinked several times to clear his vision. Confusion swamped him. He was in a bed, the pillow soft, the bedding fresh laundered, and rolled over his shoulders a white crisp sheet. Above him, on the white ceiling, was a decorative, gold trimmed, light fixture with etched glass.

How did he get here? He swallowed hard. *And where was here?*

To his right was an arm chair and a window with white, sheer, drapes which allowed the daylight to filter in. A television was in the corner, and to his left a nightstand with a glass of water. The room also had a sweet potpourri scent, like lavender flowers.

He pushed the bedding back. Groaning from the pain as he moved, he picked up the glass, drinking deeply until it was empty. Kate's bear fell off his chest, and onto the floor.

The children!

Panic set in. He set the glass down, and rolled over, placing his feet on the grey carpet. How long had he been out? The last thing he remembered was the meadow…and Tony Manatone. He started to rise, but stopped. Dizziness washed over him and he swayed for a moment, his head pounding like a wrecking ball sweeping back and forth from temple to temple. He probed the wound on his head. His hair had been shaved off, the skin smooth to the touch, and he could feel a compress bandage across the dome of his skull. His beard was gone too, his face clean shaven.

Looking down, he glimpsed more of his injuries. Dressed only in boxers, he saw two more compressed bandages on each of his sides—front and back—and his left leg was bandaged from the knee up, the white gauze blotchy from iodine. His left arm looked much the same. It was immobilized, bandaged from the wrist to the shoulder, and in a sling across his bare chest.

The door swung open. "Hey! Lay back down!"

Tom blinked in surprise. He recognized the thin, white-haired man. It was Pete Warfield, *Arc Angels* doctor, and Crude Technologies fleet surgeon. As he stepped over to lay Tom back down, pulling the bedding up around him again, Tom was speechless. Was this a dream?

Pete grinned, his hazel eyes gleaming. "If you keep staring I'm going to think I have egg on my face or something."

"But how…" Tom asked, after his head settled back in the pillow. His eyes flared and he started to rise again. "The children?"

"Easy. They're fine." Pete clarified, "You've been out for the past three days so I wouldn't move too far, too fast." He grinned shamelessly. "Sorry about cutting off all your hair, but I needed to keep that head wound from getting infected. The same applied to shaving your face. The bath however…I've left for you." He chuckled, and stood over Tom. "As for your wounds, you had no broken bones, and the gunshots, although plentiful, were all through and through and didn't require surgery. Neither was there any internal damage that I could find. All you need now is rest and you'll be up and around in no time."

Another familiar face appeared in the open doorway. Blond haired and blue eyed, with wide shoulders and an infectious smile, it was Reed Davenport his boss—both their bosses—and friend. "What's all the ruckus, Pete?" he asked, with a glint of amusement. He had a cup of coffee in his hand, and the aroma of breakfast cooking wafted into the room, making Toms stomach grumble.

"Your chief of security is obviously up," Pete answered, leaning over to check the brown and purple bruised skin beyond the bandage on Tom's head, "and his bedside manner reminds me a whole lot of someone else I know." Appearing satisfied, he gave Reed a wink, and stepped back to the door. "I'll be back in a minute with some breakfast. I expect you're hungry about now." He smiled. "It's really good to see you awake. You had lots of people worried." He turned and disappeared down the hall.

Tom remained dumbfounded as Reed stepped to the bed. "I'm thinking you have a shitload of questions, but first you have some visitors who are eager to see you."

For the first time, Tom heard chattering voices, and laughter, coming from down the hall. It sounded like organized chaos, but familiar.

A woman spoke. It sounded like Reed's wife, Olena. "Sit down and eat please. You're as skinny as spaghetti."

Utensils clattered, glasses clanked, and there were some whispers and some giggles. Then Tom's heart fluttered when he heard a boy's voice. "Yeah, you're so skinny that if you swallowed a meatball, you'd look pregnant."

There was a chorus of laughter, then another familiar voice. "He's breath jabbing me!" It was Kate, followed by more laughter.

Reed yelled through the doorway. "Tom's up."

The other room went quiet. Then there was a commotion…a flurry of activity as utensils were dropped, chairs scraped—with one falling over—and scampering feet down the hall. The footfalls stopped at the doorway, and a more beautiful picture Tom couldn't have imagined. He did a head count to make sure they were all there. Six children, with Kate and Tara in the front, Ricky and Jody on the ends, and in the back were Maria and Bridget. All were smiling except Maria, who had a hand covering her mouth, and grateful tears floating down her cheeks.

Tom barely recognized them. Gone was the dirt, the sunken eyes, and starving appearance. Gone was that glint of desperation in each of their eyes. It was quite the transformation. They now had haircuts, their clothes fit, and each had a happy glow.

To control his blossoming emotions, Tom grit his teeth together. "So this is what clean kids look like." Injuries or no injuries, they flocked to him with glee, and Tom felt no pain, as Kate and Tara jumped onto the bed, smothering him with hugs. Tom then realized he still had Kate's bear in his hand—never letting it go since he picked it up. "I think this belongs to you," he said, knowing how much it meant to her.

Her smile faded and she got serious. "We can share him. Teddy wants you to get better."

"Well, thank you. I'll take very good care of him."

Tom looked past the huddled children to Reed, who smiled at the reunion, and turned to leave.

You're right, my friend. I have a shitload of questions.

Pete brought Tom some breakfast, and for the rest of the morning Maria and the children stayed at his side, huddled around him on the double bed and, with Teddy lying on his chest, they explained what had happened after he went down in the field. They told him how they had left the cave and gone to help him. And shortly after arriving on the bluff overlooking the meadow, it was Maria—using the rifle Tom had left behind—who had shot both Ramon and the other man.

Tom listened in amazement, and considering their ages, their riveting accomplishments were nothing short of unbelievable. Like with most kids telling stories, they said it like it was, going through the highs and lows, peaks and valleys, as well as the overwhelming sadness and terror of Tom being hurt. Each had something to say, a portion of the story—usually at the same time—and even bashful Kate had proclaimed how she had carried the medical kit. They explained how Maria and Ricky had cleaned the wounds, and while Maria stitched and bandaged, Ricky prepared the IV all by himself—an IV, Pete had later told them, that had saved his life. And when they ran out of bandages, it was Kate, Tara, and Jody tearing Tom's coat to use as wraps, while Bridget guarded them all with a pistol.

But beyond each voice and addition to the storyline, Tom heard something else, too. Over and over again, even as scared as they were, whether it was facing the fear of armed men, or formulating a plan of action, was the recurring theme of them doing everything together.

Good or bad, right or wrong, they made decisions like a team, a family, and never strayed from it; even now, praising the others' accomplishments and never making it about the one. This had been the key to their survival. It was, and always would be, the well-being of the group first. They coped together; their bond strong. He also realized something else: to think of these six kids as only children, meant underestimating them. He himself had, and…obviously…so had Ramon Ramirez.

"I thought the scariest part of the trip was driving the quad," Jody said, lying on the foot of the bed with her head on Maria's thighs.

"No way!" Ricky proclaimed. "That was the best!"

They went on to tell him how they made it back to the cave, packed up like he had told them, and left. "But we didn't know what direction to go," Maria said. "We needed to get you to a doctor, and we couldn't go toward the farm because the men were coming…"

"Men that wanted to hurt you," Tara clarified with a serious look, sitting to the left of Tom with her back against the wall. "Tell him about the horses, Maria."

"Oh, yeah," Maria said. "While they were packing up supplies from the cave, I unsaddled the horses, tied all three to my quad, and took them to the southern valley you told me about. With Jessy still limping,

I had to go slow, but I figured if I got them pointed in the right direction, they could find their own way back to the farm. Once there, I took their bridles off and that's where I released them. You think they're okay?"

Maria was holding Tom's right hand and he squeezed it. He couldn't have been more proud. Again, growing up before her time, she acted like no fourteen year old he had ever met. "Your decision was perfect," he answered honestly. "That's exactly what Myra said to do when I was done with them."

"So they're okay?" Tara asked, snuggling into his injured left shoulder.

With slow and deliberate movements, Tom leaned over and kissed the top of her head. "They couldn't be better. After two or three days, I'm sure they found their way right back to the farm."

"Good. I feel better," Maria said, continuing, "so when I got back we made sure you were secure, gave you antibiotics from the other medical kit, re-strapped the IV bag up near your neck using the bridles, and decided to head north toward Canada, bypassing all the grow fields, until we finally came to a highway."

"And Maria was very careful, too," Kate said from Tom's immediate right. She sat between Jody's legs, who was leaning against the wall. "She wouldn't let us near the road. There were cars and trucks. Big trucks! And we didn't know who to trust."

"That's right," Bridget added. She was lying along Tom's side, facing the opposite direction, with her feet propped on Kate's legs. "We made everyone stay out of sight, driving the quads inside the tree line."

"That's when Tara started screaming," Ricky said. Much like Bridget on the other side of Tom, he was also facing him only with his legs on Tara.

Maria nodded. "She was behind me and you," she gestured to Tom, "riding in front of Jody's quad."

"That's right," Jody added. "It was a long, rough, ride, and we needed to continually make sure you weren't coming free from the chair. So she was our eyes, and she saw that you were bleeding again."

Maria nodded. "It was dark anyway, so we patched you up again and made camp in the woods."

"Yeah," Bridget said, "we made you a real comfortable bed out of branches, and covered you with our blankets."

"It took all of us to lift you," Maria said. "It wasn't easy, and the IV tube was almost pulled from your arm twice."

"Then I fed Tom!" Ricky said triumphantly. "Macaroni and cheese in a tube!"

Tom grinned. "It must have been good. Thank you."

"After you ate, we all snuggled in next to you to keep you warm," Kate added. But Tom knew it was much more than that. An attachment had sprouted. He felt it too, and its roots were growing stronger by the second.

"Then the helicopter came," Tara said with a glint of astonishment in her big blue eyes. "And the helicopter ride."

"The helicopter?" Tom asked.

"Yes," Maria answered. "Reed and True John. They came about four hours later, in the middle of the night. Landed just off the highway."

Kate giggled. "We almost shot them."

Maria nodded. "Seriously, we almost did."

More laughter followed.

*****

Reed came into Tom's room after the children were called for lunch. Tom was looking at the television. It was on with the volume muted. The news was covering some kind of sickness. The caption in red bold print read "Another Outbreak".

It jarred his memory. Only a month prior, and just as he went in search of his kidnapped wife, Reed and TJ had uncovered a ruthless and deadly plot to unleash the original black plague unto the world. The culprit had been Stan Rickter, who had resurrected the original plot hatched as far back as World War II by Hitler himself. Developed by the Nazi's, their plan had been to use a torpedo as the delivery method—the first bio weapon ever designed—to be fired toward the Washington coast from a submarine. The plan had failed though when the black torpedo had gotten entangled in a fishing net, and then snagged in the masses of bull kelp along the coastal waters. There it had remained, hidden for the next seventy four years, until Reed and Crude Technologies stumbled on it while cleaning up an oil spill.

Tom pointed at the television. "Does this have anything to do with Stan Rickter and the black torpedo?"

"It does, I'm afraid," Reed answered. "Stan Rickter's worldwide reach in biotechnology proved to be formidable and broad; his plan too well prepared and long in the making. So stopping it entirely had been impossible. But we can get you caught up later. How you feeling?"

"Like I've been shot six times," Tom answered flatly. He was sitting up in bed, with his back against the wall.

"That's because you *were* shot six times," Reed said, grinning. He pointed at the chair next to the bed. "You mind?"

"Please. Where is TJ?" Tom asked. "I understand he's here too."

"Was here," Reed answered as he sat down. "Unfortunately, we've been away longer than planned and yesterday there was a large fuel spill off the Washington coast near Westport." Reed glanced at his watch. "He and the skimmer, *Arc Angel,* are en route. They should be exiting the Strait of Juan de Fuca and going around Cape Flattery as we speak." Reed looked at his friend. "And you should know, he's also been looking for you—right by my side—since you left."

"I look forward to talking to him."

"And he, you. He thinks bald suits you," Reed replied with a wink and a grin.

Olena came in carrying two cups of coffee. She wore a flowered sun dress, tight around her slender waist, and her thick brown hair was pulled back into a long braid. As she approached, there was no hiding the warmth in her grey eyes. "I'm so glad you're okay, Tom. If there's anything we can do for you, just ask."

"Thank you."

She handed a cup to Reed and then Tom, whom she bent over and kissed on the cheek. "Yell if you need anything. I'm just down the hall. Maria wants to learn how to make black bread." She disappeared back down the hallway.

"Maria is quite the fourteen-year-old," Reed said.

"Yes, she is. Without her…them…I wouldn't be here."

"I know, I've heard the stories." Reed paused a moment before continuing. "The injustices that were going on out there in the mountains boggle the imagination. It should be a police matter."

"Can't happen," Tom replied.

"I'm just stating the obvious," Reed said, holding up his hand to quiet Tom's fears. "It's your call, and I get the complexity of the matter. For one, there are the kids, and I've seen the look on their faces, and yours. You have an undeniable bond, but I'm guessing you suddenly showing up with six children is going to raise a few eyebrows both legally and generally."

"One problem at a time."

Reed nodded. "Understood. I also recognize this goes far beyond what I really know." He sighed. "So what do I know? This is what TJ and I managed to put together: Tanya's abduction had something to do with your previous life working for the Manatone crime family in New York. You went there, found her, and then tracked the people responsible to the middle of the wilderness—on horseback no less." He met Tom's eyes. "How am I doing so far?" Tom nodded, so Reed continued. "You ran into the children by chance, and dealt with the people responsible for both the atrocities towards the children and also toward Tanya." He took a sip of coffee before continuing, choosing his next words carefully. "That means dead bodies. So getting back to the police…I of all people, know when there is value in not talking to them. I could probably write a book on the subject. That being said, and knowing the mob might be looking for you as well as the police, I took precautions."

Reed swept a hand around the room.

"This is a farm. Untraceable, and isolated. It's located in West Virginia—a rental I paid cash for. The owner was skeptical at first, thinking illegal activities were involved, but I reassured him this had nothing to do with drugs. It was about not leaving a paper trail. Nothing more." Reed smirked. "It also didn't hurt that it was only for a month, and I left a sizeable damage deposit. It's also why you weren't taken directly to a hospital, and why I flew Pete out here as well."

"Thank you."

Reed held up a hand. "You will never have to thank me for anything. You and Tanya have become part of our family, and when you were attacked, my family was attacked." He shook his head. "The grievance, however, that you *will* have to amend in the future was not asking for my help in the first place, but that's for another day."

"I couldn't involve anyone else…to have anyone else in jeopardy."

Reed nodded with understanding. "It was a dilemma."

Tom's face turned solemn. "Mike and Micky are dead."

"I gathered that might be the case. I'm sorry."

"So am I," Tom lamented. "They were good people. Now I need to ask…" He had to clear his throat. "You got my messages about where to find Tanya, didn't you?"

Reed sighed heavily. "First off, no man should ever have to say those words about his wife, and for that I'm truly sorry. The loss hit us pretty hard as well. But yes, I flew to New York the next day, and met with the police right away. They knew nothing of a body…"

"What? I called them myself."

Reed shook his head. "I can't explain that, but without proof and due to syndicate ownership, we couldn't get into the Red Hook Granary right away. The process took two more days to get a warrant, and when we did, TJ and I, along with the police, searched the silos from above with flashlights but didn't find anything."

Tom straightened. Doubt and guilt washed over him. "That can't be."

Reed held up a finger. "Initially. We didn't find anything initially." He leaned forward in his chair, cradling his coffee with two hands. "The police easily dismissed us because—as per your instructions—we couldn't give them my source…you…for the information, much less Tanya's name. But TJ and I did some digging on our own. Our dilemma was if the syndicate didn't remove the body themselves, then where did she disappear to? To find the answer meant getting back into the granary. Fortunately, the guards at the gate hadn't seen us in back of the police cruiser originally, so we pretended to be tourists, and after giving them two hundred dollars, they let us in for an hour. What we noticed, upon further scrutiny, was a discharge tube—only one—that was still connected to the base of one of the one-hundred-and-forty-foot silos. This was an important clue. The tubes had normally been used for filling barges; the spout hanging some ten feet over the waterway, and more than twenty feet in the air."

"I still don't understand," Tom responded, growing impatient. "I told you she fell into silo six."

Reed nodded. "Silo six *was the silo* with the discharge tube." Reed stared at his friend for a moment, but he still wasn't grasping what he was telling him. "You said on the recording, you heard Tanya hit and then a splash, but when TJ and I got there and looked down, there was no water in the silo. Nearest I can tell it must have been standing water from having the lid off for decades. Then over time it clogged, probably from leftover grain and sludge. My guess is the slope at the bottom of the silo had acted like a slide before she struck the water; the impact dislodging the blockage, and the entire contents discharged through the tube into the water basin."

"What are you saying?"

"Bear with me. So after we left, we contacted all the surrounding hospitals, more specifically the morgues." He shrugged. "It turns out a fisherman had found the body of an unidentified woman a half-mile down the waterway on the rocky shore line the next morning."

"So she's been found," Tom said, relieved, but with a sapping sense of despair growing in the pit of his stomach.

"She has, but it wasn't in the morgue."

Reed stood. "We couldn't find you, although we tried." He reached into the inside breast pocket of his Crude Technologies windbreaker. "Until we learned that you might have this on you." Removing his hand, Tanya's golden locket—glinting as it slowly spun on its chain—dangled from his fingers. "And when we discovered the signal had to be piggy-backed off cellphone's, we just hoped you would get into a service area, which you did when the children got you to the highway."

"You tracked me using Tanya's locket?"

"We did. She's the one who gave us the security code," Reed said, his face breaking into a broad grin. "Tom, she's alive."

EPILOGUE

Payback

HUNG BY HIS WRISTS, RICK Motese swayed back and forth from a chain which was hooked to the large arm of a hydraulic engine hoist. He was gagged, stripped to the waist, and with his head tilted forward, pleading to Mike Grevo for his life. But the new crime boss felt no mercy.

After putting the traitorous pieces together, Mike and four syndicate men had surprised Rick at his elegant penthouse suite. Located along the banks of the East River, the sprawling suite was at the top of Sutton Place South; a free-standing, pre-war building for exclusively rich clientele. And Rick was just that, rich, thanks in large part, Mike had learned, to both the New York mob, and also the Mexican cartel. But Rick was now learning the price for burning the proverbial candle at both ends.

Once he was captured, Mike and his grey-suited men had escorted him down the elevator, and out to the back loading dock where a white, nondescript, one-ton cube-van waited for him. Inside, he had been gagged, his hands and feet zip tied, and he was bound to an appliance dolly, which was then laid down for the trip.

Twenty minutes later, the back door was rolled up and he was wheeled through another loading dock at the back of Simon's Auto Repair—a mob front, located in a rundown warehousing district of Queens. After taking him inside, the men had leaned him casually against one of the iron-grey cement walls and waited. Facing outward, he had remained there for more than two hours, staring at a large engine hoist in the middle of the room. Beyond it, and as ordered by Mike, who came and went during this time, the four grim-faced men had waited patiently, sitting at a small folding table, making small talk; one of whom was sick—his cough echoing throughout the empty chamber.

Watching them with obvious dread, the terror had shown in Rick's wide eyes as sweat ran down both sides of his face, soaking the collar-line of his expensive suit. After all, he knew more than anyone the significance of the building, and no doubt, why he'd been brought here. Vacant for more than five years, the auto repair equipment had long since been gone, but then again, and much like the granary, that's not why the mob kept the building on the books, or the reason the engine hoist remained.

When Mike Grevo had finally returned, Rick was laid down over a grated floor drain in the middle of the room, and the questioning had begun. To ensure the answers were truthful, a towel had been placed over his face, and buckets of water brought in from the lavatory. That's when the water-boarding had begun with the water being poured onto the towel over his face. For more than an hour he had been questioned. Not that getting answers had been a problem. Rick had been forthcoming right from the start, but this wasn't entirely about answering questions. Only when Rick's body was convulsing, retching water, and near death from drowning, had Mike been satisfied.

With the questions now answered, the new crime boss watched as Rick was regagged, stripped to the waist, and attached to the engine hoist; his ankles chained to eyebolts to each side of the grated floor-drain. The answers garnered from him had been illuminating. Mike learned the takeover of the grow fields had occurred much earlier, and longer, than previously thought; almost four years. It had started for Rick when he'd gone back to visit his family outside of Mexico City. He had been approached by a man named Ramon Juan Ramirez, a member of the Tapito drug cartel, and they were interested in having a grow field operation of their own inside the borders of the United States.

Just as Frank Manatone had realized decades ago, this would simplify the distribution process, and virtually eliminate the uncertainty of border crossings. But that had only been a ruse initially—to test the waters in the manipulation process. The real plan all along was to subtly take over the New York's grow fields without Frank Manatone's knowledge—fields that Rick Motese was solely in charge of. It had taken weeks of courting and deliberations, but eventually Rick had agreed, and large amounts of money were transferred in exchange for supply routes, field coordinates, strengths and weaknesses of the forces stationed there, monthly quotas for various crops, and the biggest of all: Rick would now be working covertly for the Tapito drug cartel, running the operation to guarantee success, and make sure no one was the wiser. Three weeks later the attack…the takeover…had happened.

And they had been right, Mike thought, *no one had been the wiser. It had gone without a hitch except for the children and a girl named Maria.*

Only yesterday, Mike had gotten word from his men that the fields were now under their control again. This news had come as a big surprise because it had been done without even firing a single shot. Apparently— his man in charge had told him—the Mexican cartels force was dead and scattered between a northern meadow and the encampment of field one.

The only person alive at this field had been one of the Mexican cartels cooks, who had confirmed Tom Spears was responsible. Sneaking into the camp before dinner, he had added poisonous mushrooms to the soup, and by the next morning only twelve men remained out of thirty four; the rest sick and dying, or dead already.

Mike smirked, his respect apparent. He expected no less from the man he knew as the Shadow. The numbers were never perceived as a problem to him. One man or thirty four, he was focused and it never altered his successes. This also held true for the twelve men that remained, who ultimately went out to meet Tom Spears at the meadow. But something had obviously gone horribly wrong for those men too, including the man known as Ramon Juan Ramirez. Even Tony Manatone had been found dead in the meadow.

So where had the Shadow gotten to? It was a recurring question. What was his plan? Was Spears still an enemy? If he had been found, Mike's men had had orders to shoot him on sight. But that was only as a precaution, a reaction to a man who had gone on a killing rampage both in New York and in the mountains.

Did he understand Tom's rage? Of course. Tom wanted justice, like he himself had wanted justice for George, his dead son. It wasn't difficult to comprehend. But now what? Should he put contracts out on the Shadow…see if someone else could achieve success where so many others had failed? It wasn't a pleasant thought considering how well it had worked out for Frank, Tony, Charley Mack, and Bishop Styles.

Mike decided to wait until he knew more. It was prudent, an important decision, and not to be taken lightly. The man known as the Shadow had proven time and again, he was a force to be reckoned with, and if provoked, a trail of bodies was sure to follow. A perfect example of this were the dead men in the meadow. They probably went in overconfident and overplayed their hand. Like so many before, they had underestimated Spears, and failed to realize it was one of his greatest strengths.

Another reason to wait was that everything had worked out so far. The majority of the cartel's men were dead, including Tony Manatone, and all that remained were the few in the surrounding farms. But those men, including the cook, would all be dead by sunset.

Still lost in thought, he looked down at the cement floor under Rick Motese. The surface gleamed under the bright overhead lighting, but several dark oil stains remained near the drain—a long narrow grate that left the room smelling of solvents and oils, and in many cases, blood. Today would be no different.

He looked at the hanging man, whose eyes flicked with uncertainty back and forth. They had been friends for many years.

Now look at him.

Known as a clean cut, crisp dresser, his black hair, normally parted down the middle with a waxy sheen, was now spiked, disheveled, and damp with sweat. His once proud handle-bar mustache, twisted at the ends, now drooped uncharacteristically like a withered plant, sticking to the sides of his face pathetically like a sulking frown. And the confidence that once came from running one of the organizations' most profitable enterprises, was now replaced with fear and pitiful uncertainty.

Mike shook his head.

How had someone so promising…so powerful…been reduced to someone so weak and insignificant? Looking at him now, Mike could see how frail the man had become. The once feared man, with a muscled physique, had long since disappeared, replaced now by a fat belly and growing jowls. This said it all. He had grown soft and easy to manipulate.

Mike wasn't unsympathetic, though. Had this been about threats to his family back in Mexico, and not money, it might have altered the outcome. He would still be dead, but it might have stopped there. That was no longer the case.

A message had to be sent, violent and swift.

He pulled out his cellphone and dialed a number.

A man with a Spanish accent picked up. "We're here. Just arrived. You ready?" the man asked.

"We are," Mike answered, "pan the view." Putting the phone on speaker, he stepped up to Rick and showed him the screen. "You recognize this home."

For a moment Rick wasn't sure, then his eyes flared and he shook his head, pleading into the gag.

"Yes, it's your home in Mexico City. Home of your wife Marina, your twelve year old son, Felipe, your two daughters Caty and Arla… and home of your infant son, Rick…named after you."

The screen moved unsteadily for a moment, and indicative of the obvious terror going on in the home, shrieks along with commanding voices could be heard. Then the screen steadied and Rick's family could be seen on their knees in front of a sofa; the infant in a blanket on the cushions. Aside from the baby, all were gagged with their hands tied behind their backs.

Mike sighed. He wasn't looking forward to what was about to happen…needed to happen. "As you are aware Rick, I'm the new crime boss for the once proud Manatone syndicate, and as a first priority, it's important to reaffirm the rules, swiftly and without empathy. You, yourself, know that maintaining strength in our world is crucial. With any apparent weakness, only disaster lurks; the balance a fine line. You have crossed that line, and no one can be allowed to do what you've done ever again. A message must be sent."

Holding the phone off to the side, Mike glimpsed the screen.

The camera moved in front of Marina, and Rick jerked at his restraints.

Even with tears streaming down her face, and fear held in her wide eyes, Mike noticed Rick's wife had a warm face. Plump from middle age, she had round cheeks, and her black hair was cut short. At one time, Mike could tell she had been a striking woman. Now she was a mother, and over her soft blue dress, she wore a white apron, like she'd been cooking in the kitchen. Like Rick, she seemed to be pleading and her chest heaved in panic. Then came the shot to the back of her head, loud and intrusive, and her chest stopped moving. One moment she had hopes and dreams, full of life, and the next she appeared statue-like, with only a blank stare, before falling forward to the floor; the smoking gun still in the picture.

Mike held his phone steady. It wasn't something he wanted to see, but he had been left with little choice.

Rick screamed into his gag in anguish, tears running down his face.

More shrieks followed, hysterical and heart wrenching. The camera went in front of Filipe—a narrow faced boy, with fine bones, and green eyes. Again the gun sounded and the twelve-year-old jerked once and then tumbled forward.

As the nightmare played out in front of Rick, his emotional response was continually changing. It was a kaleidoscope of emotions, from shock and anger, to fear and sadness, and now unrealistic hope as his tone changed from hysterical to attempting to barter…to negotiate… for his family's remaining lives. The word "please" could be heard over and over again, and "I'll do anything," and "listen to me!"

Mike glared at him. "There will be no bartering. You sold us out… for what? So your family could live the good life?" His eyes narrowed. "Now they have no life...no life at all."

One of his daughters, Caty, was on the screen now. The eleven-year-old was visibly shaking and taking convulsive breaths. Another booming sound followed, making Rick jump, but Caty remained unhurt.

"Take a good look Rick at those two daughters of yours. Ten and eleven. So innocent."

Rick's eyes blinked rapidly as the camera swung to the other daughter, Arla. A pretty girl with brown hair, her eyes were squeezed shut and she was rocking back and forth.

"That's right, look real hard," Mike snarled. "The penance won't be death for these two…at least not right away. There are bills to pay, money that was stolen from us that needs to be repaid. So I've arranged for your two daughters to join a prostitution ring in the suburbs of Guadalajara; a place that even Mexico's president proclaimed was the lowest, dirtiest, crime ridden city in all of Mexico."

Rick's head whipped back and forth.

Mike nodded with satisfaction. "They will be juiced up on drugs, given an addiction, and then passed around like a soccer ball on championship Sunday. But not to worry, in between getting repeatedly raped, they'll be so strung out they won't know which way is up, where they're at, or even what day it is. This is important. Once they're addicted, they'll crave the world of dreams instead of reality, and doing anything to remain there. At that point, they'll become mindless, and respond like trained dogs with only one goal: lying down to make money for the syndicate. That's the life you've passed on to them. How long before those innocent faces have seen the worst in men?" He shook his head. "That, I guarantee, will take longer…much longer. I'll personally see to it, and it begins right after this call." He glared at Rick. "Before setting your house on fire and wiping all signs of you from this world, my men are going to break those two girls in good and proper…to get them set on their new life's course. In fact, I told them to take the entire day. It was an order. Then, all thanks to you, they are off to their new life as filthy whores."

Turning away, Mike took the phone off speaker mode, and talked to the man again. "We're done here. Enjoy yourself and have them in Guadalajara by midday tomorrow. I want them avidly working the streets by tomorrow night." He hung up and placed the phone back in the inside breast pocket of his suit. Then once again, he looked at Rick.

"As for your infant son, he also has value. I've arranged for him to be adopted for the generous fee of twenty-five thousand dollars. It's a step in the right direction, along with the bank accounts you so generously supplied, towards getting back the millions you siphoned from us." He leaned in close to Rick. "Not sure who the adopting family is, nor do I care. A sexual predator? Maybe. I can't know. It's a gamble with illegitimate deals such as this. If he's lucky he may survive. But two things are for certain: one, he'll never know who his father was, and two, your son's name won't ever be Rick—a prerequisite of the deal."

Rick's head was sagging forward and he was crying in racking sobs; snot dripping from the end of his nose. Up to now—aside from the water-boarding—the pain he felt had mostly been emotional. But that was about to change. With a flick of Mike's hand, the four grim faced men stepped forward. One manned the hydraulic controls to the hoist, while two posted up on each side of Rick, holding his shoulders to limit his movements. The last man, with wide shoulders and raspy cough, stepped in front of Rick. In his hand was a thin, long-bladed filet-knife typically used by fishermen.

The man at the controls pulled one of the levers back. A hydraulic humming noise was followed by the chain around Rick's wrists being hauled up until his feet—anchored by chains—were drawn up, pulled taut, ten inches off the floor. One of the men standing to the side grabbed Rick's hair, pulling his head back to expose his neck.

"Now it's time to deal with the traitor himself," Mike said, stepping forward. "At first I wanted to see you slowly carved up, but then I got a better idea. With your heritage, and your connections to the Mexican cartel, I thought we'd stick to a Spanish theme. I'm sure you've heard the term 'Colombian necktie'. Your compadres in Mexico have been doing this for years." He nodded to the hoist operator, who disappeared for a moment, then returned from the back room, pushing a full-length mirror; its wheels squeaking, high-pitched and grating, like fingernails on a chalkboard. He stopped in front of Rick Motese, who started to fight his bindings and squirm. But it wasn't any use. His arms and legs were stretched tighter than strings on a guitar.

"The method is crude, but effective, in striking fear into those who might think about doing something as self-serving and stupid as you did," he said unsympathetically. "An incision will be made in your neck, and then this wire," he grabbed a thick wire bent into a hook hanging from the side of the hoist; its curled end pointed and sharp, "will be inserted into your neck, slowly maneuvered up and through the base of your mouth, where it will be hooked like a fish through your lying tongue. Then it will be drawn out just as delicately back through your upper neck. The trick to doing it, so I've heard, is getting around the wind pipe and not cutting any arteries so you can witness the procedure yourself." He gestured to the mirror. "And watch it you will, as you gag and choke on your own blood. Then we'll wait patiently until you die, long and painfully, I might add."

Mike nodded to the coughing man with the knife. "Get on with it!"

Outside, along the back loading dock, and oblivious to the screams that now filled the interior, two teenage boys laughed and skateboarded down a side ramp, enjoying a quiet sunny day.

Making Things Right

Three weeks had passed since Tom had woken up at the farmhouse, and he now sat in his idling Honda SUV—reacquired from the airport parking lot—and watched Mike Grevo and his bodyguard get into the backseat of his car; a new Lincoln Town Car, with tinted windows and a driver in the front seat. They were backed into a parking stall near the wall of Buvette, the French restaurant located near the corner of Grove and Bleecker streets in New York City.

Tom looked at himself in the rearview mirror and adjusted the beanie on his head. His hair was growing back, and his injuries were healing up like Pete had said. The left arm remained stiff, and he still had a noticeable limp, but both were vast improvements from three weeks ago. Even the recurring headaches were becoming less severe.

He entered a number on his disposable cellphone, and the familiar voice of Mike Grevo picked up. "Hello?"

"How was breakfast?" Tom asked, watching him from sixty spaces away and to the front of him.

There was a notable pause, but Tom saw no signs of alarm from him as the new crime boss spoke. "I was wondering if you might call."

"You were right to think so," Tom said. "I don't like loose ends. So this is a courtesy call to make sure we're on the same page. You've obviously seen the camera footage I gave you at your home. It's proof that I had nothing to do with the assassination of Frank or your son." Another long pause followed; the death of George obviously a lingering pain for Mike. "Now I need to know if we're good, or if you're going to continue to hunt me."

Tom was grateful to hear no hesitation. "No. I consider the incident with the assassination, and even Frank's nephew to be closed. Even the attack on our server station I'm going to let slide. That's why we have insurance. However, you killed many of our men…"

"Sixteen," Tom said dryly.

"Yes, and those men had families and friends, too. So I really can't say how many of them will come looking for vengeance." He paused. "But you won't have anything to worry about with the syndicate directly."

"Worry…wasn't the case, but I'm glad to hear it," Tom said. "It was the only acceptable answer to me."

They were getting ready to leave so Tom pulled out of his spot and came to a stop in front of their car, blocking them in. Rolling down the passenger window, he watched Mike calm the driver and the man beside him into not overreacting.

"I didn't mean to alarm you, Mike, but I like to look at a man when I talk to him. It puts everything on the table…a complete perspective. That way, hypothetically speaking, I'll know if he's lying, and he in turn can clearly see the threat of my intentions. So know this," Tom said flatly as he glared across the hood of the Town Car. "If I ever find myself looking over my shoulder, you'll be my first stop, and no amount of security will stop me from killing you."

The new mob boss coolly nodded. "We have an understanding then. And as long as we're talking hypotheticals, is there anything I should worry about as far as the grow fields are concerned?"

Tom knew he was referring to the children, and even him, about alerting the authorities to the field's illegal activities. Much like Tom's threat, this was a threat of his own, and understandable considering it was a billion dollar industry. "I've known about the fields from when I worked here. Nothing new there, and I'll vouch for the children. No one will be telling the authorities anything. You have my word, Mike. You'll also find the four quads that were borrowed at mile post 162 just east of Malone on Highway 11. They're hidden in the tree line, but I wouldn't leave them there too long if you don't want the police getting involved."

"Thank you. I'll see it's done right away."

"And so we're clear about anything that might be perceived as *a loose end*, or a *liability*, those same children you just hypothetically inquired about were instrumental in taking down the force that was there. To further that, over the last four years they've lived through a nightmare and now only require to be left alone."

"Understood. Then we have an agreement, Tom," Mike said, his words sincere. "I will leave you alone, and you leave us alone. Consider this a verbal contract between two old friends. It's a new beginning, like the grow fields, which are back under our control again, with all people involved having been dealt with, including traitors."

Tom knew what "dealt with" meant. They were dead, including Rick Motese. As for the Mexican cartel and how they would be punished for taking over the fields, killing almost everyone there, and stealing the revenue, was anyone's guess. But one thing was certain, New York's retaliation wasn't a question of if, but when.

"One more thing I need to mention," Tom said. "As you know Maria was instrumental in usurping the Mexican cartel's infiltration into the fields. Without her, and her call to Frank, no one would have known."

Mike nodded. "The child will be taken care of."

"See that she is. That pain you feel for the loss of your son would be multiplied by a hundred with me should anything happen to her. To further that, her last name is Kaylor, but I want you to consider it to be Spears."

"Done. She will be treated like your daughter, and given the proper respect."

"Thank you, and so you know, I offered to take her away, but she declined. Seems she's more comfortable in the woods." Tom's eyes showed a glint of sadness as he continued. "I can't tell you what's best for your operation, but know this, there is no one more suited or qualified to run it."

Mike cocked his head curiously. "She's fourteen."

Tom grinned, letting the emotional response melt the coldness of his features like a spring thaw. "True, but she's actually fourteen going on thirty. She's also a survivor, tough as nails, knows the ins and outs of the business from supplies, production of product and packaging, to the plant fertilizers used and watering schedules. In fact, it's a subject that would make your ears bleed from her endless chatter. More importantly—as you've already learned—she's loyal; a quality you are in dire need of in the fields. She's also smart, and committed if given the opportunity."

"Message received. I'll consider it."

"You do that." Another grin cracked his grim and worn-out features. "But be forewarned, she only knows how to succeed, and might be running your entire enterprise, both here and abroad, in a few years."

"In that case, I'll talk to her tomorrow."

"Your call. You'll find her in the Presidential suite at the Grand Hyatt Hotel on Forty Second for another week," Tom said respectably. "And future children in the fields?"

"A new policy has already been implemented. We've purchased the surrounding farms that were vacated by the Mexican cartel. The estates will be used for transitional purposes. Workers will no longer stay longer than two months, and women will no longer be part of the equation. This will eliminate what occurred out there, or at least contain it."

Tom was quiet for a moment, staring forward out his own windshield. "I'm sorry for the loss of your son, Mike. I truly am."

"I know you are," Mike lamented, "and thank you for pulling him out of the building. Getting to see him one more time before burying him meant the world to me and Lucile. For this, I'm grateful."

Tom nodded. "It was the least I could do."

"Anyway, thank you, and I'm sorry about what happened to Mike and Micky," the crime boss reciprocated with equal sincerity. "They were close to you...and then the tragedy that befell your wife..." He shook his head. "Again, I'm sorry, Tom. I didn't know."

"I know that, otherwise this meeting would have gone much differently." The statement wasn't brash or even a threat. It was a fact and they stared at each other for a moment. "Take care, Mike."

"You too. I think you already know there are some that'll come after you."

"Yep, and they should pray they never find me." With that, Tom hung up and sped away, disappearing into the ubiquitous flow of traffic.

A New Life

As the taxi wound along the serpentine road through mountainous jungles and tropical rainforests, Tom sat in the backseat, thinking about the past two weeks. After the meeting with Mike Grevo, Tom had gone to a used car dealership, sold his car well below value, and hopped on a Crude Technologies jet—compliments of Reed Davenport—from New York's John F. Kennedy International Airport back to Seattle. After arriving, Reed had picked him up at the airport, and taken Tom to his house. A small moving truck was just pulling away, and a "For Sale" sign had been placed in the front lawn. The sight had saddened him—a reflection of the changes in his life, past and present.

Years before 'Tom Spears' the killer, he had been 'Allen Wittman' the soon-to-be lawyer. Then his wife Mellany and daughter Sally had been killed by drunks—a life altering experience, which had ultimately sent him to New York, where Tom Spears, and the assassin known as the Shadow, were born. For more than ten years this had become his world. Then another life-changing event occurred after taking a job to look for an abducted girl by the name of Maggie Klein—the fourteen-year-old daughter of John Wilks who would later run for governor of New York.

Tom remembered the refreshing feeling at the time. No longer was he an assassin for hire, killing for money, and he liked the new feeling—his tortured soul given a moment's reprieve. The search had taken months, but in the rescuing process, he had met Reed Davenport, and also Tanya Demitry, who would later become his wife. That path led him to Washington State, where he and Tanya would start a life together working for Reed Davenport at Crude Technologies: him as the security chief, and her as the liaison for three fleets spread around the globe. For two years, thanks to the Davenport family, this had become their life, and with normalcy came hope for the future. Then, most recently, the Manatone's had changed their world once again.

Even with Mike Grevo's personal assurances, Tom had to take the necessary precautions against any and all potential threats from New York. This meant moving, new employment, and a change of identity. It was one of the reasons he had Reed take him back to his house. Inside the paneled wall to the left of the brick fireplace was a hidden compartment, and in it a go bag with stacks of cash, and more than fourteen fictitious identities, including passports; important for the new journey to come.

The cash, aside from convenience, wasn't a need. Between the money he had hidden away in several offshore accounts, not to mention the funds acquired from Bishop Styles, he had enough for two or three lifetimes. The passports though were invaluable, including one for the Caribbean island of Dominica. Having been there on four separate occasions, it was a good place to get off the beaten track, and even better to get off the grid.

The other reason to be at the house had been to pick up the four boxes left by the movers. Prearranged by Tom, the packed items amounted to clothes, shoes, and personal items such as pictures. As for furniture, he and Tanya had little, but what they did have, were taken by the moving company to a local storage facility, which had been paid a full year in advance. And to keep his identity safe from anyone who might inquire about his storage rental, he used a PO Box as a return address.

When he was finished at the house, Reed had taken him to Crude Technologies to clear out his office and say his goodbyes to all the people who worked there, including Rusty, Brad, Marie, Olena, and Chuck, and especially Reed's siblings, James and Sarah. It had been harder than he could've imagined. Even saying goodbye to Bear had caused an emotional stirring; the big animal uncharacteristically lingering by his side the entire time. His last stop had been to the dock and the skimmer *Arc Angel* where True John waited on the bridge with an open bottle of Cognac and three glasses. Reed had joined them, and the three had toasted.

"To good friends," True John had said, and Reed had followed it with, "Any time, any day."

Reed had also been insistent about not leaving any paper trail which would occur when flying on a commercial airline. So seven hours later, the Crude Technologies jet carrying Tom and the four boxes, touched down at Douglas-Charles Airport on the Caribbean island of Dominica—a small airfield located on the northeast side of the island; its seclusion emphasized by the worn windsock, the terminal's rundown single-story-building, and the encroaching trees and overgrowth along the lone dilapidated runway. After clearing Customs—a one man operation at a corner desk—he had called a taxi for the hour-long drive to the west side of the island.

Now, for the first time in over two months, Tom was beginning to relax. He put his hand on the back of the front seat as the taxi slowed for a moment on the narrow road—one of only two that bisected the island—to get around an old man ushering three goats along in front of him. Then they were off again, heading around the hairpin turns to the other side of the island.

The driver, an elderly man with thinning black hair trimmed tight on the sides, coughed once; the sound seismic given the outbreaks that were happening around the globe.

While at the farm, Reed had filled Tom in on what he and TJ had uncovered at the Rickter's secret underground bio lab, and also the plot to reintroduce an even deadlier version of the original black plague onto the world. "The culling of the world's population," Stan Rickter had called it. And although Reed and TJ had been able to shut the bio lab down, Reed suspected now, as he did then, it wasn't over. He had been correct, if indeed this was the Rickter born virus sweeping across the lands from shore to shore—a delivery system yet unknown.

"A corrupted form of the black plague," Reed had said, "even deadlier than the original spore which had at one time killed three quarters of the European population."

Tom slowly shook his head. Even to think it seemed absurd, but he had no doubt as to what Reed had told him. He looked at the puncture mark on the inside of his arm, still visible from the vaccine Reed had acquired from the CDC.

Even with the enhancements of computers, genetics research, and bio lab technology, a synthesized version produced in volume was still a long way off, but an agreement had been struck with Reed, who had risked his life to get the lone ampule from the Rickter's secret underground laboratory before it blew up. Three ounces wasn't much, but in today's world versus years past, only a pin drop was needed of the antidote to get both the molecular structure for replication, and also for inoculations.

"A mandatory flu shot," Tom mumbled. That's what Reed had told him to call it if anyone were to ask, and the only thing he had told the personnel at the Crude Technologies Corporate Office when they got their shots, too. But Tom understood the need for secrecy. As much as Reed wanted to help everyone, it wasn't possible at the moment, and even though the ampule of vaccine had gone a long ways, the quantities were already all but depleted. So what would Reed have said to the employees who wanted shots for their family, for the friends of their family, and so on and so forth? Where would it stop? The fact was he couldn't save everyone. So until it was mass produced, and as unpleasant as it sounded, this was the only real alternative. Otherwise panic and violence would follow over the only known vaccine.

All things considered, this made Tom thankful; thankful to the Davenports, and especially thankful for the inoculations given to all six children and Tanya. To put it in further context was the fact that the bulk of the antidote probably went only to prominent people in the CDC itself, and people in top government agencies, including the president of the United States and his staff.

The sun broke clear of the clouds just as the taxi was coming down the other side of the pass. In the distance was the Caribbean Sea, blue and shimmering under the sun's rays. A large sailboat was slowly working its way along the coast; its three billowing sails of white, highlighted elegantly against a sea of blue.

A new start, Tom thought, as he took in the spectacular view.

Once they reached the coast, it was another hour drive heading south, past Pointe Michel, and Soufriere. Before getting to Scotts Head at the very southern tip of the island, they turned off onto a dirt road that wound through a thick rainforest; the huge trees creating a natural tunnel of lush green beauty.

Tom rolled down the window. Warm tropical air swept in, carrying the smell of the nearby sea and the sounds of birds in the trees above. Harmony washed over him, and like a warm embrace, the solitude was as intoxicating as it was refreshing. When the car finally broke free of the forest they were looking at the blue ocean, a white sandy beach, and a recently built, three story A-frame house, with huge lodge-style bay windows fronting the water.

Tom had purchased the property four years ago before ever meeting Tanya. It was meant to be a surprise and only recently had the house been built. Set on more than one hundred acres, there wasn't a neighbor for miles; the house perfect for raising a family.

The taxi came to a stop alongside the house, and the driver got out, unloaded the boxes and Tom's only bag. Tom thanked him, tipping him twice the amount of the fare. Then the taxi disappeared into the tree line once again.

Adjusting the baseball cap on his head to shield the glare, Tom remained standing there, feeling the warmth of the sun on his shoulders, listening to the sounds of the slow rolling surf, and staring at the surrounding beauty. A woman's voice, and laughter came from the beach to the left. Tom turned to see his wife, Tanya, walking up the beach. She was in a loose-fitting t-shirt, tied at the waist, and cutoff denim shorts; her thick brown hair cascading over her shoulders. Her feet were bare, and she walked with a noticeable limp, but that was expected after having her leg broken in two places.

Only the week before, Pete had flown out to remove the cast on both her leg, and left arm, broken at the wrist and collarbone. The fisherman who had found her, so Tom was told, had said she was near dead when he'd spotted her along the rocks of the waterway. Bleeding from the head, broken bones, and multiple contusions, he had been shocked to see her move. As he waited for help, holding her hand and comforting her, she had only whispered a single word: "Tom."

For the next two weeks she had been unconscious in the intensive care unit at St. Francis Hospital in Roslyn, New York. And when she finally awoke, she had no recollection of what had happened to her or even who she was. But as the days passed, the memory of her fall, and her life, had returned in time to greet Reed and TJ who had finally found her. Three weeks had passed since her abduction at that point, and Reed and TJ—unsure about her safety—had never left her side, sending for Pete, the fleet surgeon, while quietly whisking her away to the rented farmhouse in West Virginia. But her injuries were too severe to remain there, so Pete had her flown back to Crude Technologies in Washington State, where she could be monitored and secured at the same time. Meanwhile, Reed and TJ had continued their search for Tom, using the farm as a base of operations.

Tom thought again about Reed's words, informing him that Tanya was alive—too weak to travel, but alive. A short time later, he had called her, his knees buckling at the sound of her voice. For two long hours they had talked, and during that time tears were shed, and words of undying love spoken. Five days later, and multiple phone calls back and forth, Tom had recovered enough to go see her; a visit he'd decided that needed to be done alone. So he had left the children under the supervision of Reed, TJ, and Olena, and flown back to Washington under the watchful eye of Pete Warfield.

Tom remembered seeing her for the first time since the fall, and the thought now made him shudder involuntarily. With Bear stationed dutifully outside her door, she was in a spare bedroom at Crude Technologies, with her left leg in a full length cast from her toes to her hip and lifted into the air. The other cast went up her left arm, and wrapped around her shoulder to immobilize both her broken collarbone and left wrist. A compress bandage marked the spot where she had struck the steel edge of the silo opening with her forehead; a bump still visible, along with black and blue skin around the edge of the bandage. Covered in various scrapes, healing and scabbed over, her face was pale and swollen on the left side from the hideous impact at the bottom of the silo.

Pete had told him that being unconscious had been a blessing, and probably saved her life. Her body had been relaxed when she struck, and after the brutal impact and the slide into the water, she was carried like a rag doll easily through the pipe to the sea.

A blessing wasn't how Tom would have described her on the bed, but he was no less grateful. She had been sleeping when he walked in, but tears were streaming down both his cheeks by the time he made it to her side. Emotional pain had quickly transcended to a physical pain in his heart. Seeing her defenseless, broken, and vulnerable, was a moment he would never forget. Guilt had touched him then. Regardless of the circumstances, he should've been here with her…for her…by verifying what had happened at the bottom of the silo. No excuse. So, while standing over her as she lay in bed, he had made an unspoken vow then and there. Her safety, no matter the circumstances, difficulty, or pain, would always come first, and he would give his life freely to uphold that vow.

Then another memorable moment occurred when the love of his life opened her eyes.

For two more days, he had stayed there with her, never leaving her side; their discussions covering everything, from what had happened after her fall, to finding everyone responsible, to the trip to the mountains, where he'd found six amazing children. To Tom's delight, and just like the previous phone calls, this was the conversation they talked about the most, with Tanya eventually getting the opportunity to talk to each of them. When she finally talked to Maria, it was apparent the two had a special bond—their conversations mostly taking place when Tom wasn't present, and always finishing with happy tears.

Maria, he thought, as he watched a small flock of sea birds skim along the ocean's surface.

The two of them, Tom and she, had had several long talks at the Virginia farm, late at night while the other children slept. Maria had been concerned about her age, not having been formally educated, and the transition to suddenly being reliant on adults; something she wasn't sure she could accept. She also wasn't thrilled about trading in the mountains and forest—a life she knew—for a world of cement, buildings, and lots of people.

Another topic of deep concern came to the forefront when she asked what was going to happen to Jody, Ricky, Kate, Tara, and Bridget? "Separating them," she had told him, "was unacceptable." Tom hadn't disagreed, or responded to her question, pondering it for several days. Not that he needed to, having come up with the same answer over and over again. The fact was, he was attached to them, and being separated for even a minute filled him with endless worry and a longing pain. Moreover, the solution…the answer…the only answer…Tom kept coming up with, was to have them live with him, and later, if they approved, he would adopt them. When he had finally told Maria his thoughts, she was overjoyed, and crying with delight.

As for Maria's future plans, they had come to a temporary and mutual understanding. She would come to New York and spend two weeks at a hotel of Tom's choosing. This way, she could judge the civilized world for herself, and at the same time sleep in the most comfortable bed Tom could arrange, eat the best food she had ever eaten in her life, and mostly, be reassured; to let that guard down that had kept her and the children alive for so long. He had also left her with ten thousand dollars cash, the newest pocket dictionary from Webster, and a digital reader—rechargeable either by wall or by generator—with more than one hundred books already downloaded.

Tom sighed heavily with thoughts of her.

That had been a week ago to the day. He still held out hope she would change her mind, but that now seemed unlikely. Keeping his word, Mike Grevo had indeed paid her a visit the next day, and after talking to her in-depth about the fields, her knowledge, and her plans, had taken her to an expensive dinner, hiring her over two plates of lobster—both hers. The job would be on a trial basis, but she would indeed get the opportunity to run the grow field operation. This she had told Tom over the satellite phone he had supplied for her; his number to be called anytime, any day.

Anytime, any day, Tom thought. It was a phrase used often by the Davenports, and its meaning—it's true meaning—Tom now profoundly understood.

Making sure she wasn't getting taken advantage of, Tom had taken the liberty of calling Mike Grevo about payment, where she might live, and bank accounts. Mike had chuckled, telling Tom, "she negotiated like she had done it all her life. I couldn't have taken advantage of her even if I wanted to," he had said with good humor, and acknowledged that he had been very impressed with the young lady; her forwardness, intelligence, and like Tom had told him, her loyalty.

Regardless of the apparent good news, Tom would miss her, the children would miss her, and with her life being in further peril wasn't going to help that feeling. But, if she ever changed her mind, he was prepared. He touched the stack of newly issued passports in his breast pocket of his sport coat. As a benefit of living on the Caribbean island of Dominica, citizenship could be bought. Aside from his, there was one for each of the children, including Maria and Tanya; the stack costing him a small fortune. But it paled in comparison to having a family once again.

A family, he thought with a warm feeling. It had been a long time since it applied to him. He grinned. Although legally adopting the children in the United States would have to wait, all their new passports now had the same last name of Wittman; Tom's given name from so long ago.

"Tom Allen Wittman," Tom mumbled with a smirk. It seemed fitting. A mixture of two lives, past and present.

When Tanya saw him standing there, she waved energetically, and made her way through the deep sand into his arms. "I missed you," she said kissing him multiple times, and giving him a gentle hug with her good arm.

"How are the kids settling in?" he asked, holding her close.

"They haven't stopped smiling since they got here," she answered, drawing back to look at him, "but it's not because of the scenery."

"What do you mean?"

She smiled. "It's you. They not only look up to you, but you're their family secret and they hold that honor proudly, if not dearly. In fact, just so you know, the label "Shadow" doesn't sit well with Kate.

She thinks it's scary, and you are not. Tara agreed. So according to those two...and Teddy...you are now the Dark Angel."

"I prefer no label at all."

She laughed, a sound rich in good humor.

"I'm glad someone thinks this is funny."

"You'd laugh too," she said kissing him, "if you knew how serious they are. I wouldn't press the issue. They seem very determined." Her eyes narrowed. "What about Maria?"

He shook his head. "No. But I hold out hope that maybe one day…"

"I'll help you with that," she said with a sly grin.

"And how might you do that, my dear?" he mused, meeting her gaze.

She had rebounded well since the first time he had seen her in bed. Her visible injuries were limited to her limp, which according to Pete, would slowly improve, much like the movement in her arm associated with the broken collarbone. The glow—as radiant as the sun—had also returned to her face, and her smile, bright and dazzling, matched her brilliant her brown eyes, now full of life.

"She's already called me from that expensive phone you gave her." She smiled coyly. "Twice last night alone." She pulled away, looking serious. "Did you give it to her?"

She was referring to the gold locket Tom had given Tanya. The same locket Tom had used to track Tanya to New York, and later the same one Reed had used to locate Tom. "I did, and her exact words were, "Thank you, I will never take it off." He kissed Tanya gently on the lips. "And when I told her it was your idea, she said, "I will treasure it always.""

She nodded with satisfaction, her brown eyes gleaming. "Good. I need the peace of mind."

"So do I," he acknowledged somberly; the thought of her continuing peril as tormenting as being away from her. "Between the constant dangers of working for the mob, living in the wilderness, and growing illegal drugs, I'll have gray hairs inside of a year."

Tanya reached up and took off his baseball cap to look at his head. The hair was already growing in nicely, the scar almost hidden. "I'm thinking a few gray hairs will only add to your ruggedly handsome looks."

He kissed her hard on the lips, and, wary of her injuries, lifted her to her tip toes. "Thank you for the locket gesture," he told her.

"Don't be thanking me yet, I haven't told you what I want for Christmas." She turned at the sound of children's laughter. Kate, Tara, Jody, Ricky and Bridget, who were playing in the surf, had seen Tom and Tanya, and ran toward them, screaming with delight and waving.

Before they arrived, Tanya turned back to Tom and leaned into his ear. "I'd like a matching set for the entire family."

THE END

*****

I hope you enjoyed
Black Dawn.

Go to Brettdiffley.com for updates

Perfect Plan

Perfect Plan II

Black Tide

Black Dawn

Safe Passage

Storm Warning

Treacherous Paths (2025)

Chance (2025)

Terror Effect (2025)

Acknowledgement

- Editor: Caroline Tolley

- Proof Readers: Joseph Bouchard, Dayna Garner, John Sobeck MD

- Book cover: Ani at AV DESIGN

IT WOULD BE IMPOSSIBLE FOR me to list all the different professionals and volunteers that aided me in my research to make this book a possibility. But first and foremost I want to thank the various animal agencies for the stories incorporated into this book. These stories make the book real. I also want to give special thanks to these same volunteers for their tireless and unselfish efforts in working for the various nonprofit organizations. They make it all about the animals.

It's important to know…the plight of some animals is growing dire, but most people are unaware. Today, right now, there are several species that are so endangered they will be gone, extinct in our life time, and some in less than ten years. It makes no difference if the animals are on the other side of the globe or in our own back yard. People need to care, because once they're gone…they're gone forever. So please, if you can't volunteer, give what you can.

The Davenport Series Continues...
Excerpt from Book 5—**Safe Passage**

Reed put the survival suit on over his clothing. It was cumbersome, and with the built in gloves, hood and boots, made the simplest of movements that much more difficult. He glanced again at the radar as his ship snaked through the various channels between icebergs. The attackers were gaining rapidly, and by the looks of their closing net, at least one of them had radar tracking ability much like *Freelance*.

The grim reality was the tug would be clear of the icebergs in another half-mile, but then what? They would be caught in the open and defenseless. He turned the ships radio on once more, but there was only static. Turning the volume down, he pushed the emergency transponder, which would continuously ping their current position through both the satellite navigation system and also through the GPS tracking system on the radio. Then he thumbed the walky-talky through the bulky gloves. "TJ."

"Go ahead," his friend replied, breathing heavily. "We're in survival suits. I've also got spare gear stowed in the watertight duffle bags and the two life pods are unbuckled and ready to go."

The *Freelance* wasn't equipped with standard hard hulled lifeboats. Due to lack of space on the working vessel, life boats came in form of domed rubber rafts, which were packed in hard canisters in cradles high over the water. Before use, a small door was opened to allow water into the self-inflating, water-activating, mechanism. Then once the canisters were rolled off the cradle and floating on the surface, the eight-man raft would break free of the outer shell and fill in seconds.

"TJ, they are going to be all over us in a minute, and there is a series of bergs approaching. I'm going to snake around the first one, and then come to a stop. For a moment we'll be off their radar, and I want you, Skip, and Richard to take a raft and paddle in close to the berg. Meanwhile, I'll head for open water..."

"No!" True John replied angrily. "We'll find a way. We always do."

"This is finding a way!" Reed snapped, turning slightly to starboard to get around a massive iceberg off the bow. "They will follow the tug, and in the darkness you have a chance."

"What about you?"

"I'm figuring that out," Reed answered, working one problem at a time. "I need you to do this, True John. To keep people safe, this has to happen, and they will need you to survive. So when I get to the other side of this berg, eject the raft. Then once it's inflated, take as much gear as you can, and jump in the water."

TJ didn't respond, but Reed knew exactly what was going on in his friends mind. It came from working together as ship mates, and best friends for more than twenty-five years. A man of conviction and honor, TJ was frustrated, but he himself knew they were out of options; the thought of leaving Reed behind ripping at his very soul...

www.ingramcontent.com/pod-product-compliance
Lightning Source LLC
Chambersburg PA
CBHW030123010826

48973CB00002B/399